And
Now
There's
You

And Now There's You

A Novel

Susan S. Etkin

Published by SparkPress, a BookSparks imprint,
A division of SparkPoint Studio, LLC
Phoenix, Arizona, USA, 85007
www.gosparkpress.com

Published 2019
Printed in the United States of America
ISBN: 978-1-68463-000-4 (pbk)
ISBN: 978-1-68463-001-1 (e-bk)

Library of Congress Control Number: 2019937596

For my wonderful sons and daughters-in-law,
Howard and Jennifer,
David and Karin,
May romance continue to brighten your days.

1

Leila Brandt sat on the window seat in the breakfast nook of her carriage house, taking in the lush beauty of her surroundings. The morning sunlight beamed upon the pink and purple blossoms adorning the azaleas and rhododendrons much like stage lighting brings to life the actors in a play. A soft breeze teased the white blossoms on the large tree a short distance from the deck, encouraging a few fragile petals to let go and gently make their way to the ground below. In the distance, couples walked along the nature trail that wound its way through the community. Some strolled hand in hand, enjoying the quiet of the new day. Others moved more briskly, but even those who were not touching maintained a closeness that bespoke of their unique pairing. The couples reminded Leila of the times she'd enjoyed the same activity with her late husband, Nick, before he was struck down at too young an age by cancer nearly five years ago.

A soft knock on the glass door leading to the deck interrupted Leila's reminiscence. As she rose to respond, a smile crossed her face. Her daughter Hillary stood before her, dressed in full running gear, a pedometer strapped to her right arm.

Leila slid open the door. "Sweetheart, I didn't know you were going to stop by. What if I weren't home? You'd have wasted a trip."

"I know, but I'm in the neighborhood. Chad went to play golf, and I decided to jog, so I jogged in your direction. I want to borrow your gold evening bag for the Bradford wedding next weekend."

"What are you wearing?"

"The green-and-gold sequined dress we bought together."

Leila smiled. "Ah, yes. It looks stunning on you and brings out the green in your hazel eyes. Well, I'm glad I wasn't invited. I'd inevitably end up sitting by myself at the dinner table for most of the evening while all the 'couple' people enjoy themselves on the dance floor."

Hillary walked to the kitchen counter, retrieved a mug, and poured herself some coffee. "Mom, you have to do something about your social life. You have to get out there. You need a companion, someone to accompany you to weddings and whatever. Dad wouldn't want you to be alone. You're a woman in her prime. You're attractive, intelligent, and personable. Give dating a try!"

Leila grimaced at the thought of marketing herself on a dating site. "So, Hillary, you want your mother to fill out one of those ridiculous electronic-dating-site forms and reveal her inner and outer selves to the world? And once that's done, you want your mother to be judged on a multitude of levels by a throng of divorced men, likely in their seventies or eighties, since that's the group of potential companions that's more apt to go for a woman my age?"

"There you go." Hillary threw her hands up. "That's the attitude that will get you somewhere. You need to get with the times. The dating scene has changed since the 1970s."

Leila walked over to her daughter and gave her a kiss on the forehead. "I'm so lucky to have such a caring daughter. Run up and get the bag; it's in the top right-hand drawer of my dresser."

Hillary scooted up the stairs and came back down seconds later, bag in hand. "Later, Mom." She blew Leila a kiss and jogged out the door.

Leila gazed upon her departing daughter. Her heart swelled. Hillary, just thirty-two and already a partner in a Center City law firm. She always set high expectations for herself and didn't give up until she realized them.

❀

On Monday morning, Leila hurried to get to work on time. Michelle expected her by ten. For just over a decade, Leila and Michelle had been operating an art gallery situated conveniently in Whitemarsh, a bedroom community outside of Philadelphia. The gallery featured an array of artisan-crafted pieces. In addition, the pair offered interior design services. Over the years, their expertise had earned them invitations to participate in designer showhouse events that raised money for a variety of charities. This year was no exception. With the coming of spring, a number of possibilities had arisen. After much discussion, they'd decided to focus their energies on the Children's Hospital fundraising project. The hospital had decided to work with the executors of the estate of the late Henry Marcus; the large manor home on Philadelphia's Main Line was up for sale. The Designers' Showhouse would provide free publicity plus exposure of the property to large crowds of people for a period of two weeks—a win-win situation.

"Good morning," Leila called out cheerfully upon entering the gallery. As she made her way to the office, she heard Michelle rustling papers.

"What's good about this morning?" Michelle asked when she saw Leila standing in the doorway. "I suppose spring has sprung, because my allergies are absolutely devastating, and I've a terrible sinus headache. Last night I tossed and turned. I couldn't find a place for myself."

Michelle, a tall, striking woman with long raven hair and violet eyes, didn't look well.

"Oh, poor baby," Leila responded sympathetically. "You need to get to the doctor's office today. I'll take care of the calls and paperwork."

"You're kidding, right?" Michelle shook her head. "Today is the appointment with Janice Perkins. In fact, I had a lengthy phone conversation with her before she even considered making the appointment. She's relying on our expertise to help her overcome her renovation anxieties. She approached two other designers before us. From what I heard through the grapevine, the other two ran for their lives."

Leila laughed. She appreciated Michelle's sense of humor, which always seemed to surface when things looked dire. "I'll handle the Perkinses. What time is the appointment?"

"Well, it's for just after lunch—one thirty."

"Fine. I'll be there. You call the doctor and see what kind of appointment you can get for today. Okay?"

Michelle nodded and sighed. "Thanks, Leila. You're a dear. I just don't think I'm at my best, and when dealing with Janice Perkins, the *best* is necessary. She's very demanding."

❁

The drive to the Perkinses' house was a good forty-five minutes, giving Leila time to plan her offensive and defensive strategies. Local media sources consistently characterized Mrs. Perkins as a caring but sometimes intractable force in local and state concerns, especially politics. She expected the professionals with whom she worked to be current, knowledgeable, and confident.

"Oooh," Leila said aloud as she began to think things through.

She was in big trouble. She found it difficult to assert herself; in fact, she was often rendered speechless when confronted with aggressive client behavior. The background work, the design itself, and project management were her areas of expertise. Client relations? Not so much. Michelle was the "tough cookie," able to respond quickly to any unwarranted attacks from clients as well as remediate a problem that might otherwise lead to a client's breaking off the design relationship or threatening even worse. Michelle's feelings were never hurt. She went immediately on the offensive. Furthermore, she always felt perfectly justified in doing so. They provided top service and products, regardless of the size of the project. Consequently, no client had reason to complain, question their intentions, or challenge their professionalism or expertise.

The voice of the navigator interrupted Leila's contemplation and put an end to her pep talk. She found herself driving onto Janice Perkins's street, a secluded country lane with older homes on one side and The Meadows Golf and Tennis Club on the other. Generally, the homes had significant histories, some dating back to the early 1800s. Though various owners had lovingly maintained and reno-vated the properties over the years, they remained true to the colo-nial facades of yore, using traditional materials for the exteriors, such as natural-colored stone, brick, and mortar complemented by wooden window shutters in hues of deep red, brown, black, or green. The Perkinses' residence was no different. Leila saw immediately that it was truly exemplary.

An elaborately detailed wrought iron mailbox encircled with yellow daffodils marked the entrance to 340 Fancy Meadow Lane and offered a cheery welcome. A driveway of dark brown paver stones led to the main house. Shielded by a covered porch, the extra-wide front door was stained a rich chocolate brown, its mahogany wood framing a faceted leaded-glass insert. Espresso-colored shutters adorned the white-framed windows and contrasted with the varied tones of the natural stone. The expansive grounds were impeccably maintained—a young green everywhere, since spring had just begun to show itself. A lovely courtyard between the main house and the detached three-car garage was graced with a fountain, but the water had yet to be turned on.

Leila hopped out of her car and made her way to the entry. With a gentle push of the doorbell, chimes sounded, and a figure appeared behind the glass. The door opened, and a slender, attractive woman with a generous smile moved toward Leila, her hands extended in greeting.

"Welcome! Come in, please. I'm Janice Perkins. You must be Leila Brandt. I'm so excited to meet you. Michelle called this morning. Oh, my, she sounded terrible."

"It's very nice to meet you as well, Mrs. Perkins," Leila responded, affecting her most perky smile. "I convinced Michelle to go to the doctor, so you have the next best thing: me."

"I'm sure both of you are equally competent. And please, call me Janice. *Mrs. Perkins* is much too formal. Let's make our way to the project area, the master bath. I know you'll have to take measurements, make notes, whatever. Ayden Doyle is already up there, assessing the scope of the renovation."

"Ayden Doyle?"

"Why, yes. I guess Michelle didn't tell you my dear friend Cynthia recommended a contractor. He's also an architect. Quite talented, a true craftsman. I just went through his portfolio. I'm very impressed. You will be too."

From the large foyer, Janice led the way up a curved wooden staircase with wonderful carvings to the second-floor balcony area. A polished, multi-armed fixture made of brass and crystal hung from the second-floor ceiling, hovering ten feet or so above the foyer's herringbone wood floor. Wallpaper depicting hunting scenes and wainscoting in distressed chestnut wood covered the walls of the space.

"Your woodwork here is magnificent," Leila said. "Is it all original?"

"Oh, yes. However, there are areas that have needed repair over the years, so some modern touches have been added. The first time I walked into the house and experienced the foyer and staircase, I knew I wanted to buy the place. Marshall didn't need much coaxing before he put in an offer."

Opposite the staircase, a raised-paneled door served as the gateway to a large, window-adorned room filled with sunlight. Inevitable dust particles danced gaily in the rays of light that streamed through the windows. Leila immediately noted the color scheme's muted hues—pale beiges paired with shades of caramel and soft touches of aqua and apricot.

She gazed upon the king-size canopy bed in the center of the room, which rose majestically toward the tray ceiling above it. In spite of the extraordinary size of the bedroom and the grandeur of the bed, there wasn't much furniture elsewhere. A fine eighteenth-century French armoire occupied the opposing wall, and mirrored chests of drawers served as night tables. Two upholstered armchairs flanked a fireplace against the right wall.

"Ayden, here we are," Janice sang out. As the two women crossed the threshold into the en suite bathroom, Janice proceeded with her introduction. "This is Leila Brandt, the design consultant of whom I spoke. She's here to inspire and help with decision-making."

Ayden turned and walked toward Leila with hand extended, and she automatically reached out to him. She immediately noticed his firm grasp and liked his assuredness.

"Hello," he said, meeting her gaze.

"It's nice to meet you. I hear your work is wonderful," Leila said with a controlled smile. She relaxed her hand slowly in his before letting go, inadvertently enjoying his touch.

"Thanks. People are pleased."

Leila perceived an impish wink, complemented by a boyish grin. And twinkling blue eyes. Nice. Was he playing with her or just trying to be friendly?

At first glance, Ayden didn't present an overwhelmingly impressive appearance; he was a man of average height, maybe five foot nine or ten, and somewhere in his early fifties. Nevertheless, something about him captured Leila's attention and caused a fluttering sensation deep in her chest. His still-dark auburn hair, though sprinkled with touches of gray, had some curls, giving him a youthful air. His toned body wore his blue jeans and gray T-shirt well—something he probably knew.

"I want to redo the bathroom," Janice continued. "Update it, make it more user-friendly, but with a touch of splendor and sophistication."

"That's possible," Ayden quickly responded. "However, its present size isn't very generous."

"I'm thinking that as well," Leila said. "I'm wondering if we could annex some of the master bedroom, since it's so large. How do you feel about that, Janice?"

"Oh, I don't know. I'd have to run that idea by Marshall. How much are you thinking of taking from the bedroom?"

"That depends," Ayden interjected. "The design you choose will dictate the space that's needed."

Leila nodded. "Ayden is right. In order to zero in on the design, we need to talk at length about what you want in the new bathroom. While I'm here, let me jot down some notes, take a couple of pictures and measurements, and then let's sit down somewhere and really discuss the details—with Ayden, of course."

"Great idea. We can go to the sunroom just off the kitchen, a really delightful room. I'll bring us some iced tea and nibbles to fuel our creativity," Janice said with enthusiasm. With that, she headed downstairs.

Ayden returned to his original position, standing with his back to Leila, his leg propped up on the edge of the bathtub to support his notepad. He continued to write but broke the silence left in the wake of Janice's departure. "There's really no need for both of us to draw out the space and take measurements. I'll be happy to give you a copy when I'm finished. I'll just slip a carbon between two sheets of graph paper."

"That's very kind of you," Leila said. "In return, I'll share my pictures with you."

"I hope you don't mind, but I prefer to take my own. I can forward those to you if you'd like."

Leila pondered her response for a few seconds. Perhaps this man was a bit too full of himself. She'd not let his smugness intimidate her.

"Where's that portfolio of yours, the one Janice mentioned? I'd like to take a look at it before I take you up on your offer." She affected a tone that was half-joking and half-serious, not even sure which she had in mind.

Ayden spun around. His blue eyes were on fire. She had pushed a button. He reached down for a black leather briefcase that rested against the side of the vanity. With finesse, he retrieved the portfolio, rose to his full height, and extended it toward Leila. "I took all the photos in here. I think you'll see that I'm quite good at capturing the particulars of all kinds of spaces."

Leila took the portfolio and slowly flipped its pages—and soon found that Ayden was as masterful as Janice had described. The photos were expertly taken and showed the remarkable craftsmanship that went into each project.

She closed the portfolio and met his gaze with a faint smile. "Yes, I see you're very talented. Please, I'd appreciate both the photos and the room plan."

"Fine," he said—and with that, returned to his notepad.

"I think I'll go down and help Janice," Leila said. "I can begin our chat, take some notes, and review them with you when you join us."

Only silence.

Frustrated, Leila picked up her briefcase, gripped its handle with intensity, and quickly left the room. As she descended the staircase, her footsteps sounded heavy. Her heart raced.

Michelle had thought Janice was going to be difficult. But Mr. Ayden Doyle was proving to be no walk in the park, either.

Dishes and silverware clashed and jingled, cabinet drawers and doors opened and shut, and the refrigerator alarm rang out as Leila reached the ground floor. This cacophony directed her through the foyer and under an archway to the dining room. She stopped for a second or two to admire a beautiful Chippendale table set for sixteen. The dining chairs, upholstered in a striped blue and green silk, showed a Far Eastern influence. Over the table, a massive crystal chandelier glistened in the afternoon sunlight while a soft breeze from an open window caused some of its adornments to collide gently. The soft, chime-like tones contrasted pleasantly with the ruckus in the kitchen.

"Janice?" Leila called out.

"Here, behind the dining room, through the butler's pantry."

Leila made her way into a bright kitchen with white cabinets put into relief by yellow trellis wallpaper. Large picture windows were topped off with architectural stained-glass sections in spring-like colors. The kitchen extended into a glorious sunroom and, beyond that, a patio. Instead of a wood floor, large square terra-cotta tiles set the mood for the sunroom and patio. All the colors and textures of Janice's kitchen, sunroom, and patio flowed expertly.

Leila and Michelle preferred an air of casual elegance to permeate informal spaces. This section of the house was much to her liking, a masterpiece of design.

The grounds beyond the house captivated Leila's attention as well. They were landscaped magnificently with evergreens and a brilliant variety of deciduous trees. Flowering shrubbery added to the mix—azaleas, rhododendrons, and the like. The view was lovely.

"Leila, did you hear me?" Janice's voice broke through Leila's reverie.

"Oh, I'm sorry," Leila said. "It's just that I'm completely overwhelmed by what I'm seeing. This is the most inviting and uplifting space I've seen in a long time."

"How kind of you to say." Janice's face brightened. "This entire area is a recent addition to the original house. And by recent, I mean a project from the 1950s. We renovated it about two years ago." She spread her arms wide to embrace the scene. "The outside is paradise, isn't it?"

Leila helped her hostess carry the drinks and snacks into the sunroom, and then the two women began exploring ideas for the master bath. Leila made a list of must-have items as Janice spoke.

They enjoyed each other's company, and the time passed quickly. As their conversation progressed, Leila became more convinced they'd have to take some space from the bedroom to make everything Janice was suggesting a reality.

Footsteps moving across the wood floor caused Leila and Janice to look toward the kitchen. Ayden passed through the doorway like he owned the house, a forgotten pencil propped behind his ear, his notepad under his arm, and a briefcase in his hand. How did such a masculine man move with such grace?

"Well, ladies, I've done my thing. What have you been up to?" He placed his articles on the floor next to the chair he chose for himself. Without a pause, he reached for a glass of iced tea and a couple of crackers topped with cheese. With one hand, he released the contents of a sugar packet into his glass, rolled the wrapper up into a tiny sphere, and tossed it into a nearby wastebasket.

Leila fought her urge to smile. Ayden's performance reminded her of her engineer son, Drew. In high school, for a physics class project, he'd designed a Rube Goldberg contraption that involved a series of simple devices linked together to produce a domino effect. He'd used his body to demonstrate to his parents how the complicated system worked and had Nick and Leila laughing so hard they were in tears by the end of it.

Still somewhat entertained by Ayden's performance, Leila began relating what she and Janice had discussed. "Janice has requested that a number of things be included in the master bath makeover: a double vanity with a beveled mirror and wall sconces; a large shower with at least two heads; a private toilet area; a large soaking tub; a heated floor; skylights; recessed ceiling lights, as well as a centered, hanging chandelier; new windows; a walk-in linen closet; and, if possible, a laundry room."

"Oh, my," Janice interjected, "I now see that some of the bedroom space will need to be sacrificed. But I want what I want. As Marshall and I stand on the precipice of our 'golden years,' there should be no doing without or postponing things."

Ayden agreed. "Give me a little time to work up some ideas and illustrate them for you. Leila, when will you be available to meet with me?"

Quite surprised, Leila took a moment to gather her thoughts. "Well, as soon as possible, because I'm going to be tied up with the Designers' Showhouse next month."

Ayden pulled out his electronic planner. "How about we meet at my place in a couple of weeks—say on the fifteenth?" Ayden looked up and shot his baby blues in Leila's direction.

"That's good. It will give me a couple of weeks to research the project." She took out her traditional planner and circled the date.

Ayden tapped her arm and offered her his card.

Leila quickly reciprocated. "Here's mine."

Ayden took it and put it into the pocket of his T-shirt.

"Don't lose that valuable information in the laundry," Leila said, attempting to add some levity to the conversation.

"I'm so happy you two are working well together," Janice said merrily. "I'm anxious to hear your suggestions."

"I guess we're done here," Ayden concluded. He adeptly collected his belongings and directed a smile toward Leila, who rose on cue. Ayden gestured for her to exit ahead of him.

Did he want to speak privately? Why did his politeness seem to possess an air of arrogance?

Anxious to find out his intentions, she quickly took possession of her handbag and briefcase. Janice walked them out, and after she closed the front door, Ayden and Leila walked together down the driveway.

She broke the silence. "I think that went well, don't you?"

"Yep. Well, nice meeting you," Ayden said, and he headed toward his truck.

"Ditto," she said, but he was already whistling a tune to himself and likely didn't hear her reply.

Something about Ayden Doyle bothered Leila. She wasn't exactly certain what it was, but there was one thing she was sure about: on the fifteenth of the month, she'd find out.

2

The alarm clock gave off its unwelcome sound. Leila rolled over and pressed the off button. She reached for the remote and turned on the news just in time for the weather report. The next few days were to be bright and sunny but unseasonably chilly with gusty winds. But what did she care? Much of her time would be devoted to manning the shop or tracking down interesting fixtures for the Perkinses' new master bath. A trip to the Willow Grove showroom would be a must-do before the meeting with Ayden on the fifteenth.

Leila stared at herself in the large bathroom mirror. Her shoulder-length golden-brown hair tumbled haphazardly. She leaned forward and blinked her light brown eyes to achieve more clarity as she inspected the few gray hairs that had woven themselves into her hairline. When would she fit a touch-up into her busy schedule? She was thankful she had little gray in her hair; not bad for a woman in her midfifties. In fact, most people didn't perceive her to be in her fifties at all. She looked a good ten years younger.

Leila removed her nightgown and stepped on the scale. The reading, as usual, hovered near 130—a reasonable weight for her height of five foot four. She turned sideways and scrutinized her midsection in the mirror. It was not to her liking. However, she had learned to accept gracefully the consequences of aging, with one intervention: the surgery two years earlier that had restored youthfulness and allure to her eyes.

❁

Later that morning, Leila sat in the office discussing the Perkins project with Michelle.

"I'm so happy Janice Perkins came across as a congenial client who looked forward to working with us," Michelle said. "I don't know what you did, but apparently there was chemistry between the two of you. She's not known for her graciousness, but you got things rolling."

"Honestly, she was very nice," Leila said with a shrug. "Maybe her evil twin sister will emerge later on. In that case, you'll have to handle her."

"And what about her architect-slash-contractor?"

"Ayden Doyle? He's an interesting character. I'm certain there wasn't much chemistry between us, but in a couple of weeks I'll be meeting with him to discuss design particulars. I'll get a better read on him then. I did see his portfolio. Very impressive."

Michelle tapped a finger on her desk. "Can I change the subject for a minute?"

"Go ahead."

"Your birthday is coming up, and I've an unusual treat for you. In fact, Hillary and I are partnering."

Leila sat up. "Okay, you've got my attention. Uh-oh. Your eyes are twinkling. A warning of things to come. What are you two plotting?"

"Hillary has a light day today, so she's going to bring lunch for all of us and we can talk things over together then," Michelle explained airily.

Leila shook her head. "Tell me now."

"Shortly. Be patient. Make yourself busy and return phone calls."

Leila went about her work and tried to put Michelle's mystery plans out of her thoughts. She touched base with clients, straightened up the front of the shop, and did some bookkeeping. Michelle put together some design boards for projects already underway. The rest of the morning flew by for both of them; in what seemed like no time at all, the shop's door was chiming and a familiar voice called, "Mom, Michelle, I'm here with delicious things!"

Hillary hurried to the office. "Hi, you two. Are you hungry? I'm starving." She placed a neatly packed picnic basket on top of a small table.

"How fantastic of you to bring us lunch. You're the best." Michelle was back to being her perky self now that her allergies were under control.

"Hi, sweetheart. I'm glad you've time to spend with us." Leila paused for a moment, trying to get her thoughts together. "But honestly, why are you here? You and Michelle are up to something. What gives?"

"Don't be ridiculous." Hillary quickly turned toward Michelle. "What did you tell her?"

Michelle took on a practiced innocent look. "I simply mentioned her birthday."

"Let's set up first, okay?" Hillary proceeded to ready the table for lunch. She topped it with a brightly colored cloth and laid out three place settings, napkins, and cups that coordinated nicely. Then she unloaded the basket. A nice spring salad, crusty bread, lemonade, and fruit yogurt for dessert made up the menu.

"What, no chocolate?" Leila remarked. Chocolate was her weakness.

"Well, mother, if you *insist* rather than *resist*, I've packed some Hershey's Kisses in the bottom of the basket, but maybe you'll have no appetite to tackle them by the time we're done."

"I'll purposely save room for them," Leila said with conviction. "Now, tell me, what have you planned for my birthday?"

Both Hillary and Michelle exchanged furtive glances until Michelle finally took charge. "You've been a widow for almost five years. It's time you get on with your life."

"Oh, no, did you sign me up on some dating site? Please say you didn't."

"That's easy, Mom, because we didn't do any such thing."

"No, we didn't," Michelle confirmed. "However, we did take a like action."

Leila narrowed her eyes. "A like action? Please explain."

"Well," Michelle began, "I ran into Mimi Wexler a couple of weeks ago at the hair salon and we began to talk. She happened to mention that one of her good friends went to a professional match-maker located in Doylestown. This matchmaker found Mimi's friend an ideal mate using a meticulous process that's both discreet and effective."

"Wait." Leila swallowed and composed herself. "You sound like a TV commercial. Do you really think I'm going to take myself to this matchmaker, pay her a hefty fee—I assume that's involved—and allow myself to be test driven by strange men? This is so not my style."

"First, we've already paid the not-so-hefty fee," Hillary said. "That's your birthday present—plus a really nice lunch at a steakhouse in Doylestown. Besides, we're both going to the interview with you. We're going to support you the whole way. The three of us will agree upon the appropriate candidates. This will be a team effort."

"Really," Michelle chimed in, "I've a good feeling about this."

Leila went silent. She pushed her plate to the side. Her appetite had waned considerably. She didn't know how she truly felt, but she did know she was somewhere between appreciative and infuriated. What were they thinking?

"I don't know about this," she finally said with a sigh. "I'm not happy about the whole thing. I feel awkward. It's not that I'm against meeting someone with whom I could share my life, but I had hoped it would happen serendipitously, that coincidental forces would come into play. I'd be waiting in a supermarket line and begin a conversa-tion with a nice man standing behind me, or I'd be waiting at the car dealership for my car to be inspected and strike up a conversation with a man about our preference for Buicks."

"Get real, Mom. This is a new millennium. If you don't try the electronic dating services, then matchmaking is the next-best, perhaps better, alternative."

"Leila," Michelle said in a soft voice, her hand on Leila's shoulder, "nothing ventured, nothing gained. You may find a great guy, and you may not. But you need to be proactive and put yourself out there. Give it a go and then decide whether to continue or not. There really is nothing to lose."

Leila frowned. "That's easy for you to say. You've been married to a great man for thirty-five years. It's my dignity and self-esteem at risk."

"Well, next Monday, we're going to meet with Dr. Lola Goodwin of Heavenly Matches. Our appointment is at ten. We'll pick you up at nine. Look your very best, because I expect picture taking to be part of the interview."

Leila buried her head in her hands. "I hate the whole idea," she said under her breath.

"I think you need some comfort food to lift your spirits," Hillary suggested, and she placed a handful of Hershey's Kisses on a napkin in front of Leila.

Leila reached for one and slowly removed its wrapping.

What had she allowed herself to get into?

This was Leila's big day. She had set the alarm for seven. She wanted plenty of time to prepare for the interview. Her mind was in a frenzy. Why had she agreed to this matchmaking business?

She had tried on at least a dozen outfits the night before but still couldn't make up her mind on what to wear to the Heavenly Matches appointment. Rummaging through her closet once again, she finally zeroed in on beige ankle pants, a neutral cashmere sweater, beige kitten pumps, and gold jewelry.

By eight thirty Leila had showered, washed and styled her hair, and, for drama, applied brown eye shadows, bronze liner, and black mascara. She studied herself in the mirror one last time, grabbed her ivory handbag, and headed to the kitchen for her favorite brew and a half of a blueberry muffin.

The phone rang as soon as she took her first sip.

"Hello, Michelle. What's up?"

"Are you ready to begin the first day of the rest of your life?" Michelle's eagerness, though cloaked in humor, did nothing to ease Leila's anxiety.

"Please, try not to be so trite. I'm looking forward to spending time with you and Hillary and enjoying a great steak salad. The other item on our agenda will likely be torturous."

"Oh, don't be so negative. What are you wearing?"

"What does it matter? I'm not changing," Leila said with certainty.

"All right. I'll pick you up in a half hour. Hillary is meeting us at your house."

❁

The three women made it to Heavenly Matches at the appointed time. The office was situated on the first floor of a small brick professional building just off of Easton Road. An attractive young receptionist greeted the trio with a warm smile and a well-practiced welcoming phrase: "Welcome to Heavenly Matches. May I have your name?"

Hillary took charge as only a lawyer can do. "You should have Leila Brandt scheduled for ten."

"Why, yes, we're so happy to meet you, Ms. Brandt."

"Actually, Ms. Brandt is the woman who just seated herself across the room and is thumbing through a magazine. I'm her daughter. I'm just checking in for her."

At this, Leila looked up.

"Oh, I see," the receptionist responded. "Our new clients often come with support staff." She leaned forward and said with a smile Leila perceived to be reassuring, "Dr. Goodwin will be with Ms. Brandt—I mean, all of you—in a few moments."

Leila turned her attention to scrutinizing the waiting room's design. "It's furnished with the essentials—a few armchairs and a large table in the center topped with a variety of magazines for people to browse," she noted.

Michelle nodded. "It's unpretentious but pleasant. The green plants and the generous light coming through the floor-to-ceiling window create a nice ambience. And I really like the color of the walls. The soft green works well with the dark green carpet. Did you notice the subtle white, orange, and periwinkle dots in the carpet?"

Michelle seemed to be trying a bit too hard. "If you're trying to distract me or perhaps calm me with this design talk, it isn't working," Leila said. She rose from her seat and began to walk about the room, stopping to examine two art pieces portraying romantic subject matter. In one, a man and woman were walking through Paris in the rain, their hands wrapped together around an umbrella they shared. The other showed a bride and groom dancing their first dance as their wedding guests looked on, smiling and clapping.

Suddenly, the inner office door swung open. An older man, likely in his late seventies and conservatively dressed, appeared in the doorway. He entered the waiting room followed closely by a middle-aged woman dressed in a silk blouse and businesslike skirt. The two shook hands.

"Nice to meet you, Stan," the woman said. "I enjoyed our talk. You should hear from me in a couple of weeks."

"Dr. Goodwin," the man replied, "the pleasure has been all mine."

He gave her a wink. He turned to leave but slowed to take a sustained look at Leila, Hillary, and Michelle. He smiled politely, turned back toward Dr. Goodwin, and gave her a thumbs-up. She returned his gesture with a smile. With the wave of his hand, the man was out the door.

"Hi there," Dr. Goodwin said, approaching the three women. "I'm Dr. Lola Goodwin. One of you must be Leila Brandt."

Both Hillary and Michelle pointed toward Leila and in unison said, "She is."

3

D r. Goodwin guided Leila, Hillary, and Michelle into her office. Leila noted that its décor was similar to that of the waiting room.

"Please, have a seat." Dr. Goodwin seated herself at her desk, a rather large Louis XIV with prominent but gracefully curved legs. Its ebony wood was embellished with gilt and chinoiserie. Her desk chair, upholstered in rich apricot velvet, was also oversize. With these furnishings acting as an extension of herself, Dr. Lola Goodwin exuded confidence and captured Leila's attention.

Leila felt uncomfortable but mustered up the wherewithal to introduce her supporters. "This is my wonderful daughter, Hillary, and my equally wonderful business partner, Michelle. They're in cahoots and have brought me here under duress."

Dr. Goodwin laughed. "It's very nice to meet all of you," she said warmly. "I know, Hillary and Michelle, that you care deeply about Leila and that's why you're here with her." She then leaned forward in her chair and spoke directly to Leila. "I thoroughly understand your apprehension. Let me take a few moments to explain how the Heavenly Matches process works."

Hillary and Michelle shifted to the front of their chairs, as if inching closer would allow them greater access to restricted information. Leila, on the other hand, receded into the depth of her chair, trying to avoid the harsh reality of her present circumstance.

For the next twenty minutes, Dr. Goodwin explained how she recorded clients' answers to a wide range of questions, probing more deeply when necessary. Clients were expected to be open and honest. "This is the only way to achieve good results," Dr. Goodwin cautioned her listeners. She proceeded to explain the course of action. Once a particular client's background and criteria were fully documented, the database was activated and suitable matches were sought. Suitability was multidimensional. That is, age; physical appearance; interests; education; friends and family connections and their importance; professional and religious affiliations; hobbies; and short- and long-term goals were all explored to see where appropriate pairings could be made.

"You must all understand, though, there's one very important element upon which the process cannot exert any influence, and that's *chemistry*. This is a naturally occurring phenomenon that emerges when a match is optimal." Dr. Goodwin paused for some time to allow Leila, Michelle, and Hillary to absorb the information. Then she broke the silence. "Leila, are you ready to begin the interview process?"

"She's ready," Michelle and Hillary replied in one voice.

Leila remained silent but shrugged in assent, thinking, *Well, I guess. Do I really have a choice?*

Dr. Goodwin began her interview with basic background questions. When Leila was slow to answer, Hillary and Michelle came up with the answers for her.

"Oh, Leila and I are both graduates of Philadelphia University," Michelle said with enthusiasm. "That's where we first decided to start our own business."

"Mother is a fabulous cook!" Hillary piped up. "In fact, cooking is one of her hobbies."

With each piece of information, Leila's electronic dossier began to take shape. Dr. Goodwin learned that her new client appreciated the arts and sought out a broad range of expressions. Her preferences in music, for example, included everything from opera at the Academy of Music to pop concerts at the Wells Fargo Center. In the fine arts, she loved the pleasing colors and scenes of the Impressionists but also found the works of Expressionists, like Jackson Pollock, interesting.

"Mother loves to go to all the museums on the Parkway," Hillary volunteered.

Michelle elaborated. "She and her husband, Nick, loved to go to an art exhibition and then walk over to a nearby restaurant for lunch or dinner. Leila loves restaurants that not only have good food but also offer exceptional ambience, whether the dining is casual or formal. Right?" Michelle turned toward Leila, evidently pleased with her own commentary.

Leila studied Michelle's face for a long beat and then sighed. "Yes, Michelle, that's right." Then turning to direct her remarks to Dr. Goodwin, she continued. "All this is true, Dr. Goodwin, but lately I've shied away from the cultural scene unless a girlfriend or family member has shown interest in venturing downtown. I'm not self-assured when it comes to navigating the city on my own. I've gone to the small neighborhood theaters, but again, never by myself. I'm not afraid to call someone and suggest an outing. However, many of my friends and family are still couples—it's a *couple's* world out there—and husbands' tastes and interests must be considered. Some wives choose not to leave their husbands behind when their men don't embrace the arrangements."

"I understand completely." Dr. Goodwin's tone was sympathetic. "That's why you're here, to find a nice male companion—or companions—so you can reenter the couple's scene more often. I think we have the basics down. Shall we move on to the area of intimacy now?"

"Wait one minute," Leila interrupted. "This is really very personal, and I'm not sure I want to divulge my innermost secrets, feelings, whatever, to all of you."

"Perhaps it's best for Hillary and Michelle to wait outside. Ladies"—Dr. Goodwin nodded in their direction—"please step outside for a bit. We won't be very long. I'd say no more than a half hour."

"Of course. We understand," Hillary responded. She latched on to Michelle's arm and led the retreat to the waiting room.

With the door closed, Dr. Goodwin focused her attention on Leila. "That's a wonderful support team you have there. But let's start with another aspect of your preferences. My first question concerns your perspective on sex. Do you consider casual sex an integral part of dating? In other words, can you decontextualize the act, seeking merely to receive and give pleasure?"

This bold query propelled Leila into a stupor. She was speechless. She felt violated and annoyed. What business was that of Dr. Goodwin's—or anyone else's, for that matter?

"I know I'm taking you outside your comfort level," Dr. Goodwin said gently. "However, I don't want you to find yourself in precarious situations. Some men see sex as an extension of the dating process and nothing more."

Finally, Leila gathered her thoughts. "I don't think highly of casual sex. I've had sex with only one man: Nick, my husband. We met in high school. Though I had a significant dating life before Nick, I never felt close enough to anyone to go *all the way*. For me, sex needs to mean something. The act, for me, is the ultimate expression of love and commitment. Please don't pair me up with any man not sharing or understanding this perspective."

"That's fine. Now I have the direction I need. You sound angry. Please forgive me, but I need to understand these things in order to do my job. I'm sorry if my question caused you to feel uneasy. But I'm afraid it will not be the only one in this section to do so. Here's the next one. How important is sex to you?"

"If I'm in love and in a committed relationship, it's very important. Otherwise, the act is of no importance to me."

"In your past life with your husband, did you ever initiate sex?"

"Of course."

"Did you take charge, telling your lover what to do to pleasure you?"

"Why do you need to know that?"

"Because some men want their women to be totally passive, while others want their women to direct, even if just occasionally."

"All I can say is that Nick and I had a passionate sex life. There was a healthy balance. We communicated when we made love, either verbally or physically. We didn't go in for the kinky stuff, but we weren't totally without creativity." Leila's face was growing pinker by the moment. "I think I've said all I'm going to say about my sex life with Nick and about intimacy, in general. Have we finished? I believe it's almost lunchtime."

Dr. Goodwin nodded. "Yes, I think I have enough to begin my search for those men who have much in common with you. I'll get back to you in a couple of weeks."

"Fine." Leila rose from her seat, extended her hand, and forced a smile. "Thank you for your time and interest in my well-being. I look forward to hearing from you." *NOT*, she added silently.

"Let me walk you out. Before you leave, the receptionist will take some pictures of you for the database." Dr. Goodwin led Leila out of the office and accompanied her into the waiting room.

Michelle and Hillary rose to greet Leila, their expressions a bit concerned.

"Leila did just fine," Dr. Goodwin said, smiling. "Now I need her to take some pictures. Let me make the arrangements with my receptionist." She walked over to the receptionist's desk, jotted down a few notes, handed them to the perky young woman behind the counter, and then returned to say good-bye. "I enjoyed meeting all of you." She stepped closer to Leila and in a voice just short of a whisper said, "See you soon."

"Another face-to-face meeting?" Leila was unsettled.

"Yes, I'll need to discuss the list of candidates with you. You'll make some selections then, and we'll go from there." Dr. Goodwin squeezed Leila's hand, gave her a reassuring look, and returned to her office.

"Ms. Brandt," the receptionist called. "Please step behind my desk so I can take some pictures of you."

"Don't forget to smile," Michelle said in a weak attempt at humor.

Leila frowned and proceeded toward the receptionist. After ten uncomfortable minutes, her photo shoot was done. She emerged from behind the desk feeling relieved that the appointment was over.

Hillary jumped up when she saw her. "Well, Mom, I'm starved. Let's go to lunch."

"Yes," said Michelle. "We have much to discuss."

Leila sighed. "I think, girls, I've talked enough for one day."

4

The fifteenth of the month arrived. Leila was due to meet with Ayden Doyle at eleven. She decided on the same outfit she wore to the Heavenly Matches interview. She'd invested much time and thought into that ensemble, and the outcome had been noteworthy: both Hillary and Michelle had wholeheartedly approved, and the pictures taken at Dr. Goodwin's office had turned out well. At least a couple of satisfying things had come out of this matchmaking experience.

By nine, Leila was in her car heading to the boutique. She allowed plenty of time to ready the shop for the day's business and place the Perkins design materials into two large totes. She and Michelle had reviewed everything the day before. Both were satisfied that they'd come up with enough samples and illustrations to launch a successful collaboration with Ayden.

"I'll keep things in check here," Michelle assured Leila. "Try to get back for lunch. Have fun."

"'Fun' may not be exactly the term I'd use. Ayden appears to be somewhat standoffish. However, I'll do my best to get a synergistic relationship going."

"I love your positive attitude," Michelle said with a wink.

Leila heaved the heavy totes into the back of her car and began her drive to Old Merion. Forty-five minutes later, she pulled up in front of 108 Meetinghouse Lane—Ayden's residence, office, and workshop. The house exemplified the American Craftsmen Style of architecture; Leila guessed that it dated back to the early 1900s. She was immediately struck by the home's simple and elegant lines. The lovely front porch, constructed of natural fieldstone and supported by tapered columns, led the way to a terra-cotta front door with a row of etched glass panes at the top. The exterior was beige stucco accented with a light moss-green trim. Multi-paned windows were set in groups of three. A driveway comprised of stone pavers set off in two directions. A section to the right of the house led from the street to a detached structure in the rear that appeared to be the workshop. In the opposite direction, a section circled in front of the house; the mature evergreens and spring flowers along its edges helped to give the home wonderful curb appeal.

Leila looked at herself in the rearview mirror and decided to tidy up her makeup before pulling into the driveway. Thankfully, she had arrived a bit early. She needed time to compose herself. She wasn't exactly sure why she felt nervous, so she decided to give herself a pep talk. In a strong voice she said aloud, "You're an accomplished and respected professional. Stop this silliness. Get out there and show your stuff!"

She turned into the driveway, where a discreet sign showed the way to the office and workshop. She pulled up to the building that had likely served as a garage in years past. Its architecture mirrored that of the main house. She turned off the engine, got her belongings from the backseat, and approached the door. She heard loud noises from within and decided a knock would go unheard, so she pressed the latch on the door and inched her way through the doorway.

"Hello! Ayden! It's Leila Brandt," she called in a very loud voice. A young man with protective glasses was working at a table saw and didn't notice or hear her. As she moved farther inside, she glimpsed a male figure moving about in a second-floor loft. A glass wall allowed a full view of the area below, where she was standing. She frantically waved her arm, trying to get his attention. Finally, the figure moved closer to the glass and returned the wave. Only then did Leila recognize Ayden.

Within a few seconds, he appeared on the main floor. He approached with a smile on his face, but not necessarily one that expressed great warmth. "You apparently had no difficulty finding the place." He reached for the totes. "Let me help you carry these things upstairs, where we can talk and be more comfortable. But first, let me introduce you to my son, Daniel."

"Thanks for your help. Those totes are packed with lots of samples." Just as the words left her mouth, Leila realized that Ayden was easily carrying the totes with one hand. With the other hand, he motioned for her to follow him over to where the young man was working.

Feeling his father's touch on his shoulder, the young man turned off the machine and raised his protective eyewear.

"Daniel, this is Leila Brandt. She's the interior design consultant working with us on the Perkins project."

Daniel came from behind the table saw to shake Leila's hand. "Nice to meet you, Ms. Brandt. My dad has told me about you. We're interested in your feedback."

"Please call me Leila. I'm happy to meet you too."

"When you're done, Daniel, please come upstairs."

"I need at least twenty more minutes, Dad."

"That's fine." Ayden beckoned to Leila, and she followed him to the rear of the main floor, where both an elevator and a long, winding staircase provided access to the second-floor loft. "What's your preference?"

"If you continue to carry those totes, I'll gladly take the stairs." She wasn't about to suggest she was in need of fitness training. Ayden nodded and followed her up the staircase.

By the time Leila made it to the top of the stairs, her breathing was a bit challenged. Ayden, on the other hand, was undaunted. He moved ahead of her to place the totes near a drafting table and stool positioned against the back wall. Leila watched him as he pulled up an additional stool from the corner so they both could sit at the drafting table.

As before, his movements were precise and skillful. Why did she take notice of this? She wasn't sure, but she continued to study Ayden as he pulled out large illustrations from a portfolio already placed on the table. He was nicely built. His gray T-shirt, with the logo AD AND ASSOCIATES scrolled in navy blue above the pocket, showed off his trim, muscular frame. His hair was exceptionally curly today, making him appear more boyish than he had at the Perkinses'. And those eyes of his were an intriguing sky-blue that Leila found almost hypnotizing.

I must be attracted to this man. If I weren't, I wouldn't be thinking like this. Leila set her jaw. *I need to stay focused on my design mission.*

Ayden's words helped Leila redirect her thoughts. "I've a few ideas to go over with you."

Ayden's draftsmanship was artful and detailed. He provided three options for Leila and the Perkinses to consider. All required taking some footage from the master bedroom. The first design pushed out the wall between the bathroom and bedroom about six feet to provide for a modest dressing room and adjacent linen closet. This created a small entryway into the bathroom. A fabulous floor-to-ceiling Palladian window, to be seen from the bedroom, was placed on the far bathroom wall, which was currently windowless. The view would embrace the old trees and lush grounds of the Perkinses' property.

"I love the window idea," Leila said, excitement in her voice. "It will make the master bath seem even more spacious and bring in the natural surroundings."

"That's my thinking. The other two plans also include a majestic window, but I suggest raising the ceiling by going into the attic space above the bathroom. This second design is much more expensive because it's labor intensive, but it opens up the space even more, allowing for a larger window and an elaborate chandelier that would require additional ceiling height."

"Janice did say she's partial to chandeliers."

Ayden continued with his descriptions. Leila listened with great interest. The third alternative required stealing even a few more feet from the master bedroom to create a large dressing area, walk-in linen closet, and laundry area. This design also offered his-and-hers private toilet areas, an eight-foot double vanity rather than the standard six-foot, and a larger shower area with multiple showerheads. In addition, a large drop-in tub positioned under the original bathroom window was flanked by gorgeous cabinetry. Open cubbyholes accented by carved, twisted rope moldings allowed easy access to towels when stepping out of the tub or the shower.

"Wow, Ayden." Leila raised her eyebrows. "This last one is over-the-top."

"I always create one design that's ideal and not subject to budget constraints, especially when I think the client can afford to stretch a bit. Now, what have you got in those bags?"

Leila began to explain her vision for the interior design of the bathroom. Her goal was to establish an ambience of sophistication and elegance without ostentation. She pulled out marble, granite, and natural stone samples and an array of textured ceramic tiles with coordinating accent tiles. She showed how the fixtures and cabinetry worked well together. Ayden studied each sample and reviewed every catalog while listening intently to Leila's explanations of how each product and the various color selections contributed to her design concept. When he asked questions, even those that seemed to be testing Leila's knowledge base, she patiently provided detailed answers without being defensive.

As the meeting continued, Leila sensed Ayden becoming

increasingly receptive. He seemed to respond to her enthusiasm and appreciate her expertise. Was he beginning to see her as a valuable cohort rather than a clueless intruder?

Ayden inched his stool closer to Leila's in order to see her pencil sketches of the various ways the flooring products could be installed. Their shoulders touched. As the discussion went farther their hands frequently swept across the samples they shared, sometimes colliding. Occasionally, their knees knocked as they shifted on their stools. They grew more relaxed in each other's company and were able to laugh at one another's attempts at humor. But mostly, they were very serious.

"You've done great work of your own. The Perkinses have plenty to choose from, and I doubt you'll need to research any further." Ayden offered his assessment without hesitation.

"Thanks, Ayden. I'll take that compliment."

"A well-deserved one, I might add." He looked directly into her eyes.

Leila was entranced. Those eyes of his held power over her; she remained motionless and expressionless, almost lost in time. Her hypnotic state was only dispelled when Daniel joined them.

"Hey, you two seem to be getting along." Daniel approached the drafting table. "Can I buddy up?"

"Of course." Leila gave Daniel a shortened version of the presentation she'd given Ayden. He responded as favorably as his father had. As he reviewed a couple of the samples she'd brought, she glanced at her watch and was amazed to discover that it was almost one o'clock. "I see it's getting late. I need to get back to the shop. Where do we go from here?"

Tossing the ball into Ayden's court was deliberate. She knew his ego needed an occasional feeding. In the end, her deference would work to her advantage.

"I think we're ready to go back to the Perkinses with our ideas," he said, rising from his stool. "Do you want to set up that meeting?"

"I can."

Ayden pulled out his electronic planner and checked his schedule. "I have numerous conflicts next week, but I'm totally flexible the week after that. Why don't you try to set up something for then—unless, of course, you're unavailable then?"

Leila attempted to access her schedule in her head, to no avail. "Let me get back to you."

She began to organize her materials and repack them into her totes. Ayden and Daniel helped, and all three chatted amicably as they took the elevator down and left the workshop. Daniel said his good-byes then and walked toward the house, but Ayden accompanied Leila to her car. He opened the passenger door and placed the totes carefully on her backseat. Then he came around to the driver's side and leaned into the open window as she started up the car.

"I enjoyed our meeting. Looking forward to next time." As he drew back, Ayden reached through the window to offer a parting handshake. Leila grasped his hand, and his firm but gentle touch aroused sensations that spread rapidly through her body. She tried to dismiss her reaction and hoped Ayden hadn't noticed anything. She nodded, smiled, and nervously turned her car around to head down the driveway. Her heart pounded as she looked in the rearview mirror. Ayden remained fixed, watching her. Her face felt flushed. She'd previously thought him arrogant and rude, but her first impression was currently undergoing a radical revision.

As Hillary would say, she thought, *"That man is hot."*

When Leila pulled up to the shop, she glanced at the clock on the dashboard and realized she was almost an hour late. The drive had taken longer than it should have. Her mind had been swirling with thoughts of Ayden to such an extent that she couldn't even remember what route she'd taken. Why was she so drawn to him? Why was she so looking forward to the meeting with him at the Perkinses'?

As Leila closed the door behind her, she found Michelle waiting to greet her. "Where were you?" she asked. "I expected you back an hour ago. Did you bring lunch?"

"Oh, I'm so sorry. I lost track of time. Ayden's plans were fabulous and prompted much discussion."

Michelle went silent. She concentrated on Leila, who avoided her gaze and walked over to the corner next to her desk to find a place for her totes. That done, she sat to touch up her makeup.

She looked up to find her friend staring at her. "What's the matter?" she asked as she continued to examine herself in a mirror. "Can't you decide on what you want for lunch? I'm flexible. Want some suggestions?"

"You know, you seem different," Michelle said. "Are you okay? Your face is red. Do you think you have a temperature?"

"I'm perfectly fine." Leila wore a smile that she knew was exceptionally large. "Now, let's make a decision, because suddenly I'm ravenous."

"How about antipasto from Maria's Café?"

"Perfect! Call it in, and I'll go get it."

Michelle picked up her cell, placed the order quickly, and sat down at her desk. Out of the corner of her eye, Leila saw her fumbling with some papers, as if trying to establish a casual demeanor.

"Tell me," Michelle said, looking up from the papers, "what did Ayden include in those plans of his?"

"Well, the third plan is my favorite, but it will be very costly. It includes a wonderful Palladian window—actually, all three plans have the window, which will give a great view of the grounds—a raised ceiling, separate toilet areas, a nicely sized dressing room with adjacent laundry facilities, and a walk-in linen closet."

"I like those ideas, and I think the Perkinses will too."

"I hope so, because I'm crazy about them. I need to set up an appointment with them for the week after next. I told Ayden I'd handle that and let him know the particulars."

"It seems Ayden is growing on you?" Michelle asked, leaning toward her friend.

"I found him less annoying today and more respectful." Leila's answer carried with it an air of peaceful certainty.

"Is that it?"

"Of course that's it. What are you implying?"

"Oh, nothing," Michelle said—somewhat slyly, Leila thought— and she returned to her work.

Leila grabbed her handbag and left for Maria's. She felt Michelle had tapped into an inner sanctum, an area that she'd rather keep private. She needed to work on taming her body language and her physiological reactions to her emotions. The last thing she wanted was for Michelle to suspect that Ayden was increasingly occupying her thoughts.

❁

"I'm back with the goods," Leila proclaimed, closing the shop door behind her. As she approached the office, she overheard Michelle ending a phone conversation.

"Yes, thank you, Dr. Goodwin. I'll talk to Leila, but I think things will work out for this coming Monday. If not, Leila will get back to you."

Leila strode in just as Michelle was replacing the phone on its dock. "Did I hear you talking to Dr. Goodwin?"

"Correct. She wants us to meet with her again next week, so I chose Monday, since we've no design appointments."

"And this next meeting is to . . . ?"

"The next meeting is to review the candidates Dr. Goodwin has come up with and, based on your feedback, set up introductions. I made the meeting for ten o'clock. That time seemed to work well, right?"

"I guess." Leila dumped the bag holding their lunches onto the table next to her. "I really hate this matchmaking thing. I'll tell you this: I'm not meeting anyone I've serious reservations about just because well-meaning individuals think I need to find another Nick in order to make my life work."

"Please, cut the dramatics. We're looking for dates, just some dates."

Leila started unpacking their food. "Why are you always using the word *we*?"

"Because this is a team effort!" Michelle said, rising to join her. "You're not alone in this endeavor."

"Is the 'team' going on these dates?" Leila asked, dropping into a chair.

Michelle slid into the seat next to her. "Well, Hillary and I may be in the background, just as a precaution."

"This whole thing is absolutely ridiculous."

"Maybe so, but we're going to see Dr. Goodwin on Monday. No more discussion. Let's enjoy our lunch." Michelle opened one of the boxes of food and grinned. "I just love when anchovies are mixed in . . ."

5

Monday came sooner than Leila wanted. Despite numerous attempts, she'd been unable to deter Michelle and Hillary from bestowing their birthday gift in its entirety, and she felt totally defeated by the time she arrived at her second matchmaking appointment. Moreover, she sensed she'd become part of some bizarre ritual. Hillary once again checked in with the receptionist while Leila and Michelle found seats.

"Dr. Goodwin will be with you shortly," said the well-rehearsed receptionist. Hillary nodded and took a seat next to her mother.

"I'm excited to see the candidates, Mom. You must be a tiny bit curious, right?"

"My darling daughter, I'm much more apprehensive than curious."

A good ten minutes passed before Dr. Goodwin opened her office door and approached the trio. "Welcome, ladies. It's so nice to see you again. Come. We've much to discuss." She led them into her office and gestured for them to sit. "Please pull your chairs right up to the desk so you can see the computer screen and review the materials on the desktop."

Next to the computer rested three piles of folders. Glass paperweights anchored each one in place. "The materials are organized in identical fashion," Dr. Goodwin explained. "The last folder in each pile contains pictures relevant to the particular candidate. We'll look at the pictures only after you've acquired some insights into each candidate's attributes, accomplishments, and preferences."

"Your approach, then," Michelle interrupted, "is to sell us on the person first rather than on what the person appears to be on the surface."

"Exactly," Dr. Goodwin said. "Anyway, there's a game-like aspect to this as well. All of you will develop images in your mind as we begin to explore the candidates. Seeing how those images match the pictures in the bottom folders can be fun." She pulled up her chair and leaned forward. "So, let's begin."

Dr. Goodwin said that all three candidates had been sent Leila's information the week before, excluding her photographs. The men had been asked to review Leila's file and then let Heavenly Matches know within five days if they were interested or not interested in being introduced to her. All three had replied in the affirmative. After that, Leila's pictures had been sent to them.

"The computer generated a number of matches," Dr. Goodwin said. "I reviewed them all and selected these three candidates for your initial consideration. That's how I incorporate my personal touch in the process."

The three women listened intently as Dr. Goodwin reviewed the first candidate. He was slightly older than Dr. Goodwin would normally have chosen for Leila, but his history was engaging. Morgan Bradford was a retired family dentist currently teaching at his alma mater, Temple University's School of Dentistry. He was sixty-four years old—*Eight years older than me*, Leila thought, not sure how she felt about that—and just over five foot ten, with a full shock of dark hair, peppered with gray, that complemented his blue eyes. He was recently divorced from his wife of thirty-eight years. According to Morgan, she'd decided he'd become too predictable and had found a younger man with whom she planned to travel the world. Dr. Bradford had two sons who were married with children, making him a grandfather to five children under the age of ten. Both of Dr. Bradford's children lived out of town, so he made arrangements to visit them frequently. Luckily, they lived within a reasonable driving distance—one in Boston and the other outside of New York City.

Morgan went regularly to a gym near his apartment on Rittenhouse Square and enjoyed a round of golf now and then. He didn't smoke. He did, however, enjoy a glass of wine or two when dining out with friends, and on occasion savored a martini before his main course. He frequently made plans with friends and associates to attend the theater or see art exhibitions on the Parkway. Fine artworks particularly intrigued him, as his hobby was sketching and painting with watercolors. Dr. Goodwin directed the women's attention to the bottom folder, where they could see two samples of his work. He clearly had excellent hand-eye coordination—*All dentists must*, Leila thought—and this adeptness had helped him to create lovely pieces.

Dr. Goodwin paused, took a long breath, and then said, "I'll give you a couple of minutes to digest this information. Please, don't hesitate to have a discussion about everything you just heard." She sat back in her seat and waited.

Leila was speechless, in awe of Dr. Goodwin's fact-packed synopsis of the good dentist's life. And she wasn't the only one, if Michelle and Hillary's unusual silence was any indication.

"You'd make a great litigator," Hillary commented after a long pause.

Dr. Goodwin smiled and remained silent.

"I certainly don't want Leila to be the rebound girl," Michelle said slowly. "That may be the case with a newly divorced man. I think we need to hear about the other two. What do you think, Leila?"

"I don't know what to think, but I do feel as if I'm in some kind of absurd experiment where men in white coats are observing me through a two-way mirror."

"I can assure you, that's not the case," Dr. Goodwin said in a soothing tone. "But this process can be overwhelming. I believe in a few days you'll decide to meet at least one of these gentlemen."

Dr. Goodwin moved on to the second candidate, Chet Nickels. He was the same age as Leila. A graduate of Villanova University, he'd launched his own advertising and marketing company in 2002. Previously, he had worked in the communications industry for cable companies, selling advertising space. Unfortunately, his wife of thirty-plus years, his college sweetheart, had died of breast cancer three years earlier, leaving him to finish raising his two daughters, now ages twenty and twenty-two. Overcome with grief, Chet poured himself into his work. After more than two years, he'd decided he didn't want to live his life alone, and, with the urging of his daughters, he'd become a recent Heavenly Matches client. He'd done some dating in the past six months, but nothing had turned serious.

Chet had put on the pounds during his wife's long illness, too concentrated on helping her battle the disease to take care of himself, but since her death he'd become a fitness and nutrition enthusiast. His goal to lose twenty pounds had yet to be reached, but his height of six foot two allowed him to carry some extra weight without destroying his attractiveness. His wife had been an accomplished violinist with the Suburban Philharmonic Orchestra; consequently, over the years, Chet had grown to love music as well. He'd even tried his hand at piano and sometimes played simple duets with his wife. He also enjoyed playing chess, prompting him to join a local chess club that participated in international competitions. Since Chet and his wife liked to travel, they'd attended some of those competitions together.

"Any comments regarding Chet?" Dr. Goodwin asked. She waited patiently for a reply. Hillary, Michelle, and Leila looked at each other and shrugged in unison.

"Not really," Leila replied. "Let's go on to the last candidate."

"Just one minute," Dr. Goodwin urged. "I've a point I'd like to make. I haven't related every bit of information contained in these folders. I couldn't possibly do that in the time allotted." Turning in her chair, she spoke directly to Leila. "You'll need to read through each candidate's folder and ponder its contents. You may find you'd like to meet all three." She paused. "So, shall we proceed?"

All three women nodded their heads.

"Okay. I took somewhat of a risk offering this last candidate. He's been a client of Heavenly Matches on and off for five years or so. He's been divorced for many years, and though he's had two serious relationships, neither worked out. I just have a feeling that Leila may be the one to get him thinking long-term. His name is Ayden Doyle."

Leila forcefully inhaled and held her breath. She and Michelle shot wide-eyed glances at each other, communicating their utter astonishment.

"Do you two know this man?" Hillary asked, sounding confused.

Leila, still ardently focused on Michelle, shook her head, indicating to her friend that she wanted her to remain silent. "I may. Would that be a problem, Dr. Goodwin?"

"Not really. Ayden has already responded favorably. If he felt the situation were awkward, he'd have declined and I'd have removed him from the list."

Hillary pushed onward. "I'd like to hear more about Ayden Doyle since it seems I'm the only one who knows nothing about him."

Dr. Goodwin informed the eager listeners that Ayden Doyle was five years younger than Leila but shared many of her interests. "I don't see this age difference as significant. To your credit, Leila, you look younger than your years."

Dr. Goodwin proceeded to reveal Ayden's story. "He holds a degree in architecture from Drexel University. After a short stint with the architectural firm of White and Eagleton, he went out on his own as a general contractor. About that time, he married the daughter of a custom builder for whom he had worked during high school and college. The couple remained married for two years, just enough time to have a son named Daniel but not enough time to work out their problems. According to Ayden, his wife thought he was overly interested in drinking beer with his men friends and much less interested in being a devoted husband and father. Ayden did prove himself to be a responsible father, however, especially during his son's adolescent years. He took Daniel to work and taught him carpentry skills. Daniel eventually followed in his father's footsteps and began to work for him full-time after graduating from college.

"Ayden's company, AD and Associates, became known for its skillfulness in the restoration of older homes, especially those representing significant periods of American architectural development. Ayden built a fine reputation and won a number of design awards over the years, including 'Best on the Main Line.' Moreover, he became known as an avid sculptor, using a variety of mediums, such as clay and metal, to create both traditional and abstract forms. A number of Center City galleries currently exhibit his work. To their delight, his pieces sell quickly."

Dr. Goodwin concluded her remarks in her matter-of-fact way: "Ayden is about five foot ten and has a trim, muscular frame. The kind of work he does involves extensive physical exertion that helps to keep him in shape. He has a pleasant appearance that includes inviting blue eyes and auburn hair now beginning to show touches of gray." She rested for a moment. "Any comments or questions regarding Ayden Doyle?"

When the women shook their heads, Dr. Goodwin glanced at her watch. "It looks like our session is drawing to a close. You're sure you don't have any questions?"

Leila shook her head again, and Dr. Goodwin rose from her desk and collected all the folders. She handed one pile to each woman.

"Now let's skip to the picture folders. There isn't much time left for discussion, but I'm interested in seeing if your mental images of the candidates match their actual photos."

Michelle went through her pile and retrieved a picture of Morgan

Bradford. "I didn't picture him with glasses, but he appears to be a nice-looking man." Leila and Hillary reached for the picture, each taking a corner of Dr. Bradford's rather formal photograph. *The same one is likely featured on the dental school's website*, Leila thought.

After studying it for a few seconds, they returned it to Michelle.

"I have Chet Nickel's picture," Hillary informed the others. "His hair is thinning, but I think he still looks handsome. He cuts his hair á la Bruce Willis."

Leila and Michelle leaned over Hillary's shoulders to gaze upon candidate Number Two. Their body language indicated they agreed with Hillary's assessment.

"Mom, you must have Ayden Doyle."

Leila fumbled with her stack and brought the bottom folder to the top.

She opened it to find Ayden Doyle staring back at her, sitting on a post and rail fence wearing a light blue, collared, long-sleeved shirt and khakis. Michelle leaned over and whispered into Leila's ear, "So, this is our Ayden Doyle. Not bad."

"He's all right," Leila responded in an attempt to be nonchalant.

"Let me see, Mom." Hillary took Ayden's photo and studied it for a few seconds. "I think his eyes are his best feature."

"Well, did the gentlemen meet your expectations?" Dr. Goodwin inquired.

"Somewhat," Leila began. "All three candidates are nice-looking enough, but as you said, I must consider each in totality. I'm looking for sincerity, kindness, a sense of humor, and intelligence."

"You're also looking to see if there's chemistry, that attraction that prompts a man and a woman to explore one another further," interjected Michelle. "The draw may not be the same as you and Nick had, but it should be close."

Dr. Goodwin nodded. "Michelle is right. That's why dating is important. You may not need more than two or three dates to discover if chemistry exists or not, but you need to take the risk. Go home, take your time, and go through the folders. Let me know if you're interested in going forward, and I'll make the necessary arrangements. I hope you'll give all three candidates a chance."

The three women rose from their seats and watched Dr. Goodwin place the candidates' folders into a Heavenly Matches tote. Leila took hold of the precious cargo and extended her hand to Dr. Goodwin. "Thank you for your help and advice. I've a lot to think about."

After Michelle and Hillary exchanged handshakes with Dr. Goodwin, the group hastened into the waiting room, their impatience fueled partially by hunger pangs but mostly by the need to rehash what they'd just learned. They'd already agreed upon a deli near the design boutique as their lunch destination and soon made a beeline for the door.

⚘

Soon after Hillary drove away, Leila turned to Michelle to discuss an issue she hadn't brought into their rather benign conversation over lunch. "Do you realize the entire time I met with Ayden last week he knew Dr. Goodwin had paired us up? How embarrassing. He said absolutely nothing. No wonder he was more civil. He must have had a good laugh at my expense. How am I ever going to face him again? You'll need to completely take over the Perkins project."

Michelle's expression was unreadable. "Ayden likely felt just as awkward as you do now. Perhaps he decided to wait things out. He welcomed the opportunity to meet you in a setting other than the Perkinses' home. You should keep him in the running. Go out with him. Learn more about him. See if there is any chemistry. Have some fun."

Leila scowled. "Leave it to you to give this disaster a positive twist."

"Look, you can play the *game* just as well as Ayden has. Make the next appointment with the Perkinses. Let Ayden know about it. Avoid discussing the matchmaking situation unless he brings it up. Meanwhile, make arrangements to meet the other two guys. You need to gain some experience. Morgan and Chet appear to be nice, at least on paper, right?"

Leila considered. Could Michelle's advice be worth taking? She shook her head. "I find this entire circumstance very disturbing. I feel like I'm an adolescent, new to the dating scene and totally clueless about how to handle things." She turned and hugged Michelle. "Thanks for your thoughts. And I'll call the Perkinses tonight, see if I can set up that appointment."

"That's the spirit, partner." Michelle gave Leila a thumbs-up. When she drove away, Leila was still lost in thought on the sidewalk in front of her house, the tote filled with the Heavenly Matches folders dangling from her arm.

6

The next morning, Leila was running late. She walked in twenty minutes after Michelle opened.

"I'm so sorry, Michelle, but I didn't get the Perkinses on the phone last night; their phone just rang and rang and the voice mail didn't kick in. So I decided to try again from home before I left, and it threw my schedule off."

Michelle waved away her apology. "Not a problem. Did you get an appointment?"

"Yes. I arranged it for the first of the month at ten. Now I have to let Ayden know about it. Hopefully, that time will be good for him too." She picked up the shop phone and gave her friend a look, and Michelle made a point of leaving the office and busying herself around the shop.

Ayden's phone went straight to voice mail. Leila felt a little relieved. "Hi, Ayden, this is Leila Brandt. I've made arrangements for us to meet the Perkinses on the first of the month at ten. Please let me know if that is a good day and time for you. You can contact me at the shop or reach me on my cell. Both numbers are on my business card. Take care."

As soon as she hung up the phone, Michelle reentered the office and rattled through some notes. "So, we have two prospective design clients. Both have left voice mails. The Millers live in Radnor and the Hunters live in Blue Bell. The Millers want to rejuvenate their master bedroom and redo the master bathroom, and the Hunters are interested in updating their family room."

Leila looked up from doodling on her notepad to find Michelle staring at her.

"Did you hear me?"

"I'm sorry." Leila set down her pen. "I'm somewhere else. Two new clients?"

"Yes, the Millers in Radnor and the Hunters in Blue Bell. Do you want to schedule for next Monday?"

Leila reached for her planner and found no conflicts. "Okay. Let's try to get both of them in by midafternoon. I may want to schedule a touch-up for later that day."

"Perfect," Michelle said. "I'll take care of making the appointments. I'm also thinking of putting off other design clients until after the Children's Hospital fund-raiser is over. I think we're spreading ourselves too thin."

"I agree." Leila paused. "I know you're just dying to ask me about the Heavenly Matches stuff." She smiled at her friend. "I did come to a decision last night. First, I'll ask to meet the dentist and see how that goes. I want to take things slowly. What may seem a baby step to you is really a giant leap for me. Can you understand that?"

"Of course. I know this dating scene can be unsettling. And sharing your personal feelings or experiences with me is purely your decision. I don't want to be intrusive."

"You're the best." Leila reached for her cell phone and sat back in her desk chair. "Yes, I'd like to leave a message for Dr. Goodwin, please." She circled a finger on her desk as she waited to be connected. "Dr. Goodwin, this is Leila Brandt. I'd like you to go ahead and initiate a meeting with Morgan Bradford. I'm thinking something simple, perhaps drinks at a convenient restaurant that usually has a lively crowd. Please feel free to give Morgan my cell number and my home number. I prefer no texts or emails. Thanks so much."

Soon after Leila placed her cell phone on the top of her desk, she received a text message from Ayden: "*I'll be there. Ayden.*"

✿

Morgan Bradford called Leila two days after she gave Dr. Goodwin the go-ahead. Their conversation was short, primarily making arrangements for the upcoming Friday-night happy hour at The Grille in Plymouth Meeting. Morgan lived downtown, about fifteen miles away, but he was happy to drive out her way. Leila considered that a good sign. It indicated that he was flexible, a good trait for a possible man-friend.

A last look in the hall mirror assured Leila that her outfit—sea-green pants, matching sweater, and two-toned, neutral sandals—achieved the desired effect. The monotones helped her appear taller. The sweater's neckline was slightly seductive but certainly not brazen. Dangling aquamarine and pearl earrings added just the right touch of femininity. In sum, Leila thought she looked smashing. However, her satisfaction with her appearance did nothing for her anxiety. Her stomach was in knots.

How would she ever be able to appear casual while drinking a glass of wine and nibbling on hors d'oeuvres? Why had she allowed herself to be put in this awkward situation in the first place?

As soon as she opened the door to the restaurant, she caught sight of Morgan. He was standing near the hostess station, reviewing the available seating in the bar area. He was dressed nicely, in a collared shirt, sweater, and navy pants. Leila decided she would approach him as if he were a prospective client. She'd put on her warm smile and reach out for the handshake that would accompany her self-introduction.

Just as she moved forward, Morgan looked her way. She met his eyes, gave him a big smile, and inquired, "Morgan?" as she walked toward him.

"Yes. So nice to meet you, Leila."

He got his handshake going before Leila completely transferred her shawl and purse to her left hand. She didn't like being outmaneuvered. "Likewise."

"Say, it's really noisy in the bar area. How about we take a booth in the back so we can talk?"

Leila nodded her assent.

"What would you like to drink?"

"I'd love a glass of merlot."

Morgan approached the bartender with his request and consulted with the hostess, who confirmed the last booth was free. He touched Leila's shoulder and guided her to their space. "I'll be right back with our drinks."

Morgan returned quickly with two glasses of wine. "For you, my lady," he said with a wink. "I asked the waitress to bring us the assorted vegetables and dip appetizer. Is that all right with you?"

"That's a great choice."

"I guess I'd sound really stupid if I asked you to tell me about yourself since I have thoroughly read your bio. Is there anything you left out that I should know?"

He's trying to be humorous. "Not that I can think of at the moment," she replied with a polite smile.

"You're prettier in person," Morgan said, lifting his gaze from the neckline of her sweater to her eyes.

His line was corny but she responded warmly, "That's sweet of you to say. Listen, why don't we begin by talking about our work lives and then move on from there?"

"Sounds good. I'll go first."

Morgan rattled off a detailed description of his years in family practice. He had especially enjoyed working with children.

While Leila listened dutifully, she couldn't help but notice that he had very white, straight teeth. Were they real? Wouldn't it be hilarious if Morgan wore a complete set of dentures? The mere thought of that brought her to the brink of laughter, but she managed to ward off the impulse. *Don't be that way,* she scolded herself. *He appears to be a really nice and sincere man.*

Morgan concluded, "I enjoy teaching, but not as much as I liked practicing."

"You have the opportunity to give back, to share your wisdom with future dentists," Leila said. "That's very nice. I sometimes teach design courses at Philadelphia University. I hope in some small way I'm able to pass on what I've learned over the years."

And so went the two hours they spent exchanging small talk, sipping wine, enjoying a variety of appetizers, and getting to know each other. When the evening drew to a close, Morgan was thoughtful enough to walk Leila to her car.

"I hope we can get together again soon," Morgan said in an almost questioning manner, leaning into Leila's open window.

"I'll look forward to it." A pleasantry Leila didn't mean.

He stood back, reached through the window, and gently touched Leila's left hand, which was firmly attached to the steering wheel. "Good night, Leila."

Leila immediately recalled a similar scene at Ayden's when the aftereffect had been totally different. With Morgan, she was in control and at peace with herself. Her time with him could be likened to spending the evening with an older brother, reminiscing about the old days and catching up on current events. His touch was inconsequential. On the other hand, every fiber of Leila's body had reacted to Ayden's handshake. She'd kept him in sight using the rearview mirror as she headed down his driveway, relishing every second until she needed to turn onto the street. She thought about him on the ride back and beyond—how gentle his hands seemed when they touched hers in spite of the rugged work they performed, how intoxicating his blue eyes were, how willingly she abandoned herself to them, and how precise his body movements were, as if they'd been carefully choreographed and practiced over and over again until perfection resulted. She had even fantasized what it would be like to be kissed by Ayden—to feel his warm lips against hers, to know his scent and taste.

Such thoughts placed her in a state of euphoria that, sadly, came to an end when she discovered him to be an *undeclared* Heavenly Matches candidate. Why did she feel betrayed? Was there even a basis for such a response? Somehow, she knew that Morgan Bradford, apparently a very nice man, didn't have a chance, while Ayden was still in the running. Both dread and anticipation permeated her thoughts as she contemplated the upcoming appointment at the Perkinses.

❀

The first of the month arrived with brilliant sunshine. Summer was in full swing, minus the humidity the Northeast often experienced. Everything seemed aglow, including Leila. She sat on her deck, enjoying her muffin and cup of coffee despite how nervous she felt about the meeting at ten. She wasn't worried the Perkinses would reject her ideas or the materials she'd selected. Her apprehension? An inability to keep her crush on Ayden a secret from him. An involuntary gesture, a telling facial expression, or a verbal response not carefully thought out might provide a clue to her inner feelings. Furthermore, the Heavenly Matches situation unsettled her. Was she intentionally being made the fool? Should she bring up the subject at all, or should she let Ayden take the lead?

Leila packed the drawings and materials she needed to show the Perkinses into three totes and loaded them into the trunk of her car before going upstairs to ready herself. Once upstairs, she eyed the outfit she'd selected for this momentous day and laid out neatly on her bed: a sleeveless silk V-neck blouse the color of café au lait, a peach-colored linen pencil skirt with a tortoiseshell belt, and new bronze patent leather pumps. Together, the ensemble suggested a blend of professionalism and allure. Her confidence revved up.

❁

Leila pulled into the Perkinses' driveway just before ten. She noticed Ayden's truck parked just past the front door. She parked behind him, collected her totes and briefcase, and rang the doorbell.

Janice greeted her warmly. "Hi, Leila. Please come in."

"Good morning. How are things going?"

"Just great. Marshall and I have been upstairs with Ayden for ten minutes or so. He's explaining the floor-plan options. Why don't we leave your things here for now and join the men?" Janice motioned for Leila to follow her up the stairs and led the way at a brisk clip. Obviously, she didn't want to miss a second of Ayden's presentation.

Isn't it just like him to arrive early and begin without me? Leila thought. *How frustrating.*

Janice entered the master-bedroom suite first. "I'm back with Leila," she announced. She hurried Leila into the bathroom. "Marshall, you haven't met Leila yet."

Marshall's initial reaction was a broad smile. "Great to meet you." He initiated a handshake that seemed to last a bit longer than necessary. "I'm looking forward to working with you and Ayden. He's just begun telling us about his floor plans. I understand you have a favorite?"

"It's nice to meet you, Marshall. And, yes, there is one I especially like, but all of the plans are impressive."

"Well, Ayden, please continue now that we're all here." Marshall turned his attention back to the plans.

Ayden fiddled with his laptop, adjusting the clarity and color of an image on the screen. Once he finally achieved the effect he wanted, he turned to face the others. His blue eyes quickly shifted in Leila's direction. "Hey, Leila, where are your totes?" he asked with a wink and a smile.

"Oh, I told her to leave them downstairs for now. Should we go and get them?" Janice asked, clearly not recognizing Ayden's attempt at humor.

"No, we'll get to them soon enough," Ayden replied.

Leila knew Ayden was making a joke, or perhaps flirting with her. She offered a slight smile and an accompanying nod that meant, *Please continue.* As she gazed upon her secret beau, she wondered if there were any other men who could wear jeans and a gray T-shirt as well as Ayden. It seemed unfair that he could look that good without investing much time in deciding what to wear while she'd devoted hours to creating her *special* look for the day.

Ayden carefully took the Perkinses through the three floor plans, explaining all that they entailed. He answered all of their questions honestly, responsively, and respectfully. In short, he proved himself to be a charming and consummate professional.

Marshall and Janice looked at each other.

"I love all the plans, but I'm drawn to the last one, the one with all the bells and whistles," Janice blurted out.

"I agree," Marshall said. "Though I suppose the cost will have an impact on our final decision."

"The third option is twenty thousand dollars more than the first," Ayden said plainly. "That's primarily due to the increased labor costs. What will help you to choose *the* plan is to see the various design options Leila has created. Don't rush through the decision process. I wouldn't be able to start your project for a month anyway."

"I'm impressed," Marshall said. "I know you're our man, but you're right. Janice and I need to sort things out. Leave me all the necessary paperwork. I have to leave now to meet my golf buddies, but Janice will catch me up on things tonight." He turned to give

Janice a peck on the cheek, shook Ayden's hand, and squeezed Leila's arm before leaving.

"Well then," Janice said. "Let's meet downstairs in the sunroom. I'll get some snacks together."

"That's a great idea," Leila agreed. The prospect of spending more time with Ayden wasn't unpleasant. "The natural lighting will nicely showcase the products I've brought for your consideration."

"See you in ten minutes." Janice left Ayden and Leila alone.

"I'll be right down to help you," Leila called after her. She turned to Ayden. "Your presentation was great. I'm not usually a betting woman, but I think the third option, obviously my favorite, will win."

"Thanks. The third option is my stretch plan, but it offers a potentially great return on the investment."

"You're right." Leila paused a moment to study Ayden's pleasing face. "Well, I better get down to Janice and help her set up the refreshments."

"Did you let Dr. Goodwin know you wanted to meet me?"

Leila stopped dead in her tracks. Did she have the courage to turn around and look at him? Ayden waited patiently for her response. He had no follow-up. The ball was in her court, and she needed a strategic return.

Leila slowly pivoted; she leaned against the doorframe and crossed her arms the way a mother would position herself before scolding her child. "All right. Let's get this out in the open. My daughter and my business partner decided for my birthday they'd give me a consultation with Dr. Goodwin. They were concerned I'd become a hermit after my husband's death. I was totally against it, but I didn't want to hurt their feelings. That's all there is to it. It's unfortunate the two of us were paired up. I think you'll agree it's important to keep our relationship totally professional."

Ayden approached Leila, coming so close she caught a whiff of his lime-scented cologne. He leaned in, supporting his stance by placing one hand on the doorframe above her head and the other against the wall, almost within kissing distance. Would he kiss her?

"No," he said firmly. "I don't agree. We can have both a professional and personal relationship. You're just a bit scared. It's been a while."

How arrogant. Now she was on the offensive. She wasn't going to retreat from his challenge. "Unfortunately, I think you've misjudged me. I'm perfectly comfortable with men. What I'm uncomfortable with is mixing business with pleasure. I don't want to in any way compromise my relationship with a client."

"Now, how would having dinner with me compromise your relationship with the Perkinses?" He raised an eyebrow. "Take some time to think about it. We've already proven ourselves to be a very effective team."

Leila surprised herself with the lighthearted lilt in her voice. "Okay, I'll think about it. Would you please let me out of this tight spot so I can help Janice downstairs?"

Ayden looked at her intently with his baby blues for a few more seconds. Leila returned the gaze. Could she endure his look without withering? She'd not surrender.

Finally, he moved back and allowed her the room to make a graceful exit.

She breathed a sigh of relief after exiting the room. He'd tested her, and she'd stood her ground. But how she wished he had kissed her. Little did he know she wouldn't have resisted.

7

Leila raced down the stairs, her heart beating a mile a minute. She stopped in the foyer to pick up her totes and her briefcase and trotted through the dining room, only slowing her pace as she approached the kitchen.

A tray loaded with iced tea, fruit, crackers, and cheese was sitting on the island. Janice was still bustling around the kitchen.

"Let me help." Leila gestured to the tray. "Do you want this in the sunroom on the coffee table the way we had it before?"

"That would be great," Janet said. "Is Ayden still upstairs?"

"Yes, I think he's still checking a few things out. He should be down very soon. Let me put my things in the sunroom, and I'll be back for the tray."

Leila and Janice had everything situated on the sunroom table and were sitting on the sofa chatting when Ayden joined them. He was readied for a quick departure: his laptop case hung from his shoulder, his sunglasses rested on top of his head, and his keys jingled in his right hand.

"I know the two of you have a lot to talk about," he said. "I've got to run now. I have to be in Devon in less than an hour. We'll need to schedule another appointment. Leila, can we take care of that now?"

"Sure," Leila responded, avoiding eye contact. She gave Janice her undivided attention. "How much time do you think you and Marshall need to go over things before making any commitments?"

"I think a week will be enough. Ayden is busy now anyway, right, Ayden?"

"Yes, I'm finishing up with two clients. I need a good three weeks to a month before taking on a large renovation. If it's okay with Leila, how about we meet next week, the eighth, same time?"

"Let me check, but I think that will be fine." Leila reached for her briefcase and retrieved her planner. After a quick check, she summoned all the courage she could muster, turned to Ayden, and said with a smile, "That's fine. See you then."

"Great." Ayden turned to leave and then suddenly stopped. "Oh, one thing, Janice, the three floor plans aren't set in stone. You can take an idea from one and include it in another, or eliminate something altogether. For example, you may decide that it's not necessary to have both his and her private toilets if you opt for plan three. Just one shared private toilet may suffice. I can make all kinds of adjustments."

"Thanks for the direction." Janice clapped her hands together. "Now Leila and I can do some out-of-the box thinking."

"Later, then."

Ayden departed, leaving Leila both disappointed and relieved by his absence. She missed being around him when he was gone but felt emotionally encumbered when he was present. This man was turning her personal and work lives upside down. What was she going to do? Maybe she needed to give Dr. Goodwin a call.

❁

Leila spent another hour and a half with Janice, providing explicit guidance. Each of her three totes contained a unique design plan for the master bath. The first tote contained a neutral plan with glistening metallic accents; the second, ivory, soft beiges, and pale aqua products with chrome and gold accents; and the third, a bolder scheme of beige, brown, coffee, and caramel tones complemented by touches of peach and terra-cotta. Leila designated space on the floor for each plan, spreading about drawings, pamphlets, and products so Janice could see everything easily. Janice listened carefully to her descriptions and took notes so she could correctly explain things to her husband later.

"I love everything," she said when Leila was done. "Marshall and I will have a tough time making decisions. You've done a wonderful job. You know, you and Ayden make a great team."

The mention of her and Ayden as a team caught Leila momentarily off guard, and she froze. It was only Janice's reaching over with open arms to offer an appreciative hug that enabled her to regroup.

❁

Driving back to the shop, Leila experienced different thoughts and emotions. Those totes, at least for now, were out of her jurisdiction. She had done a good job with the design plans and had created some wonderful possibilities for the Perkinses. But there was still the burning question of what to do about Ayden. There was no doubt he had caused dormant feelings within her to awaken—feelings she had buried along with Nick. She recalled Dr. Goodwin's words: *I just have a feeling that you, Leila, may be the one to get him thinking long-term.* Yet her woman's intuition kept alerting her to the strong probability that this man liked being a free agent and would never welcome an enduring, monogamous relationship.

As soon as Leila entered the shop, she realized how important her return was to Michelle, who was trying to serve the needs of four customers at the same time. She immediately took over package-wrapping duties while Michelle processed sales. They worked nonstop for over an hour, and when the last customer finally left, they both fell onto the hand-painted bench they kept by the checkout, a resting place especially favored by husbands waiting while their wives shopped.

"Thank goodness you returned when you did," Michelle said. "I was about to have a meltdown."

Leila leaned her head back against the wall. "Everyone seemed content with their purchases. The bridal shower gift Mrs. Telford bought will be a hit, don't you think?"

"That was one gorgeous vase. Sad to see it go. I wanted it for myself," Michelle said with a sigh. "Before I forget, Morgan Bradford called and left a message. Apparently, you weren't picking up your cell phone, and rather than waiting to leave a message, he thought he might catch you here. He must have noted our business's name in your bio."

"What did he say?"

"He asked that you let him know at your earliest convenience if you're free for dinner tonight. I wrote his number down on a Post-it Note. It's on your desk blotter."

"I'm too tired. This has been an action-packed day. I think I'll put him off."

She pulled herself off the bench and went into the office to call Morgan. He was disappointed she had declined his invitation but happy when she asked about the following night.

She and Michelle spent the rest of the afternoon tidying up the shop and rearranging displays. Inevitably, the conversation targeted the Perkins project.

"How did things go with the Perkinses and Ayden?" Michelle asked.

"Great. Ayden's presentation wowed them. Janice loved our design plans. All of us will meet again next week, on the eighth, and hopefully get some major things finalized."

"That makes me happy. I can begin billing, and that means we'll start to see some money from the Perkinses soon."

Leila grinned. "I love the creative part of our business, but getting paid for having fun is even better."

"I'd like to run over to the market and get something for dinner tonight," Michelle said. "You know how grumpy David gets when I haven't planned anything. Can you close up?"

"Absolutely."

Michelle caught her handbag on the shop's door in her hurry to vacate the premises. Leila laughed and shook her head, but she looked forward to her "alone" time. A number of thoughts raced through her mind. What about Chet Nickels? Should she call Dr. Goodwin and ask her to make the arrangements? Why not? Nothing ventured, nothing gained.

And then there was Ayden. No denying there was chemistry there. Amazing chemistry. A smile crossed her face. Of late, her private thoughts had centered on him, spawned by both his interest in her and his magnetic presence, and undeterred by his blatant hubris. Who was she kidding? Morgan didn't have a chance. Maybe Chet did. She picked up the phone and dialed Heavenly Matches.

"Dr. Goodwin is tied up with a client at the moment, Ms. Brandt. Let me put you through to her voice mail," the receptionist said.

Leila waited for the beep, then began: "Hi, Dr. Goodwin. This is Leila Brandt. I just want you to know I've met Morgan Bradford. He seems to be a very nice man. I'm going to see him again. As far as the other two candidates, Chet Nickels and Ayden Doyle, I've decided to check them out as well. Thank you for arranging things. Take care."

There. It was done. She'd taken the giant leap of including Ayden. "Permission granted, Mr. Doyle. You can continue to pursue me if you wish," she said to herself.

8

L eila arrived at The Tavern a few minutes early. The hostess seated her in one of the large booths in the main dining area, where it would be easy for Morgan to find her.

"Hello, pretty lady."

Morgan was standing right in front of her; she hadn't even noticed him approaching. He leaned over to give her a kiss on the cheek and then slid into the booth. He was nicely dressed, as before, this time in a pale-blue sweater over a plaid shirt teamed up with tan pants. Certainly, this man made a good appearance.

"So, how have you been?" he asked.

"I'm fine. We've been busy, though, so I'm a bit tired. I'll rest up and recharge on Sunday. How about you?"

"This is an easy time of the year for me. I'm not teaching very much, just a couple of three-week courses. I'll find myself in over-drive fall semester."

"You know what they say: when it rains, it pours. Sounds very trite, but things do seem to come in waves—everything at once, followed by a lull. For example, yesterday when I got back to the shop, my partner Michelle was waiting on four customers at one time. An hour later all was still, and it stayed that way until closing."

"I guess we should decide on what we want," Morgan said, opening his menu and cutting off the conversation. "Anything you'd like to recommend?"

Leila didn't appreciate the move, but she tried to keep her tone light. "I've never been disappointed here. Order what appeals to you. I'm thinking about the chicken marsala."

I sure hope this conversation becomes more stimulating. He's probably thinking the same.

"How about a cocktail or glass of wine?" he suggested.

"That sounds like a good idea. A glass of chardonnay would be lovely." Leila energized her voice, hoping to liven things up.

The waitress approached, delivered two glasses of water with ice and lemon wedges, and took their dinner order. When she walked away, Morgan reached out and gently grasped Leila's hand.

"I have a couple of tickets to a community playhouse's production of Shakespeare's *Much Ado About Nothing*. I'd like you to go with me. It's for next Saturday evening."

"I love the theater, as you know from my bio"—she tried one of the smiles she'd practiced in the mirror while getting dressed—"but the shop is open on Saturdays. What time is the performance?"

"Eight o'clock," Morgan promptly responded.

"I think that's doable. Which theater?"

Morgan hesitated. "There's a slight catch. The theater is in Longport, New Jersey, about a ninety-minute drive from the city."

"We'd need to leave around six," Leila said, thinking aloud. "That would be a bit tight for me, but maybe Michelle could finish up without me."

Morgan continued to hold her hand. "I own a home down there, so rather than driving home after the performance, I thought we could stay there for the night, have a nice, leisurely breakfast the following day, and then head for home. What do you think?"

The suggested arrangements came as a surprise. She'd wanted a more stimulating conversation, and now she was getting it. Her first inclination was to withdraw her hand, gain needed distance, and chastise Morgan for even suggesting such a plan. Her inner voice told her to calm down. She didn't want to appear intimidated; moreover, she wanted her reply to sound totally sincere.

"Gee, Morgan, that sounds like a truly lovely idea, but I'm not comfortable with it at this stage of our relationship. We're just getting to know each other. I'd like to take things more slowly. But certainly, feel free to ask someone else. I'll totally understand if you decide to do so."

The waitress intervened with their wine and salads. "Is there anything else I can get you?" she asked.

Morgan released Leila's hand and sat back in his seat. "Maybe a couple of rolls and some oil for dipping," he suggested.

"Right away."

Morgan wore a slight frown. Instead of looking directly at Leila, he kept his eyes on his food. "We're both adults. I see nothing wrong with our enjoying each other."

Immediately and involuntarily, Leila found herself in the twenty-first century and forced to consider current mores. Inexperienced though she might be about many things associated with the dating scene, she understood Morgan's intentions and decided not to make this portion of their conversation easy for him.

"What exactly are you saying?"

With that question floating in the air, she firmly grasped her fork and began eating her salad.

Morgan hesitated, searching for the words to drive home his point. "I'm talking about companionship and all that goes along with it. If that includes sex, so be it."

"Oh, I see, and I agree." She sensed Morgan was surprised by her response. Suddenly, she felt empowered. "I do think sex should be part of a loving relationship. Only, you and I aren't in love at the moment, and I'm not an advocate of casual sex. For me, sex must mean something."

"I appreciate your honesty and totally understand where you're coming from," he said, his frown gone. "Let's consider a Plan B. I'll pack a snack we can eat on the way down. After the performance, we can go to a cute Italian restaurant in Margate that stays open late for theatergoers, and then we'll drive back."

Leila considered. "It would be a late evening, but the next day is Sunday. I could sleep in. Let's think on this some more, but your Plan B sounds good."

"Fine."

After the arrival of the main dishes, Morgan and Leila's conversation returned to more mundane topics—the politics of the day, a recently released movie. They lingered over coffee and shared a chocolate dessert since Leila had admitted to her weakness for chocolate.

As she finished her coffee, she glanced at her watch. "It's getting late. Tomorrow is a workday. I'd better be getting home."

"Sure." Morgan called the waitress over and asked for the bill. There was no more small talk. Silence prevailed as he handled the business aspect of the date. Soon thereafter, he walked Leila to her car and waited for her to situate herself in the driver's seat. As she lowered the window to say good-bye, he said, "I'll check in with you the beginning of next week."

"Great! And Morgan, thanks for a lovely dinner and pleasant conversation."

"You're welcome." He kissed her lightly on the cheek, and in an instant, he was gone.

As Leila drove home, she began to review the evening. A number of questions raced through her mind. Wasn't Morgan bold to suggest an overnighter so early in the game? Did he truly understand why she refused? And when they said their good-byes, had he appeared less interested in her than before?

At home, she checked her voice mail and found that Chet Nickels had left a message: "Hi, Leila. This is Chet Nickels. I'm sorry I missed you. I'll try you again tomorrow. I'm hoping we can find a time to meet in the near future. Take care."

Chet sounded nice. Perhaps a widower was a better candidate than a divorced man, who might harbor negative feelings toward women. She decided to discuss this idea with Michelle. But for now, she headed straight to bed.

❀

The weekend loomed on the horizon. Leila didn't expect to hear from Morgan until Monday at the earliest, since his theater tickets were for the following Saturday. However, she looked forward to meeting Chet Nickels. Had Dr. Goodwin given him all three of her contact numbers? Likely, she had.

"Good morning, partner," Leila called out as she entered the shop and headed to the office.

"Hi there."

Leila settled in at her desk and checked around for any Post-it Notes from Michelle. None were in view. "Any messages?"

"None, nada, zip," replied Michelle, a mischievous grin spreading across her face. "May I ask which of your candidates you expected to hear from?"

"Oh, Chet Nickels left a message on my home phone. I missed his call last night when I was out with Morgan. I thought he might have tried me here."

"You're much in demand, it seems, yes?" Michelle wasn't done with her banter yet.

Leila shook her head. "Okay, you've had enough fun. Just quit it. I need you to be serious, because I have something to tell you about yesterday's date with Morgan. I want your take on things."

With that, Michelle became all ears. She repositioned herself in her chair, grabbed her glasses so she'd appear serious, and looked intently in Leila's direction. "So? Get to it."

"Well, I met Morgan at The Tavern. Things seemed to be

going well, but then he asked me to go with him to a community theater production of *Much Ado About Nothing*. The catch?
The theater is located in Longport, New Jersey. To avoid driving
home late at night, he wanted me to sleep at his shore house and
drive back the next morning after we had a leisurely breakfast. I,
of course, was most uncomfortable with that arrangement, and
I declined."

Michelle sat silent for a few seconds, processing the information.
Then she launched her inquest. "What did he say about the sleeping
arrangements?"

"We didn't get that far, Michelle."

"Did he mention sex?"

"In a roundabout way. He said he saw nothing wrong with our
enjoying each other. The problem is, I do."

"How many dates have you had with Morgan?"

"Just two."

"How do you feel about him?"

"I don't *feel* at the moment. I'm just getting to know him. But, I'm
not gaga over him."

"So what you're saying is, the ingredient needed to launch a relationship with the dentist hasn't surfaced."

"What are you saying? Would you please avoid encrypting the
points you want to make?"

"There's no chemistry at the moment. If there were chemistry,
you might have considered his offer, right?"

"Don't be ridiculous! I've only been out with the man twice. What
woman in her right mind would spend the night with a man she
hardly knows?"

"Get real. There are plenty of women in their right minds who
would. I bet you wouldn't be so appalled at this invitation if it had
come from someone else—say, Ayden Doyle?"

Leila derailed for a moment. "What do you mean? I haven't even gone out on a date with him. We hardly know each other. At this point, our relationship is purely business."

"Okay, but I think you're protesting way too much. There appears to be a to-do about something. And by the way, all my puns are intended."

Luckily for Leila, the shop bell rang. Michelle left to attend to the customer while Leila reflected on their conversation. Would she have felt less flabbergasted if the idea for an overnighter had come from Ayden? Michelle might be right. Hadn't she fantasized about Ayden? Hadn't she wondered what his kiss would be like? Hadn't she imagined herself in his arms? She hadn't entertained such thoughts about Morgan, and she felt certain she never would.

Michelle continued her inquiry upon her return. "Well, are you going to see Morgan again?"

"We did make plans to see the play, catch a bite afterward, and drive back. He's supposed to call me the beginning of next week to finalize things."

"I'm flattered you feel comfortable confiding in me," Michelle said, her playfulness gone. "I only want the best for you. I have some thoughts about this whole scenario I'd like to share with you, okay?"

Leila nodded.

"Yes, Morgan may have been presumptuous. But he's a man, and that's how men think. He did switch things around to accommodate your feelings. That's a plus. I'd give him another chance. But if you cannot see yourself being intimate with him in the near future, I'd move on. Why waste his time and yours?"

"Does sex always have to be part of the equation?"

"I'm afraid so—and isn't it a wonderful part of a loving relationship? I don't want to stir up buried feelings about Nick. I know that can be painful. But you two had that special something. After all those years together, you still had the hots for each other. I feel the same about David. You and I have been most fortunate." Michelle reached for Leila's hand and gave it a squeeze. "You're very protective of yourself. You need to let go—whether it's with Ayden, Chet, or somebody else who makes you feel alive."

"Maybe a widower has more potential than a divorced man," Leila said, floating her new theory. "Divorced men could be bitter and harbor negative feelings toward women. What do you think?"

"Well, that's more a question for Dr. Goodwin. However, I think just because a guy is a widower doesn't mean he was a happily married man."

"I suppose you're right." Leila sighed, exhaling as if she were letting out all the anxiety that had built up inside her since her date with Morgan.

9

Chet had suggested a bar-and-grill spot in Radnor. "It's a great place for a first date," he'd said. "It always attracts a lively bar crowd, and there are booths that can give us enough privacy to talk."

Leila arrived ten minutes early. She sat in her car and checked her phone messages to kill some time. Nothing from Ayden. *Why hasn't he called? Is he waiting for the next meeting at the Perkinses to make his move? I should play it cool too.* She reached for her handbag and retrieved her cosmetic pouch. A last-minute touch-up was needed before her debut. As she looked in the rearview mirror, she noticed a tall man entering the bar. Was it Chet? She quickly finished reapplying her lipstick and headed for the door.

The man waited patiently just past the entrance, his eye on a television over the bar. A SportsNet commentator was conducting an interview with an Eagles guard. He seemed totally engrossed in the exchange, but when Leila walked in, he immediately turned and moved toward her.

"You're even prettier than your picture," he declared with an approving smile.

That must be the most overused line uttered by men, she thought. But she responded in kind. Why not? "Thank you, Chet. You look just as handsome as you did in your photograph."

"We have two seating areas to choose from." He pointed to

the back of the bar area. "We can sit at that high-top table over there, or we can sit in the booth next to the entrance. What do you think?"

"I like the cozy booth, if you don't mind."

Chet looped his arm around Leila's shoulders and guided her in the direction of the booth.

As soon as they sat down, a waiter came over with place settings and menus. "Good evening," he said in a cheerful voice. "My name is Stan, and I'll be your waiter this evening. What can I get you to drink?"

"I'd like water with ice and lemon, please," Leila requested.

"I'd like the same," Chet said, "but we'll probably want something else after we look at the menu."

"Take your time. I'll be right back with the water."

An awkward silence prevailed as Leila and Chet browsed their menus. She was grateful when he asked if she wanted a cocktail or wine with her dinner.

"I think I'm in the mood for a glass of wine," she said. "And I'm enticed by the description of the crab cakes. What about you?"

"I always seem to order the same thing when I'm here. Salmon. It's very good."

The waiter returned with the water and listened patiently to the couple's requests.

"How about a glass of chardonnay?" Chet asked after they'd placed their food order.

Leila gave him a nod of approval.

"Please bring us two glasses of the house chardonnay," he said, handing the menus back to the waiter.

The conversation evolved much like the one Leila had with Morgan on their first date. They talked about their work lives, their children, and their mutual desire to meet someone special. All the while, she made observations. Chet had lost some weight. That was good. He had likely come from work, because the sleeves of his blue-collared shirt hugged his elbows and his tie drooped. Making a good first impression wasn't at the top of his to-do list. But he seemed sincere and open. He spoke volumes about his wife, his struggles as a single parent, and his hopes for the future.

"I think about Ellen almost every day. It's been over two years since she passed, but I'm having a difficult time letting go. I'm certainly better than I was a year ago, but I want to be more forward-thinking. What about you?"

"I'm in a different place. My husband, Nick, died over five years ago. Though I miss him terribly, I've adapted to my new life. I'm able to manage alone. I try to fill the void by devoting more time and energy to work and family."

Chet nodded. "I've done the same. My business is growing and occupies much of my time. I always have homework, so my nights are less lonely than they could be. Now that the girls are in college, my parental duties are less demanding, but I do miss them. Did I tell you they are both majoring in business?"

"Yes, you did. I know you must be very proud of them."

"Yes. I can't help but think how Ellen and the girls have been cheated. They were very close. They had so much to look forward to."

"I understand," Leila sympathetically replied.

Throughout their dinner, Chet's words communicated his deep longing for his wife. Even when he asked Leila to reveal more about herself, it served only as a lead-in to what he wanted to say about his life with Ellen. She suddenly realized she'd taken on the role of a therapist. When the waiter came over to clear away the dinner plates and inquire about additional menu items, Leila welcomed the relief his courteous service offered.

"May I get you anything else? Coffee? Tea? Dessert?"

"I don't think so," Leila quickly responded. "I've had my fill. Everything was delicious."

"I'm rather stuffed myself," Chet said. "Please, just bring the check."

Leila knew all too well there was nothing left to discuss. Time to bring the evening to a swift but polite end. "Well, Chet, thank you for a lovely evening. It was so good to meet you." She hoped for a quick getaway. She'd heard enough about Ellen, the ultimate role model for women of all ages.

"I had a nice time too," Chet said. "Let's get together again. How about it?"

How might she best handle this situation and not hurt his feelings? He was a nice man, but he wasn't over his wife's death. And she wasn't interested in continuing as his therapist or playing the role of Ellen's stand-in.

"I'd like that very much when you're ready," she finally said.

"What do you mean by that?" he demanded.

"When you're ready to move on. I think you're stuck. I was in the same place myself two years after Nick died. My memories of my life with him filled every idle space in my brain. I dwelled on the past. It takes time to get unstuck, and you need more time."

He deflated. "I'm sorry I came off like that. I've really been trying."

"I know." Leila stood up, took hold of her belongings, and placed her hand on Chet's shoulder.

He attempted to rise, seeming to feel that the gallant thing to do was to walk her to her car.

"Please, sit," she said. "I can easily navigate my way to my car. It's just outside the entrance. Thanks again."

He didn't protest.

❁

Leila heard the phone ringing and raced to answer it.

"Hello," she said in a breathless voice.

"Mom, is that you? Are you all right?"

"Oh, Hillary, I just got home and rushed to get the phone. How are you, dear? Did you have a good week?"

"Yes, things went well. Where were you, anyway?"

"I met Chet Nickels for dinner at the Radnor Hotel."

"How did it go?"

Leila sighed, taking an extra moment to figure out exactly what she wanted to say. "He's a nice man who is not ready to move on. He spent much of the time reminiscing about his life with his late wife."

"I'm sorry, Mom. That must have been awkward for you."

"Well, it wasn't so bad. So, what's up?"

"I want to invite you for dinner on Sunday. Chad's parents are in from Florida, so I thought I'd cook up a storm."

"Great! What can I bring?"

"Just yourself. See you around six."

"Okay. Love you."

Leila hung up the phone, picked up her handbag, and walked toward the staircase. At first, she thought she'd get ready for bed and watch television. Then she caught sight of the baby grand piano her parents had bought for her when she was in high school, now gracing a corner of her living room. She'd never become the virtuoso her parents had hoped for, but she found enjoyment in playing melodies that soothed or energized her, depending on her mood. Tonight, she needed to be soothed, so she dropped her bag and headed into the living room.

After playing a few simplified classical pieces, she picked up the sheet music for Alicia Keys's "That's When I Knew." She'd bought it on a whim after hearing the song on the car radio. The melody was lovely, and the lyrics imparted a poignant message, focusing on how falling in love can be slow and quiet, and then suddenly, when least expected, the emotion fills one's soul. Why not take a few extra minutes to begin learning it?

As Leila moved through the music, thoughts of Ayden surfaced, prompted mainly by the lyrics she read in tandem with the notes. She recalled the meeting at his workshop—how close they'd sat to each other, causing their knees to occasionally bump, and how her body had responded when Ayden's hand lightly grazed across hers as they examined product samples together. Was it then that she'd become aware of the profound effect he had on her? Probably. After that meeting, she'd begun to feel like a woman again—to tingle when she recalled his touch, to imagine intimate embraces, and, most of all, to play over and over again in her mind memories of the few times she'd been in his company. It didn't matter if the memories focused on her annoyance in response to his arrogance, her awe in response to his talent, or her quivering in response to his touch and manly presence. She wanted it all.

The hall clock chimed twelve times. It was late. She stopped playing and headed for the stairs. No more thinking about Ayden.

Sure.

❀

Leila felt a bit blue Sunday morning. She didn't know exactly why, but she was sad.

At least she had some uplifting things scheduled. She knew dinner with Hillary, Chad, and Chad's parents—Elliot and Suzanne—would be very pleasant. Chad's parents were witty and bright, and terribly fun. Chad was just like them. No wonder Hillary had fallen for him. They'd met in court one day, each representing opposing sides. Once the case settled, Chad had called her.

"I'm really a nice, fun-loving guy," he'd said. "I'd like to show you that side of me. How about having dinner with me?"

When Hillary got home from that first date, she'd called her parents to report she thought she'd just met her future husband and father of her children.

The proclamation had meant a lot to Nick. He'd know exactly who would be around to take care of his little girl if he succumbed to his illness. Unfortunately, he wouldn't make it to the wedding, but knowing Chad and Hillary were a committed couple gave him much solace.

Hillary and Chad also lived in Leila's subdivision, a large golf course community with different types of dwellings—carriage homes like Leila's, larger attached homes, and single homes of varying sizes. Hillary and Chad's home was a moderately sized single, about 2,500 square feet, situated on a cul-de-sac. Leila had helped them renovate it. The kitchen, the most recent update, had French country cabinets in an antiqued moss green, dark granite countertops, and stain-less-steel appliances. Hillary and Chad gloated over the results.

Just before six that evening, Leila grabbed a bottle of her favorite red wine and left for Hillary's dinner party. When she arrived, Chad's parents were already there, marveling over the new kitchen. Hillary served appetizers on the island while she finished getting the dinner together. The cheerful conversation was dotted with convivial laughter—just what Leila needed—and continued in that vein as they sat around the dining room table.

"The pot roast is absolutely fabulous," Leila enthused after taking her first bite. "I'm really enjoying it."

"Mom, this is your recipe," Hillary said, chuckling.

"Really?" Leila loved to cook—or she had when Nick was around. Since being alone, she'd rarely spent time in the kitchen. It wasn't much fun going to the trouble just for herself. When holidays came around, however, she still took pleasure in entertaining large groups, trying out new recipes, and enjoying her guests and the festivities. Doing so kept her cooking talents from going downhill.

Leila noticed Hillary hadn't touched her wine. She didn't say anything at the table, but when the two of them were alone in the kitchen, she asked, "Didn't you like my choice of wine?"

Hillary hesitated, as if searching for just the right response to her mother's question. Finally, her voice filled with more enthusiasm than necessary, she said, "Oh, Mom, it was wonderful. Everyone loved it. There's nothing left." She proceeded to fumble with the coffee paraphernalia for a few moments before saying, "Listen, Chad and I have an announcement to make. Let's join the others while the coffee is perking."

Leila knew before the words came out of Hillary's mouth: she was pregnant. As happy as she was for Hillary and Chad, Chad's parents, and herself, she began thinking of Nick and how he'd have adored being a grandfather. Tears welled in her eyes, her happiness suddenly overshadowed by the idea of grandparenting without him—but she made great efforts to appear as jubilant as the others.

"I'm so happy for the two of you," she said with forced cheer. "When's the happy day?"

"Mid-January," Chad answered.

"This is wonderful news," Suzanne chimed in. "We want to help with the nursery. Leila, you take care of that with the kids, and then let us know how we can contribute."

"That's so sweet of you," Leila said, still on the edge of tears. "We can do it together—you, me, and Hillary."

Everyone hugged and continued the celebration with the special cake Hillary had ordered from the Swiss bakery, decorated with all things baby.

❁

The tears were pouring out by the time Leila reached the first stoplight on her way home. She'd never expected to grandparent without Nick. "It just isn't fair," she said out loud, sobbing.

Once home, her tears subsided, but a terrible ache filled her chest. She swooped up her cat, Melinda, and nestled her in her arms. "It's just you and me, girl," she said aloud. The cat's soft fur and purring offered some comfort. "Let's check to see if there are any voice mails."

One message from Morgan Bradford made up the queue. "Hello, Leila, this is Morgan Bradford. I'm sorry I didn't catch you in. Listen, I have to cancel for this coming weekend. An unexpected family situation has come up and may take some time to resolve. If you do not hear from me, I know you'll understand. Take care."

A perfect ending for the weekend, considering all that had transpired. Morgan was done with her and likely much relieved she hadn't been home, making his retreat less difficult. She supposed this was the reality single, middle-aged women confronted when attempting to find love and companionship. She wasn't an adolescent, but she felt like one—a rejected one. Her naivete had never appeared more pronounced.

"I'm done with Heavenly Matches!" she proclaimed to her bathroom mirror. Michelle and Hillary would just have to understand.

10

Leila and Michelle planned to meet at the shop around nine thirty. They had two design appointments scheduled: a ten o'clock with the Millers and a two o'clock with the Hunters.

Leila arrived first. She went into the office to organize her briefcase and listen to the only message—a reminder from the Designers' Showhouse Fundraising Committee to remove by the end of the month any unsold items she and Michelle had used in the design of the home office project. She wrote a hasty reminder and placed the Post-it Note on Michelle's desk.

"I'm here and ready to go," Michelle said, standing in the office doorway.

"Okay," Leila said, bustling back over to her desk to grab her things. "Let's go. I guess you're the designated driver today?"

"Yep, it's me."

They walked out together, and Leila took the shotgun position in Michelle's BMW. Once they were on the road, she thought to ask, "How was your weekend?"

"It was very nice. David and I had a romantic dinner at The Café on Saturday. It was great, just the two of us. And on Sunday, we had dinner with David's parents."

"How are they doing?"

"They're doing wonderfully. They love living at the Quadrangle. What about your weekend?"

Leila hesitated for a moment—and then began to vent. "Well, my dinner date with Chet was nice, but nothing will come of it. He's still grieving."

"How do you know that?"

"I know that because he spent much of our time together talking about his wife, either directly or indirectly. It's difficult to compete on any level with a dead person who led the life of a saint."

"Oh, and your Heavenly Matches candidates don't have the same problem? Nick is a hard act to follow." Playing the devil's advocate was Michelle's forte.

"I know my expectations are probably set too high, but I didn't spend my time with Chet highlighting Nick's accomplishments and detailing the particulars regarding the extraordinary husband and father he was. And now that you mentioned it, I think I need a rest, if not a total detachment, from Heavenly Matches."

Michelle shot her a sideways glance. "Why are you so negative? So Chet didn't work out, but there's Morgan Bradford. He seems ready to move on."

"Well, you're right there. He's moved on and will not be calling me anymore. He left a message on my voice mail. He encountered an 'unexpected family situation that may take some time to settle.' He went on to say that if I don't hear from him, he knows I'll understand."

"That's a bummer," Michelle said, unfazed, "but don't let that one rejection get you down. You rejected Chet. Sometimes you'll be the one who rejects, and at other times, you'll be the one rejected. That's life. We don't get every design job we go for, but that doesn't make us want to give up the business. Anyway, there's still Ayden."

"Ayden hasn't called. I'm not counting on him either."

"Let's see what happens when you meet him at the Perkinses' this week. You'll have to be at your best, if you know what I mean."

"Maybe you should be more explicit."

"I mean a great outfit—a bit sexy, but not overdone—dewy, fresh makeup, flowing hair, shiny nails, a warm smile . . . the whole nine yards."

Michelle's explanation, which Leila perceived as instructions, put her on the defensive. "You want me to market myself at a business meeting? Am I that desperate? This whole dating thing is beginning to turn my stomach."

"If you don't make the effort to communicate your availability or interest, what man will be courageous enough to chop down that wall of ice you've built around yourself? Look, I'm not a Dr. Goodwin, but I'm your friend, and I want you to find happiness. If that means taking a risk or two, going out of your comfort zone now and then, so be it."

Michelle's response was only semiconvincing. "I'll think about it," Leila said, not really meaning it.

❁

D-day arrived. Leila prepared for her ten o'clock at the Perkinses' with military precision. She arose two hours earlier than usual so she could perfect her appearance. She reconsidered Michelle's advice and decided to go all out: washed her hair and sprayed it with root lifter to get extra volume out of her "do"; applied dark eye shadows, navy eyeliner, and black mascara for drama; added a touch of foundation and luminescent powder to give her face a soft, golden glow; and finished her look with pink blush and lipstick.

When all this fuss was completed, she stared at her image in the mirror. *Well done!* she thought, satisfied with the result.

Now came the next challenge: settling on a suitable outfit. Something that could be considered appropriate businesswear but still have enough allure to capture Ayden's undivided attention. While lying in bed the night before, she'd reviewed her options as if she were counting sheep, but she'd soon fallen asleep. Now the moment of decision had arrived.

She selected a Ralph Lauren jacket of soft wool and silk with matching trousers—businesswear designed for the summer months. The supple material highlighted her feminine curves. A sleeveless, deep V-neck with fine navy netting—suggestive without compromising the aura of professionalism she was intent on projecting—complemented her suit. Jimmy Choo navy patent leather pumps, silver hoop earrings, and a sleek watch were the crowning touches.

Before dressing, she decided to go downstairs and have a good breakfast. A rumbling tummy never helped to reel in a client and secure a deposit.

Just as she was about to pour herself a cup of coffee, the phone rang.

"Good morning," Michelle said with a great deal of energy.

"Good morning," Leila said cautiously. "What's up?"

"I just want to wish you good luck and all that."

"The Perkinses will start things rolling today. I've a good feeling about that."

"I didn't necessarily mean good luck with the Perkinses. I know they're happy with our work. I'm really thinking about Ayden. What are you going to wear?"

"Navy," Leila responded nonchalantly.

"Navy what?"

"A navy suit," she clarified.

"Where's the sexy in that?"

"The sleeveless V-neck blouse is the sexy part."

"I hope the house is stuffy, so taking off your jacket is considered a reasonable action." As usual, Michelle laughed at her own joke.

"Anything else, partner?"

"No, but I'll anxiously await your arrival at the shop. Call me when you're on your way, and I'll order something for lunch."

"Will do. Bye for now."

Leila had her coffee, English muffin, and scrambled egg out on the deck. The day was off to a pleasant start. A few whimsical clouds floated in the sky and a light breeze rustled the leaves, encouraging her positivity. She anticipated things would go well with the Perkinses, but she wasn't so sure where the next encounter with Ayden would lead. Maybe nowhere. She lingered a while and then gathered the dishes together, rinsed them, and went upstairs to don what she thought was a "killer" outfit.

Prepared for departure, Leila stood in the front hall and examined herself in the mirror. Her satisfaction resulted in a broad smile. Her golden-brown curls rested softly on her shoulders. She'd achieved the height across her crown, making her seem just a bit taller. The navy suit looked great. The tapered pants and high heels made her legs look longer.

❁

Leila admired the perfectly manicured grounds and the many plantings in full bloom as she pulled into the Perkinses' driveway. Pots filled with geraniums and begonias adorned the steps leading to the front door.

As she took in the beauty of the surroundings, she noticed that Ayden's truck was nowhere to be seen. She liked the idea of getting a head start on him. She parked, grabbed her briefcase from the backseat, and made her way to the entrance.

"Hey, Leila, nice to see you," Marshall greeted her at the door. "Ayden called and said he'd be about a half hour late. He apologized and suggested we get started from your end. Janice is in the sunroom with all the paraphernalia you left with us."

"That's fine." She followed Marshall into the sunroom.

Janice was seated on the sofa when they walked in. "Hi, Leila," she said, rising to shake her hand. "Oh, I love your suit. It looks great on you."

Marshall nodded in agreement and smiled his usual, amiable grin.

"You're so kind," Leila said, pleased. "It's a recent addition to my wardrobe. I'm enjoying it." She looked for a moment at the various samples spread out on the floor. "What have you and Marshall been up to this past week?"

"Well, we've made decisions. We're pretty clear on things, right, honey?"

"Whatever you want, Janice," Marshall said with a bob of his head. "You have excellent taste, and Leila has given you solid design ideas. My compliments to you, Leila—and your partner Michelle, too, of course."

"Thanks, Marshall. We had great fun working on your project."

Janice went on to relate what she and Marshall had decided. They would stick with the neutral plan contained in tote one. They thought that plan would allow them to change the accent colors depending on the season. They loved all the elements of the neutral design—the classically styled fixtures, the marble tiles, the metallic glass accent tiles, and the vanilla double vanity with a slightly darker granite top.

"I believe you've made wise choices," Leila said, her mind already whirring away with plans. "And I love your idea of changing the accent colors to complement the seasons."

"Me too," Janice responded with pride in her voice. "I thought that with the large Palladian window we're installing, so much of our landscape will influence the bathroom's design, so why not let nature's colors prevail throughout the year?"

The sound of chimes interrupted the conversation. "That must be Ayden," Marshall said, already heading out to open the door for him.

Seconds later, Leila heard Ayden apologizing for his delay.

"Not at all," Marshall told him. "Leila and Janice have just about finished up discussing the design plans."

And then the two men were in the sunroom. Leila looked Ayden's way and gave him a smile. He carried his laptop and heavy briefcase in one hand, as if they weighed as much as feathers. Just as she'd anticipated, he wore his usual tee and jeans combo, looking just as virile as ever. Thank goodness mind reading wasn't one of his talents.

"Good morning, ladies. I've been told you've made progress."

"Yes," Janice said, all enthusiasm. "Come over here. Everything is spread out on the floor. We've gone with the neutral package and decided to change the accent colors with the change of season, primarily because of that wonderful window you included in our plans. So much of our outside will be inside."

Ayden set his laptop and briefcase down, propping them up against a chair. As he walked past the sofa, he stopped to give Leila one of his winks, suggesting that her exceptional appearance that day hadn't gone unnoticed. He moved into the open space.

"Very nice," he remarked as his eyes slowly surveyed the product samples before him. "Leila has done a great job. The colors are soft, and the fixtures, tiles, and hardware create a sophisticated environment that's not overstated."

"I'm so glad you like everything." Janice beamed. "You two have made a wonderful team. Marshall and I are beyond pleased."

"Well, now that the design is settled, why don't we go upstairs and talk about the renovation itself?" Marshall suggested. "It will be easier to understand what will be done when we're actually standing in the space."

"Sounds like a plan," Ayden responded energetically. He picked up his briefcase and laptop and walked alongside Marshall toward the staircase, already explaining some of his thoughts about the work to be done. Janice and Leila followed, conducting their own conversation pertaining to the chandelier that was to be placed in the center of the new bathroom.

Once everyone was together upstairs, Marshall explained they favored the "stretch" plan but wanted some accommodations. "The two private toilets are unnecessary," he said. "One will be enough, since there are two other bathrooms on this floor. We'd like to use that space as open area."

"And speaking of space," Janice added, "we definitely want the laundry area, the walk-in linen closet, and the dressing room, but Marshall and I thought if we could pare down the size of each, perhaps less needs to be taken from the master bedroom. As these areas stand now, they are generously sized."

"Sure, that's doable," Ayden said, looking up from the notes he was jotting down. "Let's take a look at the least amount of space we need to take away from the master bedroom. Everyone, follow me."

The group reassembled in the bedroom. After some discussion, and with the help of numerous sketches deftly drawn by Ayden, a decision developed. The master bedroom's width would be trimmed just four feet, leaving a length of eight from the back wall. An ample amount of wall space would remain to the left of the back window.

"I'll redo the third plan and send it to you," he said. "Please look things over carefully, then sign on the bottom of the plan and return it to me in the envelope provided. Once I get that back, we'll set up a starting date. How does that sound?"

"I'm so excited," Janice exclaimed. "I can hardly wait!"

"Well, Rome wasn't built in a day, Janice," Marshall teased, chuckling at his own humor. "I think I'm going to the office now. We accomplished a lot this morning, and in much less time than I thought." He shook Ayden's hand, waved good-bye to Leila, and kissed Janice on the cheek. "See you at dinner, honey."

Ayden's voice drowned out the faint echo of Marshall's footsteps on the staircase. "I need to take some measurements. Leila, can you help me with the retractable tape?"

"Sure." Did multitalented Ayden really need her help?

"I'll go downstairs and pack up the things Leila needs to take with her," Janice offered. "I've scattered them all over the sunroom. I'd like to keep the entire contents of tote one."

"By all means, but I want to check through some things first," Leila said. "I'll be down as soon as Ayden can go it alone."

"You two must be thirsty. I know I am. I'll get some iced tea out for us too."

"That would be great." Leila knew she'd be alone with Ayden in a matter of moments, and that thought energized her voice.

Once Janice was out of sight, Ayden made his way into the bathroom. He waved his hand so Leila would follow. She did so obediently but somewhat reluctantly. She was nervous.

Ayden walked to the back wall, but not before he'd handed her one end of the tape. She made her way to the opposite corner. Once he had measured the wall, he began to walk toward her, allowing the tape to gradually return to its housing. Leila watched him approach. His blue eyes steadily studying her face immobilized her. He stopped less than a foot from her, pulled the end of the tape from her hand, and remained silent—perhaps only for a second or two, but to Leila it seemed much longer.

Finally, he said, "Do you really think I need your help?"

Without hesitation, Leila replied, "Frankly, I thought it odd that you asked."

"But you were curious?"

"Yes."

"I want to date you." With this announcement, he went silent, stared into her eyes, and waited.

Leila felt terribly awkward. What was he waiting for? Her permission? She needed to say something in order to move the conversation forward. "That would be nice. What do you have in mind?"

"How about dinner tonight? The restaurant in Bryn Mawr in the old train station? Around seven thirty?"

"Can we make it eight?"

"I can do eight," he said with a wry smile.

"Then eight it is." She glanced at the tape measure in his hand. "Do you need me anymore?"

"I can do it from here."

"If that's the case, I'll head downstairs and get my things together."

"I'll be stuck up here for a while."

"Well, then, I'll say good-bye now."

He leaned forward. Leila waited impatiently for his kiss. She knew it was coming. When his breath touched her face, she involuntarily closed her eyes and puckered her lips. To her utter disappointment, he placed his soft kiss on her right cheek. When she opened her eyes, he had already moved away, a triumphant smile on his face. Apparently, his game plan had worked. He'd lured her in, built up her expectations, and, in an instant, delivered what she didn't expect and less than she wanted. Why? To communicate that he was in control and she subject to his whim?

Not so! The words blasted through Leila's mind. She moved toward the doorway as Ayden picked up his graph paper and began to write down his notations. She didn't look back, determined to exit as if nothing had happened.

❀

As Leila descended the staircase, her legs wobbled. Ayden had just outmaneuvered her. That realization made her angry at herself rather than at him. How could she have been so stupid? This man was a masterful player, and though Dr. Goodwin had indicated she thought Leila could be the one to tame him, she had her doubts. Still, inexperienced as she might be with the current dating scene, she possessed mature insights that should help. Morgan and Chet were easy to forget. Ayden was in another category altogether.

"There you are," Janice said as she and Leila almost collided with each other at the bottom of the staircase. She was carrying two of the totes.

"I'd have gotten everything together," Leila said, reaching for the totes. "I feel awful leaving the clean-up to you."

"Don't be silly," Janice said. "I messed up everything and needed to clean things up. Let's go into the sunroom and rummage through the first tote to make sure you can leave all the product samples with me."

The two women stopped at the kitchen island to grab the glasses of iced tea Janice had prepared, then proceeded to the sunroom. Once there, Leila carefully but quickly took inventory, making sure the neutral collection didn't contain anything she would need back at the shop. She didn't want to rush things, but she did want to get on the road before Ayden finished upstairs. Satisfied that she had everything she needed, she said, "I'm fine leaving all the samples with you. I know they're in good hands. And if by chance I'm in need of something, I'll let you know."

"Great. By the way, don't we owe you some money at this point?" Janice asked.

"Yes, you do," Leila said, glad that Janice, and not she, had brought it up. "Michelle will send you a bill for the design work. Once Ayden lets us know your project's start date, we'll invoice you and ask for a 50 percent deposit. Everything we'll be ordering is referenced in the tote. The balance will be due upon delivery."

"Do you need the tote back before you order things?"

"No, I have everything listed, and in some instances, I have backup samples. You can double-check me by going through the tote once you're invoiced."

"Well, I guess that's it."

Leila smiled. "Michelle and I will keep an eye on things as they unfold. It's been a pleasure working with you and Marshall." She offered her hand for their usual, businesslike handshake, but Janice brushed it aside and gave her a hug. Surprised, Leila returned it.

So far, Janice Perkins had been a pleasure to work with—not at all the demanding, bossy person her reputation had suggested. *Hopefully, I'll feel the same at the completion of this project*, Leila thought.

❁

The ride back to the shop gave Leila some alone time—time to consider the date with Ayden. After calling Michelle to let her know she was heading back and weigh in on lunch options, she began thinking, her brain in overdrive. Her life had been simple, routine, and without much stress before this venture with Heavenly Matches. But even if she'd never explored the matchmaking service, she realized, fate would still have brought Ayden and her to this point. The chemistry between them was evident and powerful, yet it filled her with a sense of foreboding. Why did she have this feeling—call it woman's intuition—that Ayden was trouble personified? Somehow, she'd found herself standing on the precipice of a relationship that could cause her to reexamine her principles and values—perhaps toss them aside—yet she couldn't turn away. She'd morphed into a risk taker. Hadn't Michelle advised her to be just that?

❁

"Lunch," Michelle announced as Leila entered the office. She had already cleared the small table and set it with brightly colored paisley paper plates and coordinating plastic flatware. "The bread is still warm. And luckily, no customers in the shop to cause a delay in satisfying my extreme hunger!"

Once they settled in, she inquired how things had gone with the Perkinses.

"Just fine," Leila said. "You can bill them for our design services. When Ayden determines the project start date, we'll bill them again for deposit money to begin the ordering process. Some of the items they've selected will take as many as eight weeks to come in."

"Now we can concentrate on the Millers and the Hunters." Michelle paused, slightly wary about asking her next question. "Anything happen with Ayden?"

There was no avoiding that aspect of the morning meeting. "Well, he did ask me out for this evening—to the restaurant at the train station in Bryn Mawr."

"Get out!" Michelle dropped her fork. "Tell me everything! How did it come about? What did he say?"

"Settle down," Leila said. "He simply said he'd like to date me and wondered if I was free this evening. When I said I had no plans, he suggested the restaurant. I thought it a convenient place to meet too."

Michelle narrowed her eyes. "Are you leaving something out?"

"No. I'm telling you what happened," Leila replied, looking down at her plate in order to avoid her friend's searing gaze. She didn't want her own facial expression to betray her. Michelle always figured out when she wasn't totally forthcoming.

"OMG! What are you going to wear?"

"Please, do we have to discuss my apparel like a couple of teenagers?"

"Yes! Just as clothes make the man, clothes help the woman get the man."

"I'm just going to wear a nice jeans outfit. Ayden is always in jeans. I don't expect him to be in anything else. Anyway, I'd like to unwind. Get out of business clothes."

"Okay." Michelle nodded slowly. "I see where you're coming from.

Anyway, I can't wait to hear how the evening goes. Do you think you could call me when you get home?"

"Are you serious?" Leila shook her head in disbelief. "Michelle, I'm not going to my high school prom. I'm a middle-aged woman, simply meeting an acquaintance for an informal dinner. That's it. You'll have to wait until tomorrow."

"Well, if you get home and feel you need someone to talk to, please don't hesitate to call, even if it's late."

"You're a good friend," Leila said, softening. "I appreciate your concern."

Lunch came to an end when the shop bell rang. A customer needed attention. Leila cleaned up while Michelle went to see how she could help, and it wasn't long before she began thinking about her dinner attire. What top would she wear with her favorite pair of black jeans?

11

The thirty-minute ride to Bryn Mawr went all too fast. Leila wanted more time to prepare for her date. She felt like an inexperienced defense attorney, psyching herself up to take on the shenanigans of a formidable prosecutor.

There he was, sitting on a bench near the patio area set aside for outside dining. He was dressed in jeans as she expected, but instead of his signature tee, he'd donned a pastel-plaid collared shirt.

He spotted her immediately and gave her a wave, accompanied by a smile. She responded in kind—then searched for a parking spot out of his view, hoping to gain a few extra seconds to touch up her face and brush her hair.

She adjusted her top, a pale blue sweater with a plunging cowl neckline, once she emerged from the car. The jeans coordinated well with the top and showed off her womanly curves, while her sandals created the illusion that she was taller than her five-foot-four height.

Ayden stayed seated as she approached, observing her every movement. Leila, noticing his scrutiny, added a slight sway to her walk and tossed her head. She also nervously tapped on the strap of her shoulder bag as if she were tinkering with the keys of a piano—she hoped he didn't notice that part.

He remained seated until she began to climb the steps to the patio. When she drew closer, he rose, reached for her left hand, and helped her with the last step. "You look different out of uniform," he said with a boyish grin that engulfed his face.

"I could say the same about you. Look at you, collar and all. Did you do that for me?"

"Of course." He grinned. "This is where you're supposed to say I clean up nicely, or something like that."

"Well, you do, but you don't need me to tell you that."

"Now that the niceties are over, let's decide where we'll eat. There's a booth in a quiet corner of the restaurant, or we can stay outside. The only problem with that is the sun is at a bad angle, so the glare will be in our eyes for a while. Do you mind? You'll have to look at me through sunglasses."

She paused to think. "Let's go inside to the quiet booth—that is, if you don't mind."

"That was my first choice anyway."

Ayden gently put his arm around her shoulders and guided her into the restaurant. His touch seemed to ripple through her body, but maybe it was just nerves.

The hostess took them to a booth meant for two. There were cute tieback curtains on a small window with a view of the railroad tracks. A candle glowed inside its holder, helping to create the perfect setting for romance.

A waitress approached. "Hi, I'm Emily. I'll be taking care of you this evening. What can I get you to drink?"

"I'd just like to start off with ice water with a lemon," Leila replied.

"I'd like a Grey Goose Bloody Mary and an ice water," Ayden said. He looked at her. "Are you sure you don't want something—a glass of wine or a drink?"

Leila gave a slight shake of her head. "Thanks, but let me see first what looks tempting."

How would she ever be able to consume food or drink in this man's company? Her stomach tensed. She perused the menu to settle her nerves, taking random peeks at her dinner companion all the while. He certainly was an attractive man. He looked equally good in his "dress-up" clothes, though his muscular frame was less evident in the looser-fitting shirt. The top buttons of his shirt, left undone, did expose some of his chest, however—something his T-shirts couldn't do. She liked that.

"Have you made up your mind yet?" he asked, catching her eye.

"I'm going for the Asian salmon," she said brightly.

"That sounds good. I'll get that too."

When Emily returned with the drinks and some warm bread, they placed their food order. Leila also requested a glass of chardonnay, hoping the alcohol would relax her. Unfortunately, it didn't arrive in time for her to field Ayden's next question with calm assurance.

"So, how many men have you dated since becoming a Heavenly Matches client?"

She hadn't expected him to be so blunt. She scrambled for the appropriate response and finally decided to answer his question with a question: "Does it really matter?"

"I'd like to know if I have any competition."

Are you crazy? Competition? You've already won. She worked diligently to appear composed. "I've dated a little, but I've not met that special someone yet. To clarify, I've met some very nice men, but none who have made me feel the way I felt about my late husband." She wasn't especially satisfied with her answer, but there it was.

"He's my competition, then. What was his name?"

"Nick," she answered, looking straight into Ayden's blue eyes.

"What did he do for a living?"

"He was a lawyer."

"What happened to him?"

"He died of prostate cancer."

Ayden looked out the window toward the steely tracks. He turned back and fixed his eyes on hers. "I'm sorry. I'm sure you miss him."

"Yes," Leila said. "I see you understand." She searched for something to say, something clever to move the conversation away from herself. A gloom had set over them with this line of questioning; she wanted to liven things up. And explore his past. "What about you?" she asked. "I know you've been divorced for many years. Was your ex the love of your life, and since your divorce, no one else has come close?"

Ayden seemed uncomfortable discussing his personal history. He focused on Leila as if he were in a trance or somewhere else. She returned the stare, not retreating from her desire to learn more about him.

"We were young," he said slowly. "I thought I was ready to settle down, but I wasn't. Then she got pregnant with Daniel. I felt obligated. I had worked for her father for years. He was good to me. I didn't want to disappoint him. She deserved more. I couldn't give more. End of story."

"I hope she found someone else to share her life with." Leila wanted to know if that was the case.

"She did."

"What's her name?"

"Sara."

"That's a nice biblical name." Ayden didn't respond, so she decided to be bold. "I'm curious. You're a successful man, nice-looking—why did you go the matchmaking route?"

His response was brusque. "Efficiency. I don't have time to do the research or spend hours reading emails or writing them."

"I know. The arena of electronic dating requires an enormous amount of time, not to mention commitment and persistence."

"You prefer using a matchmaker?"

"To be honest, I'd prefer to meet someone by happenstance. I told you before, I went the matchmaking route because it was a birthday gift from my daughter and my business partner. I didn't want to hurt their feelings. They had good intentions."

"We met by happenstance," he pointed out.

"That's true."

"You got your wish." His eyes gleamed.

"Try not to be so smug," she said, stifling a smile.

"I was surprised to find out you're unmarried."

"Why? You're not married," she shot back.

"You are talented, very attractive, and self-assured."

"Right back at you." She decided to test a hypothesis of hers. "I believe you're unmarried because that's the way you choose to live your life. I'm unmarried or unattached because I haven't yet met a man with whom I want to share my life—since losing my husband, that is."

"So, you think I'm a player?"

"Somewhat."

"I've had a couple of serious relationships," he said, a bit defensive. "Unfortunately, they didn't work out."

"Why was that?"

"I didn't want more kids and they did. Daniel is enough for me."

Their food arrived then, and Leila decided to take the focus off Ayden for a while. As they dined, she talked about Hillary, Chad, and the fact she would be in uncharted waters shortly, taking sail as a grandmother.

"You don't look old enough to be a grandmother," Ayden said.

"Well, I am, but thanks for the compliment." She wanted him to know that he wasn't with a woman who was ashamed of her age, that is, as long as she could maintain her youthful allure.

"Daniel has a girlfriend. I suppose if he marries, I'll find myself in the same position in the not-too-distant future."

Emily approached the table, dessert menus in hand. After they ordered coffee and she left, Ayden asked if Leila wanted dessert.

"I'd share something, if you're interested."

He handed her a menu and opened the other for himself. After a quick review, he informed her of his choice. "I'd like apple pie à la mode. Vanilla ice cream. Does that do it for you?"

"Sounds great," she said with enthusiasm. The conversation had gotten a bit too heavy, and she was happy to lighten things up.

"Do you want to see me again?" Ayden asked.

Emily showed up right then with the coffees. Leila received her cup with gratitude in her eyes; now she had some time to organize her response.

With his eyes still focused on Leila, Ayden placed the dessert order: "Please bring us one apple pie, warmed, with vanilla ice cream."

"Certainly," Emily said, and she was gone again.

"I'll likely see you many times as we move forward with the Perkins project," Leila said, smiling.

"You know what I mean."

"Yes, I guess I do." She hesitated. He waited patiently for her to continue. She ached for him to touch her, knowing that if he did, she'd say *yes* without further thought. Was he a risk worth taking? Finally, she admitted to herself that the attraction was so strong, she'd be crazy not to investigate further. "I'd love to see you again."

An enormous smile crossed his face. "Good. How about this coming weekend?"

"Do you have a plan?"

"Yes. Let's go to the races in Delaware on Saturday. I've a friend whose horse is entered in the sixth race."

"I'd like that. The races are always fun."

"Can you meet me in King of Prussia? It would be a good place to park your car."

"Fine. What time?"

"Let's say three thirty."

Emily brought the dessert. Armed with their forks, Ayden and Leila began their gustative adventure. At times, they dueled over the small puff of whipped cream that decorated a corner of the rectangular dessert plate. This prompted spontaneous laughter unaccompanied by words. When their eyes met, all that needed to be said was said.

The dessert was soon devoured. Leila sat back after finishing her coffee and glanced about the restaurant. Most of the patrons had left. She looked at her watch. Where had the time gone? It was almost eleven. Ayden was in the process of settling the bill. She continued to watch him, and in spite of feeling exhausted, she didn't want the evening to end. She loved observing him. His graceful movements intrigued her—how he retrieved his wallet from his jeans pocket, flipped it open, slid his charge card out, and tossed it on the tray containing the bill using only his right hand. When it came time for him to sign the slip, his artful penmanship attracted her attention. Most men scribbled their names. Not Ayden. Everything he did was precise yet effortless.

"I'll walk you to your car," he declared as he glided from the booth. He waited for her to stand. Then he took her left hand in his and led the way out of the restaurant. Leila contemplated his grasp. It was gentle, like Nick's. She glanced at the finger where she'd worn her gold wedding band for over thirty years. Her eyes began to water as she filled with emotion. She fought the tears. She needed to be in control.

"I parked at the end of the second row," she told him as they emerged from the restaurant.

Ayden continued leading the way without uttering a word. She felt the steady, warm pressure of his hand.

"Give me your keys," he said when they were standing beside her car. "I'll start it up to make sure everything is in working order."

She obeyed but felt sad when he let go of her. The car responded as she expected. The engine hummed in readiness. Ayden emerged from the car as though an air current had lifted him out of the seat.

"Thanks for dinner. And the conversation," she muttered softly, her heart beating in anticipation of his good-bye kiss.

"You're welcome."

He placed his arms around her shoulders and pulled her close to him. His warm lips met hers, and her body went limp. She savored a bit of cinnamon left over from the apple pie, making his taste even more delightful. She wished his kiss would last forever.

With that thought, a profound realization came to her. She wanted romance in her life again. She wanted someone to manhandle her in the same loving way Nick had done. She was like a dry river-bed suddenly filling with water after years of drought. This emotional flow was awakening every nerve in her body; she tingled all over.

Leila didn't know exactly how well she transitioned from fantasy to reality. Hopefully she hadn't just made a fool of herself.

Ayden took her shoulder bag, tossed it onto the passenger seat, and gently directed her into the driver's seat. He pulled the seat belt out and Leila finished securing it.

"I'll call you later in the week," he said as he closed the door.

"Okay," she said, unable to manage more words than that.

She lowered the window and inched her car forward. It was late, and there were only a few cars left in the lot, allowing her to achieve a graceful exit. She looked in the rearview mirror and noted that Ayden was standing watch, just as he had the day she left his work-shop. Like before, she dwelled on his reflection until he faded away. When that happened, her memory took over, and she replayed the entire evening in her head, driving home on autopilot.

❀

Leila didn't get a good night's sleep; she tossed and turned through to morning. When the alarm went off, she arose feeling unsettled. She thought about Nick as she showered and dressed for work. In an odd way, she felt as if she were being unfaithful, desiring another man when memories of Nick had seemed to suffice until now. Her close friends and family had long encouraged her to move on, telling her she had a life to live. Moving ahead was difficult, but staying in the past wasn't a healthy alternative.

She dressed and ate quickly, then headed to the shop. As she neared the office, Michelle heard her and called out, "I'm on the phone."

She walked in to find Michelle scribbling on the Post-it Note she'd left on her blotter the other day.

"Yes, Eugene, so you'll be able to pick them up and drop them off at the shop on Friday? That's great. See you then." She hung up the phone and stared at Leila.

"What?"

"How did last night go?"

She decided to present a concise summary. "Dinner was nice. The conversation went well. We learned more about each other. He asked me to go to the races with him this weekend. I need to take off early on Saturday."

"Fine, I'll close up," Michelle said, a bit gleefully. "What did you learn about him that you didn't already know?"

Leila dutifully reported her findings. "His ex-wife remarried and found happiness. His other serious relationships fizzled because he didn't want to father more children. He enlisted the help of Heavenly Matches because he doesn't have the time to search himself. He has a friend who owns a racehorse."

"Well, then, we have the beginning of an open and honest relationship."

"I wouldn't go that far. He has potential, but I'm wary of how sincere he is about finding a person to share his life with. I admit I'm very attracted to him. Without a doubt, there's chemistry. But he's a bit too masterful . . . as if he's had too much practice dating."

"What do you mean by that?"

"For example, he walked me to my car, asked for my keys, and started it up for me to 'make sure it was in working order' before he left."

"I think that's very gallant. He considered your safety."

"Okay, but I feel it's a *move* he's done many times before."

"You're being hypercritical. Just go out with him and enjoy yourself. Have fun! And if that includes sex, I'm fine with that," Michelle said with a wink.

"I'm so glad I've gotten your approval," Leila said, her voice laden with sarcasm.

"Enough with Ayden," Michelle said, seeming to understand that a change of topic was necessary. "Let's go on to the Hunters and their needs."

"Great idea," Leila said, relieved.

12

The weather forecast had predicted a beautiful, warm weekend with low humidity. This was especially good news for the thoroughbreds competing in the night's races. As soon as Leila pulled into the mall's parking lot, she caught sight of Ayden sitting on the low retaining wall near the entrance.

He didn't notice her arrival. His focus was elsewhere, actually—on a brochure of some type. She was happy about that. Sneaking up on him enticed her. The unexpected always adds a measure of thrill to any experience.

"Hello there."

He instantly looked up and smiled. Leila, dressed in beige linen ankle pants, canvas wedges, and a sleeveless pink top with a plunging neckline, was confident that she presented an eye-pleasing image. Around her shoulders she wore a matching pink cardigan; on her arm, an oversize straw and leather satchel swayed back and forth, a repository for the artifacts needed for the day's outing at the racetrack. Large Jackie O tortoiseshell sunglasses shielded her eyes from the afternoon sun and added a touch of casual glamour.

"You look great." He was obviously impressed.

"Thank you." Instinctively, she assessed Ayden's appearance. "You look ready for a day at the races as well."

Ayden wore a short-sleeved, olive-green shirt; olive pants in a deeper hue; and loafers without socks. He looked camera-ready. She pictured him posing for a man's cologne ad, peering through binoculars toward a racetrack, a dust trail created by thoroughbreds on a dry summer day serving as the backdrop.

"What's in that bag of yours?" he asked, eyebrows raised.

"What every lady needs when venturing far from home for a day," Leila replied flirtatiously.

"And that would be?"

"Oh, standard equipment—makeup, hair brush, sun visor, sun block, keys, extra pair of shoes, bottled water—that kind of stuff. Oh, and a little money."

"Well, I see you're prepared and armed. That bag has the potential to be deadly." Ayden smiled at her as he slid off the wall, grabbed the satchel, and pretended to lose footing, leaning heavily to his right side. Leila followed him to his car, enjoying his humor.

"Where's your truck?" Leila took a few moments to survey the silver-gray Mercedes convertible in front of her whose passenger door Ayden had just opened for her.

"The truck is for work. *This* baby is for play."

Leila got into the "baby." Ayden quickly found his place behind the steering wheel and lowered the top. He glanced at himself in the rearview mirror, pushed his hair back, and donned his movie-star sunglasses before beginning to reverse out of the spot.

"Wait," Leila blurted out. "I need to get my sun visor or my hair will be blowing in the wind." She twisted in her seat to reach for her satchel, which Ayden had placed in the backseat of the car. He waited patiently for her to find it. After some searching, she secured her visor and placed it just above her forehead. "Ready."

Ayden zoomed ahead. Leila was conscious of what a great-looking pair they made; some heads in neighboring cars even turned as they made their way down the highway. Conversation was difficult, however. With the engine roaring and the fast-moving air making a whistling sound, they had to raise their voices significantly to communicate.

"It will take us just over an hour to get there," Ayden shouted over the wind. "I thought we'd stop at the casino for an hour or so and then get a bite to eat. There are a number of restaurants to choose from. You'd like Legends. The races begin at eight. I told my friend Mark we'd stop by his stall around then. You'll be able to meet his horse, Wings of Hope."

"That should be fun," Leila said, trying to make her voice loud enough for him to hear her without actually shouting. "I've never been to the park in Delaware. There's lots more going on than horseracing. It seems somewhat like Las Vegas."

"There's gambling, but not much entertainment," Ayden said. "Another racetrack offers more quality entertainment. Quite a variety of well-known personalities perform there."

"Like who?"

"LeAnn Rimes and Dennis Miller have passed through recently."

"That's impressive."

Thirty minutes into the drive, the two settled into quiet companionship. Leila mindlessly took in passing images, happy to be free of the business duties she'd had to deal with earlier that day—consequence of Saturday shoppers eager to take advantage of the summer sale. Ayden clearly enjoyed driving his weekend toy.

On occasion, she looked his way. She tried to do so only when he was very much focused on his driving. She didn't want him aware of her gaze, but she so enjoyed the view—his curly hair blowing about, the way he placed his right forearm on the top of the steering wheel, the rise and fall of his chest when he took a deep breath, and the occasional adjustment of his sunglasses, which caused his nose to wrinkle up in such an adorable way that he fleetingly appeared more boy than man.

They arrived at the park just after four thirty. Ayden pulled up to the entrance of the clubhouse and casino and requested valet parking. Once that business was taken care of and they were out of the car, Ayden reached for her hand and led the way.

Inside, a bustling economy was in full swing. The casino was large. There were a number of bars and restaurants. Across from the entrance, a pianist played show tunes in a bar area, accompanied by the vocals of a group of intoxicated patrons. They were clearly enjoying themselves.

"Do you like to gamble?" Leila asked Ayden.

"I enjoy blackjack. Perhaps we can sit a while at a five-dollar table."

"I'm game," she replied with a wink.

Once Ayden found a spot with two empty seats, he grabbed them quickly. Leila could tell she surprised him when she took out some money and became an active player. She even won a couple of hands. *You're not the only one with diverse talents*, she thought, pleased with herself.

After thirty minutes passed, she was ready for a new adventure. "I'm going to try the roulette table. When you're done here, will you cash in my chips and meet me over there?" She pointed to a table roughly ten feet away. She touched Ayden gently on the shoulder and then made her way to her destination.

She felt his eyes on her as she assumed a position at the roulette table, nudging herself between two men who were all smiles and eager to give up some room for her. She hoped their reaction to her generated a bit of jealousy in Ayden.

He stayed fixed where he was for longer than she expected, but at six, he wrapped things up, cashed in the chips, and reconnected with her at the roulette table. She was reveling in the action and had actually begun to build a stack of winnings. Ayden, too, had been successful; they were both up from where they'd started.

"We need to get something to eat," Ayden said. "It's after six."

"Time flies!" Leila laughed. "Yes, let's eat. I just need to cash in my chips and stop by the ladies' room."

Ten minutes later, they met outside the casino entrance and decided to have dinner at Legends, an upscale restaurant with nice selections of beer and wine. The atmosphere was lively, but a booth away from the bar provided an area more conducive for conversation.

"This is a fun place," Leila remarked.

"I'm glad you like it. You seem to be quite a gambler."

"I have luck now and then," she said playfully.

"Do you think you'll be interested in placing some bets at the races?"

"Certainly, especially since charities will benefit from tonight's races." She swirled the wine in her glass. "Tell me about your friend, Mark."

"We met at summer camp after our freshman year in college. We were both specialty counselors. He handled horseback riding, and I took care of boating and fishing. It's been easy to remain friends, since we both live in the Philadelphia area. Mark owns a stable in Blue Bell where horses are boarded and trained, and his staff provides riding lessons. He's also a veterinarian—quite an accomplished guy."

"Is he married? Children?"

"Yes. He has a very nice family."

Leila didn't press further for information, but Ayden's answers had sparked her curiosity. Was he an anomaly among his acquaintances—the only singleton? She had a feeling he was, but she hadn't yet gathered enough evidence to confirm her suspicion.

❁

A shuttle to the track waited outside. The driver passed around copies of the racing schedule, a time-saving measure Leila appreciated.

"Are you as successful picking winners as you are at the gaming tables?" Ayden asked, smiling, as they settled into their seats on the bus.

"Not really. I don't know much about horseracing. I just pick a name I like."

"Can you come up with names for the first three races?"

"If pushed, I can." Leila opened the pamphlet and studied the entries. Each race had eight horses competing. There were ten races in all.

"Do you have a pen?" Ayden asked, eyes twinkling. "I'm assuming you do since you have everything else in your bag."

"Are you making fun of me, Mr. Doyle?" She opened her treasure trove, dove in, and discovered a ballpoint pen that she quickly handed over to her new sidekick.

"Okay, give me the names. I'll circle them and place our bets before we visit Mark. I'm also going to place my bet on Mark's horse; he's running in the sixth race."

Leila dutifully supplied the necessary information. "I like My Little Sunshine in the first race, Nick's Boy in the second, and Total Rapture in the third."

"Got it," Ayden said. Leila couldn't tell if her including a horse with her late husband's name in its title bothered him or not.

❁

The bus pulled up to the racetrack only twenty minutes before the start of the first race. Ayden guided Leila to the betting stations. Afterward, he took hold of her hand and headed toward the paddock and stalls. She walked slightly behind him, brimming with curiosity. How would he introduce her? Would he say she was his friend? Would he continue to hold her hand in his?

With her free hand, she managed to extract a pink lipstick from her satchel and freshened the color on her lips. First impressions were important, and her debut this evening was no exception. Ayden, focused on finding his friend, didn't seem to notice her small exercise in vanity.

The paddock was bustling with activity. An air of excitement prevailed. She could only assume that the charity aspect of the event was the cause. The media were there. Owners and jockeys gave interviews. Trainers sweet-talked their animals and rubbed their heads and necks, trying to ward off prerace jitters. The protocol prior to each race involved the eight horses assembling and parading in front of the grandstand to allow onlookers a preview before placing bets. The first group of horses was beginning to line up.

Amid all this commotion, Ayden spotted Mark and quickened his pace, pulling Leila along, his grasp intact.

"Mark," he shouted, waving with his free hand. His hold on Leila ended shortly thereafter. Within moments the two men were vigorously shaking hands and bear hugging. Leila stood to the side while they reconnected.

After this friendly ritual was complete, Ayden said, "Mark, I'd like to introduce you to Leila Brandt."

Mark approached and extended his hand. "Very nice to meet you, Leila. I appreciate your coming today and cheering on Wings of Hope, who will be running his heart out. I think he has a good chance of winning, but what do I know?"

"It's nice to meet you too," Leila said, impressed by the firmness of Mark's handshake. He was a good-looking man, tall and lean with salt-and-pepper hair.

"Why don't you two come over to the stall and give our pony some encouragement," he said, smiling widely.

They followed Mark to the enclosure. Leila's first glimpse of Wings of Hope overwhelmed her. The word *majestic* popped into her head. The horse was tall and muscular. His coat gleamed a beautiful, dark coppery color.

"What a magnificent animal," she said, eyes wide. "I didn't expect him to be so large!"

"Thank you. We think he's pretty special too. He's a stallion, which means he hasn't been castrated. We hope to breed him down the line. But first, he needs to establish a reputation for himself."

"May I pet him?"

"Yes, on his forehead would be a good spot."

Leila approached the horse and, standing on her tippy-toes, she baby-talked him as if she were speaking to her Melinda. After allowing him to get used to her scent, she gently slid her left hand up the side of his face. He didn't react. When she stepped back and Mark came over to caress him, however, the horse showed much more enthusiasm.

"Hey, Wings," Mark said softly, scratching the horse under his chin. "Wings," in response, nudged his nose into his owner's shoulder. They indeed had a relationship.

A man and his horse, Leila thought—*a truly heartwarming sight.*

"Hey, Ayden," a woman called from some distance away. Leila turned to see a tall brunette approaching. She greeted Ayden with a hug. "Where have you been keeping yourself? It's been ages since we've seen you."

"Nancy, it's so good to see you," he said. "The truth is, I've been crazy busy. I haven't had any free time. But look, I'm here now, and I brought my friend Leila Brandt with me. Leila, this is Mark's wife, Nancy."

"It's nice to meet you, Leila," Nancy said, wearing a welcoming smile.

Instantly at ease, Leila returned the smile. "I'm so happy to share this exciting time with you." She met Nancy's extended hand with hers. "Your horse is awesome."

"Thanks. We've been preparing him for months for this event. We're nervous but hopeful."

"Hey, stop talking like that," Mark interjected. "We need to think positively. Victory is near. Let's go up to the owners' lounge, get a drink, and relax. The trainer and the jockey can stay with Wings."

The foursome walked toward the grandstand and took the elevator to the top floor, where owners and their guests watched the races from a cushy spot furnished with auditorium seats and cocktail tables laden with dips and hors d'oeuvres.

Just as they arrived, the first race began. Everyone was in a festive mood and committed to cheering unabashedly for their favorite horse. Although My Little Sunshine didn't win, the horse at least came in third and paid some money. But it was Nick's Boy in the second race that drew Leila's special attention, and she screamed him on to victory as he came in first by more than a length.

"You were really into that race," Nancy commented.

"My late husband was named Nick, so I guess I had a special connection with Nick's Boy."

"You're a widow." Nancy's voice filled with sympathy. "I'm sorry. You may be the first widow Ayden has dated. How long have you been a couple?"

"I wouldn't go so far as to say we're a couple. This is only our second date."

"How did you meet him?"

Leila wasn't offended by Nancy's curiosity. She understood that she and Mark were Ayden's good friends. "Through work. I'm an interior design consultant, and my clients hired Ayden to take care of their renovation. He came highly recommended by a close friend of theirs."

"That's so nice. You likely have much in common."

"Beyond our work interests, we may not have that much in common," Leila cautioned. "We'll have to see how things work out."

The cheering began again as the third race got underway. Total Rapture came in fourth, just missing third.

"Two out of three ain't bad," Ayden told Leila. "Do you want to sit out the next two races, or do you want to do a little more betting?"

"Why don't you see if you can do as well as I have?" Leila teased. "You pick the horses."

Ayden rubbed his hands together. "I'm up to the challenge. But I think I'll consult with Mark before I make my final decisions."

"Isn't that against the rules? It seems somewhat like insider trading if you take any advice from Mark."

At that, Ayden took out his racing form and began to study the data. He looked up at Leila. "Okay. I've made my decisions. Do you want to hear the names of the horses on my wish list?"

"Sure."

"I'm going for Second Date in the fourth and My Hero in the fifth."

"Let me see that form," Leila demanded.

Ayden handed the sheet to Leila and walked over to Mark for a brief discussion. To her surprise, Leila discovered there were indeed horses running with those names. When he returned, she said, "If those horses win, higher powers are at work."

"Maybe so, but I've never considered Mark to be one—even if he is a bit taller than I am."

Leila cracked a smile.

As it turned out, Second Date came in fifth and My Hero won. The tension in the Dawsons' circle of family and friends increased as the sixth race approached. The merrymaking gave way to studious silence as Nancy and Mark surveyed the competition, until the announcer's voice broke their concentration: "And they're off!"

At first, Wings of Hope held back, keeping pace but not leading. Then, as the pack rounded the bend, the stallion took off, the jockey allowing him to be himself.

"Look at our boy go!" Mark blurted out. "Go, Wings!"

Everyone shouted the same. All were in motion. Arms waving about. Feet stomping. Bodies jumping up and down. The group's connection with the horse was exhilarating.

Wings of Hope and Lady Lucy were neck and neck as they headed for the finish line. "It's Wings of Hope and Lady Lucy. Still Wings and the Lady," the announcer informed the crowd. Mere feet before the finish line, with a sudden burst of energy, Wings of Hope took the lead and won the race.

Pandemonium set in. Mark uncorked champagne. One pop— and then another, and yet another—burst forth. The clinking of glasses seemed endless. Seconds later, Mark and Nancy departed for the Winner's Circle while their guests stayed behind, continuing the revelry.

Ayden took hold of Leila and eagerly pulled her to him. Champagne rained on them, but they didn't care. He gave her a robust hug and passionate kiss that lingered much longer than she expected. Every fiber of her body filled with delight. She responded to his hold by wrapping her arm around his neck and pressing her body against his. She felt his tongue part her lips. She didn't resist. The sweet taste of champagne intensified the experience. She wanted to freeze this point in time, but the embrace came to an end.

Ayden's blue eyes met hers, and she remained mesmerized.

"More champagne?" He reached for an open bottle in a nearby stand.

"Yes," she whispered, still recovering from the kiss.

Ayden filled her glass. "I think we should start back after the eighth race to avoid the traffic. Even with valet parking, the wait can become a real nightmare since everyone is leaving at the same time."

"That's a good idea. Besides, all this excitement is exhausting."

"Really? It has had the opposite effect on me. I'm up for anything." A boyish grin appeared.

Leila knew what he meant, but she didn't acknowledge his message. Her eyes focused on the glass in her hand. Momentarily, Mark and Nancy returned, forestalling a potentially awkward situation. More handshakes. More congratulatory words. More races. Finally, Ayden and Leila said their good-byes, collected their winnings, and headed for the shuttle bus.

❁

The valet retrieved the car in a timely manner. As soon as they settled in, Ayden put the top up. The sky was clear. The night air had a slight chill. "I thought we could listen to some music on the way home," he said—and to Leila's surprise, he chose Rachmaninoff's Concerto No. 3. "I hope you like Yuja Wang," he said. "She's playing with the Venezuelan orchestra. Their partnership is phenomenal. Sit back and relax. I think you'll find it enjoyable."

"The piano is my favorite instrument," Leila said. "I play every now and then." She paused a moment, then decided to clarify her previous remark. "I don't want to deceive you. I am no Yuja Wang." Her voice involuntarily took on a tone she'd always reserved for Nick, a mixture of warmth and serenity. She surprised herself.

"Well then," he said, "I've made a very good choice."

The music added just the right touch of romance to the drive home. The car's dark cabin served as the perfect envelope, an archive for lustful but private thoughts. Surely, they didn't need to have conversation. Their body language communicated it all—the exchange of occasional looks, smiles, winks, and seemingly innocent touches. When they arrived back in King of Prussia, Leila regretted that the drive had taken but an hour. She relished Ayden's quiet company and the opportunity to fantasize about him in his presence. She searched his face for insights into his thoughts, but no clear read emerged. Reality set in when she noticed he'd pulled up next to her car.

She turned to retrieve her satchel from the backseat; by the time she had it in hand, Ayden already had her door open. He helped her to her feet and grabbed the large bag at the same time.

"Can you find your keys? I'll start up your car."

She did have to search a bit but soon handed them over. He unlocked her car and tossed the satchel onto the passenger seat. Soon the engine was purring, assuring her that the trip home would be a safe one.

Without a word, Ayden glided out of the driver's seat, took her in his arms, and pressed her body against the car. Her heart pumped with excitement. She could feel his arousal. His breathing became heavy as he placed his mouth on hers. His kiss wasn't as gentle as it had been earlier in the day. He was forceful and controlling; Leila had no wiggle room. But she didn't care. She wanted him as close as possible. His tongue moved brilliantly inside her mouth, and she reciprocated with equal passion.

Ayden stopped and pulled away just enough to look her straight in the eyes. "I'm crazy about you, Leila. I think you're feeling something as well. Where do we go from here—my place or yours?"

Leila froze. Another Ayden zinger. She had anticipated getting into her car, somewhat lightheaded and giddy; driving home while reviewing the romantic events of the day; getting ready for bed; and then entering dreamland until morning arrived. Now, an uncomfortable situation for which she wasn't prepared had unfolded.

Her eyes continued to look into his, but she was frantically thinking. How presumptuous of him to make such a proposal. Why did he think she'd be ready to take such a leap after only two dates? His arrogance—a trait she'd tried to forget or ignore—had resurfaced.

She knew she had to say something. He waited, patiently, for her answer. Finally, she gave him one.

"It's true: I find myself very much attracted to you. I enjoy your company. I like kissing you. I like being close to you. I like your arms around me. However, I'm not ready to have sex with you. We've only been on two dates. I need more time. I'm unsure of myself—unsure of these new feelings you've stirred up in me. But one thing I do know—and I want you to keep this in mind—I'm looking for more than a sex buddy. I want a relationship that will last a lifetime."

He went silent for a while. Finally, with a slight smile, he said,

"So, you kind of like me. I'm getting to you, and that's unnerving. Am I correct?"

"Yes. But what about the rest?"

"I'll wait until you're ready. But honestly, I'm not sure I'm the marrying kind."

"I don't need marriage, but I do need commitment," Leila said matter-of-factly. "Not now, but later on, if we find ourselves in love with each other."

He studied her face and pondered her words for what seemed to be forever. Then, his voice low and soothing, he asked, "When can I see you again?"

"Next week? Maybe Friday or Saturday evening?" Leila put her arms around his neck, drew him to her, and placed a kiss on his warm lips. With him still wrapped in her embrace, she said, "Thank you for a wonderful day. I thoroughly enjoyed it—and you."

Ayden kissed her back—a kiss that said "good night"—and stood aside as she inched her way into the driver's seat. "I'll call you in a couple of days," he said before gently closing her door.

❁

The trip home, which Leila had thought would be filled with joyful thoughts of the evening's excitement, was actually quite disconcerting. Heavy thoughts raced through her mind. She realized Ayden had a difficult time accepting her terms. His track record showed that he was adept at wooing and bedding a woman, but not so great at committing himself to one. And another realization hit her: she wanted to go to bed with him. Her body ached for him. But a voice inside her head screamed, *Be sensible. Don't be too easy. He'll lose interest.*

Already, waiting for his promised call was agonizing. A terrifying idea struck: *What if he doesn't call?* A range of emotions overtook

Leila as her imagination went wild—rejection and hurt, loneliness and despair, anger and frustration.

She miraculously found her way home in spite of her inner turmoil. Her cheeks were on fire. "I don't need to have these feelings," she screamed as she climbed the stairs to her bedroom.

Still, she decided to shower in the morning. Traces of Ayden's scent remained in her hair and on her neck and arms, and she wanted them to linger.

After preparing for bed, she slid under the covers and clicked the remote, hoping a favorite movie would lull her to sleep, but thoughts of Ayden persisted. Desire raced through her veins. As she stared at the shadows on the ceiling, her hands gently circled her breasts and moved slowly to her thighs. She imagined Ayden caressing her. This fantasy prompted her to reach for a pillow. She pulled it close to her and moved against it. How would she deal with these emerging physical sensations?

Luckily, sleep made the decision for her. As she drifted off, lines of Shakespeare, committed to memory long ago, found voice in her head:

Sleep that knits up the ravell'd sleave of care,
The death of each day's life, sore labour's bath,
Balm of hurt minds, great nature's second course,
Chief nourisher in life's feast.

13

Leila heard the phone ringing in the distance. She opened her eyes and adjusted to the dawn of a new day. The clock read nine. Stretching toward the night table, she answered with a groggy, "Hello."

"Mother," Hillary said in an annoyed tone, "what took you so long to answer? I was totally freaked out."

"I'm sorry, honey. I got to bed late. It's Sunday, right? On Sunday, most people sleep in. Why aren't you?"

"I'm sorry I woke you, but curiosity got the better of me."

"What are you so curious about?"

"Your date yesterday with Ayden."

"How did you know about that?"

"I stopped by the shop yesterday afternoon to discuss the design of the nursery, and you weren't there. Michelle told me you left early to go to the races with Ayden."

"That's true. We went to the track in Delaware. A charity event. Ayden's friend's horse ran in the sixth and won. Very exciting. I had a nice time but got home late."

"Is that it? Did anything romantic happen? Did you kiss him?"

"Hillary, I don't feel comfortable discussing such things with you." Leila fidgeted where she lay. "I'll admit I'm attracted to him and kissed him good night."

"Fine," Hillary said, seeming resigned to not getting any juicy details. "I'm glad you find him attractive and good company. Anyway,

Chad and I thought we'd bring brunch over to you and discuss the nursery. How does that sound?"

"Sounds great. How about eleven thirty? I need to shower."

"Wonderful. See you later."

Leila hung up the phone, relieved that she had some more sleep time. But the recurring idea that Ayden may not call as promised unsettled her and thwarted her efforts. Finally, after some tossing and turning, she left her cozy haven to shower.

A half hour later, the phone rang again.

"How did it go?"

"Good morning to you too, Michelle. I had a very nice time. Ayden's friend has a horse that ran in the sixth race and won."

"Great. Let me speed things up. Did you have sex?"

Leila reddened. "Sometimes you can be a real pain in the you-know-what. I'm uncomfortable discussing intimate things with you. You've got to respect my privacy."

"I'm sorry for being intrusive. I promise to do better. That being said, did you at least kiss him?"

"Yes," she admitted. "I enjoyed kissing him very much. I'm attracted to him and find his company entertaining. However, I need to take things slowly. We've only been out on two dates. What's the rush?"

"Well, our world is fast-paced. Men don't really court women in the traditional way anymore. They know what they want, and they ask for it."

Oh boy, is she right on target. "I know what you're saying is true. Let's see if this relationship even lasts a month."

"Okay. I'll move on to business matters. Do you want to work on our new projects tomorrow?"

"I'm up for that," Leila said, her tension easing. "Why don't I meet you at the shop around ten?"

"See you then."

Leila went back to her grooming. She finished her hair and makeup, dropped her towel, and reached for her underwear—but didn't put it on right away. Instead, she scrutinized her nakedness. Would Ayden find her unclothed body attractive? She became filled with self-doubt.

She was a savvy woman who knew how to dress to play up her assets. She selected tops that tastefully accentuated her ample breasts. Her outfits always strategically hugged her curves, calling attention to her femininity without being overly tight. Nonetheless, she was a middle-aged woman with a body that matched her years, though she made every effort to keep it in shape. Ayden's previous relationships had involved women of childbearing age. How could she successfully compete with such young women? Her outer layer presently enchanted Ayden—but once he began to peel off her attractive facade, would he remain interested? This unanswered question unnerved her.

She slipped into her gray-knit loungewear, put on gray socks, and slid her feet into furry pink slippers. Dressed to enjoy her Sunday, she made her way downstairs to set up for brunch.

The smell of coffee soon permeated the air. Leila set three places at the kitchen table and opened the shutters to let in the morning light. The summer flowers she'd planted were in full bloom—begonias, petunias, geraniums, and hydrangeas. Her yard appeared Eden-like. The beep of the coffee maker enticed her to pour herself a cup and take a seat at the table to enjoy the view.

Thoughts of Ayden soon disturbed her serenity. Why had this brazen man taken hold of her emotions? Yes, she was lonely, but there was something more powerful at play here. She'd had the same chemistry with Nick. But the two men differed significantly. Nick, over six feet tall with twinkling hazel eyes flecked with green and thick black hair shot with gray, had possessed a distinguished look. His presence had mesmerized a jury when he'd addressed them, and—though he'd never lacked for skill in his practice of law—his outer appearance had certainly contributed to his success.

Ayden, on the other hand, stood at five foot nine, maybe slightly taller, and had a smaller—albeit more muscular—frame overall. What unique elements of his being drew her to him? His talents and skills, oh yes. Those marvelous blue eyes, oh yes. And—*aha!*—the way he moved: with grace. She enjoyed watching him. He was a man in tune with his body—a body that took him about with ease, never faltering. Yes, his remarkable, seemingly effortless agility bewitched her.

A soft knock on the front door interrupted her contemplation. Hillary and Chad had just arrived, armed with two shopping bags of food.

"I guess I'm eating for two for sure," Hillary joked. "I couldn't decide what I wanted for brunch, so I bought everything in sight."

"Do you have anyone else you'd like to invite to this party?" Chad asked jovially. "There's plenty." He gave Hillary a sweet kiss on her cheek before walking to the counter to pour himself a cup of coffee. Leila waved him over to the table while she and Hillary found serving plates and created an inviting spread across the island: Danish coffee cakes, bagels, smoked salmon, cream cheese, tomatoes, cucumbers, diced onions, a spinach-and-egg quiche, and mixed fruit.

"This is absolutely wonderful," Leila said, looking at the impressive spread. "What a great way to start a summer Sunday!"

"We need this nourishment to fuel our creativity," Hillary said, already picking up a bagel half. "We'd like to leave today with some definite plans. If the nursery is done by Christmas, we can really enjoy the holidays."

"I'm more than happy to help," Leila said, beaming.

The three filled their plates and settled into their chairs.

"Hillary and I decided not to learn the sex of the baby because we want to be surprised," Chad began. "So the nursery design has to be flexible until the baby arrives. We can add finishing touches then."

Leila felt her own sense of urgency growing inside her. "I understand. We need to choose gender-neutral colors that will coordinate with more feminine or masculine ones later down the line. What do you think of using soft tones—grays, beiges, off-whites—with pastels? Why not get a light wood crib and dresser and accent them with soft aqua to start? Then we can use darker beige tones and bold stripes for a boy, or add lots of ruffles and girly prints with off-white backgrounds for a girl."

"And the walls and woodwork?" Hillary asked.

"Paint the walls a very pale aqua, and all the trim and woodwork off-white. We can look for area rugs with those colors too."

"I like it!" Chad proclaimed.

Hillary popped up to give Leila an appreciative hug and kiss. "Anything Mom designs comes out great."

The particulars regarding background work occupied the remainder of the morning's conversation. The wood floors needed refinishing, and the current baseboards needed replacing. The walls, ceiling, closet, and woodwork needed painting. An electrician needed to provide more outlets, as well as wiring for a ceiling fixture and wall lighting on both sides of the changing table.

"We'll call my parents and tell them what we've decided so far," Chad said, rising to clear plates. "I know they want to be part of this."

"Of course. I'll follow up with a call myself," Leila said. "And I'll schedule the craftsmen and supervise their work so you two can continue with your work responsibilities without any interruptions. When we're ready, we can have the closet finished inside with shelves, drawers, and cubbyholes. What do you think?"

"Mom, you're the best. That will be so helpful." Hillary sighed with relief.

Leila helped Hillary pack up the leftovers, waved her and Chad off, then returned to her bedroom, where she nestled into the comfy chaise beside the picture window to read a book, listen to her Sunday news programs, and, yes, recall the pleasure she'd experienced when Ayden had held her close and kissed her passionately.

But when would he call?

Leila met up with Michelle in the parking lot on Monday morning just before ten.

"Are you ready for a productive work day?" Michelle asked, full of energy.

"I suppose. Mondays are always difficult for me," Leila admitted. "But don't worry. I'll be slow to start but will get a handle on things soon enough."

"Great. I think we should start with the Millers. We have an appointment with them next Monday, late in the afternoon."

The two women worked nonstop for three hours. By the time they were on the third design board, Leila was compulsively looking at her watch and eyeing her cell phone, which rested nearby. These furtive glances didn't go unnoticed.

"What's with you?" Michelle asked, hand on hip.

"What do you mean?"

"You seem nervous or anticipatory. Does Ayden have something to do with this?"

Leila wanted to remain closed-mouthed, but her need for friendly advice got the better of her. "On Saturday, he made a move. He wanted sex. I felt the same. OMG! The chemistry is amazing. But ratcheting up the relationship to that level after just two dates? I'm not comfortable with that." Leila scrutinized Michelle's face, trying to read her reaction. "There's something else. Ayden's a player—has been for over twenty years. I might not be as easy as other women he's dated, and perhaps that's holding his interest for now. But I don't know for how long. Anyway, he's not going to commit to a middle-aged woman who's soon to be a grandmother—"

"Stop it right now," Michelle commanded. "You're beating yourself up. Most men are jerks; that is, until they fall in love. Right now, you don't have anyone else lined up, so go out and have fun—romantic fun. Take a chance."

Leila turned aside to avoid showing the tears beginning to well in her eyes. "And get dumped in the end?"

Michelle's tone softened in response to her friend's evident distress. "There are no guarantees in life."

"Just like there's no guarantee he'll ever call again, even though he said he would in a couple of days. Here we are, two days later, and no call."

"So that's why you keep looking at your watch and phone. I knew something was up." Michelle walked over and put her arms around her, gave her a sisterly hug and a quick kiss on the cheek. "Today isn't over yet. Wait and see. One thing's for sure, though: you're hooked."

"What do you mean?"

"Leila B., you've fallen in love again."

14

Leila arrived home just before six and immediately went to the phone to check her voice mail. One message, from Drew. He was considering coming home for the weekend. She opened the freezer to check its contents and pulled out a container of pot roast. With the dilemma of what to eat for dinner solved, she headed upstairs to get into more comfortable clothes and return Drew's call.

To her disappointment, when she dialed her son's number, instead of Drew himself, she had to settle for a recording.

"Drew, this is Mom. Hope things are going all right. I'd love for you to come home this weekend. Let me know your schedule. I'll be home all evening."

Leila placed the phone back in its caddy and decided to review the materials she'd brought home and go through her mail.

Five minutes in, she heard her cell phone chirp. Retrieving it from her handbag, she discovered a text message from Ayden. Quite impersonal of him, but he was not a conventional guy.

The message read: *Been busy. FYI—starting date for the Perkinses will be after Labor Day. Dinner this Saturday? Let me know. Take care. Patient Ayden.*

At first, Ayden's making light of the sex situation caused her to smile. But then. *Wait.* Was he downplaying her feelings?

She'd respond later. After she heard from Drew and learned about his weekend plans.

She rummaged through her mail while the pot roast defrosted in the microwave. She felt relieved Ayden had checked in as he said he would. On the other hand, she realized she'd rather have heard his voice.

The ringing of the phone jolted her. When she looked at the caller ID, she smiled and answered.

"Hi, Drew."

"Hi, Mom, how's it going?"

"Just fine, dear. So, you're coming in for the weekend?"

"Think so. I called Michael and Sam to see if they were free Saturday night. They are. We're going to hit a new bar in Center City around nine. Can I borrow your car?"

"You're flying in, then?"

"Yes, Friday evening. Chad said he'd pick me up. The plane gets in around seven. He suggested we all meet for a late dinner. You don't need to cook."

"Sounds like a plan. Be safe. I'll see you soon. Love you."

"Love you too."

Leila set down the phone and wandered to the kitchen, where she poured herself a glass of red wine and sat down to eat her pot roast. She leisurely made her way through her meal, contemplating how she'd reply to Ayden's text message. A tone needed to be set. If it were business, she'd gladly accept text messaging. But she required personal communication between the two of them to be more intimate. Their conversation could be brief, but she needed to hear his voice and know that he found it important to hear hers.

She called his cell phone. It rang and rang and then went to voice mail. A pang of disappointment gripped her chest. Why wasn't he anxiously awaiting her answer?

"Ayden, I'd like to discuss plans for this weekend when you have a free moment or two. I won't have a car Saturday evening. My son,

Drew, is flying in for the weekend and meeting up with friends down-town, so he needs to borrow my car. Talk to you soon."

There. She hung up. Her concise message, delivered in a cordial manner, implicitly informed Ayden of her expectations. *Well done!*

❀

Leila was wrapping up some work on the Miller project when the phone rang. *Ayden.* She felt a flutter of excitement as she answered, "Hello?"

"It's Ayden," he said. "How are things?"

"Just fine."

"So, you'll be without wheels on Saturday? Looks like I'm the des-ignated driver." He spoke as if he were an adolescent proudly taking on a responsible role. "What time and where do you want to have dinner?"

"How about eight? There's a gourmet Italian restaurant near me that's wonderful."

"I totally trust your judgment. Now, I need your address."

What had been her private world was about to become quite public. She took a deep breath and gave Ayden the information he needed.

"I'll target seven thirty. How's that?"

"Perfect."

"Great. See you then."

Leila pondered her level of satisfaction with the brief exchange after they hung up, considering whether those few moments on the phone had been more fulfilling than Ayden's previous text.

Hearing his voice, even for a few moments, had made her tingle all over.

Yes, much better.

❀

Drew's plane landed on time, and the Brandt clan met up at a favorite Asian fusion restaurant in Plymouth Meeting at eight. The reunion was festive. The arrival of the baby was the prime topic of conversation, followed closely by their plans for the nursery.

"Have you thought about names?" Drew asked.

"We've had some discussion, but nothing's definite. We do want the name to connect with Dad's in some way, though." Hillary squeezed her mother's hand.

Leila tried desperately not to become too emotional. "You don't have to do that. But I greatly appreciate the thought."

Drew, always sensitive to her moods, seemed to sense that the talk needed to be redirected. "Mom, you don't mind my borrowing your car tomorrow?"

"Not at all. I'll try to get out of work earlier and be home by five."

Hillary, looking a bit mischievous, asked, "Are you going out with Ayden tomorrow?"

"Yes, dinner in the neighborhood." Leila felt the tips of her ears begin to burn.

"Has he been to the house before?"

"No."

Drew jumped in. "Who's this Ayden?"

"A man Mom began dating recently."

"A man, really?" Drew leaned forward. "What's his line of work?"

"He's an architect," Hillary answered for her mother. "Mom met him through a client."

At least she didn't mention the matchmaking service.

"Will I meet him this weekend?" Drew asked.

"I really don't know. We're leaving around seven thirty. No need to adjust your plans based on that. Look, all of you. He's a nice guy. We enjoy each other's company. I'll let you know if anything develops."

"We want you to be happy, Mom," Hillary said, shooting a look at Drew that Leila didn't miss. "That's all."

"I know. You guys are the best. Now, how about some dessert?"

15

It was a surprisingly busy week. Usually summer days meant less business. Labor Day was on the horizon, however, and their semi-annual sale attracted a good number of customers, mostly people shopping for themselves.

Saturday turned out to be no exception. When a small window of opportunity for a break popped up around noon, Leila and Michelle pulled out their brown-bag lunches, eager to refuel and relax for a few minutes.

"Drew got in without problems?" Michelle asked.

"Yes, thankfully. Chad and Hillary picked him up at the airport, and we met for dinner. Actually, do you mind if I leave a half hour early today, so I can give him my car for the evening?"

"No problem. By four thirty, people will be thinking about their evening plans." Michelle paused. "And yours?" She wore a devilish smile.

Leila gave her friend a studied look and finally decided to tell her about her plans. "Yes, I'm having dinner with Ayden. And yes, he'll need to pick me up at home. I feel that arrangement is a form of home invasion, but unavoidable if I want to see him."

"Don't be silly. Relationships inevitably progress."

"Or end."

The door chimed, signaling a customer. Leila took care of things, allowing Michelle to relax a bit longer.

A steady flow of business over the course of the afternoon made the time pass quickly. At four thirty, Leila gathered her belongings, went over Monday's schedule with Michelle, and left.

❀

She found Drew in the family room, channel hopping. She knew he was anxious to get on the road.

She held up her keys. "Drew, dear, the car is yours."

"Thanks, Mom," he said, jumping up. "I want to get to the mall before I meet up with Michael and Sam. I'll see you later tonight." He kissed her on the cheek and promptly left.

Leila didn't waste time. In just a little over two hours, Ayden would be knocking at her door. She had to get started with her preparations—tidying up the downstairs, selecting just the right outfit, and redoing her hair and makeup. She intended to capture his attention the instant he laid his fantastic eyes upon her.

She started with a relaxing milk bath. That step accomplished, she washed her face and applied a mask. The instructions said to leave it on for ten minutes, so she used the time to get her outfit together. The restaurant was upscale. She could dress up a bit. After serious thought, she took out navy linen trousers and a sleeveless white cotton blouse with ruffles around a deep-V neckline. A navy, white, and lime-green tweed cardigan served as the perfect topper and added splashes of color. To give her stature a boost, she chose navy slingback pumps with two-inch heels, keeping in mind that Ayden was of average height. She didn't want to challenge his ego in that regard.

Satisfied with her wardrobe choices, she returned to her grooming, removing the mask and applying foundation and a blush with a sparkling effect that would be enhanced by the candlelight in the restaurant. Then she moved on to the last area to be addressed: her hair. She decided to wear it up, but to soften the effect, she added some flirtatious bangs and wispy tendrils. This gave her quite a different appearance—a surprise for Ayden, who was unfamiliar with her chameleon-like abilities.

With only twenty minutes to go before Ayden's arrival, Leila hurried downstairs and surveyed the first floor, hoping to catch anything that would detract from her design work. An air of spaciousness existed. The rooms merged just past the entrance, and the color scheme of navy blue, terra-cotta, vanilla, and willow green with touches of black flowed throughout. The overall traditional style, spiced with imaginatively placed abstract wall art, hand-blown glass, and antique treasures, created the air of casual elegance Leila favored. She possessed a special fondness for a Victorian tea set she'd lucked upon at a flea market in the quaint town of Skippack. To show it off to its best advantage, Leila placed it on the glass-topped fishbowl on a stand that served as the living room's cocktail table—a conversation piece many admired.

Hunger pangs prompted Leila to secure a chocolate-covered mint from a candy dish on the large ottoman in the family room. Just as she popped it into her mouth, the doorbell rang. She finished it quickly, downing it in one gulp. If Ayden decided to greet her with a kiss, the lingering taste of peppermint and chocolate would enhance his experience.

Leila opened the front door and was immediately satisfied that she'd successfully wowed Ayden. His eyes gave him away, widening as he took her in.

He soon regained his composure, of course. "You look so different with your hair up. At first, I wasn't sure it was you," he teased. "You look wonderful." He leaned close and gave her a kiss on the cheek.

"Thanks. Please, come in."

Just as she expected, he looked around with his expert eyes, taking in the elements in each room. "You've done nice work here."

"What you see is an accumulation of finds over the years. It works, right?"

"Yes, it does. You're eclectic and sophisticated."

"I suppose so." She paused to take in his handsome presence. "Are you hungry?"

"I'm ready to indulge," he responded with his usual boyishness.

"Well, let's go." She reached for her bag and sweater—placed strategically on the entry hall table—and led the way out the door.

Ayden's snazzy convertible was parked in her driveway.

"I see you have your convertible with you tonight." The top was down. She was glad she'd worn her hair up and secured it well.

He opened the car door, as any gentleman would. "I'll put the top up. You've gone to such trouble to look fabulous, I don't want to undermine your efforts in any way."

With Ayden seated next to her and the top back in place, the space inside became more intimate. Leila appreciated his efforts to please her.

"So, where to?" he asked.

Leila was happy to direct.

❁

The maître d' led them to a window table draped with a crisp white linen cloth, matching napkins, and gleaming silverware. Tea candles encircled a low bouquet of flowers. A lovely garden, just outside their view, contained a dark wooden bench and a small replica of one of the fountains in Rome's St. Peter's Square. Tiny lights wound their way up a white birch tree. Once night fell, they'd illuminate the area, adding a magical touch to the setting.

"Good evening," their waiter greeted them. "My name is Alberto. I'll be waiting on you this evening."

"Hello," they said in unison.

"May I get you something to drink besides water?"

Ayden gestured to Leila to go first. She thought for a moment and then ordered the house merlot, her usual choice. Ayden asked for a shiraz. Alberto handed them menus and promised to return very soon with their wine.

"I got your message about the starting date for the Perkins project," Leila said. "I'm excited for them."

"Their project is challenging. It'll take some time, at least four to six weeks. But in the end, our team will pull it together." Ayden gave her a wink.

Indeed, they were a team in more ways than one. Leila felt comfortable in his company. He seemed equally relaxed. They shared at least some history, though it was still in its infancy.

"Have you spoken with the Dawsons since last week's victory?" she asked.

"I sent them a congratulatory email and thanked them for their hospitality."

"I sense that you're not a fan of the old-fashioned phone call."

"The new technology allows people to save time, be more efficient."

Emboldened, Leila leaned forward slightly and tilted her head, searching his eyes. "I enjoy hearing your voice."

"I'll keep that in mind." He sat silent for a moment. "I have a question for you. You may think it more a request or an invitation . . ."

Alberto returned with their wine order, interrupting the conversation. "Are you ready to order?"

"I'll have the tomato, avocado, and mozzarella salad to start," Ayden said. "And the blackened tilapia."

Leila was anxious to hear Ayden's question, so she quickly delivered her requests. "I'll have the same salad to start, please, and then the veal medallions with prosciutto."

"You both made excellent choices. Please enjoy your drinks."

With that, Alberto gathered up the menus, taking care to leave the wine list on the table.

They were alone again. She could hardly contain herself. Inside she was aflutter, but on the outside, she knew she appeared composed. "What's the question?" She fixed her eyes on Ayden and made sure the corners of her mouth were turned up into a warm smile.

"Did I ever tell you I own a small home in St. Michaels, Maryland, near the bay?"

That was the question? Her thoughts began to wander. *Does he want decorating advice?* "No," she replied, trying to sound neutral.

"Well, if you felt comfortable with the idea, we could spend Labor Day weekend there. What do you think?"

At first, Leila had no response, feeling somewhat guilty for thinking he was trying to benefit from their relationship. On the other hand, such an invitation was unexpected. How could she get through a weekend with Ayden without having sex with him? It would be awkward, and therefore not doable. If she were honest with herself, she'd admit to wanting Ayden and just get on with it. She looked across the table at him. What would she say?

"That sounds like a wonderful idea. But what would the arrangements be?"

"Meaning?"

"Meaning, what would the *sleeping* arrangements be? And what about sex?"

Ayden leaned toward her and lowered his voice. "The cottage has three bedrooms. I like sex. But I don't expect it . . . unless you want it too." With a completely straight face, he added, "But keep this in mind. I'll not be your plaything."

The sip of water Leila had just taken in sprayed over the table as she burst out laughing.

Ayden grinned. Clearly, he'd achieved his goal: to lighten up the table talk.

After she composed herself, Leila felt the need to express her concerns. "I've only been intimate with my husband. That part of our marriage was wonderful, but sadly, it ended over five years ago. So I'm out of practice. You, on the other hand, have likely been active over the past five years. Perhaps with multiple partners?"

"I see where you're going with this." Ayden turned sober. "You want assurance I'm not dealing with any STIs. I can provide that. And we can take things slow, too—that is, if we decide to be intimate." He fell silent and trained his hypnotic eyes on Leila.

"Is there a deadline for my answer?" she asked, already trying to convince herself that a weekend getaway with Ayden need not be a dangerous undertaking.

"Not really."

"Then let me think about it for a while."

"Fine."

Alberto returned with their meals, and the conversation took yet another turn as Leila provided more details about her children and Ayden talked about his parents and siblings.

"Funny." Leila tilted her head. "I pictured you as an only child."

"I'm the *only* one who's remained single for quite some time."

"Your choice, Mr. Doyle."

"Yes, but I never met someone I truly wanted to marry."

"And I've never met someone who made me feel I could let go of Nick."

Ayden looked carefully at her and, with obvious sincerity, said, "Well then, I guess we're both kind of stuck for now."

After Alberto removed the dinner dishes, he returned to ask if Ayden and Leila wanted coffee and dessert. Leila glanced at her watch; the evening was still young. It was just nine thirty. "I'm set at the moment. How about you?"

"I'm quite content for now."

"Why don't you take me home and we can have coffee there?"

"Sounds good." Ayden turned to Alberto and asked for the check.

As they walked out, Leila touched Ayden's arm. "How did you like the restaurant?" She was curious to see if she'd made the right choice.

"I liked it very much. Great food, courteous service, and nice atmosphere."

"My thoughts exactly. And I especially enjoyed the company," she said, letting a teasing glint enter her eyes.

A smile crossed Ayden's face. "Me too."

The two sat in silence for the short ride home. Leila was, of course, thinking of how the remainder of the evening would go, and she suspected Ayden was too. She had no qualms inviting him in for coffee since she knew Drew would likely be home by midnight. He was departing for Boston the next day on a two o'clock flight; she was sure he'd want a good night's sleep.

Once inside the house, Ayden followed Leila into the kitchen and took a seat at the island while she set about making coffee. No Drew yet. *Nice.* Ayden didn't exactly seem ready for the family thing yet.

"I just bought a customized brewing system that uses pods," Leila said, pointing to the machine. "We have lots of options."

"What are my choices?"

Leila provided a detailed explanation.

Ayden, looking overwhelmed, put his hands up. "I'm easy. Just give me regular, black—no cream, no sugar."

"I took you for the more adventurous type." Leila laughed.

"Not when it comes to my coffee."

Leila's choice—an espresso topped with whipped cream—showed her to be more daring. After placing Ayden's drink in front of him, she sat down next to him with hers in hand.

Ayden wrapped his hands around his mug. "I may have a new client for you."

"How so?"

"The Perkinses' friend, Cynthia, recommended me to another friend of hers."

"Oh?"

"Her name is Susan Fredericks. She is recently divorced and has bought a Tudor home in Wynnewood, but it requires extensive renovation. She needs a designer to help her out because the bridal shop she owns takes up all of her time. I mentioned you and Michelle to her, and she seemed very interested."

"Does she want me to call her?"

"Yes, definitely. Go get your phone. I'll give you her contact info."

Leila pulled her phone from her handbag and handed it to Ayden, who tapped in the information. When he handed the phone back, she smiled warmly. "I appreciate the referral. I may be able to return the favor shortly. Michelle and I have a project underway that will eventually require the demolition of a master bath and perhaps the installation of some custom cabinetry in the master bedroom."

"Great." Ayden smiled back.

"How's your coffee?"

"It needs a bit of sweetening."

"Really? I thought you liked your coffee black."

He responded by leaning forward and kissing her gently on the lips. She kissed him back—and her feelings for him took the path of passion. She put her arms around his neck and drew him close to her in a prolonged embrace. His hands slipped under her blouse and eased their way to her breasts. She had no intention of stopping him. Instead, she encouraged him by moving onto his lap. She wanted him to explore, to feel the softness of her skin, to enjoy her fragrance.

Is this lust or love or both? She didn't need an answer.

Just as she felt Ayden's hands slip from her breasts and travel across her navel to the warm, moist place between her thighs, she heard the garage door open. Leila instantly retook her seat and rearranged her disheveled clothing. She blotted her face with a napkin, reconfigured her hair as best she could, and took a long sip of her espresso.

"I suppose this will be Drew?" Ayden asked quietly.

"Yes, perhaps just in time." She smiled nervously in his direction.

Ayden appeared his usual, cool self. Leila was amazed by how easily he regained his composure. The door from the garage opened, and Drew emerged. He seemed to realize immediately that he'd just interrupted something intimate, because he stopped short when he saw Leila and Ayden sitting at the island.

"Hi, sweetheart! Come meet my friend, Ayden Doyle." Leila turned to Ayden and finished the introduction. "Ayden, this is my son, Drew."

Drew approached Ayden and extended his hand. "Nice to meet you, Ayden."

"Great meeting you."

Drew took a seat at the island. "The coffee smells pretty good. How about making me a cup?"

"Of course. There are a number of options," Leila said, overly enthusiastic, still feeling flustered. "Did you notice my new beverage maker? I just had an espresso with whipped cream. Delicious."

"That sounds good," Drew said, eyeing the new appliance admiringly.

"Drew, how do you like Boston?" Ayden inquired politely.

"I like it very much. In many ways it reminds me of Philadelphia, so I felt at home rather quickly. I live north of the city, in West Peabody."

"And your job with GE?"

"It's going great. I'm a test engineer—quality control and all that stuff."

"That's impressive."

"Drew is quite an accomplished man," Leila interjected. "He

graduated from Penn State at the top of his class and is earning a master's at MIT."

"Mom, stop with those accolades," Drew protested. "It's embarrassing."

"Well, I'm proud of you." She carried his coffee over to him.

Drew shook his head and sipped his espresso.

Ayden finished his coffee. "Well, it's getting late. I'd better get home. Have a safe trip back, Drew."

"Thanks, Ayden. You too."

"I'll walk you to the door," Leila said, knowing her nervousness was evident.

At the door, Ayden looked around to make sure Drew hadn't moved from his place in the kitchen, then gave Leila a quick kiss good night on the cheek. Before withdrawing, he whispered into her ear, "Your skin felt so wonderful. Come to St. Michaels with me. We'll be alone and free from any distractions."

Leila wanted to verbalize the depth of her feelings, but Drew's nearby presence stifled her response. "It was a fabulous evening. Call me soon."

"I'll call you in a couple of days."

Leila watched Ayden head to his car and pull away from the house. She regretted his departure but was thankful Drew had come home when he did. She needed to keep Ayden at a distance for a while longer. Leila knew where a "yes" to St. Michaels would lead. She needed to prepare herself, physically and emotionally, for that leap. Her mind told her to resist, but every other part of her body ached for her to go.

She returned to the kitchen, her heart still beating rapidly. "How was your evening, dear?"

He answered, but she heard nothing.

16

Leila and Michelle both breathed a sigh of relief as they hooked their seat belts. The Millers had praised the design plans. Madeline Miller had particularly voiced her delight with the option that expanded on the color scheme in her master bedroom, which she loved.

"That went well," Michelle remarked.

"Yes, it did. Ayden must be at the next meeting. Now that the Millers see a completely new master bath is necessary, we need all the possibilities highlighted. His expertise will help."

"I agree. Let's try to set something up after Labor Day. You'll be talking to him soon?"

"Yes, within a couple of days."

"Drew got off without a hitch?"

"Yes."

"And what about your time with Ayden?"

"Very nice. We came back to my place for coffee. He gave me a lead for a possible new client. I'll need to give her a call."

"Who is it?"

"A divorced woman who's had to downsize. Her name is Susan Fredericks."

"Wait. I think I know her. Does she own a bridal shop?"

"Yes. Ayden mentioned that."

"She's very attractive. Talented too. My niece bought her wedding dress from her. It was gorgeous!"

Leila struggled to keep her sudden, swelling interest in Susan Fredericks from becoming obvious. "Really? What else do you know about her?"

"Not much. She's younger than we are, in her early forties. I went with my niece for one of her fittings, so I met her. She's petite and has a nice figure. She has an accent of some sort, but I'm not sure where she's from."

"I may be able to use some of that information to endear us to her."

"You're good at that. Now you've two important calls to make and hopefully two meetings to arrange."

Leila decided a discussion regarding Ayden's invitation might be worthwhile. "I have something to tell you. I have a big decision to make." Leila paused while Michelle impatiently waited for her to unload. "Ayden invited me to spend Labor Day weekend with him at his vacation house on the Chesapeake Bay."

"Wow! That's so romantic!"

"Do you know what this means?"

"Of course. He likes you and may be on his way to falling in love with you. And, he wants you. Sex is on the horizon."

"I think so. But I'm not sure I'm ready."

"Well, get ready. Leila, you're not a kid. You've known this man for almost six months, and you've had the hots for him the whole time. Let loose."

"It's not easy. I have my reservations. He might move on once he's conquered me. That will hurt. I'm not sure I can deal with that."

"I know. Rejection is horrible. On the other hand, you might eventually reject him. Or, you two may find happiness with each other. Without taking a risk, the unknown will remain unknown. Can you deal with *that*?"

Leila fell silent. Michelle wasn't expecting an answer anyway. The rest of the ride back to the shop was void of conversation, both women deep in thought. Leila continued thinking about Ayden's invitation. Would she accept? She still wasn't sure.

Leila's attraction to Ayden made it impossible for her to say no to going away with him for Labor Day. A few days after their romantic dinner, she sent a simple text message: *"It's a go!"*

Michelle and Leila discussed closing the shop Friday through Tuesday, giving both of them some well-deserved downtime. Business would be slow anyway. They posted the closing on their website and changed their outgoing voice mail, freeing themselves to make plans for the holiday weekend.

Ayden and Leila decided to leave early on Friday morning for the three-hour trip to St. Michaels. The weather report for the locale contained mixed messages. Friday and Saturday promised to be lovely—sunny with highs in the mideighties. A cloudy day and intermittent showers were forecast for Sunday, but on Labor Day, sunshine and pleasant temperatures would return.

Ayden said there was plenty to do in St. Michaels, rain or shine. He also offered some wardrobe advice: "The dress code is casual, so pack light."

Leila conjectured the hefty satchel she'd taken to the races had prompted Ayden's guideline for this excursion of more than one day, but she had no intention of roughing it. Everything would be packed into a duffel bag she could easily carry over her shoulder. The bag had small wheels that could be deployed if necessary. This option would allow her to maintain her independence. She didn't want Ayden to perceive her as a helpless female who needed his assistance whenever the going got a bit rough.

She removed her colorful Vera Bradley toiletry bag from the top shelf of her closet and filled it with her specially purchased travel sizes of shampoo, conditioner, and a heavenly scented citrus body lotion—perfect for the last weekend of summer. She filled the matching makeup bag with all the essentials and located her small blow dryer and a handful of curlers, just in case there was time to primp a bit before dinners. Ever the designer, she focused her clothing selection on two color schemes: black with neutrals and denim with neutrals. She packed two pairs of jeans, a variety of cotton knit tops, two sweaters, two dresses, two bathing suits, and two cover-ups. Limiting the shoe selection was difficult, but she finally decided on her favorite bronze-metallic sandals with two-inch heels; pewter ballet flats; black flip-flops for padding around the house; and athletic shoes designed for walking, just in case. Only a couple of things still needed to be included, and they were crucial items: sleepwear.

She'd avoid anything provocative. That left out the full-length see-through black nightgown with rosettes on the shoulders she hadn't worn since Nick died. After perusing her bedtime apparel, she opted for soft gray patio pajamas. She could easily sleep in those. Her second choice was a long white lace-and-satin chemise with pink spaghetti straps and a scalloped neckline and hem. She liked how it draped across her body without clinging and how it flattered her figure just so.

She placed her sleepwear at the bottom of the bag, as if she were hiding contraband from the Maryland State Police.

Just after nine, the doorbell rang. Leila was in the kitchen finishing up a cup of coffee and a muffin. She'd already brought her gear into the hall. She opened the door and energetically greeted Ayden. "Good morning!"

"Well, good morning to you. All packed and ready to go?"

"I'm just finishing my coffee and muffin. Do you want a little something to eat?"

"No, thanks. I have coffee in the car and already finished a jelly donut."

"My things are in that bag near the entry table." Fighting back her own impulse to laugh, she said, "I tried my best to pack light."

Ayden walked over and picked up the bag. He wore an expression of pleasant surprise. "I must be truthful. I expected more. I cleaned out my trunk, wanting to make sure there was enough room. Now, there's plenty."

"Good" was Leila's simple response. Although she knew Ayden was teasing her, she'd endured enough of his chauvinistic humor. "If you don't mind taking my things to the car, I'll just do some last-minute tidying up and meet you outside."

Her quick scrutiny of the house confirmed that all was in order. Melinda had enough food and water. Hillary would check on things Sunday morning during her run. She grabbed her handbag, sunglasses, visor, keys, and remote and locked up.

Ayden stood beside the open car door, waiting to tuck her in. As she walked down the path, Leila hoped he appreciated how she looked in her denim capris, white tee, and open-toed shoes with kitten heels. Her hair, which she was wearing half-up and half-down, was held in place with a large tortoiseshell barrette. Today, she felt, she looked particularly youthful.

She approached the passenger side of the car, and Ayden unexpectedly moved forward, put his arms around her, drew her in, and gave her a passionate kiss on the lips. "I'm really glad you decided to go. I promise you we'll have a really nice time."

She stood silent and still for a few seconds, enjoying his tight hold and dreamy blue eyes. "You're a man who keeps promises, so I expect we'll have fun. Most of all, I'm looking forward to spending time alone with you." She gave him a quick kiss on the lips and slipped into the car.

Ayden handed the seat belt to her and closed the door. Once in the driver's seat, he put on his sunglasses, adjusted the air conditioner, and slipped in a Yuja Wang CD. "We're off!" Ayden proclaimed.

17

During the first leg of the trip, Leila and Ayden sat quietly and enjoyed Yuja Wang's *Fantasia*, an album of her favorite encores. The music complemented the wonderful scenery along the way. An occasional puffy white cloud dotted the blue sky—it was a picture-perfect day. The warmth of the summer sun, streaming through the windows, touched Leila's right cheek, contrasting pleasantly with the cool air inside the car.

Ayden's prized possession took to the road like a young stallion just released into an open meadow. They sped joyfully toward St. Michaels. Though the car provided a very smooth ride, Leila knew her companion was testing the speed limit. She also understood that a person couldn't be timid when driving such a car, however, so she said nothing.

When the CD ended, Ayden put his hand on her knee. "We're just about two hours from St. Michaels, so we should arrive around lunchtime."

"I'm really excited. I've heard the town is absolutely charming and has wonderful restaurants and shops."

"It is. Most of the shops and restaurants are on the main street—that's Talbot Street—or one of the little side streets. Let's eat outside and enjoy a nice view when we get there. There's a surf-and-turf place I particularly like for lunch."

"You're in charge. Just lead the way." She communicated her vote of confidence with a smile.

Fifteen minutes away from their destination, Ayden suggested putting down the top and breathing in the fresh air. "Any objections?" he asked Leila.

"None." As the top folded back, a whiff of air from the bay teased Leila's sense of smell. Exuberance and liberation rushed through her, feelings she hadn't experienced in a long time. "I'm looking forward to seeing your home. You haven't said much about it except that it's close to the water."

"Your reaction will let me know if I've achieved my goal of creating a charming place to unwind in after a busy workweek."

Before long, a sign appeared: *Welcome to St. Michaels.* The surroundings turned out to be just as Leila imagined: structures with weathered shingles, characteristic of an old but enchanting seaside town. Ayden left the main thoroughfare and, after a few turns, pulled into a short driveway. A charming shingled cottage with white trim and cranberry shutters stood before them. A storybook picket fence set off the cobblestone walkway leading to the front door.

"This is lovely." Leila lit up. "I can't wait to see the inside."

"It's a work in progress, but I can show you some startling before-and-after pictures."

They hopped out of the car and Ayden opened the trunk to retrieve their things. Leila insisted on rolling her duffel bag herself while Ayden carried his luggage and the supplies he'd brought along.

Ayden unlocked the door and pushed it open. Leila's heart raced with anticipation. Once she stepped over the threshold, she suspected, her life would change course.

She took a deep breath and stepped inside, into a large room. Sunlight poured in through the expansive paned windows in the front and sliding French doors leading onto the deck in the back. A soft moss green on the walls contrasted wonderfully with the white woodwork, and as she looked up to take in the high ceiling, a loft came into view. Honey-colored wood floors spread throughout the open first floor, with only a plush moss-green sectional sofa to mark the space between the living room and formal dining area. She walked toward the back and into an inviting kitchen with a small island topped with black speckled granite. A wall of white cabinets with beadwork doors served as a backdrop for the island. Her mind raced. In the morning, she'd have breakfast there with Ayden and sit on the barstools tucked under the countertop.

Leila spun around and lifted her arms in the air. "This is a wonderful space. I love everything you've done."

Ayden smiled, obviously pleased with her enthusiasm. "I guess you can see that one of my favorite colors is green."

"Yes. It's a rich, quiet green. Perfect for a home near water."

"I still need a few lamps and area rugs, but what's really missing is some great artwork for the walls." He pivoted suddenly to the right, as if a thought had just struck him. "I have something to show you." He opened up a drawer in the island and took out a photo album. "This is what the place looked like a couple of years ago."

Leila pulled out a bar stool and began to view the album.

Ayden retrieved a bottle of water from the refrigerator. "Are you thirsty?"

She nodded. "I could go for some water."

He took out two glasses and added some ice. "Lemon?"

"If it's not too much trouble."

He opened a flavoring packet and sprinkled some lemon zest into the glasses. "Presto! Lemon-flavored water." A triumphant smile crossed his face.

The first page showed the cottage in ruin and a large sign nailed to the front door: *Condemned! Danger! Beware!*

The home's former condition shocked Leila. "Only an expert craftsman like you could have given this place new life. Who owned it?"

"The town took possession of it. Years of back taxes were due. The elderly man who owned it died without a will or heirs. And that was that. It went up for auction on a wintry day, and I bought it for two hundred thousand. I thought one of the owners of the adjacent inns would snatch it up, but I outbid them. Truthfully, I lucked out."

"To think this adorable retreat almost became a parking lot! Show me more."

"Come this way."

Ayden headed toward a door in the front corner of the living room that opened into a spacious hallway. Immediately to the left was a small powder room with a white pedestal sink and whimsical hand towels embroidered with skiffs used for crabbing and oystering. The doors facing one another at the end of the hallway opened into equally sized bedrooms, each with its own dressing area and bathroom, one with a walk-in shower and the other with a tub. Leila surveyed each and noticed the room facing the back of the house had French doors leading onto a deck.

"I love the French country furniture, and it goes well with your mix of white-on-white patterns for linens. Stripes, plaids, and dots— what we call in the trade *casual elegance*. Is that a hot tub I see out on the deck?"

"It is."

"Is it in working order?"

Ayden's boyish grin appeared. "I thought we'd try it out later this evening."

"That will be nice," she said, her heart skipping a beat.

Ayden continued providing details of the renovation, clearly taking great pride in his work.

"The transformation is amazing," Leila said as they walked back down the hall toward the living room. "You should see if one of the design magazines would be interested in your story. A little publicity never hurts."

"I'll give that idea some thought."

Had Ayden wooed a throng of women here in the past? How could she discover the truth?

"Do you get down here often?"

"Not as often as I'd like. It's not a place I readily share with others."

Now seemed the appropriate time to discuss her need for her own space. "Do I have my choice of bedroom suite? Because if I do, I opt for the one with the tub. You can have the better view, hot tub and all." She spoke her words as innocently as possible.

Ayden said nothing for the longest time; Leila continued to look at him, waiting patiently but nervously for his response. He appeared to be contemplating a suitable reply. Finally, he placed his hands on her shoulders and looked directly into her eyes. "I want you to feel at home here. If you want your own space, fine."

She felt weak in the knees looking into his blue eyes, but she gathered herself together and offered her appreciation. "Thanks for understanding."

Ayden gave her a tender kiss on her forehead. "Let's take a look at the loft."

He had an uncanny knack for defusing an intense or awkward moment or situation. Taking her hand in his, he led her back to the living room and up the staircase.

"I use this mostly as a den, but it can also be a third bedroom."

The airy feel of the space wowed Leila. She looked up to find sky-lights on either side of a large ceiling fan, revealing the afternoon's blue sky with its wispy white clouds. The walls were primed for paint. The wood floor matched the downstairs. The space included a nicely appointed bathroom with colorful tile work.

"Incorporating a private bathroom for each bedroom was wise."

"That had to be. If I decide to rent the place out, I can demand top dollar."

"Is this room to be green as well?"

"What do you think?"

"I think you can change color here since it's a space unto itself."

"What would you suggest?"

"Something light but neutral. And since you are thinking about setting up this room to function as both a bedroom and a den, maybe you should consider a sofa bed."

"That's likely the way I'll go."

Leila decided enough time had been devoted to indoor sightseeing. "I don't know about you, but I'm getting hungry. Let's go and have lunch at that place you suggested earlier. Are you ready?"

"More than ready."

Once downstairs, Leila picked up her bag and swung it over her shoulder. "I need just a couple of minutes to freshen up."

"Me too."

They paraded toward the bedroom wing, belongings in tow, and closed the doors to their own personal sanctuaries at precisely the same time.

❀

The restaurant was situated on the marina within walking distance of the cottage. Ayden asked the hostess to seat them at an umbrella table on the deck.

Leila studied the menu for a few moments, her hunger compelling her to make a quick decision. "Everything on the menu is appealing. I'm going for the Trio Salad. It has shrimp, crab, and chicken, so I can have it all."

"I think I'm going for the burger with crabmeat on top."

"That's a fine, manly choice."

"I'm glad you approve." He gave Leila one of his sexy smiles and moved on to another topic. "Can we talk about tonight?"

"Sure."

"Since we're having a late lunch, I thought we could delay dinner and spend time at a local bar overlooking the harbor. The drinks and appetizers are really good there. Live music as well. Maybe dance some. Then we can go back to the house. I'll make dinner, and we can try out the hot tub. I just installed a pretty impressive grill on the deck. What do you say to that?"

"That sounds wonderful." She gently placed her hand on his and said in a low voice, "I didn't know you were a grill master too."

"Oh, but I am." He winked. "After lunch, let's take a walk to the open-air market. I'm thinking kebabs."

"Then kebabs it is."

The waiter arrived with water. "Hi, my name is Jeff. Are you ready to order?"

Ayden took charge. "The lady would like the Trio Salad, and I'd like the burger with crabmeat topping but no cheese."

"Anything to drink besides water?"

"I'll have a beer, something dark on draft. How about you, Leila?"

"I'm fine with water."

They sat quietly, looking out at the harbor scene, until the food arrived.

An hour later, they began their walk toward the market. As they waited for a light to change, Ayden grasped Leila's hand more tightly. She turned toward him and smiled.

"Having fun?" he asked.

"Yes."

"You know, I'm falling for you."

Once again, he'd delivered one of his zingers—to purposely unnerve her, she suspected. And on a street corner crowded with pedestrians and traffic. Her heart pounded. "What does that mean, exactly?"

Ayden sighed, knowing Leila didn't intend to make things easy for him.

"It means I care about you very much. I don't want you seeing anyone else."

"Do you think Dr. Goodwin would approve of that arrangement?"

"The hell with Dr. Goodwin. It's really not up to her, is it?"

Uh-oh. Ayden had missed her attempt at humor. He was being sincere and forthright, and she had unwisely interjected what she thought was a witty comment into the conversation. She had hurt his feelings.

"No, of course not," she said gently. "However, that's quite a commitment for both of us, don't you think?"

He gazed intently into her eyes. "Yes."

Leila had the guilts. She needed to set things right. "I'm sorry. I didn't mean to be dismissive. To be honest, I'm having difficulty dealing with my feelings. You're now Nick's rival. I'm thinking more about you and less about him. Then there is the ever-present fear of loss. I'm not sure I can deal with that again." She paused for a moment to think how she could better handle the situation. "Can we revisit this on our way home, after our weekend? We may have a better sense of where our relationship is going then."

"Not a problem." He seemed happier after her apology and admission. "But for now, could you stop walking for just a moment and kiss me?"

Leila turned to face him and placed her arms around his neck. Ayden pressed his lips to hers and gently nudged his tongue into her mouth. A passing motorist whistled and gave a thumbs-up. They both broke out laughing; Leila felt like they were a couple of teenagers caught behind the grandstand at a football game. Ayden took her hand again, and they headed to their destination.

The market bustled with activity. A variety of local produce, seafood, and fresh-baked pies stocked the shelves, all in abundant supply. Ayden picked up a shopping basket and soon filled it with lettuce, tomatoes, cucumbers, assorted kebabs, corn, French bread, apple pie, and fruit and muffins for the next day's breakfast.

Leila audited the contents of the basket. "Do we need to pick up any wine?"

"No, I brought some from home. We're set for the weekend."

Leila recalled similar marketing trips with Nick; it was an activity they'd enjoyed, simple as it was. She'd missed it. Her current companion was making today's experience especially pleasant. She took a moment to appreciate his presence—warm, sexy, handsome—and realized how much better her life seemed now that he was in it.

❁

A row of tall evergreens separated Ayden's property from the grounds of the adjacent inns, but all the greenery seemed to collide, giving the impression that Ayden's backyard spread out extensively. The outside ambience suggested peace and tranquility in spite of the slight intrusion of the faraway sounds of laughter and splashing from the pool of a nearby inn.

Two lounge chairs faced the hot tub. Leila stretched out on one of them while Ayden busied himself preparing the hot tub for later. He removed the cover and turned on the filter system. A low hum began; the motor seemed to be functioning just fine. Ayden gave Leila the "okay" sign, then moved on to test the water.

Leila watched him for a while, enjoying, as always, his physique and agile moves, but soon she drifted off to sleep. The car ride and the walking around town had tired her out. She rarely needed a nap, but today was an exception.

Quickly, she fell into a dream.

Lying on the bed in her private quarters, she relished how the sleek white bedding cooled and soothed her warm body. Suddenly, she realized she wasn't alone. Ayden stood in the doorway wearing long white pajama bottoms. She hadn't heard the door open. He said nothing. His look was steady as he waited for permission to enter. Leila slowly lifted the white sheet, and he moved toward the bed. Her body tingled all over, anticipating his skillful touch.

"Leila. Leila. It's time." Whispers in her ear.

"Ayden?" she whispered back.

Leila felt a gentle nudge and then another, rousing her from her deep sleep. Ayden's blue eyes were there when she opened hers. She blinked to get a clearer view.

"You fell asleep," she heard him say. "You looked so peaceful. I didn't want to wake you until the last minute. It's seven. Do you still want to go to the bar?"

"I'm sorry. I usually don't doze off like this. I was deep in a dream."

"About me?" He chuckled.

"Yes, as a matter of fact. Tell me, do you own a pair of white pajama bottoms?" Her smile lit up her face.

"No. Why do you ask?"

"Well, you should, because that's what you wore in my dream."

"Really? We'll have to go shopping tomorrow." Ayden bent over and gave her a kiss on her cheek. "Are we going out for drinks?"

"Yes. Give me a half hour."

❁

Leila spruced up in record time. She retrieved a fresh white top from her duffel, took a quick sponge bath, used some of the citrus body lotion, and redid her makeup. She kept her hair up but brought down some bangs and a few strands she twisted and sprayed with setting lotion to hold the curls. With five minutes to spare, the results she saw in the mirror pleased her. She grabbed her sweater, stuffed her lipstick into a side pocket of her purse, and headed out.

She found Ayden on the sofa, watching a golf match on TV. He looked up and smiled. "I like it when you wear your hair up."

"It's just easy when time is short."

Had he gone out of his way for her? Her answer came quickly. She noticed a hint of lime within his aura. He placed his arms around her, and she nuzzled in close to enjoy the feel, warmth, and smell of his body. He kissed her first on one side of her mouth, then on the other. He knew what she wanted—to be kissed fully on the lips. He delivered, and delivered well. The third kiss was exquisite. It began as a gentle breeze that swept across her lips as he exhaled, its force strengthening along with his embrace. He explored the inside of her mouth, and she began to feel as if she had returned to her dream.

All too soon, Ayden withdrew, stopping to bestow one last, light kiss on her lips.

"Shall we go?"

She nodded—all that she was capable of at the moment.

❀

The bar at the harbor's edge bubbled with activity. Locals and tourists of all ages were drinking, eating, listening to music, dancing, and joking. Retractable doors had been folded to blur the line between outside and inside areas. More people sat at colorful umbrella tables on the deck. Inside, a stand-up comedian concluded his act. A musical group hastened to take his place.

Ayden and Leila found a table for two near the stage and small dance floor. A waiter came by and took their order. Soon the musicians began a medley of songs from the 1990s. The dance floor filled rapidly. Ayden pulled Leila to her feet, and before she knew it, they were dancing in a mad swirl to Cher's "Believe." He showed himself to be a great dancer. Not a surprise. He moved gracefully and led expertly. Leila responded well to his strong lead.

The music ebbed, and Ayden pulled her close for their first slow dance. She anticipated a sensuous encounter—and it proved to be just that. She pressed her body against his. His heart lay below her fingertips. His hand tightened around hers and rested on her breast. She sensed a wild thumping deep inside her. Could he feel her heart's thunder?

The song was "Someone" by the Rembrandts. The lyrics told their story: loners at last finding someone to love. Leila and Ayden moved back and forth to the slow beat, staying in the space they'd claimed for themselves. The other couples on the dance floor revolved around them like planets circling a sun. Ayden made love to her there in an unconventional way. Sensations she'd never expected to feel again arose as his body moved against hers, his arm firmly around her waist. He continued to kiss her gently on her left ear and down the side of her neck. The experience was orgasmic.

The song came to its end, and Ayden kissed her one last time, then gently led the way to their table, where their drinks and appetizers waited for them.

❀

They walked back to the cottage in silence, arms entwined.

Why did she allow him to play with her—to manipulate her body and her senses? She remained committed to controlling the pace at which their relationship was developing. What was he thinking at this very moment? Did he feel victorious on some level? She looked at him. He didn't appear to be gloating.

"I'll get the grill started," he said as he ushered her into the house. "Why don't you change into your bathing suit?"

"I'll be quick. I want to help you with dinner."

She entered her suite and went straight to the bathroom. She sat on the toilet, her head in her hands, tears streaming down her cheeks. Her emotions swirled in different directions. On the one hand, she was crazy about Ayden. She had fallen in love. There was no longer any doubt about that. On the other hand, she had pangs of uncertainty regarding his true feelings, his ability to commit to her for the long term, and his trustworthiness. He'd been on the prowl for over two decades. *Does a leopard change its spots?*

Time was up. She went to the sink, wiped away the streams of mascara, retouched her makeup, and stepped into her navy-blue bathing suit, a stunning one-shoulder bandeau with a gold-toned buckle grasping the strap. She knew she looked great in it. She donned a matching ankle-length cover-up and headed for the kitchen.

Ayden had changed into loose-fitting bathing trunks and another T-shirt. Nothing too revealing, thank goodness.

Amazingly, he'd already made the salad. In addition, corn rumbled on the stovetop; bread filled a basket; and a glass of red wine waited for her on the countertop.

"What's left for me to do?" Her conscience bothered her. "You certainly accomplished a lot in fifteen minutes."

"I aim to please."

"Don't I know that!" she replied. Her conflicted feelings over having so easily succumbed to his touch likely fueled the boldness in her voice.

He didn't seem to take issue with it. "Let's eat out on the deck. Grab the place mats and table settings. I'll bring the corn."

Leila set the table and then seated herself at it to sip her wine and watch the grill master. Soon he joined her, bringing along the kebabs and barbecue sauce.

"I'm anxious to see what's underneath," he said in a low voice as he sat down across from her.

At first, Leila didn't know what he meant. The day had been a long one. However, she soon understood his message. She simply smiled at him and focused on eating her salad.

"You know, we don't have to do the hot tub thing tonight," he said, the teasing tone gone. "We can put it off until tomorrow."

Wasn't that just like him? Always trying to be so conciliatory. No wonder she had trouble resisting his overtures. "I'd like to try it for a little while and then call it a night."

"It's very relaxing. Trust me, you'll sleep like a baby."

"I'm looking forward to that." She couldn't keep the tremor from her voice.

"What's wrong?" Ayden cocked his head to the side. "You're not yourself."

Leila put down her fork and looked directly at him. "For the past five years, I've been alone, but I've grown stronger because of that. I've called all the shots. Now, there's you. I've let you in, and I'm terrified."

"Stop right there!" Ayden took a breath. "I'm sorry. I sounded harsh just then; I didn't mean to. But look, I feel unsettled too. I've been a free agent for many years. And now there's *you*. I think about you all the time. I enjoy being with you. To tell you the truth, it scares the hell out of me."

"Are you going to hurt me in the long run, Ayden?" Leila held his gaze. "Your track record isn't the best."

"I'm not about to defend my past. I admit I've been a *me* person. But lately, I'm happier. It's because of you. You've stirred up feelings in me I thought myself incapable of having. I promise not to intentionally hurt you. Even you said I make good on my promises." He smiled hopefully.

Leila reached across the table for his hand. "I appreciate your

honesty." She paused. "I have an idea. Let's drop this discussion for
now. We'll take it up again when we're not so tired. Come on, the hot
tub is waiting." She stood up and dropped her cover-up to the floor.

Ayden raised his eyebrows appreciatively. "Very nice."

"I'd thought you'd like it." She poured some more wine into her
glass. "Are you going to join me?" She tilted her head to the side and
gave him a wink.

"Was there ever any doubt?"

❁

Relaxed from the hot tub and exhausted from the long day, Leila and
Ayden walked slowly to their separate quarters, leaning on each other
as if they needed help to arrive at their destination.

"I'm taking a shower and hitting the sack," Ayden said.

"I'm exhausted too. But we did have a wonderful day. Thank you
for that." Leila squeezed his hand.

His cute smile emerged once again in response to her sincerity. He gave her a kiss good night—not a simple peck on the
cheek but the kind of kiss that said, *I want you. You'll miss me
when I'm gone.*

Leila found it difficult watching him disappear through his bedroom door, but she needed some alone time. She closed her door and
eyed the lock. Did she need to use it? *Don't be silly!* she scolded herself.
He's never been anything but respectful.

She took off her suit and got things together, though all she
wanted was to fall into bed. When she emerged from the bathroom
fifteen minutes later, she stopped in her tracks. An envelope had been
slipped under the bedroom door.

She reached for it and tore it open. Lab reports for Ayden, along
with a summation paragraph confirming his excellent health—absolutely no indication of any STIs. She refolded the report and placed it

back in the envelope. She felt relieved but, in another way, somewhat ashamed for making him go through a certification process.

Suddenly awake, she lay in bed and thought about the last few hours. Much had transpired. Most important, Ayden had confessed to having strong feelings for her. He wanted to keep her all to himself.

What else had she come to realize? He was gentle, loving, considerate, and generous. And he knew when to back off. In the hot tub, he'd avoided more intimate contact and kept the conversation light while they sipped their wine. He didn't know it, but had he attempted anything, she wouldn't have mustered much resistance. Thankfully, he hadn't tested her. However, she did want him—and she'd have him before the weekend was over.

Taking this perspective allowed her to believe she was in control, which gave her a sense of both comfort and liberation. If she could hold on to this feeling, she'd be able to move forward into the realm of risk-taking.

Just as she was about to begin strategic planning, she fell asleep.

18

Something smelled inviting. Leila struggled to rouse herself from her slumber. She remained somewhere between dream and reality. Slowly, she opened her eyes and turned toward the window, where some light filtered through the blinds. She thought she'd awakened too early, but when she looked at the clock on the nightstand, she discovered morning had arrived some time ago. *Nine thirty already?*

A whiff of brewing coffee teased her nose. How had the aroma traveled all the way down the hall and slipped under the door into her room? She needed her morning boost.

Leila hurried into the bathroom to freshen up. A perfectly made-up face wasn't her goal. Ayden should know what she looked like without the help of cosmetic wizardry. All women had imperfections, and she wanted to be honest about hers.

On second thought, perhaps a bit of assistance would be wise.

She washed her face, applied a tinted moisturizer, a dusting of translucent powder, and a dash of lip-gloss. A simply applied eye gel gave the areas around her eyes a subtle glow. She put her hair up the way Ayden liked it, twisting her ponytail into a knot and securing it with a barrette. She allowed some bangs and wisps of hair to fall where they might.

"Done," she whispered. "Go get him!"

Emboldened, she opened the bedroom door and headed down

the hall. The door to the large room was ajar. She peered through and saw Ayden sitting at the island reading a newspaper, his back to her. She didn't want to sneak up on him, so as she approached, she said softly, "Good morning, Mr. Doyle."

He turned and offered a warm smile. "Good morning to you, sleepy head."

Leila moved in and gave him a quick hug and kiss. "The coffee smells really good." She walked over to the coffee maker, where he had left a mug out for her. She filled it and joined him.

He'd set out some plates on the island, along with the blueberry muffins and sliced melon they'd bought the day before. When she sat down, he filled the empty plate in front of her.

She sipped her coffee and turned to gently rub Ayden's back—almost out of habit. Nick had always appreciated this type of attention on mornings when they had breakfast together.

Ayden leaned into her touch. "That feels good."

She leaned in close to his ear, as if sharing a secret. "What's our schedule for today? The weatherman hasn't kept his promise. We've got clouds and drizzle."

"It's a good day to visit the shops and art galleries. We'll take the car, park in the center of town, and find a place for lunch in between exploring. There's always the museum too."

"Sounds great."

He looked intently at her, studying her morning face.

She suddenly became self-conscious. "What's wrong?"

"Nothing. You look wonderful even without makeup."

Leila blushed on the outside, but on the inside—relief. "Thanks, but at the moment, I'm not completely without some help."

Ayden chuckled, leaned forward, and kissed her on the cheek. "How did you sleep?"

"I passed out the moment my head hit the pillow. But I feel well rested and ready to start our new day."

"There's a colonial inn just a short ride from here that offers an upscale restaurant and a nice view. We should go there for dinner."

"What's it like?"

"The food is eclectic. Naturally, there are a number of seafood specialties. Great atmosphere. Large windows. Past the gardens, there's a nice view of the Miles River and the bay; even if the rain continues, we'll have something pretty to look at. I'll make a reservation on the later side."

Leila gazed into his blue eyes, which seemed to be twinkling at the moment. "You sure know how to show a girl a good time." Studying him, she realized the evening would hold more for her than fine dining. Without question, she was ready to take the plunge.

❀

They headed out just before noon, carrying their umbrellas and dressed in rainy-day clothes—jeans, long-sleeved tops, and athletic shoes. Luckily, a good parking space appeared right away when they arrived downtown.

The light rain sprinkled their faces in spite of the umbrellas they held as they strolled along Talbot Street, popping in and out of the galleries and boutiques. In one, a striking watercolor of the Inn at Perry Cabin captured their attention.

"This is where we're going tonight," Ayden said.

.   Leila examined the piece. "This is beautiful. The colors are soft, and the fine strokes wonderfully detail the leaves and blooms on the trees and shrubs. This or something similar would look nice in the cottage."

"Let's look the place over and see if there's a spot we can agree on." He approached the proprietor and asked if he'd be willing to bring the piece over Sunday afternoon so he could see how it looked.

The proprietor nodded his head. "I'd be happy to do that." He took down the necessary information, and the two men shook hands.

They continued their explorations. Tucked away among the old buildings, they stumbled upon a charming little restaurant in what had once been someone's cottage home. They decided to stop there and grab a quick lunch before taking in the maritime museum.

By the time they reached the museum, the dismal morning had given way to some afternoon sun. "No need for the cumbersome umbrellas," Ayden commented as he tossed them into the car.

The museum, a mammoth complex spreading over eighteen acres, had countless exhibits. They didn't have the time or energy to see everything, but they did their best. For Leila, more important was the fact that they were together and enjoying each other's company. Their friendship continued to blossom, helped along by their shared appreciation of fine design and craftsmanship. They had become good friends on their way to becoming lovers.

❀

At five o'clock, the twosome returned to the cottage. Their eight-o'clock dinner reservation left them a little over two hours before they'd have to leave for the inn.

Ayden immediately headed for the kitchen. "I'm thirsty. Do you want something to drink?"

"I'd love some ice water with a bit of that lemon zest."

He prepared her drink, placed it on the island, and took a seat next to her. "Maybe I should've mentioned this before, but people dress up a bit when they go to this restaurant. In other words, I need to wear a sports jacket."

Leila poked him playfully in the chest. "I have a couple of dresses with me. I won't embarrass you."

"You always look great."

"Thanks." She gave his back an affectionate pat and frantically began to think of the best way to return the compliment. "I can't picture you in a sports jacket, but I'm sure you'll look quite handsome."

At that, Ayden put down his glass, turned to her, and locked his arms around her torso, drawing her closer to him. He kissed her lips hungrily. Leila moved onto his lap, wrapping her legs around the back of his stool. He explored under her top, caressing her breasts, and she responded in kind, running her hands over the solid muscles of his chest. Their emotions spiraled in intensity. Ayden lifted her off of the stool and carried her to the sofa, where their bodies crashed onto the pillows. He unfastened Leila's jeans and moved his fingers over her belly.

"Ayden," she whispered, her mouth still pressed to his. "Ayden, let's stop. Not now."

"What's wrong?"

"I'm not ready," she said breathlessly. "I need to prepare."

"I'll prepare you," he replied with confidence.

"Please. I promise. Tonight."

With that, he withdrew his hand and sat up, heeding her request though obviously frustrated. Leila stood up, fastened her jeans, and returned to the island. She grabbed the lemon water, gulped it down, and brought Ayden's glass over to him.

"I'm sorry. I didn't anticipate this happening. I'd never lead you on. I want you and aim to have you," she said in a lighthearted manner, hoping to ease the awkward situation. "I've got this issue—a postmenopausal thing. I need to take some medication and . . . oh, this is embarrassing. Must I explain myself any further?"

"No, I understand. And your doctor's report?" He asked the question with a straight face.

Leila responded with a very surprised and serious look that made him chuckle. "I'm joking, Leila."

She took his face in her hands and gave him a short, intense kiss.

"I love that you are always able to save the day with your humor." She looked into his eyes. "I'm going to start getting ready for our wonderful dinner. I'm really looking forward to it. I'll meet you here in an hour or so, okay?"

Ayden nodded, reached for the remote, and settled in to watching television.

❁

An hour and a half later, Ayden was back on the sofa, but now dressed in gray pants and a white shirt, his navy blazer neatly placed behind him. He looked quite different—but terribly appealing.

"I almost didn't recognize you," Leila teased as she entered the room.

He turned his head, responding to her voice, and found himself momentarily speechless. Then he simply said, "Wow."

"I assume you approve. I'm dressed appropriately for our destination?" Leila had chosen an espresso-colored jersey knit dress with a dusting of black sequins on its halter-top for the evening.

"You're perfect." Ayden beamed. "I'm proud to be your date."

"I feel the same." She took him in with smiling eyes. "You look very handsome this evening."

"Thank you." He approached her, gave her a tender kiss on the forehead, grasped her hand, and led the way out to the car.

❁

The inn, a mere watercolor image in Leila's mind, came to life as Ayden pulled up to the valet station. Quaint, charming, yet elegant— yes, Leila decided, those words would do.

The restaurant's décor created an environment conducive for romance. White floor-length cloths topped with gold metallic napkins, glistening place settings, fresh flowers, and tea candles graced the tables. Crystal chandeliers offered subdued lighting and occasional tinkling sounds when the fans moved air currents in their direction. Massive windows provided an extraordinary view of the grounds and beyond. Glimmering white lights intertwined in the branches of the trees and shrubs, adding an air of enchantment to the mansion's exterior, while lanterns on boats moored across the bay twinkled like distant stars.

Leila turned to Ayden. "This place is magical."

"I knew you'd like it."

The hostess showed them to a table in a secluded corner that afforded both privacy and an unobstructed view of the picturesque seascape. The service proved impeccable; the cuisine, prepared exquisitely, was also superb.

"What shall we do tomorrow?" Leila asked as the dinner wound down.

"As long as the weather is nice, let's go to Tilghman Island, wander around there for a while, and maybe take a boat tour."

"That will give me a chance to test my sea legs." She laughed and kept her eyes on him, hoping he'd appreciate her attempt at humor.

He reached across the table and took her hand. "You know, your sense of humor is almost as good as mine."

"Well, another perspective would be that mine is equal to yours."

"Perhaps." He gave her hand a slight squeeze.

"Do you hear music?" she asked.

"I believe I do. Let's ask where it's coming from."

The waiter informed them there was a wedding on the property. He suggested a walk to a nearby terrace. "People often dance out there to the party music if it's loud enough."

"Thanks for the tip." Ayden fixed his eyes on Leila. "What do you think? Should we give it a try?"

"Absolutely."

They found the terrace and discovered that the music level was perfect for dancing. The DJ had just selected Alicia Keys's "Brand New Me." For a moment, they stood slightly apart, each appreciating the other's dressed-up look—but that didn't last long. Ayden took off his jacket and tossed it on a chair. Leila did the same with her black lace shawl and small purse. At first, they took formal dance poses, as if about to enter a competition, but the need to be as close as possible quickly took over. Ayden pulled her in. His hold was firm. Leila yearned for that kind of envelopment, choosing to believe it was Ayden's way of communicating the intensity of his feelings for her. He kissed her gently on the neck but didn't attempt to make this dance experience like the one in the bar the night before. She relaxed in his arms and fantasized about what would happen once they returned to his cottage.

When the song ended, Leila whispered in his ear, "Let's go."

He smiled, knowing what she meant.

The ride home was a silent one. They didn't need conversation. Ayden concentrated on his driving. Leila's private thoughts took over and began to undermine her confidence. Memories surfaced in the form of random clips of intimate times with Nick and then with Ayden. She'd always known exactly what Nick wanted. After all, they'd had many years together and lots of practice. How would she be aware of Ayden's desires? She felt timid and apprehensive, just as she had on her wedding night.

She fiddled with her clothing, slumped in her seat, and twirled a tendril of hair around the index finger of her right hand—all signs she lacked assurance. She suddenly realized her body language was giving too much away. She straightened her posture and regained control. *I can do this.*

Ayden opened the passenger door, disrupting her deep concentration. He extended his hand to help her out of the car and then put his arm around her shoulders as they walked to the front door. Once inside, he released his hold on her and they made their way to the kitchen.

"Would you like some wine?" He held up a bottle.

"I think I've had enough. But I'd appreciate some of your famous lemon water on ice."

He poured himself some wine and prepared Leila's drink. They took seats at the island.

"Thanks for a lovely evening, Ayden." She clinked her glass against his.

"You're welcome."

Silence reigned as they sipped their drinks. Ayden appeared subdued and less bold than he had earlier in the day. Was he waiting for a signal from her? His hesitation gave Leila the sense of control she needed to move forward.

"I think I'll get ready for bed," she said.

"Do you want to watch some television?"

"Maybe. I'll check in with you in a few minutes."

"I'll get comfortable too."

Again, they strolled together down the hallway, each making a slow turn into their bedrooms. Ayden left his door slightly open. Leila closed hers completely. Her heart pounded as she undressed, put her clothes away, and washed up. She didn't want makeup to get all over Ayden's lovely white bed linens, so she repeated her "morning after" application, since it had been successful. She took one last look at her naked body before slipping into her white lace-and-satin chemise. The gown wasn't see-through, but her body appeared as an alluring shadow underneath the opaque material.

She carefully opened her door. Ayden's was still ajar. She walked over and tapped on it. "Ayden?"

"Yes." His voice sounded garbled.

Leila pushed the door open and entered. Ayden appeared in the bathroom doorway in long pajama bottoms. He didn't look exactly as he had in her dream, but it was close enough. His toothbrush dangled from his lips and white foam peeked out from the corners of his mouth. He quickly turned and headed to the bathroom to rinse. She followed and stood in the doorway, watching him. As he finished, she moved in with a towel and dried off his mouth. They stood facing each other, not saying a word. She reached up and put her arms around his neck, drawing him to her. He kissed her eagerly, pushing her against the wall as he turned off the bathroom light. He moved against her as he had on the dance floor.

She'd have been happy making love on the bathroom floor, but he pulled away, took hold of her hand, and led the way to his bed.

He began kissing her on the neck—soft kisses that lingered. "I like your nightie."

"We forgot to buy those white pajama bottoms for you."

"We can do that tomorrow." He placed his lips on hers, and the passion soared.

Ayden's French-kissing technique was so arresting that he managed to remove Leila's gown without her being aware of it. His hands caressed her, moving slowly around her breasts and then down toward the treasure buried between her thighs. She groaned, delighting in his touch. He carefully tested her when he thought she was ready for him to enter. With each forward movement, she became more welcoming. Their lovemaking evolved into an adventure of sensuality and lust, each one gradually discovering how to pleasure the other.

Some time later, spent, they lay quietly in each other's arms and fell asleep.

❀

The morning light streamed through the French doors onto Leila's face, coaxing her to open her eyes and greet the new day. Ayden was still fast asleep on his stomach. She studied his muscular back but resisted the urge to disturb him. She slid carefully from beneath the covers and walked across the hall.

A warm, soothing bath topped her agenda. As she soaked in the tub, she began to relive the night before. Ayden had been a considerate lover—gentle and attentive yet enormously passionate. She'd abandoned herself to him and had no remorse over it. She had fallen in love with him.

The way Ayden treated her indicated he had sincere feelings for her. However, neither of them had used the word *love* yet. Perhaps it would come up before the weekend ended.

She finished dressing and proceeded in the direction of the kitchen. She peeked into Ayden's room, saw that he'd left the bed, and surmised he was getting ready to shower. She wanted to get breakfast ready for him.

Upon entering the kitchen, she realized it didn't feel like a strange place anymore. She knew exactly where things were. In no time at all, she arranged place settings on the island and started the coffee.

She'd just found the fruit and muffins in the refrigerator when Ayden's arms circled her waist. He leaned in close and kissed the back and sides of her neck.

"Good morning," she said, turning slowly toward him with her finds in her hands.

He took the fruit and muffins, placed them on the island, and took a seat. "How are you feeling today?"

She responded cheerfully. "I'm fine." No need to let him know that a trace of discomfort still existed. She could deal with it, especially when romantic memories of the previous night surfaced. She poured them both coffee and brought the mugs to the island.

"Do you think you can go another round tonight?" That boyish grin she loved so much spread across his face.

Leila took her seat. Her mind raced. She turned to face him. "If you're able, I'm willing." She gave him a cute smile followed by a light kiss on the lips—hoping to forestall any serious critique of last night's lovemaking, if that was his intention.

He laughed and kissed her back. "Listen, let's discuss today. The gallery owner is coming at the end of the day with that watercolor we both liked. We've got enough time to drive to Tilghman Island, explore a shop or two, have a quick lunch, and take a tour by boat. It's a nice day. What do you think?"

"Sounds like a plan to me."

The day was warm and sunny, so, naturally, Ayden put the top down before they set out for the eleven-mile drive to Tilghman Island. He also handed Leila a brochure highlighting points of interest on the island—something to keep her occupied during the journey, since top-down road trips made it difficult to carry on conversation.

Leila learned the island's history dated back to the seventeenth century, when it had been granted to a settler named Seth Foster. It had been known as Foster Island until the Tilghman family purchased it in 1752. Since then, farmers, oystermen, boat builders, all kinds of entrepreneurs, and even vacationers had contributed to its growth and development.

"How picturesque!" Leila called out when they arrived.

Ayden, in high spirits as well, said, "Hope your shoes are made for walking."

They parked and began their tour. They investigated the Phillips Wharf Environmental Center, where people learned about the area's sea life, and finally ended up at a waterfront eatery for lunch.

"We can take a short sailboat tour that leaves from a nearby wharf," Ayden said, gesturing in the direction of the water. "Still interested?"

"Certainly, just as long as you think we have time."

Leila glanced across the table at her man. *Her man.* She had started thinking of him as that without even realizing it. Though she was enjoying the outing, she longed to be in his arms again.

A somber thought hit her. Her weekend would soon draw to a close. Tomorrow night she'd be back home, sleeping alone and reclaiming her routine. Her time with Ayden would become a mere collage of memories. Funny, they'd taken no pictures to serve as mementos.

His voice called a halt to her private thoughts. "Ready? A new adventure is calling us."

"Aye, aye, sir."

❁

The tour lasted ninety minutes and was very pleasant. The skipjack sailed deftly through the water while the captain elaborated on the historical information Leila had read in the brochure, with a number of his own, delightful embellishments. The excursion perfectly ended their day at Tilghman Island.

They returned home just before four thirty. Ayden called the gallery to ask if the proprietor was still planning to bring the art piece out to the cottage while Leila went to the kitchen for water.

"Do you want something to drink?" she called out.

"Water will be fine, thanks."

She now waited on him, much like she had for Nick. She'd fallen into the groove without thinking. Perhaps she needed to contemplate this behavior. Her self-doubt emerged once again. Would Ayden be put off by this semblance of wifely attention? Did she have what it took to keep his interest for the long haul?

A knock on the door and then low voices distracted her and prompted her investigation. She observed Ayden helping the gallery owner remove brown paper from the painting. After some pleasantries, the three of them set about determining where the

Inn at Perry Cabin might go. They finally settled on a wall in the dining room.

No sooner had the door closed behind the gallery owner than Ayden took Leila in his arms and kissed her passionately. How had she gone the whole day without one of his kisses?

"Did anyone ever tell you that you're a really great kisser?" She wasn't truly interested in an answer; she was more intent on giving him a compliment.

"You really think so?"

"I know so."

"I'm hoping you'll allow me to keep on honing my skills." With an arm resting on her shoulder, he turned to examine his new acquisition. "You know, this painting is doing double duty."

"How so?"

"First, it's adding nicely to the decor. Second, it's a keepsake, a way of remembering our weekend here—and last night."

Leila hadn't expected him to express such a sentiment and wasn't sure how to respond. She moved again into her frantic thinking mode. "I'm glad you felt our time together worthy of remembering, and in so lovely a way. It's a beginning."

Ayden continued to focus on the artwork. Apparently, this didn't strike him as the perfect opportunity to delve into a conversation about their budding relationship. "What shall we do for dinner?" he asked.

"You're hungry now?" Leila asked, almost in disbelief.

"No, but it's inevitable, right?"

"Can we stay in, order Chinese, and watch a movie?"

"Yes, if you like. We've been going nonstop. Tomorrow, I'd like to be on the road by noon. Maybe it's good we chill out this evening."

"Then it's settled." She gave his arm a squeeze and returned to the kitchen for her drink.

Ayden took a seat on the sofa, turned on the television, and flipped through the channels. He settled on a baseball game. Leila joined him, becoming a silent partner until a commercial came on. Then she headed into completely new territory. "Ayden, do you suppose we could discuss some business for a few moments?"

"What's up?" He seemed open.

"Do you remember I told you a new client of ours would likely need your help?"

"Yes."

"Well, the Millers live in Radnor. They need their master bath renovated. Can you meet me at their home this week or next to explore some ideas with them?"

"Likely not this week, but toward the end of next week is doable. I'm starting the Perkins project in a couple of days, and I've got a lot to do."

"What about Susan Fredericks? I planned to give her a call."

"If she hires you, we'll go from there."

Leila didn't say anything else. The baseball game came back on. She made herself comfortable in the corner opposite Ayden and decided to rest, maybe even take a short nap.

❀

"Leila, it's seven thirty. Let's order dinner."

She opened her eyes and saw Ayden already looking at a menu from a nearby Chinese restaurant they'd passed the day before. She scooted down to his end of the sofa to investigate. "I'll be happy with wonton soup and chicken chow mein, maybe a spring roll too."

She snuggled up against him, resting her head on his shoulder. Once he called in the order, he began to pay more attention to her and less to the television. He took her in his arms and brushed her lips with a series of gentle kisses that somersaulted one into the other, but they were just a prelude to his more passionate ones, bringing

Leila once again under his spell. They were making out like two crazy teenagers when a knock on the door interrupted their fun.

"It's dinner," Ayden said, gently disengaging himself from her arms before standing up. "I'll take care of it. Why don't you start to set up?"

Leila straightened her clothes and headed to the kitchen. She arranged two place settings on the island. Ayden set out the food cartons in a nice row and placed the condiments in a small bowl.

"How about some wine?" he suggested.

"All right. You pick what you think complements Chinese food."

"I think a white will do. Maybe a Riesling." He waited for her approval.

"Sounds fine to me."

They sat down like a long-married couple, sharing with each other from their own stash of favorites. Ayden used chopsticks. *Of course, he would. He's such a dexterous devil.* Leila felt slightly awkward relying on the standard fork, knife, and spoon, but at least she'd enjoy her food rather than fighting with it.

"So, you want to leave around noon tomorrow?" she said after swallowing a bite of chow mein.

"Yes. Otherwise, the traffic will be horrific."

"How much time do we need to clean up the cottage?" She wanted him to see her as a considerate guest, perfectly willing to take on some chores.

"None. A cleaning service will come in on Tuesday, take care of the linens, clean out the refrigerator, dust, and sweep. I've already scheduled them."

"Are you sure? I really don't mind housework. And I must say, I'm pretty darn good at it. Years of practice." She gave him a wink.

"Don't be ridiculous. You're my guest. Anyway, I don't stock cleaning supplies."

The *guest* label Ayden had just assigned to her stung a little; she decided to throw out a zinger of her own. "You've been the perfect host. I appreciate all your efforts. This weekend has been loads of fun and more. But I'm curious. What am I to you besides a guest?"

He hesitated, took a sip of wine, and turned to face her. "Are you serious?"

"Yes. I'm quite serious," she said in what she hoped was a non-threatening tone.

"I guess you're now my girl." He paused for a moment. "Maybe I should rephrase that. Will you be my girl, Leila?" He was dead serious. He stared her down and waited for an answer.

Warmth filled her body. "Yes, I'll be your girl. For two reasons."

He waited patiently for her explanation.

"First, I've grown very, very fond of you and want you in my life. Second, you're a wonderful lover, and I'd be a fool to let anyone else have you." This last line she delivered in a cheerful, almost girlish way in order to add some lightheartedness to the discussion.

"So, we're going steady?" he asked as if he were a teenaged boy needing clarification.

"I suppose. Which one of us will alert Dr. Goodwin to this new arrangement?"

"Maybe we both should send her an email."

"You're so wise. That's the way to go." She leaned over and gave him a quick kiss on the lips.

❀

After cleaning up the kitchen, they decided to relax on the sofa and find an old movie on TCM. A romantic comedy—*That Touch of Mink*, starring Cary Grant and Doris Day—captured Leila's attention. The story centered on a handsome executive not particularly looking for marriage or commitment and a woman who was. In the end, Cary Grant had no choice but to fall for Doris Day and become her steady forever.

"Such a cute movie," Leila said as the credits rolled. "I hope you liked it. I realize it's likely not your usual fare."

"A chick flick, but enjoyable. I'd like to pick up the pace somewhat." Ayden grabbed the remote and began to surf for action entertainment.

Had the movie affected his mood? He seemed a bit cool. "Interested in some coffee?" she asked, hoping to recapture his attention.

"Not now, but thanks for asking."

"If you don't mind, I'm going to get ready for bed."

At this, he perked up a bit. "Are you going to wear that cute nightie again?"

She headed down the hallway. "That's the only one I have with me, so yes."

"Doesn't really matter," he called after her. "You won't be wearing it for long anyway."

"Who says?"

"Me!" he bellowed.

She let him have the last word. He was right, after all. She'd fall into his arms once again and let him have his way with her.

❁

Upon her return to the living room, she found Ayden exactly where she'd left him. A pleasing aroma floated in the air.

"Do I smell coffee?"

He leaned back and smiled up at her. "I thought you might enjoy trying coffee with a twist."

"And you?"

"I'll join you."

He'd prepared a chocolate-flavored brew that tasted especially wonderful with the addition of some Baileys Irish Cream.

"This is truly decadent," Leila purred, sipping from her mug.

"It's the Baileys," he said with a wink. "We have to be careful not to make it a habit."

"That may be difficult, since it's among my favorites."

They sat in silence, enjoying one another. When Leila noticed that Ayden's mug was empty, she knew the time to make her move had arrived. She slid onto his lap and put her arms around his neck. She began to kiss the corners of his mouth and tease his lips with her tongue; then she began to explore further. In the midst of their embrace, she slid her hand down toward his zipper.

Ayden shifted in his seat to make it easier for her to touch him. Moments later, Leila moved from his lap, took hold of his hand, and led him toward the bedroom. Once there, she pushed him onto the bed and crawled on top of him like a cat on the prowl.

He spoke softly into her ear. "I told you I had no intention of being your plaything."

With that, he rolled over and took command.

19

Leila looked around the bedroom she'd called her own for the last three days to make sure she'd tidied up sufficiently for the cleaning service and not left any belongings behind. She made the bed, but not so perfectly that the housekeepers would overlook the need for fresh linens. Satisfied, she took her duffel and handbag and headed to the car.

Ayden placed things strategically into the trunk while cheerfully humming a favorite tune. One of his fabulous smiles crossed his face as Leila approached.

"I've made a nice spot for your bag." He placed the bag inside and closed the trunk. "I'll be right back. One last check and we're ready to go."

Leila faced the cottage and took a long, last look. She'd miss its charm but hoped for a return in the not-too-distant future. She felt close to Ayden in this place, and she doubted that her home, or his, would provide the true safe haven from the rest of the world their nascent relationship needed.

"Hungry?" he asked as he pulled out of the driveway.

"Not yet. The coffee, melon, and that terrific muffin should hold me for a while."

"Maybe when we get close to your place, you can suggest somewhere to get a bite."

Leaving the enclave of harbor homes and speeding up the highway, a sense of melancholy invaded Leila's thoughts. From now on she'd have to share Ayden with his clients, friends, and family. Most of the time, she'd be sleeping without him and missing the warmth and feel of his body. Could he be thinking similar thoughts about her?

They stopped for lunch in Plymouth Meeting. Their conversation focused on the Perkins project. Both looked forward to creating a spectacular space and meeting their clients' expectations.

"I'm going to hire extra help," Ayden said. "Without more crafts-men, the project will take much longer than the Perkinses expect."

"Anything I can do to help it along, please don't hesitate to ask. Both of us know happy clients often tell their friends, family, and business associates about their contractors and designers. Word-of-mouth advertising is the best and most cost-effective way to pick up new clients!"

"That's for sure. I spend very little on marketing my business. There's always a client waiting in the wings."

"I'll check in with the Perkinses once a week to see how things are going." She tried to keep the worry from her face as she added, "I think we should keep our relationship very low-key when we work with the Perkinses—purely professional. Toward the end of the proj-ect, we can be more open. Do you agree?"

"Fine. But you better not get too close to me when you visit the site." Ayden wagged a finger at her. "I may lose it, and then the secret will get out."

"I'm serious."

"Me too." His eyes twinkled with amusement.

❁

Leila stood in the front hall, knowing she had to bid farewell to her lover and wondering if he'd say something heartfelt to help her deal with what would seem to her a long separation.

Ayden placed her duffel bag at the foot of the stairs and turned to her. He seemed to regret having to leave, but Leila suspected her own feelings might be influencing her perception of the scene.

"I can take your bag upstairs for you if you need me to," Ayden said, lingering.

"I can manage, but thanks anyway." She gave him a tiny smile.

He hugged her tightly. "I'm finding it difficult to leave you." He pulled away, cradled her face in his hands, and placed a long kiss on her lips.

"I'll miss you too."

"Maybe we could have a sleepover this weekend?"

"That would be fun."

"I'll call you tomorrow." He kissed her again and left, closing the door behind him.

Leila stood motionless, listening to his car pull away. *Whoever said love hurts was so right.* She ached for him. Was she really going to have a second chance at love? Doubt overshadowed any positive vibes she entertained. Few people were lucky enough to have just one true love. It was crazy to think she might get two.

She turned, picked up her bag, and climbed the steps to her bedroom. Once there, she placed her bag on the bed and began to empty it. Her king-size bed with its lofty mattress and ornate, antique gold headboard had always been her favorite retreat. She felt safe there. Today, however, in the afternoon light, the bed seemed quite imposing. Why?

It needs him.

Everything had changed in a matter of three days. She'd grown strong in the wake of Nick's death. Now uneasiness set in again.

Momentarily, the ringing of the phone pulled her out of the self-pity she was wallowing in.

"Hello?"

"Mom, you're back! How did your weekend go?"

"Oh, hello dear. It was lovely. You and Chad must go to St. Michaels before the baby comes. There's a romantic inn there, and even though the town is a quiet place, there are things to do and see."

"Sounds like Ayden showed you a good time?"

Leila knew Hillary hoped she would provide some details. She didn't intend to indulge her. "Yes, he was the perfect host. How about your weekend?"

"Relaxing. We took a ride to the shore on Saturday and met some friends."

"Good. And you're feeling well?" Leila easily made the switch to her mothering mode.

"Yes, Mom. I'm fine. Chad and I thought we'd come over and have dinner with you. Do you feel like company?"

"Sure. Why don't you come over around six and we can figure out what we want to eat?" She needed them. Having dinner alone would be too depressing.

"Great. See you then."

❀

"Good morning," Leila called out as she approached the shop's office.

"Is that my long-lost pal and partner?" Michelle rounded the corner and gave Leila some quick scrutiny. "Well, look at you. You're all rested . . . and *glowing*!"

"All right. Stop being cagey. You want details, right?"

"Only if you feel comfortable filling me in."

"Well, he had his way with me. That's all I'm going to tell you."

"OMG!" Michelle shouted out. She composed herself and persisted in a softer tone, "How was it?"

"Like riding a bike. You may not do it often or for a very long time, but once you get into the seat, it all comes back."

Michelle fell silent. She took a seat and faced Leila, her mouth agape and her eyes in a fixed stare.

Leila became curious herself now. "What are you looking at?"

"The new you. You've put your heart out there. You've become a risk taker. You're courageous. I'm proud of you."

"Thanks for the encouragement." Leila felt the heat rising in her cheeks. "Now, let's get to work. I noticed some new inventory in boxes out front that needs to be unpacked, tagged, and displayed."

Michelle pushed on. "Are we done discussing Ayden and your weekend?"

"For now. I'll tell you the rest at lunch."

"I can live with that."

When they decided to take a break for lunch, Michelle ran out to get sandwiches while Leila stayed behind to straighten the office and bag remaining trash from the merchandise they'd spent all morning unpacking.

As she worked, she contemplated the conversation to come. How much more should she reveal to Michelle about her weekend with Ayden?

Her phone buzzed. She rushed to retrieve it from her handbag.

"Miss you."

Leila hadn't expected Ayden to take the time to communicate during the course of his workday. She provided a simple response: *"Ditto."* She wanted to write more—to pour out her heart, to ask him to spend the night. However, she feared that if she came across as needy or suffocating, he'd pull away. The short, to-the-point reply she'd sent seemed best.

"I'm back." Michelle entered the office just as Leila was putting her phone back into her handbag. "A business call?"

"Just a text from Ayden. He wanted to touch base with me."

"What does that mean? Something about Susan Fredericks or the Millers?"

"No, but you've reminded me I need to make those calls."

Michelle finished unloading the lunch bag and quietly began to eat her sandwich. She listened patiently as Leila offered a detailed description of the town of St. Michaels, Tilghman Island, the Inn at Perry Cabin, Ayden's renovated cottage, and the watercolor they'd purchased together—but eventually, seemingly tired of the superficial travel log, she began to delve deeper.

"I'll have to ask David if he'd like to go there. It sounds like a really romantic place, especially that Inn at Perry Cabin." A short pause. "I think you're totally in love with Ayden, and you're concerned about his staying power, right?"

Leila almost fell out of her chair. "Where did that come from?" Michelle never ceased to surprise her.

"You've been skirting the issue, so I'm getting to it without further delay."

Leila sighed and fiddled with her lunch. "He's been single for years."

"You may be the person he's been looking for all his life."

"I'm crazy about him."

"I know. You have to ride this wave and see where it takes you." She bit her lip, thinking. "How about we go out as couples—you and Ayden, me and David?"

"I think it's a bit early for that. But in a few weeks, the Perkins project will be finished. Why don't we have a celebratory dinner then?"

"Perfect!" Michelle clapped her hands together. "I'll look forward to that."

Leila reached for her cell phone. She brought up Susan Fredericks's home number, not wanting to interrupt her at work, and left a voice mail: "Hello, Ms. Fredericks. My name is Leila Brandt. Ayden Doyle suggested I contact you since you've expressed an interest in working with an interior-design consultant as you begin the process of personalizing your new home. My partner, Michelle, and I would like to offer you a complimentary consultation. We hope you'll consider meeting with us."

After leaving their contact information, Leila hung up.

Michelle shook her head. "You're so good at that kind of thing."

"I may sound smooth and confident, but on the inside I'm all jitters. I find cold-calling nerve-racking. Now, on to the Millers. Hopefully, I'll be able to schedule an appointment for the end of next week."

❀

Leila sat at her kitchen island with a mug of homemade vegetable soup and some crackers: her dinner for the night. She hadn't heard from Ayden beyond his text message. He'd spent the day preparing for the start of the Perkins project. She knew he was busy ordering materials, planning out the work schedule for the week, and discussing the plans with the other craftsmen—but knowing all this didn't make their prolonged separation any easier. The empty stool next to hers reminded her of the evening she'd slipped onto his lap and Drew's early return home had interrupted their passionate kissing. She was impatient. She wanted back the life she had with Nick—a life filled with love, passion, companionship, and evenings out dining or enjoying the theater with friends and family. She'd thought she could meander through the remainder of her life without those things, but now Ayden had stirred up wants and needs that had lain dormant in the bottom of her womanly soul since Nick's death.

You're wallowing again. You must stop.

Almost on cue, the most astounding thing happened: the phone rang, and when she lifted the receiver, she heard Ayden's voice.

"Hey, how's it going?"

Leila stirred her soup. "Fine. It's hard getting the groove back after a long weekend."

"Tell me about it. We're ready for the Perkinses tomorrow, but it was a long day getting there." He continued in a lower, more subdued tone: "If I weren't so damn tired, I'd pack my bag, drive myself to your house, and spend the night holding you against me—that is, if I were welcome."

"You've read my mind." Leila was glad he couldn't see the huge grin on her face. "But you have a big day ahead of you. Maybe you better get a good night's sleep. I hope we can spend a night or two together over the weekend. Do you think that's possible?" She needed him to confirm, so she'd have that to look forward to.

He responded with conviction. "Not only is it possible, it's probable."

"Great! Oh, I almost forgot. Do you think I can come out and see your progress Friday afternoon? Maybe check in with Janice?"

"Of course. I think you'll see the old bathroom completely demolished, the ceiling raised, and the new Palladian window installed by then."

"I'll call Janice tomorrow."

"I miss you, Leila, crazy miss you."

"And I miss you."

He ended the call with a simple, "Good night."

20

F riday finally arrived. It seemed to take forever, even though there had been plenty of work to do.

Leila's heart began to pound with anticipation when she pulled into the Perkinses' driveway. Ayden's truck sat in the courtyard area next to a dumpster that two men were filling with debris.

She looked in the rearview mirror and gave her makeup and hair a last check. She'd purposely put her hair up the way Ayden liked and donned a simple black linen pantsuit, white silk blouse, and black patent leather sandals—a professional look that still possessed a feminine seductiveness Ayden wouldn't be able to help but notice.

She reached in the backseat and grabbed the file folder containing a list of items ready for delivery, a list showing those still in transit, and a payment schedule providing a clear explanation of what monies were due and when.

Janice swung the door wide open before Leila even reached it, her face alight with excitement. "Hello there. Wait until you see what has happened in only three days. Ayden and his crew are amazing!"

"I'm so excited for you," Leila said, smiling.

Leila followed Janice up the staircase and into the master bedroom suite. She found Ayden working along with two other men. He stood atop a ladder, his back to her. The din of power saws, the pound of a hammer, and the hum of other construction equipment permeated the atmosphere. Leila's attention immediately turned to the magnificent arched window they'd installed. It gave a fantastic view of century-old trees sheltering the house. She touched Janice's arm to get her attention and pointed to the window, nodding approvingly. Janice responded by clapping her hands with glee.

Ayden, noticing them standing there, stepped down from his ladder and signaled to his men to stop working for a few minutes.

"Welcome," he said, no hint of flirtation in his voice. "We've gotten a good deal done in three days."

"Yes, you have," Leila responded, matching his professionalism. "That window is absolutely breathtaking."

"I just love it," Janice chimed in. "The higher ceiling is also remarkable, don't you think?"

"Absolutely. Any unforeseen issues?"

Ayden shook his head. "No, things have gone off without a hitch so far."

"That's a relief." She looked into his blue eyes and knew she needed to move on before she gave herself away. "Janice, let's go downstairs and let the guys finish up."

It took all of her willpower to cut her visit short and leave Ayden to his work. He gave her his boyish smile and a nod before she turned away.

Once in the foyer, she gave Janice the folder with the fee schedule and other information so they could go over it together. "I'll try to check in with you next Thursday or Friday and bring over anything new that will fit into my car," she said.

"Thanks," Janice said. "You're the best."

Janice didn't know Leila would be perfectly happy coming by every day if it meant stealing a few moments with Ayden.

Leila was steering her car along the circular drive, about to leave, when Ayden emerged from behind his truck and waved for her to stop.

He pushed his head slightly inside her window, close enough for a kiss. "Can we discuss tonight?"

"Sure."

"I'd like to go home, shower, pack, and then head out to spend the night with you. Another thing. I've errands to run on Saturday. I thought if you didn't have any plans, you'd keep me company?"

"I have to work, but we can have dinner together." She paused for a few seconds while an idea formulated in her head. "Let's get back to this evening. Perhaps I'll put something on the grill. How does that sound?"

"Great. A quiet evening at home is just what I need. I'll see you around seven thirty."

To her dismay, he didn't attempt to kiss her. She reminded herself that he was honoring her wishes, staying totally professional while on the Perkinses' property. She gave him a smile and left for the market. Her menu had to be uncomplicated since she'd only have a couple of hours to prepare, but she still wanted to show off her culinary talents at dinner.

❀

Leila raced through Whole Foods in record time and made it home by five thirty. She'd settled on steaks, baked sweet potatoes, green beans with almonds, and a salad for dinner. She decided to make her own apple-and-blueberry galette for dessert and let Ayden select the wine from the nice array she kept on hand. A velvety merlot might be nice with the steaks.

After bringing out the paraphernalia she needed to prepare the feast, she ran upstairs to freshen up the master bedroom suite. She changed from her work clothes into jeans and set about smoothing out the bedding, putting everything in its place, and running a vacuum quickly over the rugs. She checked out the bathroom as well, and gave the entire area a spritz of home-and-linen mist. Before returning to the kitchen, she slid into a pair of soft, furry slippers.

She arranged place settings on the table in the breakfast nook, made the fruit tart, and put it in the oven along with the sweet potatoes. Hurrying, she placed the meat in a marinade and assembled the salad ingredients. She looked at the clock. In only fifteen minutes, Ayden would arrive. Just the vegetables were left to prepare. *Perfect.*

The doorbell rang. Leila hurried to answer it. Filled with excitement, she neglected to take off her oven mittens before opening the door.

Ayden stepped inside, carrying a small gym bag and wearing an amused smile. "I really like how your slippers and oven mittens work together. Most women couldn't pull off that combo." He leaned forward and gave her a kiss on the cheek.

She answered playfully. "Designers have a heightened fashion sense. Why don't you hang your jacket in the hall closet and meet me in the kitchen?"

"And my bag?" he asked, displaying his boyish grin.

"Just toss it on the steps."

Ayden soon took a seat at the island.

"Help me decide on a wine for this evening. We're having steak." Leila lined up a half dozen bottles for Ayden to scrutinize.

"Do you have a preference?"

"Not really. I'll leave the choice up to you."

Ayden selected a shiraz and began to open it. "Smells good in here."

"The fruit tart and sweet potatoes cooking in the oven are what's enticing you."

"It's not just that." He pulled her close to him and kissed her in earnest. Then he pulled back a bit and stared at her for a few seconds. "Boy, did I miss you!"

"Likewise." She took the time to appreciate his presence. "Are you hungry?"

"Yes."

"Well then, you mustn't distract me with any more of those wonderful kisses of yours. I've got to get dinner together." She reached for the salad bowl and served him. "Start with this."

❁

Ayden dabbed at his mouth with his napkin. "Everything is delicious."

"I wanted to make you a manly meal. Did I succeed?"

"Yes, you did. Thanks for going to all this trouble."

"It's no trouble. I enjoy cooking. Anyway, you did the same for me in St. Michaels."

"We did have a nice weekend. I kept my promise, right?"

"You take your promises to heart. That's one of the things I love about you." She shared her feelings without hesitation.

"Enlighten me. What are the other things you *love* about me?"

"Do we need to venture into that territory?"

"All right. I'll go first." He deliberated for a few moments. "Let's see. There are many things I love about you. Not necessarily in order of importance . . . I love your sense of professionalism, your design talents, your sense of humor, and your looks. I love the smell and feel of your body. And now I can say I'm pretty impressed with your cooking skills." He watched for Leila's reaction. "It's your turn."

Leila assembled her thoughts. "I greatly appreciate the sentiments you've expressed." She took a deep breath. "I love your craftsmanship and creativity, your passion for your work, your extraordinary sense of humor, and your total presence, which is a charming combination of boyishness and manliness. I love the way you kiss . . . but you already know that." She reached for her wine glass; she needed to refuel.

"Thanks." He waited a few seconds before offering another of his zingers. "We may be falling in love with each other. What do you think?"

"I think it's a real possibility." She examined his face, hoping to find deeper insight into his feelings.

Ayden looked at her but said nothing more. Instead, he pulled her onto his lap. Leila put her arms around his neck and kissed him gently on the mouth. He kissed her back.

"How about I help clean up the kitchen so we can go upstairs?"

❀

Leila led the way to her bedroom. As she climbed the stairs, a sobering thought occurred to her. Another man would soon slip into the bed she'd shared with Nick. The word *betrayal* popped into her head.

Nick had purchased many of the things that made their house a home. His influence had left its mark in room after room. The articles in the bedroom seemed the most sacred: mementos of special events in their life together. A small, crystal frame showcasing their wedding picture; a photo album documenting the children growing up; a collection of art pieces they'd discovered during their travels; even the jewelry in her jewelry box was mostly gifts Nick had given her over the years for birthdays, Mother's Days, and anniversaries. Though she'd given away all of his clothing, some of his belongings remained, hidden in a carton on the top shelf of the walk-in closet— yearbooks, degrees, awards, and other things. Ayden likely wouldn't notice the special keepsakes or learn of the stored items, yet his entry into this particular room suggested a trespass.

She opened the doors of the armoire across from the bed, revealing a flat-screen TV, and tossed the remote onto the bed. "Just put your bag on the chaise." She watched as Ayden surveyed his lodging for the evening.

"This room is nice. It's not overly feminine, as some master bedrooms can be. There is a nice balance—complementary forces of yin and yang." He turned to face Leila.

She tried very hard to conceal her uneasiness, but Ayden wasn't fooled.

"My presence here, in this room, is troubling?"

"Somewhat," she admitted.

"We could stay in the guest room, if that helps."

"No, that won't be necessary. I'm trying very hard to look toward the future and not dwell in the past."

Ayden took a few moments, as if considering how he could best express his own feelings. "I want to be in your future. Right now, I'm here for you—to hold you, to comfort you, and to make love to you, if you let me."

Leila walked over to Ayden, put her arms around him, and kissed him on the lips. Looking squarely into his hypnotic eyes, she said, "Let's get ready for bed."

❀

The alarm, in the form of a Piano Guys CD, went off at eight. Leila found it difficult to leave Ayden, who remained in a deep sleep. She lifted his arm from its secure position around her waist, turned off the music, crept out of bed, and headed for the shower. She'd have enjoyed running errands with him today, but her absence from the shop would have been unfair to Michelle, especially on such short notice. The fall selling season started with brisk sales. People looked forward to sprucing up their homes for the upcoming holidays and getting an early start on gift shopping.

As Leila reached to turn off the water, Ayden surprised her by stepping into the shower with her. She took the opportunity to enjoy his physique, gently washing him everywhere with her suds-filled sponge. In a matter of moments, their showering turned into lovemaking.

"I'm going to be late for work," she murmured.

"Do you want me to stop?"

"No, of course not. I'm yours."

They finished with a long, passionate kiss. Leila wanted to say "I love you," but she held back, even though the words begged to be said. Her inner self called for restraint.

Let him declare himself first.

She rushed through her usual routine and managed to get downstairs in enough time to make coffee, defrost her emergency blueberry muffins, and take out some fruit. Ayden soon followed. His hair, wet and unkempt, highlighted that boyish quality of his she liked so much.

"I didn't want you to leave before we had a chance to talk about tonight. Can we meet in King of Prussia? I have some shopping to do."

"Fine. How about The Cheesecake Factory—say seven thirty?"

"Perfect." He poured himself a cup of coffee.

Leila studied her lover as he ate his breakfast, devouring every inch of his presence, and soon found herself entertaining a rather selfish idea: Call Michelle and ask for the day off. She'd understand.

No. Not a good idea.

Her sense of duty returned. She finished her breakfast, gave Ayden a quick hug and kiss, and set out for work. "Just turn the lock when you leave. Don't worry about the alarm. Have a good day." She regretfully closed the garage door behind her.

❀

A busy day came to an end. Michelle and Leila began readying the shop for closing. Michelle secured the sales slips with a rubber band.

Leila pulled the window shades. Michelle organized merchandise on shelves and in display cabinets. They took turns using the vacuum cleaner. Chitchat led to the topic of their future dinner plans.

"David and I are really looking forward to our celebratory dinner."

"I am too. You both need to get to know Ayden. I'm thinking we should try the French café in Lafayette Hill. How's that?"

"Wonderful choice. Great food and an intimate setting."

They cleaned in silence for a few minutes more, and then Michelle made Leila an offer she couldn't refuse: "Why don't you go home and freshen up before meeting Ayden? I'll take care of the last-minute things."

Leila brightened. "Are you sure?"

"I'm sure. Go."

Leila gathered up her belongings and gave Michelle a grateful hug. "You're the best."

"I know, I know," Michelle muttered under her breath. "Ain't love great." A big smile crossed her face.

❁

Leila sighted Ayden just inside The Cheesecake Factory entrance, a beeper in his hand.

"We have about a twenty-minute wait," he said, rising to greet her.

"Well, let's sit down," she said. "I have a couple of business items to talk over with you."

They sat on a bench across from the hostess stand.

"Just to confirm, you and I have an appointment with the Millers next Friday at four thirty. We should be there for about an hour or so."

"Got it," Ayden said as if he were marking off a checklist.

"I thought I'd check in at the Perkinses' around three or so and then we could head out from there."

"Sounds like a plan." He leaned over and gave Leila a kiss. "You didn't allow me to say hello," he scolded her lovingly.

"I'm sorry. I'm wound up. We had a busy day."

A few minutes later, the beeper went off and the hostess sat them in a secluded booth, an oasis from the generally noisy crowd. After a leisurely dinner, during which the conversation focused mostly on the Perkinses and the Millers, Ayden changed direction. "Come home with me. You can leave early tomorrow morning. I've got things to do tomorrow to prepare for Monday at the Perkinses' anyway, but I want you with me tonight."

"I don't know. I'd be really out of my comfort zone . . ."

"I understand, but I think you're feeling like that because you've never spent the night at my house. Hopefully, you'll soon feel at home there."

"I don't have anything with me, and I'm not driving home *and* over to your house. It's too much after a long day."

"What do you need besides me?" Ayden asked, entirely sincere.

Leila began thinking frantically once again. "A toothbrush, for example." This time, she meant for her response to be more of a joke than a statement of fact.

"I have extras—unused, of course." A broad smile crossed his face.

"What if Hillary calls and I'm not there to answer the phone? She'll worry. I haven't discussed our relationship with her yet."

"Just text her and let her know you're out with me. She'll understand."

Leila thought a bit longer and finally acquiesced. She texted Hillary, turned off her phone, and took hold of Ayden's hand. He walked her to her car and, after settling her in the driver's seat and pulling his own car around, led the way to his house. She observed him occasionally adjusting his rearview mirror, checking to see that she kept up with him.

"I love you, Ayden Doyle," she said aloud. The words needed voice, even if only she heard them.

21

Ayden had furnished his home tastefully but sparingly. Each room resembled a page from a Pottery Barn catalog. Decorative plants, flowers, candles, and tabletop accessories were limited. A handsome sculpture of a horse rested on one end of a credenza; a collection of photographs hanging on an adjoining wall focused on the natural environment—trees in a forest, small streams flowing over rocks, and a sunset over the ocean. Area rugs rested strategically atop the chestnut-brown wood floors—one in the living room seating area, one under the dining room table, and a third in a small study off the living room.

After the downstairs tour, Ayden asked, "What do you think?"

"It's very nice and just as I imagined it would be—an accomplished craftsman's retreat. I especially like the sculpture of the horse. Is that Wings of Hope?"

"Not necessarily. But I did create two, and I gave one to Mark."

"I forgot you're also a sculptor. And one of some renown," she added. "I discovered that info in your Heavenly Matches bio. We never discussed that aspect of amazing you." She ran her hands over the art piece, marveling over its detail.

"I'm glad you like it. Let me show you the upstairs." He put his arm around her and guided her toward the staircase.

Upstairs were three bedrooms and two full baths. Pleasing, neutral colors flowed throughout the master bedroom suite. Dark mahogany furniture with a just-polished look, complemented nicely by brown, cream, and white bedding with an ikat pattern, indicated that a man slept there. The soft tones of the master bath echoed those of the bed covering. The neatness and orderliness of the space captured Leila's attention—the bed made and even the accent pillows in place.

"Lots of testosterone went into the design of this suite," she joked. She pivoted to face him and smiled warmly. "It's great. I like my night's accommodations very much."

His hypnotic eyes fixed on hers as if attempting to communicate something profound. Had she become essential to his happiness? Was that the intended message?

"I'm glad you like the house, and I'm thrilled you consented to spend the night. I'm lonely without you."

"And I without you." She put her arms around his neck and brought his lips to hers.

After their long embrace, Ayden's attention turned to her needs. "Let me get you one of my pajama tops, and I'll even throw in a couple of towels so you can get ready for bed."

"Thanks. I'm really tired."

Ayden placed towels and toiletries on the top of the vanity, including a toothbrush—still in its wrapper, as promised. He returned to the bedroom to ready the bed while Leila washed up.

She soon emerged from the bathroom to find him dressed in the pajama bottoms that matched her top. He thought nothing of it, but she found the sight endearing—and humorous. She had to laugh.

"Are we not a perfectly matched pair?" he said, laughing now too.

"Yes, we are, and we can thank Dr. Goodwin for that," she teased as she poked him in his belly. "The bathroom is all yours."

They didn't make love that night; instead, they nestled into each other's arms before falling asleep. Their relationship had evolved into another configuration. Though desire still reigned, Leila found immeasurable contentment in simply being with Ayden, and it seemed he felt the same.

❀

The aroma of brewed coffee awakened Leila. She slipped out of bed, freshened up, and made her way downstairs. Ayden had just finished preparing scrambled eggs sprinkled with bacon when she surprised him in the kitchen.

"I was just about to get you." He kissed her on the cheek. "How did you sleep?"

"Wonderfully! Having you near me made all the difference." She slid into a seat at his kitchen table.

"Likewise." Ayden affectionately tapped her nose as he set a plate in front of her.

"This looks wonderful. You're going to spoil me."

"It works both ways." He joined her at the table. "I have a busy day ahead of me. I have some things to organize for the Perkinses. What's on your agenda?"

"I'm headed home. I need to take care of some chores, touch base with my kids, and hit the supermarket."

They sat quietly as they ate breakfast. Ayden rustled through the Sunday paper. Leila found pleasure in simply watching him. They cleaned up the kitchen together—*Like a real couple*, Leila thought—then headed back upstairs, where she helped him make the bed and straighten the bathroom. Ayden still strove to be a perfect host, while Leila continued to make every effort to be a considerate guest. However, now she'd become more than his guest. She was his lover and his companion, and she was ready to share this news with those near and dear to her.

She studied Ayden's reflection in the rearview mirror as she pulled away from the house—a habit she'd gotten into with no regrets. Ayden had fallen into a similar routine: he stayed where he was in the driveway, watching her depart. Both remained focused on each other until completely out of one another's view. At that point, her longing for him began anew.

After arriving home, Leila took a quick shower and pondered the best time and place to confide in her daughter. Finally, she called her. She was a bit relieved when she got her voice mail.

"Hillary, this is Mom. I'd like you to give me a call when you have a chance. I thought we could meet for lunch tomorrow, if you're free. Maybe Michelle can join us. I haven't mentioned anything to her yet, but I want to show off your cute belly. Love you!"

She went about her household chores, made a shopping list, and headed out for groceries. In the meat department, she glanced at the prepared kebabs and was reminded of her time with Ayden in the St. Michaels market. How nice that experience had been—so much nicer than this solo outing.

Hillary called just as she finished putting away the groceries.

"Hi, Mom. How was your weekend?"

Her carefree tone, an attempt to mask her eagerness to discover all the details of her mother's weekend, didn't fool Leila. "Very nice. And yours?" She matched her daughter's tone, hoping Hillary would get the hint and let things be for now.

"Nothing exciting. We met our friends Sally and Jeff for dinner on Saturday."

"That's nice. Where did you go?"

"The restaurant in Broadaxe. So, about tomorrow. I'll be through with work around one. Can you meet for a late lunch?"

"Absolutely. Where shall we meet?"

"I'm thinking the deli near your shop. Around one thirty. How does that sound?"

"Sounds great. Everything else okay?"

"Yes, everything is fine."

"Then I'll see you tomorrow."

Leila got in touch with Michelle and arranged for her to join them. "Let's meet at the shop first," Michelle suggested. "I think we need to tie up some loose ends."

"Fine. Listen, Michelle, I want to talk to Hillary about Ayden and me. The relationship is getting rather serious. I may need your help in case Hillary has qualms about her mom being intimate with a man who's not her dad."

"No problem. But I think you're not giving Hillary enough credit. She's a shrewd lawyer. She already knows that you're smitten but has decided to give you some space."

"Maybe so."

❀

The next day, Leila and Michelle pulled into the shop parking lot at the same time. Once inside and settled, they began to organize their week. Michelle checked the phone messages, jotting notes as she listened.

"Anything earth-shattering?" Leila asked when she finally replaced the phone on its receiver.

"We heard back from Susan Fredericks. She'd love to meet with us. She's hoping next Monday will work."

"That's good for me. How about you?"

"That's fine. Let's try for ten o'clock."

Leila nodded. "I'll call her now. Maybe I can catch her at home."

"Hello." The throaty, sultry voice at the other end of the phone surprised Leila. She remembered Michelle had mentioned an accent, but this woman sounded absolutely seductive. Perhaps she had a cold.

"Good morning, Ms. Fredericks. This is Leila Brandt—"

"Please, call me Susan."

"Okay, Susan."

Their conversation was brief; they agreed to a Monday-morning meeting, exchanged a couple more pleasantries, and disconnected.

"So, it's a go?" Michelle asked after Leila hung up.

"We're all set."

Leila broke into a broad smile when she saw her pregnant daughter waiting near the entrance to the deli.

Michelle eagerly embraced Hillary. "Oh, don't you look adorable!"

"Thanks, but I'm eating for hordes!"

"Don't you worry," Michelle reassured her. "You're the type that will be back in shape in no time."

Once seated, orders placed, Leila broached the subject of her relationship with Ayden. "Hillary, I have something to tell you."

"What is it?" Hillary clearly didn't know what to think.

"I've fallen in love with Ayden." Leila waited, allowing her daughter a chance to digest her declaration. "We've been seeing a lot of each other lately, and our relationship has become very close."

"Really, Mother, do you think this is a surprise?" Hillary burst out, smiling. "I hoped for this. I want you to love and be loved. I don't want you alone anymore. Wasn't that the whole reason for getting involved with Dr. Goodwin? Ayden just better be good to you."

Michelle turned to Leila. "See, I told you she'd be cool with it."

"We need to let your brother know," Leila added.

"Mother, he knows. He knew the night he surprised the two of you in the kitchen. You were all aglow. Engineers are detail people. Not much gets by them." She leaned over and placed a daughterly kiss on Leila's cheek.

Leila let out a sigh of relief. "Well, that settles that."

"One more thing, Mom. Chad and I would like to get to know Ayden. Maybe you could have Sunday dinner and bring us all together. What do you think?"

"That's a good idea. But the timing has to be right. Perhaps when Drew is home for the holidays. Let me think about it."

22

L eila loaded her car with some bathroom items for the Perkinses—
the widespread faucets, tub and shower assemblies, vanity light
fixtures, and sinks. The plumbing distributor would deliver the rest
on Monday.

"I'm packed up and ready to leave," she informed Michelle, who
was going through the week's sales slips.

"We had a great week," Michelle noted. "In spite of that, please try
to get the Perkinses to give you a check for what you're dropping off
today, and for Monday's delivery too."

"I'll do my best."

"Try not to let your favorite distraction undermine your efforts."
Michelle couldn't contain a broad smile despite her obvious effort to
appear serious.

"He's my weakness. I confess. But business is business, right?"

"Right on!" Michelle cried out, her arms raised in cheerleader
fashion.

"Fine. Make jokes." Leila winked. "I'll call you and let you know
how both appointments went on my drive home."

"I'd appreciate that, partner. I'll be out of here by five thirty, so
call me at home if you're running late."

"Will do."

Ayden and Leila had spoken every night that week, but they
hadn't seen each other since Sunday. She couldn't wait to be with

him, to touch him, to kiss him. Of course, they'd have to maintain a professional demeanor in front of their clients. That was the deal. She envied his ability to keep his feelings from showing. Her solution required a fast exit from any professional setting where he participated. Did he wrestle with his emotions as she did with hers, and to the same excruciating extent?

Leila pulled up the Perkinses' driveway and hopped out of the car. Janice answered the door and extended a warm greeting. "Great to see you. Come on in. I'm anxious to show you this week's progress. Everything is framed out!"

"That's wonderful. The area is taking shape and the excitement is mounting," Leila teased, following Janice up the stairs.

"Absolutely."

Leila extended a general greeting to the crew as she walked in: "Good afternoon, everyone."

Two other craftsmen, going about their tasks, looked up. One gave Leila a wave hello while the other simply communicated with a generous smile. However, these two men didn't matter. For Leila, Ayden was the only man in the room.

He approached, looking his ever-sexy self. "Hi, Leila."

Not too close. Not too close.

"Let me go over our accomplishments."

"Yes, please do," she responded, a slight tremble in her voice. She hoped Janice didn't pick up on that.

Ayden proceeded to go over the layout—the linen closet, the laundry room, the tub and shower area with its built-in shelving, the private toilet, the location of the vanity, and the remaining open space. Leila marveled at the raised ceiling and recessed lighting, now complete.

"The higher ceiling makes such a difference. The room is majestic." She slowly surveyed the area, trying not to catch sight of Ayden's baby blues.

Janice's eyes twinkled with delight. "I think so too."

"I'm glad you two are pleased." Ayden glanced at his watch and turned to Janice. "Leila and I have an appointment in Radnor with a new client, so we have to head out. The guys will finish up here in a couple of hours. We'll be back bright and early on Monday. Is there anything you'd like to ask me?"

"I don't think so, but if anything comes to mind, I'll give you a call. Marshall and I are very pleased. Thanks, Ayden."

"You're very welcome. See you Monday."

Ayden began to gather his belongings together, and his doing so reminded Leila of the items in her car.

"My trunk and backseat are loaded with products for the bathroom, Ayden. Where should they be stored?"

"I'll take care of it," he said, striding over. "Give me your keys."

She retrieved her keys from her handbag and gave them to him. His touch, though fleeting, made her quiver. An instant later, he was out the door.

She tried to focus. "Janice, if it's convenient, would you be able to give me a check today?"

"Sure. I'll get the folder you gave me last time and we can go over things. I'll meet you in the foyer. I need to grab the folder from my office."

Downstairs, Leila opened the front door and saw Ayden moving items into one of the garages. She wanted to help, but Janice tapped her on the shoulder. "Here's the paperwork. I'd appreciate you going over things with me."

It didn't take very long for Leila to explain what she'd brought with her and what Monday's delivery would entail. Janice took notes and wrote Leila a check.

"Thank you again for everything, Leila," she said as she handed it over. "Have a terrific weekend."

"You too." Leila hurried outside, only to find Ayden already finished and waiting for her by his truck.

"Okay, ready for the Millers?" She kept her distance, striving to keep things totally professional.

"Do you have an address I can put into my navigator?"

"Yes. I've written it down." She pulled a small notebook from her briefcase, tore off the sheet in question, and handed it to him. "See you there in a half hour or so?"

"Sounds good." He looked at the information. "We can discuss tonight afterward."

Leila returned the notebook to her briefcase; its lock clicked just as Ayden finished his last remark. She looked up and caught a smile slowly crossing his face. She wanted to go to him, put her arms around him, and kiss him.

The sound of one of his men throwing scraps of lumber into the nearby dumpster snapped her back to reality. She smiled and said, "Certainly," managing to sound very businesslike.

Leila left the driveway first. If Ayden followed her to the Millers', she'd be able to enjoy seeing his face in her rearview mirror for the next thirty minutes.

❁

Traffic and roadwork put Leila and Ayden at the Millers' slightly behind schedule. To Leila's delight, Ayden had followed her the entire way.

John and Madeline Miller gave them a warm welcome. Leila introduced Ayden, and the four soon found themselves upstairs in the master bedroom suite.

John immediately talked finances. "We have a rather tight budget, but I've done some research and think it's workable. We're hoping you can provide some innovative ideas that will help us update the bathroom without taking drastic measures. Our bedroom is not very spacious, and we really want to maintain its square footage."

"I understand, and I already have some ideas for you to consider. How about going up—raising the ceiling and adding a couple of skylights and recessed lighting? That will make this bathroom seem much larger and, frankly, much brighter. In addition, we can install a larger, more architecturally interesting window than the small double-hung you now have. A large mirror over the vanity will also help to create the illusion of space."

"I love those ideas," Madeline said.

"Me too," John said. He glanced at his wife. "I'm concerned with the cost of such an ambitious design, though."

"I think you'll find it doable," Ayden said. "Let me draw up some plans. There are always options and trade-offs. In the end, your renovation will increase the value of your home."

Leila loved how Ayden's calm, encouraging manner put his potential clients at ease.

"One other thing," Madeline interjected. "I'd like custom bookshelves around the doorway on the bedroom side for our book collection. I'm willing to give up some space there. It's really only dead space right now anyway."

"I can do that," Ayden said confidently. "Even though your bedroom is average in size, bookcases will not encroach on anything. In fact, I think that's a great idea. We can use beautiful moldings and maybe carry them around the perimeter of the ceiling."

"Oh, I'd like that very much." Madeline was clearly on board with all the ideas Ayden was presenting for her new master bedroom suite.

Ayden and Leila set up a future appointment to go over Ayden's plans, and by five thirty, they'd said their good-byes and left.

Ayden walked Leila to her car and waited for her to settle in.

He leaned into the window. "What's next?"

"Dinner is next. I'm really hungry."

"What about tonight? You know, after dinner."

"Are you interested in spending the night at my house?" A girlish smile lit up Leila's face.

"I most *certainly* am," he shot back, making fun of her extremely formal use of the word earlier.

"Since we're close to your house, why don't you go get your things and then come over. Maybe we'll order in from the Chinese restaurant near me." She deliberated before articulating her inner thoughts and decided to go for it. "And, Ayden," she called after him, "make it quick, because I've really missed you."

His face lit up in response to her declaration. He hopped into his truck and sped away.

23

They sat at the island, Ayden with his chopsticks and Leila with her silverware, an array of cartons lined up in front of them. Their conversation focused on the two clients they had in common, the Perkinses and the Millers.

"They are such nice people," Leila said. "Both couples are considerate and appreciative."

"Nice people, I agree."

"By the way, I have some news. Michelle and I have an appointment on Monday with Susan Fredericks."

"Really? Great. I know you and Michelle will win her over. Susan has a good sense of design, but she needs direction and support."

"Where are you with her?"

"I'm drawing up plans to reconfigure the downstairs. I want a more open concept for her. She hasn't said anything yet about upstairs. I'm meeting with her again in a couple of weeks. I've already been out there twice."

"If she hires us, I'd like to see the plans before you present them to her. Is that possible?"

"No problem. We should collaborate."

They finished dinner, cleaned up, and settled in the den to watch TV. Leila looked at the man relaxing in Nick's chair, and somehow, he seemed a good fit. Her loneliness had become a thing of the past—for now, at least. Suddenly, the celebratory dinner plans popped into her head.

"Michelle and I thought after we finish up with the Perkinses, the four of us—you, me, Michelle, and her husband, David—could meet for dinner at the French café in Lafayette Hill to celebrate," she said. "What do you think?"

"Sure." Ayden smiled at her. "Mid-October is good."

Leila filled with happiness, her face aglow. Ayden seemed comfortable meeting her friends for dinner. She entertained the idea of mentioning a dinner with her children as well but decided to wait on that. It seemed a bit premature. Perhaps when she did propose it, she'd ask Ayden to bring Daniel and his girlfriend along.

"How about going to a movie tomorrow night?" he asked.

"What were you thinking of seeing?"

"I'll check it out tomorrow and let you know. What time will you be home from work?"

"Around six. We can have dinner before or after the movie. I don't have a preference. I'll leave the details up to you." This last remark boomeranged back to her, and a pang hit deep within her chest. She'd often deferred to Nick when weekend plans needed fine-tuning. Then the realization hit: Ayden was slowly becoming Nick's replacement—sitting in Nick's chair, taking over Nick's duties, making love to Nick's wife. "Will you be staying with me tomorrow night?" She wanted Ayden to say *yes* without any hesitation.

"Any objections?"

His wonderful eyes inspired her quick response. "You know I can't get enough of you."

Leila rose from the sofa and sat on his lap. Her mouth found the contours of his cheek and soon his lips.

"It's bedtime," Ayden said. "Let's go up."

She knew what he meant. They turned off the lights and walked the stairs together, each anticipating falling asleep in the other's arms.

Leila and Michelle pulled up in front of Susan Frederick's house just before ten. The house, a darling cottage design, had a turret with a stone facade. Through the turret's leaded glass windows, a staircase could be seen winding its way to the floor above.

Michelle commented first. "How charming."

Leila nodded her agreement. "I'm anxious to see the inside."

Michelle reached for a notepad and retractable tape measure and placed them inside her large handbag. "Well, let's get to it."

Susan took a while to answer the door. Leila thought the bell wasn't working, so she lifted the front door knocker and pounded away. Finally, the door swung open, and a petite woman began her apologies.

"I'm so sorry. I had the blow dryer going upstairs and didn't hear the doorbell. Please, come in," she said in a breathless voice that had a slight trace of an accent Leila couldn't quite place.

Susan Fredericks had an adorable face and figure. She had dressed in jeans, ballet slippers, and a long-sleeved black tee, reminding Leila of the late Natalie Wood—just over five feet tall, large brown eyes, thick brown hair that bounced when she moved, and an engaging smile. Her makeup, artfully applied, accentuated her eyes and lips.

Michelle tried to put their prospective client at ease. "Don't worry, Susan. We weren't outside for very long."

"I'm so glad. Well, where shall we start?"

"Why don't you give us a tour of the areas you're interested in renovating?" Leila suggested.

"Will do." Susan waved them inside. "So, here we are in the foyer, small as it may be. I'd like to do something here—enlarge it, if possible. I'm really interested in opening up the entire downstairs so the living room, dining room, kitchen, and small study meld into one another."

Leila and Michelle followed Susan as she led the way through an arched entry into the living room, and then through another archway into the dining room. To the right was a 1950s-style kitchen that looked as if June Cleaver had just cleaned up after breakfast and left to join her friends at the Women's Bowling League event. The kitchen sink was situated on the back wall. Above it, a small window revealed a nicely sized backyard. In the corner, to the right, a door led onto a brick patio.

Susan guided Leila and Michelle through another archway at the far end of the kitchen, and they found themselves in a hallway leading to the garage, laundry room, a small study, and then back into the foyer.

"Great house. I can see why you wanted to live here. And the turret adds especially to its charm." Leila's enthusiasm seemed to comfort Susan—who, Leila surmised, wasn't completely convinced she'd made the right decision buying the place.

"It needs a lot, but I'm hoping the two of you, along with Ayden, can get me through the renovation period. I have enough going on taking care of my ten-year-old daughter, who is going on twenty-five, and my shop."

Michelle lent her support. "We understand. Can we sit down, perhaps in the kitchen, and talk about how we can help you with this project? We'll explain our fee schedule and throw out some ideas once you've told us what you have in mind."

"Of course," Susan responded, as if apologizing for not being more proactive herself. "I've gotten things ready to make us some coffee. Come with me."

The three women sat in the kitchen and talked for two hours. Michelle took copious notes. Susan repeated her desire for an open concept as much as possible. She liked an eclectic décor. Pottery Barn was her favorite furnishings store. She wanted to achieve a similar look, and she took out a catalog where she'd folded down some pages to show them. She was contemplating including an antique piece or a smartly executed reproduction. For her kitchen, she envisioned cabinets with a country English look, possibly with a vanilla antique finish and pewter hardware.

Leila and Michelle projected warmth, doing their best to put Susan at ease.

As Michelle put her notepad into her handbag, she said, "You probably don't remember, but I once accompanied my niece to your shop. Her name is Tracy Oliver Carson. The gown you made for her was exquisite."

"I do remember Tracy. A lovely girl. She was different from most girls her age. Strapless wedding gowns are still in vogue. Tracy wanted one with a high, suggestive neckline—a Grace Kelly look."

"That's Tracy." Michelle smiled. "A true traditionalist."

Leila chimed in with additional accolades. "You've established a fine reputation. You must be very happy with your success."

"That's so nice of you to say. I am. However, my mother is the one who started the shop. She still works with me, but not as much as in the past. She taught me everything about dressmaking. In Lithuania, she worked in a top-notch salon, truly haute couture. Many of the salon's creations shipped to France, England, and Italy. But Lithuania wasn't the best place for my father. He's Jewish, a medical doctor, and wanted to immigrate to the States and go into research. We came here when I was around my daughter's age. Before long, Mother opened the shop, and things went well. I feel obligated to carry on, but I also enjoy the creative aspect of the business—so much so that I find dealing with the less-fun things tolerable."

"We totally understand," Leila sympathized. "Entrepreneurship can be stressful. Can I return to the project for a minute?"

"Sure."

"I think the backdrop is the first step. We need to look at color options, perhaps select one core color and team it up with complementary tints, going lighter and darker on some walls and so forth.

We can bring in all the other colors you like through accent pieces. How does that sound?"

"Sounds wonderful."

"We'll team up with Ayden and come back when he's ready to present his ideas. I know you'll be pleased with him. Right now, he's working on a large renovation, and it's coming along fabulously." Leila was careful to communicate these words in the most straight-forward manner possible.

"I've met with him twice and loved all his suggestions," Susan reported. "He's one gifted guy." Her eyes glowed with admiration.

Leila felt a small twinge of something. Jealousy? "We'll need at least a couple weeks to get things together. Please be patient."

Leila and Michelle shook hands with Susan and made their way to the front door. As she ushered them out, Susan thanked them once again. "I appreciate all your ideas and the time you've taken with me."

"It's been our pleasure," Leila replied.

Once in the car, Michelle and Leila sat for a few moments to reflect.

Michelle spoke first. "She seems very nice."

"Yes, I believe we'll have no problem working with her." Even Leila heard the hint of annoyance in her voice.

Michelle clearly sensed that something about Susan bothered Leila, but she didn't comment on it for the time being. She started the car and drove toward the shop. Leila sat in silence for most of the trip, thinking—mostly about Susan's remarks concerning Ayden, and the look she'd had on her face when she made them.

24

Leila made herself a cup of bedtime tea, settled into the comfy sofa in the den, and reached for a new copy of *Traditional Home*. Momentarily, the phone rang. Ayden.

Touching base, just as he'd promised.

Leila picked up the phone and purposely spoke in a soft, sexy voice. "Hi there, handsome."

"I'm lonely. What about you, beautiful?"

"Ditto. How was your day? Did everything go well at the Perkinses'?"

"Yes. We're on schedule. I think we'll finish up in a few weeks. Why don't you set up that dinner with Michelle and her husband for later this month?"

Ayden seemed eager to meet her friends, a pleasing step in the right direction. She'd allowed Susan Frederick's enthusiasm earlier in the day to fuel her imagination in unproductive ways and cast a shadow over their relationship. *Don't be paranoid.*

"Great. I know you'll like them. In fact, you'll meet Michelle next Monday. We're going to stop by together. She's anxious to see how the design plans are playing out—yours and ours."

"What time are you planning on? I want to make sure I'm there."

"Around ten. Will that work for you?"

"Yes. Any other news for me?"

"Well, you may know this by now, but Susan Fredericks decided to work with Michelle and me." Leila waited before saying anything else. She wanted to see if he had been in touch with Susan.

"I really had no doubt that she would. I'll get cracking on those architectural plans. We can go over things this weekend."

"Sounds like a plan." Leila hesitated. A nagging—and, she knew, unfounded—doubt about his trustworthiness drove her to ask the next question: "Do you think we should meet with Susan as a team or do you prefer separate appointments?"

"I think the team approach is more efficient," he said right away.

Leila exhaled with relief. "Yes, it is, even though I sometimes have difficulty concentrating when you're close to me." Her question answered, she wanted to lighten up the conversation.

"Bring your sidekick along," he teased. "She'll help you stay focused."

Leila perked up at his mutually playful tone. "That's a wonderful idea. I'll try to make appointments for Mondays, when we don't have the shop to worry about."

"Problem solved. Now, let's move on to more important matters. Can you spend the weekend with me? It will be more convenient tackling the Miller and Fredericks projects in my office. We can reward ourselves for our hard work if we're together. What do you say?"

Leila imagined him wearing his boyish grin. "Of course, my answer is yes," she purred into the phone. "I do need to work on Saturday, though, at least for part of the day. Let me talk to Michelle."

"Good. Sweet dreams."

"Good night." She stopped short of what she really wanted to say—*I love you.* Those words reverberated in her head after she hung up.

She sat in the chair a while longer, pensive. She loved again, and that was good. But what did her man do on the nights they weren't together? Curiosity mixed with uncertainty about her future with Ayden bothered her. A restful night's sleep would likely elude her.

✿

Leila found Michelle listening to their voice mail when she entered the office. She settled in quietly and waited until she finished.

"Well, no urgent messages," Michelle advised. "However, the warehouse called to say that Chad and Hillary's baby furniture is there. It's been moved into storage for now."

"I better make arrangements to have the floor refinished and the room painted. Our little one will be here before we know it."

Michelle must have perceived a sadness in Leila's tone. "Thinking about Nick?" she asked.

"He'd have loved being a grandfather. I'm sad he's missing out."

Michelle looked filled with empathy. "I know. Perhaps Ayden will rise to the challenge and stand in for him."

"Hopefully." Leila didn't elaborate on the many doubts plaguing her. "Speaking of Ayden: We're going to spend time this weekend going over the Miller and Fredericks projects. He'll have things almost completed on his end. As for us, the Millers are nearly set. Do you think we can get enough done for Susan Fredericks by then to have something to show Ayden?"

"I think so. Why don't you spend your time on Susan, and I'll organize all the materials for the Millers, okay?"

"Fine. Oh, and about Monday: don't forget we're going to the Perkinses' around ten."

"I won't forget. I'm looking forward to meeting Ayden."

Leila went about her tasks, but she knew she had to talk to Michelle about the weekend. "Hey, Michelle—"

"I know that tone of voice," Michelle said. "You're going to ask me for time off this weekend, right?"

"Yes, but it's not for pleasure. I really do want to finalize the Miller project, since we're due back there in a couple of weeks, and get into sync with Ayden regarding Susan Fredericks."

"Lucky you!" Michelle said with a wicked smile. "You're able to work and play with the same guy."

"I'm totally serious," Leila declared.

Michelle began to think, her eyes focused on the ceiling. "How about this . . ."

"Get to it, already."

"Let's split the day. You work from nine thirty until one thirty, and I'll finish up."

"It's a deal. I promise I'll have things organized and ready to go before I take off." She couldn't wait to tell Ayden she'd be at his place midafternoon on Saturday.

The week passed quickly, especially for Leila, who had the task of translating Susan Fredericks's wishes into concrete design plans. She spent a highly productive Friday evening in her home office but couldn't stop thinking about Ayden. Anticipation raced through her veins. Her weekend would be a wonderful mixture of collaboration, companionship, and lovemaking, so she packed accordingly. She filled her overnighter with casual, comfortable clothes plus a favorite sexy black nightgown, long relegated to the back of the dresser drawer that contained her sleepwear.

The next morning, during short reprieves from waiting on customers, she found herself a bit frantic as she tried to gather together the materials she wanted to bring to Ayden's. She was unaware of the time until Michelle announced her arrival.

"I'm back here," Leila called out, "still packing up."

When Michelle rounded the corner, Leila looked up from her spot on the floor with a look of chagrin, an array of design materials fanned out in front of her. Their small office was awash with papers.

Michelle's eyes widened. "Goodness, there's so much. Maybe you shouldn't work on both clients this weekend."

"It looks this way because I've not gotten as far with my packing as I wanted," Leila said. "We were pretty busy this morning. Anyway, the whole point of this weekend is to get back to *both* clients as soon as possible and help them make decisions that will move the projects forward."

"You're beginning to sound like me."

Leila stood up and surveyed the scene. "Help me out?"

"Of course."

Both worked in dedicated silence for almost an hour. Finally, Leila pulled out her clipboard and double-checked the totes.

"You labeled and numbered each bag?" Michelle asked, her tone somewhere between incredulity and admiration.

"Well, I don't want to present things in a haphazard way to Ayden."

"Right." Michelle turned her head, unsuccessfully trying to avoid showing Leila her smile.

✿

As Leila made her way up the driveway to Ayden's workshop and office, she noticed an SUV parked in front of the door. It couldn't belong to Daniel; he always parked in the circle by the house. She took a space next to the mystery vehicle and removed her cardigan to cover her overnight bag before getting out of the car. Thank goodness she had prepared for the autumn chill the late afternoons had recently taken on. No need to suggest to anyone else that her visit was for anything other than business purposes. Just as she retrieved her purse from the backseat, the shop door opened, and she heard a distinctive voice: "Thanks so much for seeing me on such short notice. I just had to show you the picture from the design magazine before you worked further on my project."

Leila knew the voice belonged to Susan Fredericks even before she saw her talking to Ayden. She felt as though she'd been punched in the stomach. For some reason she didn't fully understand, she saw Susan as her rival.

"No problem," Ayden said cheerfully. "I'm happy to accommodate you."

At that exact moment Susan spotted Leila across the driveway, standing motionless between the two cars. "Hey, Leila, how are you?"

"I'm wonderful, and you?" Leila forced an air of sincere interest.

"Fine. I just brought Ayden a picture of an interior I fell in love with. Make sure he shows it to you." Susan's gaze swiveled from Leila to Ayden and back to Leila. "So, are you guys getting together on my account?"

Leila pumped up her voice with professional enthusiasm and purposely put on a happy face. "We'll certainly be discussing the information you gave to Michelle and me, as well as some really exciting ideas we've come up with for your home. I'll call you after the weekend and set up a tentative appointment. How does that sound?"

"Sounds great. I'm getting really excited. Well, see you later." With a small wave—meant only for Ayden, Leila was sure—Susan hopped into her SUV and headed out of the drive.

"You're traveling light," Ayden said, striding over with a grin.

"Not so. My trunk is packed," Leila warned. "I think we should focus on one client at a time." She put her arms on Ayden's shoulders and gave him a passionate kiss. She wasn't about to let Susan Fredericks's surprise appearance spoil her time with him. Pushing slightly backward, she took time to enjoy his wonderful eyes before asking, "What's on the agenda?"

"The Miller project is rather straightforward. It's really a mini-version of what's going on at the Perkinses'. Why don't we take care of that this afternoon?"

"Okay. Let's get to work."

❁

As Leila and Ayden wound their way through the shop floor, Daniel emerged from behind a storage bin. He caught a glimpse of Leila and greeted her with a smile. "Hi there. Do you need any help?"

"I think we have everything for now. Please come up when you can, though. I'd like your opinion too."

"Will do. I'm almost done cleaning out useless scraps of decorative molding from the bin. I need another fifteen minutes."

Ayden suggested using the elevator. Leila knew that if he were alone, he'd have easily climbed the stairs despite his load—but she nodded and up they went. In no time, everything had been strategically placed to the right of the drafting table. Ayden pulled over a stool for Leila and then unfurled his drawings for the Millers' master bath and bedroom bookcases.

"Gorgeous!" Leila exclaimed. "The large window opens up the room, and the raised roof and skylights add more splendor."

"Take a look at this molding for the bookcases." He placed a three-foot piece on the table for her examination. "There are small Grecian urns carved into the wood—a classical motif to complement their book collection."

"Dad's pretty happy about that molding," Daniel said, smiling, as he walked in.

"You two are the best. That's all I can say." Leila slid off the stool and brought a couple of bags over to the table. "I think our selections will work fabulously with your designs."

Leila could tell her presentation impressed both men. She showed them the paint colors she and Michelle had selected—a subtle combination of two neutrals applied to the bathroom walls using a faux-marble technique—and the Italian provincial vanity on legs, finished in a cream color with a bronze glaze, that they planned to order. The colors in the Millers' bedroom would coordinate with the plum and yellow tints of the upstairs hallway; those shades would be incorporated into the bathroom's design with iridescent glass accent tiles. The granite for the vanity had deep brown hues dotted with specks of white.

"I'd like the baseboards and moldings to be white. I think the tub, toilet, and sink can be white. That will save them some money." She waited for Ayden and Daniel's comments.

"It's elegant without being ostentatious," Ayden said right away. "I think you and Michelle hit the nail on the head."

"All the elements work great together," Daniel added.

"Absolutely." Ayden nodded.

Daniel looked at his watch and turned to his father. "I'm out of here, Dad. Isabella and I are meeting friends for dinner."

"Have fun. And thanks for working today." Ayden gave him a fatherly hug and pat on the back.

"See you, Leila," Daniel said, waving good-bye. Leila watched through the office window as he sped down the stairs to the shop floor, demonstrating he'd inherited his father's uncanny agility.

Now it was just the two of them. Leila began to collect the samples and return them to the bags. Ayden rolled up his drawings and placed them in a storage tube. They stood opposite each other for a few seconds but soon fell into a passionate embrace. How had they managed to remain so cool in front of Susan and Daniel when all they wanted was each other?

"You feel so good." She nuzzled his neck and kissed him softly just below his ear.

"Do you want to order in or go out for dinner?" he asked, holding her close.

"A change of scene may do us both some good," she suggested.

"The Tavern?"

Leila tilted her head back and smiled her approval.

"After we get these things back in your car, I'll call for a reservation."

"Make it on the later side."

A devilish smile lit up his face. "I'm glad we're on the same page."

❀

The next morning, the two of them sat in Ayden's kitchen drinking coffee while a quiche from a nearby farmers market baked in the oven. A picture window in the breakfast nook looked out onto the deck and well-manicured yard. Tall, fluffy evergreen trees around the perimeter of the property helped to ensure privacy and reduce noise from the workshop.

"This view is lovely and peaceful," Leila said.

"I think so." He took a sip of his coffee. "Are you up for working on Susan Fredericks?"

"Yes, of course. We'll need to return to my trunk."

"No problem."

"Her home is just adorable. When the first floor is opened up, its appeal will grow exponentially." Leila looked across the table and studied Ayden's face, trying to see if he expressed an unusual interest in their mutual client. She detected nothing.

The timer went off. Ayden retrieved the quiche and brought it to the table. As he began to slice it into servings, Leila reached into the fruit bowl and started to cut up a large apple.

"That quiche smells heavenly."

"It should be terrific. It's loaded with diced ham and vegetables."

Leila's professional and personal curiosity soon got the best of her. "Why don't you give me a preview of what you have in mind for Susan's house?" Her eyes remained fixed on the apple.

"It's easier for me to just show you what I've considered when we're in the office. It just so happens the interior picture she brought over is much like what I came up with. I just have to tweak my plan a bit."

"Give me a hint or two."

"Basically, creating that open concept you spoke of, enlarging the entrance hall using curved half-walls and pillars, and installing new wood floors."

"I like the house's rounded motif. It starts even before one gets inside with that fabulous turret."

"And what do you and Michelle have in mind?"

"One of our suggestions is to work with lighter and darker tints of Susan's preferred color on different walls to add interest. White trim everywhere."

He reached across the table and gave her arm a tender squeeze. "Now that we've enticed each other, let's eat up so we can get to work!"

The hours in Ayden's office flew by. He showed Leila the magazine picture Susan had brought over; it depicted a typical English cottage look using wonderful floral chintz with bold colors and coordinating patterns. Leila pulled out a very similar fabric from her samples. Ayden nodded and smiled.

They had fun working together, often inspiring each other's creativity. One of Leila's plans called for a rustic-looking painted cupboard in the dining room. "I'll have to research the source for this," she said. "I know of at least one company that replicates old pieces."

"If there's a problem, Daniel and I can build one for her," Ayden said casually.

Leila looked up from her position on the office floor, an awe-struck look on her face. *Of course you can.*

Ayden didn't notice her admiring look. He was busy at the drafting table, putting final touches on one of his illustrations.

They finished up around five and decided on a simple dinner at the neighborhood deli.

"We accomplished a great deal, don't you think?" Leila asked after they ordered.

"I'm quite satisfied with our progress." His blue eyes were fixed on her face, drinking her in.

"I think we're ready for Susan Fredericks next Monday. Does that work for you?"

"Make it early morning. I'll be finishing up at the Perkinses' this week."

"And the Millers of Radnor?" she inquired, as if she were announcing the couple at a charity ball.

"This week, late Friday. How's that for you?"

"It will work. I'll make the appointment tomorrow."

❁

Once they returned to Ayden's house, Leila faced the inevitability of returning home. She didn't want to, but both of them were tired. Their time together had been productive. A special working relationship continued to develop, bringing out the best in both. She sensed he, too, was keenly aware of it.

She checked her overnighter to make sure she had repacked everything. Ayden carried it outside and placed it in her backseat. He tossed her handbag onto the passenger's seat and took the keys from her hand so he'd be able to start her car—a gallant gesture that had now turned into a ritual Leila found endearing.

Satisfied the car was idling smoothly, Ayden got out and turned to Leila. She didn't move; she just took in his baby blues one last time. He returned her gaze.

"Did you ever see the movie *Jerry Maguire*?" he asked, a serious look on his face.

Where's he going with this? "Yes, Tom Cruise played a sports agent and Renée Zellweger his love interest."

"Yes." He stood silent for a moment and then delivered his zinger lines. "Leila, you complete me. I love you, and I hope you feel the same."

There, he'd said it—and what was so delightful about his admission was that it seemed from the heart and had been delivered at a time she least expected it. She pulled him to her and kissed him with all the gusto she had in her. He returned her fervor, pressing her against the car, its running motor serving as background music for the climactic scene.

"And I love you, Ayden Doyle," she uttered softly between kisses.

"Good." A simple word sealed the deal.

"I better go." Leila pushed him slightly away, her arms not ready to release him.

"I'll see you tomorrow at the Perkinses', around ten?"

"That's the plan."

He leaned down to give her a last passionate kiss and closed the door. Leila looked up at him and smiled, but tears began to fill her eyes. She hoped he didn't notice; she quickly put the car in reverse and backed up—skillfully, in spite of her blurred vision—and began her exit. He appeared in the rearview mirror, watching her depart. Then the dreaded need for the turn onto the street arrived, and upon its execution, he was gone.

25

On the drive with Michelle to the Perkinses', Leila described Ayden's architectural plans for Susan Fredericks as well as the Millers. She also discussed her new ideas for their clients, inspired by her time with Ayden.

"Everything sounds fabulous. I can see you used your time off wisely."

Leila shot her a look. Sometimes she couldn't tell if Michelle was being sincere or sarcastic.

They pulled into the Perkinses' driveway. Before making their way to the front door, both took a minute to make sure they looked their best, checking out their makeup, hair, and apparel.

"Ready?" Michelle asked.

"Ready," Leila replied.

Janice welcomed the team in her usual warm manner. "Michelle, I'm so glad you've come too. The renovation is almost finished." She led them upstairs to the master bedroom suite, praising Ayden all the while.

"Seems like your Ayden has quite an effect on women," Michelle whispered in Leila's ear.

"Hush!" Leila admonished, fighting off the urge to smile.

Janice made her usual announcement: "Here we are." She summoned the two women into the bathroom with a wave of her arm.

Ayden and one of the workmen were balanced atop high ladders, installing a chandelier; two more were standing below and keeping things secure. Michelle and Leila knew to remain quiet while the difficult installation was underway. In the interim, they surveyed the space and exchanged approving nods and smiles with Janice.

"How does it look from down there?" Ayden called out.

Leila assumed the first responder role. "Looks great. It's even, if that's what you're asking."

"That's what I'm asking. Thanks."

Ayden descended the ladder and walked over to the three women, who had formed a small audience. "You must be Michelle," he said, reaching out to shake her hand.

In her stocking feet, Michelle was five feet nine. In high heels, she was an imposing figure indeed. The fact that she loomed over Ayden didn't seem to bother him.

"You're right. I'm Michelle. I'm happy to finally meet you."

"Likewise." He smiled. "So, what do you think?"

"I couldn't be more impressed."

Ayden took Michelle on a tour of the suite, explaining how the space had been transformed. "Your design details really made things pop."

"Leila had more to do with that than I did," Michelle confessed.

"You all have made our dreams come true," Janice declared, "and we're delighted."

Leila smiled; a sense of satisfaction filled her designer's soul. "It's been our pleasure."

Janice glanced at her watch. "I have an appointment. I hope you'll all excuse me. Is there anything else we need to discuss?"

Ayden shook his head.

"No," Leila said, "not that I can think of."

"Fine. Ayden, I'll touch base with you when I get home."

Once Janice left, Ayden explained the status of the project. "We don't have much left to do. We need to finish up the trim and then paint. We'll definitely be out of here next week." He moved closer to the women and said in a subdued voice to avoid being overheard by his crew, "I see our celebratory dinner on the horizon." The boyish grin Leila loved spread across his face.

Michelle quickly took advantage of Ayden's overture. "Great. How about next weekend? I'll make a reservation for eight o'clock."

"We're set, then. Anything else?"

"No," Leila said, "but let's talk later. I'm going to confirm appointments with the Millers and Susan Fredericks."

"I'll call you tonight." Ayden focused his baby blues on Michelle. "Again, nice meeting you."

"Same here."

Ayden returned to his work. Michelle and Leila headed to the car.

Michelle buckled her seatbelt, waited a moment or two, and then spoke. "There's something about him. I'm not sure if it's his eyes or his smile, probably the combination. Whatever. I understand why you fell for him."

"You don't know the half of it. He has his ways. For example, when I started for home last night, he told me he loved me and hoped that I felt the same."

"Get out!"

"It's true. He used that famous line from *Jerry Maguire*."

"He didn't?" Michelle's jaw actually dropped.

"Yes. He said I complete him. To you, the phrase may sound corny, but it's what I'd been waiting to hear."

"What about you? Isn't your life better now that Ayden is part of it?"

"I never thought I'd find someone I could love as much as I loved Nick. But I'm crazy about him," Leila conceded. "Still, I do worry about our relationship ending, more often than I'd like to admit." There: her innermost fear revealed.

"Stop being so pessimistic," Michelle countered. "Enjoy the

moment. You have a second chance at love. But he's the lucky one, Leila. You're quite a catch. Don't you forget that."

That evening, Leila sat in the den waiting for Ayden's call, eager to report her success with the scheduling of appointments. The ringing of the phone startled her. For some reason, she was on edge. When she saw Ayden's name appear on the caller ID, she took a second to compose herself, then hit the "talk" button.

"Hello, you," she said softly.

"Hello, beautiful. How was your day?"

"Productive. And yours?"

"Things went well at the Perkinses'."

"That's good to hear. I have some good news too. I confirmed those appointments—the Millers this Friday at four thirty and Susan Fredericks on Monday at ten."

"Things are moving along. We'll be busy for the rest of the year." He paused. "Are you all right? You sound tired."

"I wish you were here," she confessed.

"I wish I were too. How about a sleepover at your house this weekend?"

"It's a deal," she said, a lift in her voice. "I guess I'll check in one last time at the Perkinses' on Friday, and then we can go over to the Millers' from there."

"Fine. Well, I'm headed to bed. Sweet dreams, Leila."

"You too."

26

O n Friday afternoon, Leila pulled up to the Perkinses' house and immediately spied Ayden leaning against the back of his truck. He looked quite sexy. A tool belt hanging slightly below his waist enhanced his usual outfit—jeans and a close-fitting T-shirt with his company's logo. A smile crossed Leila's face when her private thoughts likened her lover to a gunslinger from bygone days, standing alone, proudly displaying a set of six-shooters and daring anyone to mess with him. She definitely wanted to mess with him, but she'd have to hold back until later in the evening.

Ayden's face lit up as she approached. "Hi there, beautiful. How's your day going?"

"Much better now that I'm in your company," she replied with a wink. She noticed a small object in his hands. "What do you have there?"

"It's my digital camera. I've taken some pictures of the Perkinses' bedroom suite."

"Can I take a peek?"

"Of course, but doing so requires you to come closer," he warned in jest.

Ayden opened his arms and directed Leila to stand next to him. As she moved into position and leaned against the truck, his arms enclosed her. He held the camera out in front and presented the shots he had taken.

The pictures were impressive, capturing all the fine details of the renovation. But Leila couldn't concentrate on them. Ayden's aura reached out to all her senses, and she wanted him.

"Wonderful shots. They'll be great additions to your portfolio. I'd love a couple for Michelle and me."

"Just let me know which ones you'd like. Shall we go up and see everything in person?" He still had his arm resting across her shoulders.

"Absolutely. We need to watch our time, so we're not late for the Millers."

His arm remained in place as they walked to the front door. As much as Leila loved feeling it there, she was uncomfortable at the same time. "Ayden, I love your arm around me, but—"

"Janice isn't home," he interrupted. "No one else is here except my two workmen."

"Well, that's a relief." She turned to face him and placed a lingering kiss on his lips. "That should hold me for a while."

❀

Ayden's suggestions impressed the Millers, who also went gaga over his illustrations. Madeline especially liked the molding for her bookcase. "How did you ever find trim with carved Grecian urns? It's absolutely sensational!"

Ayden smiled, obviously enjoying Madeline's admiration. "I have my sources."

"When can you begin?" John asked, ever the practical one.

"Within the next couple of weeks. You need to read over the proposal and sign. Take your time and don't hesitate to call me with any questions." Ayden handed a prepared proposal to John, and the two men shook hands.

"It seems to be my turn now," Leila declared lightheartedly. "I know you will find the design plans that Michelle and I created for you filled with exciting options—all of which work wonderfully with Ayden's ideas."

As the Millers listened intently to Leila's presentation, Ayden, too, fixed his gaze on her. She felt his eyes burning into her, and it almost derailed her, but she managed to get through without a hitch.

"I really like the incorporation of the glass accent tiles and the subtle touches of color they bring to the area," Madeline commented. "You're right. Everything you've suggested goes well with Ayden's plan. I'm sold on everything." She turned toward her husband. "What do you think, darling?"

"I'm on board."

John's reply earned him a hug and kiss from his wife. Leila and Ayden glanced at each other and smiles crossed their faces, prompted by the realization that their teamwork had closed the deal. With that, they organized the samples and drawings for the Millers to review and said their good-byes.

Ayden helped Leila carry her materials out to her car and waited until she settled into the driver's seat. He leaned in close, holding the door open. "We do make a great team."

"The Millers seem to think so." She looked into his delightful blue eyes for a few seconds. "Are you staying with me tonight?"

"I'll be over by seven thirty. What should we do for dinner?"

"It's been a long day. I'll make something at home. Any requests?"

"Not really. Surprise me." He gave her a quick kiss and closed the door.

Leila glanced at the clock on the dashboard. Almost six o'clock. In less than two hours, Ayden would be all hers. She'd stop by the market and pick up a few things for the sautéed chicken dinner she had in mind. First, she'd play chef and make Ayden a great dinner. Later on, she'd parade about in her sexy black nightgown and take on the role she most preferred: Ayden Doyle's lover.

Just past seven thirty, Ayden rang the doorbell. His eyes instantly expressed his delight with Leila's whimsical cooking ensemble: apron, oven mitts, and furry slippers. This particular evening she appeared even more girlish, she knew, since she'd tied her hair up in a high ponytail with a wide ribbon.

"Hi there. Is your mom at home?" He gave her a cute wink.

"No." Leila returned a sly smile. "She's out for the entire evening, so we can do anything we want."

"Great." He proceeded to give her a quick kiss on the cheek. "Smells good in here. What's for dinner?"

"Follow me. You must be patient."

In the breakfast area, Leila arranged two place settings lit with tea candles. She poured two glasses of French chardonnay. Gold-rimmed salad plates displayed an enticing mixture of greens, dried cranberries, and pine nuts dressed with a tarragon vinaigrette of her own creation.

They began to sample the first course. Ayden closed his eyes in contentment after the first bite.

"You like?"

"It's very good. I love the vinaigrette."

She followed that success with sautéed chicken breasts, spinach, and cubed sweet potatoes. Ayden reached for a fragrant piece of focaccia from a straw basket. He had a compliment and a confession to voice. "You're a great cook. I'm one lucky guy."

"And so you are," Leila said coyly. "But I'm just as fortunate."

They finished with coffee and miniature iced brownies made from a mix. Leila kept that little secret to herself. Her mother often reminded her that a wise woman knows when to keep a secret, and so a smile crossed her face when Ayden praised her baking skills.

"I'm glad you're enjoying them," she carefully replied.

After dinner, he readily moved into kitchen-help mode. He cleared, rinsed, and stacked the dishes in the dishwasher in record time. Once they went upstairs, he tossed his bag on the chaise and turned down the bed while Leila brought out towels and toiletries for him, setting them on what had become his side of the double vanity in her elegant master bathroom. On top of the towels she placed white pajamas still in their store wrapping, a gift she'd purchased for him to set the tone for their weekend together.

"What's this?" Ayden inquired as he reached for his towel.

"I thought it was time for those white pajama bottoms." She giggled.

He pulled her to him and kissed her deeply. She could feel the warmth spread throughout her body. A moment later, he slipped on the bottoms, affecting a model's stance.

She clapped with delight. "Perfect! Just like in my dream." She reached for the black nightgown she'd purposely hung on the back of the bathroom door and let it slowly slide down over her naked body, suspecting Ayden would enjoy watching its descent. Her suspicion became a fact as she eyed his reflection in the bathroom mirror.

"Are you interested in watching TV for a while?" she asked.

"Not tonight." He switched off the bathroom light, took her hand, and led the way out. They parted when they reached the bed. In a synchronized manner, they climbed into their accustomed sides of the bed, lifted the covers over themselves, and twisted toward their own night tables to turn off the bedside lamps. In the still of the night, with just enough moonlight streaming in to add an air of magic to the room, they enjoyed finding each other once again.

27

Monday turned out to be a glorious day. The bright sun warmed the brisk morning air so typical of autumn. The leaves on the deciduous trees had just begun to turn yellow, orange, and red. The cheerful day served as a good omen. The Fredericks appointment would be a total success.

Leila had labored over her outfit, since Ayden would be there too. One thing required no deliberation: she'd wear her hair up, the way he liked it. Finally, she donned her most recent splurge: an Elie Tahari pantsuit. Its sienna color was perfect for the season. She picked black crocodile pumps with two-inch heels—high enough to flatter her figure but not so high as to interfere with her ability to handle the products they'd be showing—to go with it. A last look in the hall mirror assured her she'd have the desired effect on Ayden that day.

When she pulled into the shop's parking lot, she found Michelle waiting patiently. Totes filled with all the materials they would need that day rested at her feet.

"Good morning," Leila said brightly. "Everything organized?"

"I have everything you put by the door. Four bags, right?"

Leila got out of the car and surveyed the lot. "That's everything. Let's put them in my trunk."

"You look very lovely today." Michelle clearly knew that Leila's obvious extra effort was for Ayden's benefit.

"Why thank you. And so do you. But then again, you always do."

Michelle was dressed more casually: black pants, a camel V-neck sweater, and a chic black quilted jacket with multicolored buttons. "Well, I hope Susan appreciates my efforts." Michelle looked at Leila and burst out laughing.

"Stop teasing me," Leila pleaded. "I'm sure you make certain apparel decisions at times with David in mind."

"Okay. Let's move on. How was your weekend?"

"Wonderful. We stayed around the house and enjoyed each other's company. I cooked Friday night, and Ayden cooked Saturday night. We spent an hour or so yesterday reviewing the Fredericks project. He left on the early side to organize himself for today. What did you and David do?"

"Nothing out of the ordinary. We took in a movie and then had dinner at The Redstone. Madge and Charlie Simon met us there."

"That's nice. How was the movie?"

"It's definitely worth seeing."

The rest of the conversation focused on the ideas they'd present to Susan Fredericks. Ayden's truck was already parked in the driveway when they arrived at Susan's house, leaving just enough room for Leila to park her car directly behind it.

Susan answered the door in high spirits. "Hi there."

Leila pasted on a smile. "Good morn—"

"I'm so excited," Susan cut her off. "Ayden just started to explain his plans. And his drawings, beyond incredible! Wait until you see them. Come in. Come in. Let me help you." She reached for one of Leila's totes.

Leila and Michelle followed Susan into the dining room. Ayden's drawings, pamphlets, and samples covered the draped dining table.

"Good morning," the designers said in unison.

"Good morning, ladies." Ayden's broad smile exuded confidence.

Leila and Michelle placed their totes under the table and brought their full attention to bear on Ayden. He had reimagined the cottage using elements common to homes in the English countryside, including some from the magazine Susan had dropped off at his shop. Drawings with vivid details brought each room to life and supercharged his presentation. The outstanding features of his plans included new wide-planked wood floors of medium color for the entire downstairs; ivory chair rails and crown moldings for the living and dining areas; a large, elaborate stone-and-cement mantel for the living room fireplace; petite, discreet recessed lights for every room; large French doors for the back wall of the dining room to replace the small, no-statement window; custom bookcases for the small office off the foyer to give it the feel of a library; a curved half wall to enlarge the entry; and custom cabinetry for the kitchen, to be finished in a rubbed vanilla and accented with pewter hardware. Susan repeatedly used the words *awesome* and *fabulous* when moved to comment while Leila and Michelle fell silent, enthralled with the artistry inherent in Ayden's work.

"Of course, we'll make adjustments to the plans," Ayden said as he wrapped up the presentation. "We'll add here, take away there, until you're comfortable with everything, including the cost."

"You're phenomenal," Susan said. "You've gone beyond what I've envisioned." She walked over to Ayden and gave him a short but intense hug. Leila didn't fail to notice how she slid her fingers down his arms and gave his hands a little squeeze before turning away and looking in Leila and Michelle's direction.

Michelle jumped in on cue. "The grand concept is masterful. I especially like the idea of reconstructing the fireplace to look as if it were reclaimed from an old country house on the outskirts of London. This project begs for publication. Once things are finalized, we should contact one of the design magazines—with Susan's permission, of course. What do you think, Susan?"

"I'd love to share my soon-to-be wonderful home with others.

Right now, I'm almost jumping out of my skin to see your ideas. How about something to drink before we start?"

"I could use an ice water," Ayden said with a nod.

"I'm fine for now," Michelle said.

Leila shook her head. "Nothing at the moment."

Susan returned in a flash with Ayden's water, a lemon slice perched on the edge of the glass. His eyes twinkled with self-satisfaction as he took hold of the glass. He obviously knew he had wowed everyone.

Leila and Michelle reached for the bags they'd placed under the table.

"Let's all take a seat," Leila suggested.

Once everyone was comfortable, Leila began to present the various options she and Michelle had prepared. Susan had mentioned she favored shades of soft green. Leila showed her a moss green of medium intensity, with lighter and darker contrasts for accent walls, above and below chair rails, and wainscoting. The tints looked exceptionally nice with the color of the wood flooring Ayden suggested. Leila brought out an ample array of colorful fabrics in chintz floral patterns, plaids, stripes, small geometrics, and toile de Jouy of hunting and pastoral scenes. She demonstrated various combinations of materials, fanning out the samples on the floor and pulling out specific fabrics for window treatments, accent pillows, and upholstered pieces. Her own pencil sketches illustrated the different applications.

Susan was ecstatic. "I love them all. I'm going to have a difficult time narrowing my choices."

"You'll need to take your time," Leila said. "But you know fabric, Susan. You work with it day in and day out. Yes, you are dealing with wearable fabrics, but home materials are their kissing cousins. You'll be able to narrow down the ones you want to live with, not just for their eye appeal but also for their texture and durability."

Michelle took over the design presentation, explaining the ways to arrange the living room furniture. "We can use some of the pieces you already own—refurbish them if necessary. We may also want to buy some new things."

"I want to get new seating for the living room. I like the plan that calls for two large sofas placed on either side of the fireplace," Susan said unequivocally.

"That plan is my favorite as well," Michelle said. "It will create a cozy conversation area for you to enjoy with your family and friends."

Susan offered drinks again, but everyone declined. "Are you gals sure you don't want anything to drink?" she asked. "You've been explaining things for almost an hour."

"No, I'm fine," Michelle reiterated.

"Me too," Leila said. "Michelle and I should go, anyway. We'll repack the totes now and leave the samples for you to review. Perhaps we can get together in a week or two and go over your choices. Does that sound workable?"

"That sounds great," Susan said with enthusiasm.

Ayden, who had remained quiet during the design presentation except for an occasional "that's very nice," began to organize his materials as well. Susan went to help him.

"What do you want me to leave with you?" Ayden asked.

"Please leave me the drawings. You can take the more technical architectural drafts with you, since I'd need you with me to truly understand them. After I process everything, will you come back and discuss things with me again?" Susan spoke with a lost-girl look on her face.

"Sure," he said. "How about the same time next Monday? Does that give you enough time?"

"Fine. It's a date," she said, a large smile crossing her face.

While Leila kept a close eye on Susan's persistent flirtatious behavior, Michelle busied herself arranging the totes so Susan could easily understand the combinations and options.

"Susan," she called, "can you come here for a minute? I'd like to explain how I organized things for you."

Leila, now standing on the other side of the dining room table, watched Ayden slide his drafts into tubes and put samples in his briefcase. "Got everything?" she asked in a subdued tone. On the inside, her heart pounded, sending her blood rushing through her veins.

Ayden, as always, sensed something was up. "What?"

"Nothing."

Susan's parting remarks diverted their attention. "Thank you all so very much for your hard work and wonderful ideas. I'm truly blessed to have found such wonderful people to help me make this house into a home in which I'll find comfort and joy."

How poetic. Leila forced a smile in response to Susan's remarks, though it was clear to her that they were aimed solely at Ayden. Susan couldn't take her eyes off him.

Everyone shook hands and walked toward the entry. Leila remained silent as Michelle offered good-byes for both of them.

As they walked away, Leila could hear Susan praising Ayden for his work again and promising to review everything over the weekend so she'd be totally prepared for their next meeting.

In the process of securing her seat belt, Leila noticed Susan had accompanied Ayden outside, and the two were still steeped in conversation. Ayden leaned against the side of his truck near its open door. Susan stood close enough to him to speak in a whisper.

Michelle noted the cozy situation as well. "What are you thinking?"

"I'm thinking Susan Fredericks is not my favorite person. You may need to take the lead on this project."

"I understand," Michelle said. Uncharacteristically, she said nothing more.

Leila backed out onto the street and slowly headed for the shop.

She reached up and adjusted her rearview mirror, keeping an eye on Ayden and Susan Fredericks until she no longer could.

❀

The two women sat in silence at the deli, waiting for their order to arrive. Finally, Michelle couldn't stand it any longer. "Okay, Susan Fredericks is on the hunt, and from what we saw today, Ayden is her prey. However, that doesn't mean your relationship is doomed. He acted low-key, didn't he?"

"Somewhat. He didn't seem to communicate to Susan that he was pressed for time and needed to get back to work the way he did at the Perkinses'. He lingered."

"I'd linger too if someone kept telling me I was one cloud lower than God," Michelle said.

Leila looked down. She was in no mood for jokes.

"Look," Michelle tried again, "Susan doesn't know you and Ayden are a couple. You've wanted your relationship to remain private. Perhaps you should let her in on it. Then she'll back off."

Leila didn't respond right away. "Why wouldn't Ayden, in some way, inform Susan that he's in a serious relationship and unavailable?"

"Why?" Michelle shot back. "Because he's a man, and men are stupid about these things."

"He had to realize she was coming on to him, right?"

The waitress came with the food. "Can I get you anything else?"

"No, thanks, we're fine," Michelle responded. When the waitress left, she continued. "Bring this up when you speak with him. Don't let it slide. It's much better to be honest with him. Have this discussion before our celebratory dinner on Saturday. Okay?"

"Okay."

❀

The rest of the day at the shop moved all too slowly for Leila. After work, she took refuge on the sofa in her den, mulling over how she'd reveal to Ayden her resentment over the exuberant attention Susan Fredericks had been paying him, and how she found his laid-back response just short of disloyalty.

She questioned her reasonableness. Was she being too hard on Susan? After all, she knew nothing of their relationship. She was recently divorced, and likely lonely and just plain sad; she was seeking companionship. She appeared to be a strong and forward-looking person, but life without a loving companion wouldn't be the choice someone as young as Susan would make. So she'd zeroed in on Ayden, knowing he was unmarried, and was now trying to gain his interest. Nothing out of the ordinary.

But then there was the unnerving flip side. Why hadn't Ayden given Susan Fredericks some meaningful feedback? Why did he continue to let her make overtures? Was he enjoying the pursuit? The attention?

The phone rang and brought Leila into the moment. She caught sight of the time and was surprised it was after seven. She'd been so deep in thought she'd missed dinner. But she ignored her growling tummy for the moment; Ayden was waiting for her to pick up the phone.

"Hello," she answered without emotion.

"Hi, Leila. How was the rest of your day?"

"Fine. And yours?"

"After the Fredericks appointment, I headed to the Perkinses' to finish up and hand them a final bill."

"I'm sure the Perkinses are happy their renovation is completed. I know they're quite satisfied with everything, but it's not easy opening your home to strangers for weeks and sacrificing your privacy. It starts to get old." Leila's didn't deliver her words in her usual upbeat tone, and Ayden picked up on it.

"You don't sound like yourself. What's wrong?"

Leila wasted no time getting to the point. "I know Susan is a very nice woman. Our presentations today made her happy. But didn't you sense she had more on her mind than renovating her new home?"

"Meaning?"

"Ayden, you're a pretty smart guy. You know exactly what I mean."

"You think she was coming on to me?" His words were in the form of a question, but it was clear now, to Leila, that he was quite aware of Susan's behavior.

"Yes." Leila stayed silent, giving him the opportunity to set the direction of their conversation.

"You've got nothing to be jealous about, Leila. I'm in love with you."

"If you truly are, you'll give Susan the feedback she needs so she can conduct herself more appropriately in the future," she said stiffly.

"You know, I seem to have this uncanny effect on women. I don't really understand it," he said lightheartedly.

"That's my guy," Leila said, not amused. "Humor is the best antidote." She waited until her courage level reached maximum. "I'm going to be serious one last time and then we can drop this topic. Susan needs to know where you stand. I know we've discussed keeping our relationship private when we're working with mutual clients, but I'm okay with you being more open in this situation if it helps."

"I'll take care of it."

Leila couldn't help but notice that Ayden's voice had a hint of annoyance in it. "Thanks. You're always so understanding. Now, how shall we handle the sleeping arrangements this weekend?"

"I'll come to you on Friday."

"Wonderful." The enthusiasm returned to her voice. "I'll cook us something new and exciting."

"I love you."

"And I love you."

28

Leila and Michelle sat in the shop office, unpacking new items. "I love these picture frames." Michelle held up a silver frame dusted with multicolored crystals. "They make great gifts, don't you think?"

"Yes, I do. If I remember correctly, I think I had to twist your arm a bit to get you to order them."

"Well, sometimes I need a little coaxing." Michelle began tagging the merchandise. "I'll put the new things out front once I organize the inventory slips in the binder. What are you wearing tonight to our celebratory dinner?"

"I think I'll wear the black knit pantsuit I wore to the Designers' Showhouse opening and jazz it up with some fun jewelry. What about you?"

"I'm thinking of wearing my long brown skirt with the off-the-shoulder top that matches—you know, the outfit I bought when David and I were in Naples last Christmas."

"I remember. It's stunning."

"I'll wear my large amber earrings. How does that sound?"

"You'll look smashing," Leila assured her. "The autumn neutrals always come off so rich and elegant." She was doodling now, but productively, sketching some ideas for the Hunters' den. "I'm glad you made the reservation for eight. We don't have to rush out of here this afternoon."

"Right. We may even be able to take a power nap. David is playing golf this afternoon and may need to recharge. He's really looking forward to meeting Ayden." Michelle hadn't brought Ayden up since their post–Fredericks appointment lunch, but now, it seemed, her curiosity got the best of her. "Did you see Ayden last night?"

"Yes. He's spending the weekend with me. He's out now doing business errands."

"Did you have your talk?"

"Yes. He said he'd take care of it. He admitted that he knew Susan was coming on to him and then joked about it. He did say he loved me again before we hung up."

"Super. Things are back on track." Michelle closed the inventory binder and turned her attention to setting up displays for the new merchandise while Leila continued her sketching.

❀

On the drive home, Leila pondered the evening ahead. Nick and David had been good friends and golf partners. Inevitably, David would find himself comparing Ayden to Nick. She also knew he'd felt protective of her since Nick's death; she hoped he wouldn't interrogate Ayden during their celebratory dinner. David was very personable and funny. If he allowed those qualities to surface, Ayden would feel comfortable.

Ayden's truck was parked in her driveway. She pulled her car in next to it, looking forward to seeing him. In the morning, while she'd readied herself for work, he'd stayed in bed, watching the news. She hadn't had the chance to enjoy breakfast with him. She'd left muffins, coffee, and fruit on the island, along with a loving note wishing him a nice day.

As she came through the garage door into the kitchen, she saw Ayden relaxing on the den sofa, watching a football game. "Hi there." She hung up her jacket and walked over to him.

"Hey," he muttered under his breath. "Yes!" he yelled out when an attempt at a field goal didn't meet with success. He looked up to find Leila staring at him with her hands on her hips. She wanted more of a welcome than he'd just delivered.

He focused his attention on her. "How was your day?"

"Busy. I'm thinking about taking a nap for a half hour or so—you know, to recharge myself for our evening." She looked at Ayden, eagerly awaiting his response.

He stared back at her with his baby blues and finally gave her the response she hoped for: "Sounds like a good idea. I've had a pretty tiring day myself. I think I'll join you." He hopped up, gave her a quick kiss, and, with his arm around her shoulder, accompanied her upstairs.

❁

Ayden had shown no signs of feeling uneasy about spending an evening with Leila's friends. He remained his confident self, which put her, too, at ease.

When they arrived at the café, they found Michelle and David seated in a cozy corner in the back room.

Leila proudly introduced her companion. "David, this is Ayden Doyle."

"Nice to meet you, Ayden." David stood to shake hands. Then he turned to Leila with what she thought was an especially warm smile and gave her a kiss on the cheek. "How's it going, doll?"

"Just fine."

"Good evening, Michelle." Ayden extended his hand to give hers a gentle squeeze.

"Nice to see you again."

Ayden deftly pulled out Leila's chair and seated her. Always the gentleman. If first impressions counted, Ayden had made a positive one.

As they enjoyed their wine and appetizers, Leila looked around at her dinner companions. Everyone wore a smile. David uncorked a bottle of his favorite shiraz and kept their glasses filled. An air of joviality permeated their small corner of the café. The men began a congenial conversation. The celebratory dinner seemed to be going along nicely.

"I hear you're quite an artist," David said to Ayden.

"I like to work with my hands."

"Michelle said the Perkins job showed expert craftsmanship. Top-notch in every way."

"Well, I'm glad everyone was happy with the results. How about you, David? What's your line of work?"

"I'm a CPA, a numbers guy. I hit the links when I want to escape."

"So, you're a golf addict?"

"Do you play?"

"I have, but I really don't have the time to devote to the game."

"If you find some time, give me a call. The Meadows has a really nice course. You'd enjoy playing it."

"Thanks. I'll keep that in mind."

The rest of the evening's conversation went well. Sometimes all four participated in a lively discussion. At other times, the talk was just between the men or between the women. When the old French clock on the wall above their table struck eleven, the four found themselves the only ones left in the dining room.

"I think it's time we headed home." David fought back a yawn.

Leila agreed. "You're right. It's late." She pushed back her chair and stood up. "But we did have fun, right?"

"Absolutely. The food delicious, and the company, the best." Michelle rose and gave her a hug.

The foursome thanked the owner for a wonderful evening and made their way to the parking lot, where they lingered a while longer before saying their good-byes. The sky was clear; the air was crisp.

Moonlight danced across the lush grounds, and the stars twinkled in the sky above. A perfect night for such camaraderie. Ayden held Leila's hand, gently massaging her palm. His touch indicated more pleasure to come once they returned home.

29

Ayden looked across the table at Leila as she gathered the breakfast things together. "I'd love to spend the day with you," he said, "but the Miller project begins tomorrow. I have to get back to the workshop by noon and get things ready." He reached out for Leila's hand and gave it an affectionate squeeze, his reluctance to leave her apparent.

"I understand," Leila said. "I've got things to do as well. I may go over to Hillary's and see how the nursery is coming along. The floors have been refinished, and the painting is almost done."

"I know you'll be a wonderful grandmother, even though you won't look the part."

"Is that a compliment?"

"You bet it is." His boyish grin made a comeback.

She rose to clear their dishes, and Ayden followed her to the sink. Once she had put the dishes down, he wrapped her in his arms and gave her a deep, lingering kiss.

"So, this is my good-bye kiss?" She didn't want him to let go of her.

"Unfortunately." He gave her another quick kiss on the forehead.

Leila walked him to the foyer and retrieved his jacket from the cloak closet. "Don't forget this. It's chilly outside."

"I suppose you'll come out to the Millers' sometime this week?" he inquired as he put on the jacket.

"Yes. I have some things to drop off. I know their faucet sets and shower and tub assembly are in. More should arrive by the end of the week."

"Good. Now I have something to look forward to." With that, he swung his bag over his shoulder, gave her a last kiss, and left.

Leila watched Ayden depart, then returned to the kitchen to finish cleaning up. That's when her thinking started. Their relationship had continued to evolve since their weekend in St. Michaels, but she longed for Ayden to be more than a weekend guest. Why couldn't she have what Michelle and the rest of her married friends had? Now more than ever, she realized how lonely a life she'd led over the past five years. In spite of the fact she and Ayden spoke nightly, she missed him terribly during the week.

Try to be patient. All in good time. Things will work out in the end.

She picked up the phone and dialed Hillary. "Hi, it's Mom. I thought I'd come over and check out the nursery. Maybe the three of us could have dinner together as well."

"That's a wonderful idea, Mom!" Hillary sounded delighted.

"Oh, I'm glad you think so. I'll see you around five. Love you!" Leila sighed with relief. Tonight, she wouldn't have to eat alone.

❁

On Monday, Leila stayed home most of the day and worked on the Hunters' den. Though a small project, it had its challenges. Coming up with fresh and unexpected ideas was one. In the end, she found three new ways to arrange the room; she looked forward to showing Michelle the plans in the morning. Colors, fabrics, and furniture would still require their attention during the coming week.

The next morning, Michelle came in fifteen minutes after Leila. "Good morning," she chirped as she burst into the office. "Sorry I'm a bit late. I stopped at the dry cleaner's."

"Not a problem," Leila said.

Michelle didn't waste time with pleasantries. "David really liked Ayden. I think our couples' dinner was a success."

"I do too. Ayden thought David was a great guy as well. He mentioned he hoped the two of them could get together for golf before the winter sets in."

"That would be so nice. What did the two of you do on Sunday?"

"Ayden went home in the morning to get ready for the Millers. I went to see the nursery and had dinner with Hillary and Chad."

"How did the floor and walls turn out?"

"Just wonderful! The refinished floor has a nice honey-colored stain. The soft aqua on the walls is very soothing and contrasts nicely with the white trim."

"I'm looking forward to seeing it, but I think I'll wait until the furniture and bedding are in place."

Michelle returned to the books for a few minutes. Suddenly, her head snapped up, as if an idea had just struck her. "I'd like to buy something for Hillary and Chad. Any suggestions?"

"I'm sure Hillary has an idea or two. I'll speak with her about it. That's very sweet of you. You're the best."

"By the way," Michelle said, switching tracks, "I'd like to take the morning off on Friday. Would that be a problem?"

"No. What time do you expect to come in?"

"No later than noon, probably earlier. Afterward, you can leave for the Millers', and on your way back, bring lunch. What do you say to that?"

"I say that sounds like a plan, but I'm afraid if I agree to it, I'll be spoiling you," Leila replied playfully.

"Spoil me. I don't mind."

On Thursday evening, Leila had just finished dinner when the phone rang. Caller ID unexpectedly showed Ayden's name. Why so early?

"Hi, beautiful," he greeted her cheerfully. "How's it going?"

"We had a good week. People are gift shopping already."

"That's a good sign, right?"

"Yes. How are things going at the Millers'?"

"Great. Are you coming by tomorrow?"

"In the afternoon. I have some things to drop off—the hardware, the lighting fixture, wallpaper, and accent tiles."

"Good. We'll likely be ready for them by the end of next week." He paused and then, as if the idea had suddenly come to him, asked, "Do you want to meet for a quick lunch tomorrow?"

"Where?"

"The new place in Haverford Square. It's not far from the Millers'. You can swing by their house afterward."

"Okay. I can pick up a sandwich for Michelle while we're there. I promised her I'd bring something back. I can be there by twelve thirty."

"That's good. We can discuss our weekend plans over lunch." Ayden went silent for a moment, then said, "I've really missed you."

"Me too. Get my hello kiss ready."

"Will do."

❁

The next morning, Leila loaded her trunk with the items she wanted to take to the Millers'. She kept things tidy in the shop, hoping to leave as soon as Michelle arrived.

"Good morning," Michelle sang out as she entered the shop. She made her way to the checkout counter, where Leila was furiously moving her pencil on a page in her sketchbook. "I can still say good morning, since it's only eleven. Happy?"

"I'm thrilled." Leila closed her sketchbook. She looked up and discovered her friend wearing a slightly different hairstyle than usual. "Say, your hair looks great. Did you change the color?"

"I trimmed and layered the mop and put in some red highlights. I feel rejuvenated."

"That's good; you'll need a burst of energy since you'll be alone for a couple of hours. I think you'll be busy."

"Let's hope so."

"I'll bring back a sandwich for you. Ayden and I are meeting up for a quick lunch at that new place in Haverford Square."

"Oooh, I like the chicken salad there. How about that on whole wheat and a Diet Coke? When do you think you'll be back?"

"Since I'm getting an earlier start than I thought, I should be back no later than two. Can you hold out until then?"

"Absolutely. I had a late breakfast."

After wrapping things up, Leila started out for her lunch date. She texted Ayden to let him know she'd be arriving around noon, a half hour earlier than expected, but told him not to rush. She filled with anticipation, imagining his warm hello kiss and the feel of his muscular arms around her. A tingling sensation spread through her body. Even though she'd likely be the first to arrive, she wanted to get there quickly—all the better to enjoy watching him approach.

❁

Leila felt fortunate to get a parking spot directly in front of the restaurant when she zipped into Haverford Square. As she made her way into the café, she removed her sunglasses and took a few moments to adjust to the softer interior light.

It was a busy day. All the servers' activities made it difficult to see which tables, if any, were available. She hoped Ayden would arrive soon. In the meantime, she decided to take a seat on the bench near the entrance so she could look out for him.

Once situated, she picked up a menu on the table beside her and began looking at the items under the lunch specials. Then it happened. She glanced up from the menu, and through a clearing in the crowd she saw Susan Fredericks seated across from Ayden at a small two-seater table in the opposite corner.

POW! She felt as if a lightning bolt had struck her. Large papers, sprawled across the tabletop, became displaced as they moved them about, pointing to specific spots vital to their conversation. Leila saw Susan throw up her hands and nod enthusiastically, a broad smile brightening her face. Ayden laughed in response to something she said. He reached out and squeezed her arm with one hand, and with the other he pointed to something on one of the papers that lay between them. He angled it a bit so she could see more easily.

What was he doing here with Susan Fredericks? Why did it seem they were having such a good time together? She made the decision to stay where she was and observe the two of them. Ayden glanced at his watch at least twice. Was he worried she'd arrive too soon and spoil their fun? Her heart began to beat a mile a minute.

Five minutes later, Ayden pointed to his watch and began rolling up the sheets and placing them in tubes propped up against the wall behind him. Susan took her handbag and retrieved a pair of sunglasses and car keys. She stood up. Ayden did as well. Susan embraced him, wrapped her arms around his waist, and moved her lips to his. Leila felt ill.

When they finally stood apart, Leila saw Susan mouth the words, "Thank you." Ayden took his seat once again. Susan put on her sunglasses and sped toward the door. Leila raised the menu in front of her face, hoping Susan wouldn't catch sight of her as she went out. She didn't. Through the front window, she saw Susan walking away toward the parking lot.

Leila glanced at her watch. It was twelve twenty. She decided to sit on the bench a few minutes longer before she met Ayden. She needed time to regroup—time to think of how she'd handle what she saw and the hurt that had found its mark.

Just a few minutes shy of twelve thirty, Leila approached Ayden's table. Quietly, she slipped into the seat formerly occupied by Susan Fredericks and looked directly at him, forcing a pleasant smile.

Ayden immediately looked up and smiled at her. "Hi! Right on time." He handed her one of the menus to browse. "Let me know what you want and I'll order for us. It's busy in here. I think I'm going to have the grilled vegetable sandwich."

Leila realized he hadn't seen her text. She questioned whether she could manage to eat anything after what she'd witnessed.

"Please order me the same thing you're having, and also a chicken salad sandwich on wheat bread to take to Michelle."

"What would you like to drink?"

"I'd like a Diet Coke. Order another to-go for Michelle."

"Fine. I'll be right back."

She watched him walk over to the self-serve counter to place their order. He returned, his boyish smile gracing his face. He sported a look of innocence.

"We're number ten, so it may be a couple minutes. Meanwhile, I have that hello kiss for you." He gently lifted her chin and pressed his warm lips to hers. It was a long kiss—longer than the one Susan had given him. Was his public display of affection prompted by a guilty conscience?

"You're so good at that," Leila said once Ayden took his seat.

"I try."

Leila remained in deep thought for a moment. She wanted to stay calm and in control. "How was your morning?"

"Things went well at the Millers'. I left two men to finish putting up the new wallboard. This afternoon I'll begin to prepare the floor for the tile on Monday. What about your morning?"

"Things were slow, but I expect this afternoon to be much busier. I need to get back to the shop as soon as possible." Leila looked at the tubes resting against the wall behind Ayden. "Are those your tubes?"

"Yes. Don't let me forget them. I've been working on Susan Fredericks's main floor. She's ready to finalize her decisions and schedule a starting date."

"That's wonderful," Leila said with feigned cheer. Inside, her blood boiled. Ayden wasn't being forthright. He was avoiding telling her about his meeting with Susan Fredericks—for obvious reasons.

"Number ten," the manager called out.

Ayden rose. When Leila moved as if to help him, he waved her back into her seat. "Sit, Leila. I can handle things."

Leila knew he could. She watched him closely as he gathered up all the items, balancing them one on top of the other with his usual finesse.

"Here we go," he said upon his return. "Michelle's lunch is in the bag."

He eagerly began eating. Leila nibbled away at hers, forcing down bites. Should she be direct with him? Overlooking things would only eat away at her.

She remained cool for a while. After all, she didn't want to turn things upside down before he had a chance to finish his lunch. *That would be so inconsiderate*, she thought sarcastically.

"Aren't you hungry?" he finally asked. "You've barely touched your sandwich. I think it's good."

"I'm hungry but not famished. I agree, though, it's very tasty."

"What about our weekend? I guess I'll come to you." He waited for her to confirm the arrangement.

"Maybe we should be creative. Let me think on this a while longer. Before I leave the Millers', I'll have something interesting to share."

Ayden's wonderfully hypnotic blue eyes studied her face for a few seconds. "I do like surprises." A smile shot across his face.

If he only knew what she was thinking, he'd be totally surprised. She was seriously considering not spending the weekend with him. She needed time to think. Why hadn't he admitted to meeting with Susan? Why had he allowed her to embrace him, to kiss him? All kinds of thoughts and emotions surged through her mind, but she made every effort to appear composed.

As soon as Ayden finished his sandwich, she suggested they get going.

"Are you done?" His tone suggested disbelief. "You have another half to go."

"I'm happy. I'm anxious to get to the Millers' and back to the shop." Leila stood up and took out her keys. Ayden stood just behind her. "Don't forget your tubes," she dutifully reminded him.

He placed the tubes under one arm, slipped the other around her waist, and escorted her out of the restaurant. "I see you found a great parking spot," he said, immediately spotting her car. "I'm all the way in the back of the main lot. Wait for me. We'll drive there together."

Leila saw Ayden coming and let him pass. Then she pulled out directly behind him. The tears she'd fought back while in the restaurant began to roll down her cheeks. She knew she'd need to fix her makeup before she faced him again; for now, though, she was entitled to a good five-minute cry.

❀

Ayden stopped to talk to one of his crew as soon as they arrived at the Millers'. Leila took advantage of this delay and powdered her face and redid her lipstick. She checked in her rearview mirror. Though her eyes were wet and slightly pink, she doubted Ayden would notice anything unusual.

A tap on her window startled her. She turned to find Ayden smiling at her.

"Pop your trunk for me. I'll unload the Millers' things, and then we can check out the project."

Leila watched while Ayden and one of his men carefully moved the products from her trunk to the Millers' garage. Soon thereafter, she followed Ayden into the house. Both John and Madeline were at work, so she didn't have to worry about niceties.

Ayden was clearly eager to show her his accomplishments: he climbed the stairs two steps at a time. Leila had no doubt she'd be impressed. His workmanship always surpassed that of any other craftsman she knew.

She delighted in what she found in the new master bath. "It's wonderfully transformed," she said, spinning around to take it all in. "The ceiling height makes such a difference, just as it did for the Perkinses. And the new window—now there's a view of their lovely backyard."

Ayden seemed to revel in her appreciation of his work. "I'm pleased with the way things are coming along."

Leila walked the perimeter of the room, noting the elements that made the project especially remarkable: the reconfiguration of the space to allow for a vanity with his-and-her sinks, an enlarged linen closet, and an alcove for a new soaking tub. Her hurt and disappointment momentarily disappeared—until she came full circle and faced Ayden once again.

"Walk me out?" she asked in a soft voice, her eyes staring into his. She turned, and he followed.

When they reached her car, she leaned against it. She needed something rock solid to support her while she confronted her lover.

"I need to discuss something with you."

He came close. "Why do you look so serious all of a sudden? You're not ill, are you?" A deep look of concern spread across his face.

"Did you get my text message this morning? I sent it around eleven thirty."

"I turned my phone off last night and forgot to reactivate it this morning. Let's see." He reached into his pants pocket, pulled out his phone, and turned it on. "It's here. You thought you'd get to Haverford Square early, but you didn't."

"But I did. At first, I didn't see you were there. I sat on the bench near the front door and waited for you. Then I saw something disturbing.

"What are you talking about?" He became impatient.

"I saw Susan Fredericks and you, together, seated at the table where we had lunch. You pointed to your watch. She rose from her seat. You rose from yours. She approached you. She hugged you. She gave you a long kiss on your lips." Leila went silent. She simply looked into the face of the man she loved and hoped he'd say something that would put her worst fears to rest.

Ayden's eyebrows drew together. "Okay. I'll explain. I know you don't like the way she acts with me, so I didn't tell you about meeting her to discuss concerns she had with her project. She called me on Wednesday. For convenience's sake, I arranged a meeting at the café since I had to be at the Millers' after. I'm sorry I didn't mention it."

Leila continued to look at Ayden, not saying a word.

He finally understood his explanation had not appeased her. "The hug and kiss were just her way of thanking me. You obviously saw I didn't reciprocate."

"What I saw was you readily accepting her warm embrace and tender kiss."

"Are you reprimanding me, Leila?" He sounded annoyed.

"I'm hurt, terribly hurt, that you would allow another woman to engage you in such intimate behavior."

"You needn't be hurt." He leaned in very close and placed his hands on the roof of her car, encircling her. "I'm in love with *you*," he said in a whisper.

His closeness was almost unbearable. She wanted to kiss him. She wanted his arms to envelop her. "I know you have feelings for me." Her voice was low and soft. "I also believe you enjoy the attention other women give you, and you encourage rather than discourage it. That belief is unsettling and makes me feel inadequate."

"You're blowing this whole thing out of proportion. I'll set Susan Fredericks straight when I'm with her again. I promise." He backed away, as if he knew a kiss at this time wouldn't fix things. "We'll talk later. I need to get back to work."

"Let's take a break tonight," Leila suggested. She realized her plan could backfire. But she needed to communicate that she simply wouldn't—couldn't—ignore what she'd seen. Furthermore, she needed assurance that she was the only woman who mattered to him.

Ayden's baby blues opened wide. She'd obviously hurt him, and his hurt quickly turned to anger. "You don't want to be with me tonight? Is that what you're saying?" The intensity in his voice escalated.

"I want to be with you tonight more than ever. I'm madly in love with you, and you know it. I just think we need time to reflect on what's happened today."

"Fine. I'll call you tomorrow." He turned away and walked back into the house.

This was the first time Ayden had lost his cool demeanor in front of her. Had she done the right thing or a very stupid thing?

❁

Leila amazed herself. She returned to the shop without having an accident in spite of the continuous stream of tears blurring her vision. She began doubting her decision to break that night's plans with Ayden. Was she being childish or principled? If she called him and told him she'd changed her mind, she might appear weak. She'd worked on being strong and independent for over five years, and she wasn't about to regress. Perhaps Michelle would see things more clearly and provide some needed direction.

Michelle was handing a customer a wrapped gift as Leila entered the shop. "Please stop in again, Mary. Let me know how your sister likes her birthday present."

"Will do, Michelle. Thanks again." The smartly dressed customer exchanged hellos with Leila, then exited.

"Where have you been? I'm starving. It's almost three," Michelle blurted out when the door closed. She approached Leila and took the lunch bag from her hand—then looked up and saw the expression on her friend's face. "Oh, my, something's happened. Come in the back with me immediately." She grabbed Leila's arm and pulled her into the office.

Once they were both seated, she charged in. "What? What? Out with it!" she commanded.

In a very soft voice, fighting back a massive urge to cry, Leila explained what she'd observed between Susan Fredericks and Ayden. Michelle gobbled down her sandwich and soda while she listened intently to the story. After Leila finished, both women sat in silence for a few moments.

"Well, here's my take on things," Michelle said, her tone thoughtful. "I believe Ayden loves you. I observed how he acted toward you during our dinner last Saturday. He appeared to be a man in love, and he behaved like a man in love. You can rest assured that his feelings are genuine. On the other hand, he has been a womanizer for many years. It's in his blood. Now and then, he seems to need a fix. Hopefully, he can work this out of his system."

"Am I supposed to accept such behavior? Allow him to treat me and our relationship with disrespect?" Leila's voice had grown as loud as it could go.

"How did you handle your response?"

"After I surveyed the Miller project, I asked him to walk me to the car. Then I confronted him. He hadn't read my text message. He didn't expect me until twelve thirty, so he continued with Susan until twelve twenty or so, bringing their discussion to a close before he thought I'd arrive. He said he didn't mention a meeting with her because he knew I didn't like the way she acted toward him."

"Did he say anything else?"

"That he loves me. That Susan Fredericks just thanked him in her own way. That I was blowing things out of proportion." Leila let out a sob.

"Anything else?"

"He became annoyed and defensive and not sure of what to say except that he needed to return to work."

Michelle pushed on; she knew Leila too well. "What aren't you telling me?"

"I told him I thought we shouldn't see each other this evening— that we should reflect on this incident and revisit it tomorrow. That made him very angry. I suppose he thought I was trying to punish him. He walked away and said he'd call me tomorrow." Leila looked down and shook her head. "I was so hurt. My judgment might have been impaired."

Michelle rose from her seat and put her arms around Leila. "I know, I know. You thought he'd have put Susan in her place by now. But he didn't. He made a mistake, a severe error in judgment." Michelle pulled her chair right up to Leila and took hold of both her hands. "You need to work through this, my friend. You need to forgive him. Maybe not seeing each other tonight will do you both some good. You and Ayden will realize what you're missing and how important you've become to each other."

"I feel stupid and childish for pushing him away. What if he doesn't call tomorrow?"

"You could send him a text."

"And say what?"

"Something simple, short, to the point."

Leila took out her phone and typed, "*I miss and love you. See you tomorrow.*"

"Perfect," Michelle assured her.

30

Leila moped around all evening. She continually checked her cell phone, hoping there would be a text message from Ayden. Nothing. She lifted the telephone several times because she thought she heard it ring, only to discover it was her wishful thinking. Finally, she decided to check in with Drew.

Voice mail.

"Drew, it's Mom. Nothing important. I was just calling to see about your Thanksgiving travel plans. Get back to me when you can."

At nine, she called it a night and locked up. She turned down the bed and turned on the television. The flat-screen would be her company. Her empty bed would make her feel lonely and disconsolate. Would a bath help?

She gave up after twenty minutes. She fell asleep with the television on and didn't awake until her alarm went off.

❀

She met Michelle in the parking lot just before ten.

"I come bearing gifts," Michelle announced. She had a picnic basket on her arm filled with comfort food: fresh-brewed coffee, cinnamon-apple muffins, and iced brownies.

"What have you done?" Leila feigned horror.

"We need cheering up. Likely, our day will be busy. I thought we should start it off with comforting and yummy edibles."

"You left out 'terribly fattening,' wouldn't you say?"

"We'll work it off."

They indulged themselves for nearly thirty minutes before the customers began streaming in, sometimes in groups of two and three. The robust sales excited Michelle, the overseer of the bottom line. The constant activity helped Leila forget Ayden for a while but eventually exhausted her.

"I need to sit down and recharge," she said, touching Michelle on the shoulder, when the shop finally emptied at twelve thirty. "I'm going in the back."

Michelle nodded. "I'll join you in a few minutes. I just want to straighten up before the next wave begins."

Leila heard Michelle running the vacuum for a while. Then the noise cut off, and a few minutes later she entered the office, a delighted expression on her face. "Guess what?"

"What? Did you make another sale?"

"No, nothing like that." She paused but soon blurted out the news: "Ayden is waiting in the parking lot to speak with you. Check out your makeup and then wow him."

"I didn't even know he knew where our shop was." Leila tore into her handbag and pulled out her cosmetics case. A bit of powder and lipstick did the trick. Her face flushed in anticipation of seeing him. Luckily, she'd fixed her hair the way he liked: up, with a few wavy tendrils brushing her cheek.

"Go! Go!" Michelle urged. "I'll take care of things. Take as long as you need."

Leila rose, slipped into her heels, and headed out.

Her heart began to thump once she caught sight of him. There he stood, in all his magnificence, leaning against the side of his sports car. Sunglasses shielded his eyes from the afternoon sun, hiding his full expression.

She walked right up to him, taking bold, confident strides. "Hello," she said, her voice just above a whisper.

"Hi, yourself." He removed his sunglasses and stared at her with his wonderful eyes. "Can we talk?"

"Sure."

"I'm sorry I hurt you. I mismanaged things. I'll do better."

What could she say to that? The man was taking responsibility—and doing so with humility. She'd expected there to be more discussion, a bit of arguing, and then the customary makeup words, followed by a kiss or two. Now her response needed to be just right.

"Thank you for those caring words," she said. "I love you and would so much like you to give me one of those fabulous kisses I've come to adore." She moved closer and put her arms around his neck—and he did as she asked, and then some. More than ever before, she felt his kiss revealed the depth of the feelings he had for her.

"I love you," he murmured. "There's no one else but you. You got me."

"Well, I'm glad." Her arms remained around his neck and she pressed against his body, enjoying the warmth his arms provided as they held her close to him. "What plans do you have in mind for tonight?"

"I'll meet you at your house after work. We can go from there."

"Okay. I'll be home by five thirty."

He gave her one last kiss, pulled away, donned his sexy sunglasses, and got into his car. She turned toward the shop, trying to maintain her composure, as he drove away. The sweet words comprising his apology reverberated in her head and prompted tears to fall.

"What happened?" Michelle asked, her face full of concern, when Leila stepped back into the shop with red eyes. The tapping of her foot on the floor indicated her impatience.

"He apologized," Leila said. "He said he was sorry he hurt me, he mismanaged things, and he'd do better. He seemed totally sincere and humble. I could ask for nothing more."

"How sweet." Ever the romantic, Michelle teared up a bit as well. "This calls for a celebration. Let's have brownies. All's right with your world."

"It seems that way." Leila sighed and relaxed for the first time since the previous afternoon.

❀

Leila pulled into her driveway alongside Ayden's car. He sat in the driver's seat, talking on his cell phone. Leila could tell from the notes he was jotting down that the call was business-related. She caught his eye, gave him a smile and a wave, and pulled her car into the garage.

As she closed the car door, she felt Ayden's arms encircle her waist. He leaned in close and said softly in her left ear, "Good evening, Ms. Brandt. I've been waiting for you. I'd like to take you to dinner."

Leila turned and put her arms around Ayden's neck, looking into his dreamy eyes. "That's very nice of you, Mr. Doyle. Where would you like to go?"

"How about that nice Italian restaurant we went to when we first started to see each other?"

"Perfect. Just give me a couple of minutes and I'll be ready."

"I'll wait for you here."

Leila hurried into the house. She unloaded her materials from work, took the cosmetics case from her handbag, and scurried into the powder room to freshen up. In less than ten minutes, she and Ayden were on their way.

❀

The table next to the window overlooking the garden was available, so the maître d' accommodated them by seating them there. As before, Alberto waited on them.

"Good evening," he said with a slight bow. "I believe you have dined with us before?"

"Yes," Ayden replied. "We're back because we thoroughly enjoyed our evening."

"That's so nice to hear. Here are the menus. No specials tonight, but there's much to choose from, as you know. Can I get you something to drink while you're deciding?"

Ayden looked at Leila. "I'll have a glass of chardonnay, please."

"I'll have the same."

"I'll be back shortly," Alberto said. He gave them a wink and swept out of sight.

"How did your day go?" Ayden began to check out the menu.

Things appeared to be back on track. Leila was happy to keep them that way. "Busy," she said. "People are gearing up for Thanksgiving. I can't believe the holiday season begins in less than two weeks."

Ayden made no comment regarding the upcoming holiday, which Leila found odd. She decided to do some investigating.

"Have you made plans for Thanksgiving?"

"I usually spend Thanksgiving at my sister's house. She picks up my parents and brings them there so they can see everyone."

"I'm the head chef for my family, but I had a thought."

Ayden looked up from his menu. "A thought?"

"What would you think if I made dinner on Saturday of Thanksgiving weekend for my kids and for you, Daniel, and his girlfriend? I thought it might be time for us to start sharing occasions with the important people in our lives."

Ayden didn't rush in with a positive response; he took his time to think things over. Perhaps he wasn't ready to include family in their relationship. That notion bothered her. They had known each other for eight months and had dated seriously for five. Spending time with each other's loved ones seemed like a natural progression.

"It's a nice thought," he finally said. "I don't want you to go to a lot of trouble."

"It's no trouble. You know I enjoy cooking."

"I'll ask Daniel if he's available and let you know." Ayden returned to the menu.

Leila was gearing herself up to challenge Ayden regarding their relationship and how family and friends fit into the scheme of things when Alberto returned with the wine and a basket of bread. "Have you decided?" he asked, looking in Leila's direction.

"I think I'll have the chicken marsala."

"I'll go with the veal Parmesan. Thanks." Ayden handed Alberto the menus. When they were alone again, he lifted his wine glass for a toast. "Here's to the sexiest girl I know."

Another Ayden zinger. Leila needed to return the serve. "That's very nice. Are you hoping to score tonight?" She paired her question with a flirtatious smile.

Ayden appeared taken aback by her remark, but he had a stinging comeback: "Am I to be punished, or am I forgiven?"

Enough of this verbal jousting. "You're loved and forgiven." She reached for his hand and gave it a squeeze. "Let's stay on track for a moment. We both have families. We need to include them in our future. Don't you want to introduce me to your family?"

"They can be very intrusive," he said, frowning. "I'm not sure you'd appreciate them."

"I think I can handle them with grace and diplomacy." She paused for a moment, took a sip of wine, and followed up with a piece of bread. She needed to set the stage for her next question. "I have a very nice family. Are you interested in spending time with them, getting to know them, and allowing them to know you?"

"I guess so."

That was it? That was his answer? Leila started to squirm inside. She could push him into an argument about the future of their relationship, but she didn't want a repeat of the day before. "I love you. I'm proud of you. I know my kids and other family members would welcome you with open arms. What concerns you?"

"Nothing. I just like having you all to myself."

"That's unrealistic. It can't be like that all the time." A disturbing idea crossed her mind. She had to share it. "I told you before, I'm not looking for marriage, just commitment—a life partner. I thought we settled that early on."

Their dinners arrived before Ayden could respond. "Anything else?" Alberto inquired.

Ayden shook his head. "I think we're fine. Thanks."

"Good. Please enjoy."

They began their dinners in silence. Leila hoped Ayden would continue the conversation. Finally, he did.

"I want to be there for you. I'll do my best to make you happy."

"Thank you. Please ask Daniel about the dinner, then. Okay?"

"Will do."

The dinner conversation became more uplifting as they talked about going away between Christmas and New Year's, perhaps to St. Michaels; a possible new client referred by the Millers; and a dinner date with Mark and Nancy Dawson.

"I'd enjoy spending time with your friends," Leila said, placing her hand on top of Ayden's. "Let's try for early December."

❀

Leila sat silent on the ride home, thinking about Ayden's hesitation to include family in their future plans. Was this a red flag that meant their relationship was at risk?

She'd bury her concerns, at least for tonight. Tonight would be filled with passion.

Leila emerged from the master bath wearing a sheer black nightgown Ayden had given her. He'd already turned down the bed and positioned himself in it. The bedcovers were pulled slightly over his legs, so part of his white pajama bottoms still showed.

With a cute smile on his face, he lifted the duvet so Leila could scoot in and find her place next to him. "You know," he said in a soft but lighthearted tone, "makeup sex is generally considered the best kind."

"Really?" She nuzzled closer to him. "I'll be interested in discovering if that's just an old wives' tale or actually the case."

He kissed her gently on the neck. She wrapped her arms around him and pulled him closer yet, kissing him passionately on the lips. His hands caressed her breasts. She murmured with pleasure. Soon their legs became intertwined, and they moved against each other.

"I love you," Ayden said softly.

"I know," she whispered.

31

"Good morning," Michelle said brightly when Leila came in Monday morning. "We've something to discuss regarding Susan Fredericks."

"What?"

"She left a message saying she's ready to meet with us. She's made all of her decisions and has a few questions. She'd like to keep the samples of what she's selected and return the rest of the materials. Do we meet with her as a team, or do I go solo?"

"Did she give you an idea of when she'd like to meet?" Leila injected professionalism into her voice and posture.

"She'd prefer a morning this week rather than next Monday, since Thanksgiving is next week. She wants to get ready for the holiday."

"I'll mind the shop and you go. It's best, don't you think?"

"Absolutely."

❁

Leila was flipping through an art catalogue when Michelle came back from her meeting with Susan the next day around noon.

"Guess what?" Michelle looked like an adolescent who was about to share the most secret of all secrets. "Ayden told Susan he's involved with a woman, but he didn't elaborate."

"She told you that?" Leila asked in disbelief.

"Well, I had to set her up somewhat, but she did ask me if I knew who Ayden's girlfriend is."

"No, she didn't." Leila grimaced. "What did you say?"

"I told her I certainly couldn't elaborate either, but the woman is quite lovely. That was that."

"Ayden did as I asked. That's comforting. Thanks, Michelle."

A sense of relief washed over Leila. Ayden had lived up to his word. Their relationship seemed to be on more solid ground. Her thoughts shifted to the family dinner she had suggested. If that worked out, Ayden would be ready to fill in for Nick on yet another level.

The garage door had just closed when Leila heard her phone ringing. She picked up the phone in the kitchen and discovered Drew on the other end, calling about Thanksgiving weekend.

"You've decided to drive in? When?"

"I'm planning to leave on Tuesday after work. That should get me in around midnight. Is that too late, Mom?"

"No. You know your mother is a night owl." Leila chuckled. "Why don't you call me from the road and let me know your progress?"

"Sure. What are the plans for the weekend?"

"I'll make Thanksgiving dinner. Your grandparents, Aunt Caroline, your sister and Chad, and Chad's parents will be here. I'm not sure about your cousins."

"What about Ayden?"

"No, he'll be with his family—but maybe on Saturday he'll join us for dinner. I'll let you know in enough time for you to make other plans if that doesn't work out."

Drew took on the role of investigator-protector. "Have you been seeing anyone else?"

"No." Leila paused for a moment to think. "Sweetheart, is there a reason you ask?"

"I'm sorry. I didn't mean to sound like an interrogator. I'm just looking out for Nick's girl."

The way Drew phrased his apology made Leila quiver. When Nick died, Drew had just been finishing up his engineering studies. She'd continued to provide parental guidance then—ask the questions that needed to be asked, set limits, and support her son until he landed a job. Now a role reversal of some kind seemed to be in progress.

"I see," she said slowly. "Well, don't worry, dear. I'm doing a pretty good job of looking out for myself. I love you, and I can't wait to see you. Please drive carefully."

"I will. Talk to you soon. Bye."

Leila set down her handbag and briefcase, hung up her coat, and went into the den, where she took a seat in Nick's chair—her second-favorite place in the house when she needed to think. Apparently, Drew didn't share the same enthusiasm as his sister when it came to Ayden. Had he picked up on something Leila had missed? Drew and Ayden's brief encounter that night in the kitchen had seemed to go well, but she'd sensed some hostility in her son's voice just now.

Perfectly natural. That will change. Ayden and Drew just need to get to know each other.

The family dinner she wanted to arrange took on a new urgency.

❁

On Friday, Leila rushed home from work to get dinner ready. She hadn't seen Ayden since Sunday, and she missed him terribly. He'd been busy finishing up the Miller project. She'd experienced a demanding week as well, and she looked forward to a quiet weekend with him before the demands of the Thanksgiving holiday intruded. Though she derived pleasure from cooking for her family and bringing them together to celebrate the many blessings they enjoyed, she knew her physical and emotional stamina would be tested by the following week. She and Ayden would spend time apart. With Drew home, she didn't feel comfortable having her lover stay with her. Her motherly instincts were pitted against her need for Ayden.

The doorbell rang. She hurried to let Ayden in, anxious for her hello kiss.

"Hi, beautiful." Ayden threw his belongings on the floor and wrapped his arms around her, giving her exactly what she wanted: an enthusiastic kiss. "I missed you."

"I missed you too."

He reached for his overnight bag and pulled out a bottle of wine. "May I offer my beautiful hostess a glass of wine?" He wore the grin she'd come to love so much.

They walked into the kitchen arm in arm. He opened the wine and took glasses from the cabinet. Leila tossed the salad she'd planned for the first course and brought a basket of their favorite Italian bread to the table. She dimmed the lights and lit tea candles to create a relaxing atmosphere.

"What did you cook up this evening?" His curiosity didn't stop him from tackling his salad.

Leila looked at him. He appeared especially handsome in the candlelight. How she adored him! "A small filet roast, baby potatoes, and wonderful-looking green beans from the farmers market."

"Perfect!"

Once everything was on the table, they set about enjoying their meal and each other. Leila was about to turn her attention to readying the coffee and dessert when she noticed Ayden eyeing the roast remaining on the serving dish.

"Would you like a bit more?"

"As a matter of fact, I'd like a bit more of everything."

"You don't have to do that." She smiled, pleased and surprised at the same time.

"Do what?"

"Overreact to my cooking."

"Believe me. I'm not doing any such thing. Everything is delicious, and I'm especially hungry this evening."

"I see. An appetite for all things pleasurable is a very attractive trait in a man."

Ayden gazed at Leila with his hypnotic eyes. He reached out for her hand and gently rubbed the inside of her wrist. His soft touch aroused her. She wondered whether he could tell how much. She took a sip of wine and continued to enjoy his face while he finished his dinner. There seemed to be no need for conversation. All they had to say passed through the way they looked at or touched each other.

Toward the end of the meal, Ayden refilled his wine glass and sat back in his chair. "I spoke with Daniel about that dinner next weekend." He glanced away before delivering the bad news. "He and Isabella are going to St. Michaels, leaving on Friday for a getaway they planned weeks ago."

Leila felt a tightening in her throat. Though terribly disappointed, she made light of it. "Maybe we'll be able to do something with our kids between Christmas and New Year's."

Ayden took a long sip of wine before placing his glass back on the table. His face took on a serious look. "Let's not rush into this, Leila. I think it's best we take the family introductions gradually and casually. We need to be realistic. Remember the TV show *The Brady Bunch*? That's not going to happen here. I'm sorry, but that's the way it is."

Leila sat quiet, keeping her eyes on Ayden. She would stay strong and think things over before responding. The man who sat across from her had completely captured her heart and soul. He surfaced in her daily thoughts and nightly dreams. When they were apart, she spent her time summoning forth all the memories of him she could to fill the void his absence created. How could she convince him that their life together would be richer and more satisfying if others they loved shared in their happiness?

Baby steps were needed. Pushing him too hard would likely be disastrous for their relationship. She'd already lost a man she loved deeply. She didn't want to experience that anguish again. On the other hand, would her beloved Ayden ever live up to her expectations when it came to family?

"I understand." Her response seemed simple, but for her, it carried many layers. She rose from her seat and sat on Ayden's lap. She put her arms around him and kissed his warm lips, savoring every second. "Interested in coffee and dessert?"

"Yes, but you're all I really need."

She gave him another kiss. "Go relax in the den. I'll bring it in there."

Ayden settled himself in Nick's chair while Leila straightened up, brewed the coffee, and warmed the apple pie she'd baked earlier. She loaded everything on a tray and set the dinner's finale on the ottoman in the den.

Ayden stopped channel surfing when dessert arrived. "Warm pie à la mode," he exclaimed. "You know that's my favorite dessert."

"I know. It's what you ordered on our first date."

"If I recall correctly, you enjoyed it as much as I did."

"I enjoyed everything about our first date," she said definitively. She nestled into the corner of the sofa. "See if you can find us a movie."

Leila nodded when Ayden settled on a romantic comedy featured on the Hallmark Channel. She appreciated his willingness to take on a chick flick. After the movie ended, he put on the news and joined Leila on the sofa.

"I don't want you to cook tomorrow. Tell me what you think of this plan: we can go to the mall, take care of some shopping, and have dinner at the grill there."

"I'm fine with that. I'll just need a few minutes to change from my work clothes. I could be ready around—"

Suddenly, Ayden's lips were on hers, his mouth open and warm, his tongue probing, ending all conversation. With one deft pinch of the clasp on her bra, her breasts tumbled into his expert hands, and soon she felt the button of her jeans give way. His fingers, sure and purposeful, moved gently down her belly and slipped beneath the elastic of her panties, caressing her until he settled between her legs. Leila moved in response to his touch, moaning with pleasure. Her loins were on fire. As Ayden guided both of them to the floor, Leila felt as though she were being transported on a cloud. He undressed her slowly, showering her breasts with delicate kisses and her nipples with tender nibbles. Shudders of pleasure rippled through her body. His jeans were on the floor now, and she reached for him, the familiar hardness. She longed to feel him inside her. He began tentatively, to be sure she was ready for him. Soon he held her close, his thighs against hers, and with deliberate motion pressed them toward ecstasy. Their abandon moved them and all that was in their wake. Faint tinkling sounds, like those of a porch chime moved by a soft wind, emanated rhythmically from the chorus of dishes and silverware resting on the tray next to them.

They finally slid apart and fell into one another's arms, their bodies glistening, and the air redolent with the scent of their passion.

"Leila . . ."

"No, be quiet," she murmured.

"I love you."

Without another word, the lovers rose and, hand in hand, went to the bedroom. There they fell asleep, Leila's head on Ayden's chest, until their passion renewed as the first rays of sunlight peeked through the foliage outside the bedroom window.

32

On Tuesday morning, Leila discovered Michelle up to her elbows in ribbons, assembling hostess gifts for the Thanksgiving holiday. A production line had been arranged on the gift-wrap counter—tissue, cellophane wrap, ribbons, and gold and silver containers, all within easy reach.

"Good morning," Michelle said with her usual cheerfulness. "I'd appreciate some help."

"Of course. I'll be back in a flash." Leila dashed off to the office to unload her handbag and briefcase.

Once she returned, Michelle explained her method.

"I've organized three collections: kitchen-oriented; spa package; and my favorite, assorted chocolates."

Leila looked admiringly at her partner's work. "You're definitely the brains behind this business," she teased as she plunged into the fray.

"So, out with it. Tell me about your weekend," Michelle said over the crinkling of the gift wrap. "Details!"

"Wonderfully romantic," Leila said coyly. "We stayed in Friday night, went shopping Saturday, and then had dinner at the grill in the mall. Ayden left around noon on Sunday, since we both had things to do."

"That's nice." Michelle proceeded with caution. "And how are you handling the upcoming holiday weekend?"

"Ayden will be with his family on Thursday. We haven't made other plans as of yet." Leila's voice lost its previous bounce.

"Something's wrong," Michelle said. "One minute you sound up and the next minute you sound exactly the opposite. What is it?"

"I don't know. It's just my mood." Leila continued to work on the packages, but her ability to hold in her worries only lasted a few minutes. "Michelle, can I run something by you?"

"Absolutely."

"I know Ayden cares for me. He devotes his weekends to me. He takes me to nice restaurants. When we meet up with friends, we have a wonderful time. Our lovemaking is fantastic. The chemistry between us is quite powerful."

"But?"

"But he avoids anything to do with family, his or mine. He doesn't seem interested in knowing my kids. He doesn't care to introduce his son to Hillary, Chad, or Drew. What will happen when the baby is here? He's shown no interest in introducing me to his parents or his siblings. This is worrisome. I'm crazy about him, but I still need a meaningful life—one that includes family and friends."

Michelle pursed her lips, as if weighing the information, then said, "Look. I happen to want the best for you. I said months ago that Nick would be a hard act to follow. He adored you and his family. He loved to play golf with the guys and entertain friends at home. And he was great-looking: tall, handsome, distinguished. He always reminded me of Tom Selleck."

"Really?" Leila sighed as memories took over. "I miss him—miss the life we had together. In many ways, Ayden has taken over for Nick. He certainly has made me feel loved and desired."

Michelle walked over to Leila and gave her a warm, sisterly embrace. "Let's take a short break. Come sit with me on the bench."

They sat quietly for a minute or two, both looking through the front windows at the sunny day and the colorful foliage on the trees across the street.

"I like Ayden," Michelle said. "I've nothing bad to say about him.

He treats you well, and I know he cares deeply for you. He's at his happiest when spending time with just you. He handles himself well when he's with other people, but he's not as gregarious as Nick was. That's okay."

"But will I find myself going it alone when holidays come around or when family obligations arise? Will I ever become part of his family?" Leila was thinking aloud more than seeking Michelle's insights.

"There are no guarantees in life. Maybe Ayden can be coaxed into the family-man role."

"I hope so, but—"

The door chimed, interrupting Leila's thought. She whispered, "I'll take care of this customer. You continue with the packages."

❁

At the end of the day, Leila went straight to the market. She had some last-minute items to pick up for Thursday's holiday dinner.

The produce looked as if it had just been picked, and the abundance of choices pleased her. Everything she needed for her opening course was there for the taking. Her salad would appear as a work of art, filled with an array of shapes, sizes, and colors.

She made her way up and down the aisles. The market, surprisingly, wasn't crowded, in spite of Thanksgiving being just a couple of days away; she had no difficulty maneuvering her cart around the store and getting what she wanted.

Running her pen down her list, she stopped at *cookies*. By this she meant the popular jelly-filled shortbreads exclusive to Whole Foods. She absolutely had to have them, so before targeting anything else, she hurriedly made her way to the aisle displaying imported delicacies.

With purpose, Leila moved up the aisle to the cookie section. She was reaching toward the top shelf, where the shortbreads were housed, when her cart suddenly pushed into her, catching her off-guard. Her hand knocked two boxes to the floor. "Damn," she whispered aloud and immediately stooped down to retrieve the boxes—only to bump heads with someone else.

"Ouch."

"I'm so sorry," a deep voice said. "I didn't realize my cart rolled away."

Leila stood up, rubbing her forehead and preparing to politely scold the perpetrator—but when she caught sight of him, she gasped. Standing in front of her was a very attractive man: tall, likely in his early sixties, with salt-and-pepper hair and hazel eyes. He looked very much like her beloved Nick.

"Are you okay?" he asked. "I know we bumped heads, but I didn't think the encounter was too forceful."

"I'm fine, thanks." Leila blushed. "I can be very clumsy. I've been racing though the market without paying too much attention to what's going on around me." Nervous jitters spread like lightning throughout her body.

"I see you like those cookies too. My wife got me hooked on them. When I run out, I almost go into a panic. That's why I stopped here after work."

She nodded. "They're very good. I thought they'd be a nice addition to my holiday dessert menu."

"I agree." He reached above her to secure two more boxes of the cookies.

She couldn't take her eyes off of the stranger. His relaxed manner resembled Nick's. He moved confidently and cocked his head to the side ever so slightly when speaking. His left hand rested inside his pants pocket, a stance Nick had often taken.

"Have you tried the other varieties?" he asked.

"Just the cinnamon swirls. They're very good, but I like the fruit-filled ones more."

"My wife loved all things cinnamon." He paused. "I lost her last year, so I've become a discerning food shopper out of necessity."

Leila noticed his firm hand on the boxes before he placed them in his cart. "I understand," she said gently. "Widows continue to use the shopping skills they've honed over the years, but the challenge for us is not to buy more than we need. I tend to throw away food, which I hate. So wasteful."

Why was she sharing this information with a total stranger? She needed to move on.

Just as she grasped the handle of the shopping cart, the stranger said, "You're a widow? How long?"

What business was it of his? He was obviously nosy and needy, but she answered him anyway. "Five years."

"Oh, I'm sorry."

"Thank you. Well, I need to finish up." Leila began to move her cart down the aisle, once again consulting her list. She couldn't help but hear the wheels of another shopping cart rattling close behind her.

"My name is Eric. What's yours?"

"Are you following me?" she asked in an annoyed tone, not slowing her pace.

"I don't mean to upset you. Simply put, I think you're a very pretty woman, and I'd like to chat with you some more."

"You're trying to hit on me!" She wasn't accustomed to feeling flustered like this and immediately regretted her sharp delivery.

"I guess I am." He sounded abashed but determined. "Why don't you give me a chance? Can't we sit down like two sensible people and have coffee together? I'll even share my favorite cookies with you."

Leila turned around, ready to stop the man named Eric in his tracks, but when she saw the warm, friendly smile on his handsome face, she softened. "Look, I'm seeing someone right now. I'm sorry."

"I've been dating someone as well. I'm just asking you to join me for a cup of coffee. It's the least I can do after bumping into you."

Leila couldn't understand why, but she told Eric her name and then agreed to have coffee with him. Conceivably, it was because Eric looked so much like Nick—or because she was intrigued by his pursuit.

"Leila. That's a lovely name. It's nice to meet you, Leila." Eric extended his hand for a handshake and pulled his cart up next to hers. "May I walk with you to the coffee shop?"

Leila nodded and smiled. But she felt uneasy giving in to Eric's invitation. She'd have to set a time limit.

They pushed their carts toward the coffee area and found a table. Once they settled in, Leila decided to assert herself.

"Look, Eric, my son is driving in from Boston for the weekend, and I need to get home very soon. Please don't think me rude if I don't stay long."

"No problem. How do you take your coffee?"

Leila looked him straight in the eye. "Decaffeinated, cream, one pack of sugar substitute."

"I'll be right back."

He returned a few minutes later with her coffee and a colorful assortment of biscotti. "I'm most willing to open one of my short-breads as well, of course," he said. He tore into one of the boxes and placed it between them.

"So, Eric, what's your last name?"

"Lowell. And yours?"

"Brandt."

"Leila Brandt. Nice."

"What kind of work occupies your days, Eric Lowell?" She dipped a chocolate biscotti into her coffee.

"I'm an orthopedic surgeon. I'm in a practice associated with Einstein. And you?"

"I'm an interior designer. I have a partner; we run our own business."

"An entrepreneur. That's impressive."

Leila searched for a way to take the focus off of her. "What happened to your wife?"

Eric's face took on a frown. She'd obviously hit a very sensitive spot.

"Lindsey died of pancreatic cancer just over a year ago." His voice was soft. "Late diagnosis. Somehow, I feel guilty, but the disease is difficult to detect at its onset." He looked down at his coffee cup.

Leila felt she'd been too bold; she decided an equally sacred revelation was needed. "I know how you feel. My husband, Nick, died of prostate cancer. In retrospect, I feel I should've done more research and urged him to question his test results sooner than I did."

"I suppose it's quite common to feel the way we do. We're still here, and they're not."

"Do you have children?" Leila asked, hoping to turn the conversation in a lighter direction.

Eric's face brightened. "Yes, I have two girls. Jessica and Marie. They're both married, each with two children."

"You're a grandfather. How nice. My first grandchild is due in January."

"You don't look like the typical grandmother."

"So I've been told." She could feel the blood rushing to her cheeks as she dealt with his compliment.

An awkward silence fell upon them. Leila glanced at her watch. An hour had already passed since she arrived at the store. How could she graciously bring this friendly discussion to a close?

Just as she decided to say she needed to take care of the rest of the items on her list, Eric stunned her by saying, "Tell me about him."

He focused intently on her face.

"Him?"

"The man you're seeing now."

"I'm really not comfortable giving you details, but I've developed strong feelings for him. We've known each other for over eight months. I hadn't dated for five years. Then I met him, along with two other men, through a matchmaking service—a birthday present from my daughter and my business partner—and we fell for each other." A smile spread across her face. She exhaled and focused on her coffee, avoiding Eric's gaze.

"He could be your rebound guy." He said this with absolute seriousness.

Leila finished off the cookie resting on her napkin. *Be bold*, she told herself. "And your current friend?"

"She's an operating room nurse at the hospital."

"I'm going out on a limb here, but I sense she may be significantly younger than you. Am I right?" Leila waited with nervous anticipation for Eric's reply, feeling like she had just been very nosy.

"You're correct. I've determined that she's likely my rebound girl. Anyway, my daughters aren't exactly happy about our relationship."

"How old is she?"

"Forty-five. She's divorced with two teenagers."

"Charlie Chaplin married Oona O'Neill when he was fifty-four and she was only eighteen," Leila informed him. "They had eight children. The marriage lasted over thirty years, until his death."

"Really? I'm not familiar with that unconventional love story."

"Yes. Sometimes a significant age difference isn't a detriment to a lasting relationship."

"Well, I'm not in love with her. Not like I was with Lindsey."

"If so, you should end it and move on. It's not fair to either of you."

"I'm trying to move on, but you're making it difficult." His playfulness here didn't charm Leila the way he obviously hoped it would.

"Everything in life is about timing. It's been very nice chatting with you, but I need to finish my shopping and get home." Leila rose from her seat and grabbed her shopping cart. "Thank you for the coffee and treats."

"Leila, wait a minute." Eric reached into his pocket for his wallet. He pulled out a business card. "Do you happen to have a pen?"

Leila opened her handbag and fumbled with its contents until she found a pen.

He took the pen, wrote for a moment on the card, and then handed both items to her. "I wrote my home phone number and personal email address on the back. Please get in touch with me if your current relationship doesn't work out. I think we might hit it off."

Leila took Eric's information and placed it in a zippered compartment inside her handbag. "Thank you. It was nice meeting you. All the best." She smiled and extended her hand. Eric took hold and gave her hand a gentle squeeze.

Leila took him in one last time. Yes, she felt an attraction. But what did it matter at this point? She took a deep breath, pushed her cart in the direction of the grocery aisles, and didn't look back.

33

The sun had set when Leila finally emerged from the market. She had spent over two hours there, much longer than she'd anticipated. Her decision to have coffee with Eric Lowell perplexed her. She didn't fully understand how she, a woman so much in love, could sit down with a complete stranger for over one hour and share such personal information with him. Was her acquiescence due to Eric's uncanny resemblance to Nick?

She'd enjoyed Eric's company. He seemed to be more of a family man than Ayden was. It was likely that this attribute had drawn her in, she reasoned.

But what did her willingness to engage another man in intimate conversation say about her relationship with Ayden?

All this thinking didn't stop Leila from loading the groceries in the trunk, but it did prevent her from seeing the flat left rear tire that had somehow come about while she was shopping.

"Oh, damn it," she voiced in an uncharacteristically high-pitched tone when the reality set in. The perishables could spoil. She immediately dialed the auto club. "Yes, I'm in trouble. I have a flat tire and have just finished up a week's worth of grocery shopping. Can you please send someone out immediately?"

The patient auto club travel associate took Leila's membership information but delivered some disheartening news. "Ms. Brandt, I can put the alert in for you, but tonight has been extremely busy. I estimate your wait will be a good forty-five minutes to an hour."

"What?" Leila responded shrilly.

"I'm sorry. Maybe a friend or family member could get there more quickly and take care of the groceries for you. Is that possible?"

"If it were so easy to round up help, why would I have a membership with your organization?" Her exasperation found its voice. "Just put me in the queue. I'll call back if my situation changes."

Leila slammed the trunk closed and began her wait. Tears formed in her eyes as she reviewed her situation. She wasn't too far from home—only a fifteen-minute ride. Maybe she could call Hillary and Chad and see what they were doing?

A somewhat familiar voice interrupted her desperate thinking.

"Can I be of some assistance? You seem to be having some trouble."

Leila looked around to see Eric Lowell approaching. She felt embarrassed and out of control. Embarrassment? Why should she feel embarrassed? *Having a flat tire is a perfectly normal mishap*, she rationalized, *and no cause for humiliation.*

"I've got a flat and a trunk full of groceries," she explained begrudgingly.

"Are you a member of Three A's?"

"Yes. I already put in the alert. An hour wait. Just the way I want to end my day." She didn't even attempt to keep the frustration from her tone.

"Do you live nearby?"

"Not far, a fifteen-minute ride or so."

"I've got an idea. Why don't you let me help in this way? I'll load my trunk up with your groceries and drive you home. You can quickly unload and put the frozen and refrigerated things away. I'll drive you back. The auto club should be here when we return. How does that sound?"

Leila considered his plan. She had some reservations, but the offer was tempting.

"I couldn't bother you to that extent," she finally said. "It's quite an imposition, don't you think?"

"Not at all. I'd be happy to help."

Leila reviewed her situation. She and Ayden had no plans for the evening, and he lived a good forty-five minutes away. There was no chance he'd find out about this. Everything would be taken care of in an hour, and she could go on with her evening as planned—some light cooking for the holiday and the wait for Drew's arrival.

"Well, I must confess, your plan sounds enticing."

"I'll bring up my car."

Eric and Leila transferred the food into Eric's classy silver-gray BMW, and they were on their way in ten minutes.

"I'm sorry you had this trouble, Leila. If I hadn't detained you, your flat tire would've happened once you were home."

"It's not your fault. It's just the way it is."

"Maybe fate had something to do with it." He turned to her and winked. A cute smile crossed his face.

"I think it was more serendipity than anything else." She looked straight ahead. "Turn here, and then take the second left."

"Nice neighborhood." The guardhouse and gatekeeper clearly impressed Eric.

Immediately upon turning onto her street, Leila dove into her handbag for her keys. A few seconds later, she looked up and felt a pang of shock ripple through her chest. Ayden's car was parked in the driveway, and Ayden was seated behind the wheel.

"Looks like someone is waiting for you. Is it your son?" Eric asked nonchalantly.

"No," Leila responded weakly. "It's my significant other."

"Your rebound guy? You're kidding, right?" Eric looked over at Leila, whose deportment made it clear that she wasn't joking. "Well, this certainly *is* serendipitous."

Leila erupted from the car and headed toward Ayden, who, at the same time, alighted from his vehicle.

"You look troubled," Ayden said, his forehead creased. "What's going on?" Before Leila could answer, he noticed Eric opening the trunk of his car and filling his arms with groceries. "Who's that guy? Where's your car?"

"His name is Eric Lowell. He was kind enough to drive me home from the market. Just after I filled my trunk with my groceries at the store, I noticed I had a flat tire. I called the auto club. The agent said I likely wouldn't be serviced for an hour. I need to put things away and hurry back to the parking lot." Leila took a deep breath and continued. "Now that you're here, Eric can be on his way and you can take me back for my car."

"Hello," Eric said cheerfully. "I'd extend my hand, but as you can see, I'm pretty loaded down. You must be Ayden. Leila's not stopped talking about you."

"Really," Ayden said, a suggestion of doubt in his voice. "You two had enough time together to approach the subject of *me*?" With a quizzical look on his face, he looked first at Eric and then straight at Leila.

"Well, I explained to Eric that you live forty-five minutes away or else I would've called you. And by the way, you've surprised me. We didn't have plans for this evening . . . or have I forgotten something?" Leila tried to correct the nervous quiver in her voice.

"I did intend to surprise you. Guess I accomplished what I set out to do."

"I'd like to let Eric get on his way, Ayden, so please help with the groceries." She ignored his last comment for the moment.

Leila started up the path to the front door, her keys jangling and clinking in her hand. She was obviously rattled. Eric walked close behind. He followed her to the kitchen and placed the bundles on the island. Within seconds, Ayden did the same thing.

"Your trunk is now empty," Ayden said to Eric, his tone flat.

"Glad you were here, Ayden. You saved me a trip." Ayden didn't receive Eric's attempt at humor very well, but Eric extended his hand anyway.

Ayden took hold of Eric's hand and gave it a firm shake. "Thanks for helping out," he said politely but coldly.

"No problem. Nice meeting the both of you." Eric turned and headed for the front door.

"I really appreciated your help," Leila said, scurrying after him. "I'm sorry if you've been inconvenienced."

"I was happy to help. Good night."

Leila watched Eric walk to his car. She wanted a few moments to gather strength for what she suspected might be a confrontation with Ayden in the kitchen, so she made a call to the auto club and reconfirmed her need for assistance. They told her the service would arrive soon and encouraged her to hurry back to the parking lot. *Saved for now.*

"You're fortunate a good Samaritan was in the parking lot," Ayden commented once their return trip was underway.

"Yes, very fortunate."

"It's interesting."

"What?"

"You getting into a car with a perfect stranger. It's not like you. I guess you weren't able to reach Chad and Hillary or Michelle."

"I didn't want to bother them. Besides, I bumped carts and heads with Eric in the cookie aisle, which led to conversation. So he wasn't a total stranger. He's an orthopedic surgeon at Einstein."

"You asked him his occupation?"

"No, silly. He asked if I was hurt and told me he was a doctor."

"Leila, the guy was coming on to you. Are you that naive?"

"The man was just trying to be polite. Can we drop this interrogation?"

"Fine."

Ayden waited with Leila while the auto service installed the temporary spare. "You're good to go," the technician said. "Just sign this service report."

She signed, the technician left, and she turned to Ayden with an exhausted sigh. "Thanks for your help."

He gave a tight nod. "Are you hungry?"

"Hungry for one of your kisses." She wrapped her arms about his neck and gave him a passionate kiss on the lips.

He held back. She didn't expect that. The Eric situation had gotten under his skin.

"Are you angry?" she asked.

"No, disappointed."

"Disappointed? How so?"

"You allowed that guy, the *doctor*, into your life. You apparently enjoyed playing the part of a helpless coquette, even if only for a little while."

Leila had never seen this side of Ayden. He'd become accusatory and unreasonable. In short, he was showing signs of jealousy. His limited view of her motivations bothered her. She was much deeper and more principled than he suggested.

"You're just jealous. Let it go. Let's have dinner." Her tone was purposefully light; she was hoping to lessen the intensity of their discussion.

Ayden remained silent. His blue eyes studied her face for what seemed like forever. "Maybe it wasn't such a good idea to come over and surprise you."

"I loved your spontaneity," Leila said with enthusiasm. "We always seem to arrange to see one another by using the appointment approach. I suppose it's because we conduct our business lives that way. We need to work spontaneity into our relationship from now on. Let's eat at the grill here. Simple and easy."

❀

The events of the evening influenced their dinner conversation. Ayden remained sullen. How long would he brood?

Just as Leila was about to broach the subject of his less-than-cheerful self, her cell phone rang. "Sorry, it's Drew," she said to Ayden before taking the call. "Drew, sweetheart, where are you?"

"I'm just outside of New York. I should be home by midnight."

"How's traffic?"

"Not bad. I'm glad I decided to leave today rather than tomorrow."

"Definitely a wise decision." In her most motherly tone, she warned, "Pay attention to the road. No antics with your cell phone, okay?"

"Yes, Mom. See you soon."

The waiter brought their salmon burgers and beers. Ayden tackled his food.

"I'm so excited Drew is on his way," Leila said. "I've missed him. His job is wonderful, but he's so far away."

"Maybe it's time to cut the cord. I rarely follow Daniel's shenanigans."

His remark stung. "What are you saying? I shouldn't mother anymore? Listen, pal, once a mother, always a mother. The same goes for you. Once a father, always a father."

"I don't happen to see things exactly that way."

"Family is important to me, Ayden." Her response was soft but firm.

"I prefer to keep my family at a distance. They can become very intrusive. My parents and siblings disapprove of my single life and believe true happiness eludes me because I'm not married."

"Maybe this isn't the perfect occasion for what I have to say, but I think I need to lay my cards on the table." Ayden had to know there was no compromise when it came to family.

"Go for it." He spoke with more sarcasm than encouragement.

"I love you very much. However, I have expectations about the future. I expect you to become part of my family—to join in family celebrations and maybe even help when I'm asked to babysit for Hillary and Chad's baby because they need a night out. And I expect you to make me feel a welcomed part of your family, allowing me to get to know your siblings and your parents and nurture a closer relationship with Daniel." She took a breath and exhaled slowly. "There, I've said it."

Ayden mulled over Leila's words for a few seconds. "I'm not like the dad in *The Brady Bunch*," he finally said. "What I'm good at is loving you—fully, deeply, and for as long as you'll have me."

Leila pushed her plate away. Her appetite had vanished. She sat quietly, staring at Ayden's handsome face while tears welled in her eyes. "I'm happy you've declared your commitment to me. Those sentiments are very endearing. But I need you by my side through everything. I need you to be more like Mike Brady."

Ayden paid the bill and walked Leila to her car. They embraced and kissed, a long and passionate kiss that sent tingles throughout Leila's body. She burrowed into his neck and whispered, "Please think about what I've said. I love you." With that, she got into her car and drove away, her eyes fixed on the rearview mirror and on Ayden's image until she turned onto the highway.

34

Leila locked up, left some lights on for Drew, and went upstairs. She threw her handbag on the bed, kicked off her shoes, and headed to the bathroom to undress and get ready for bed. Ayden might call to say good night. Perhaps on his drive home, he'd think over what she'd said.

She walked out of the bathroom and stopped to stare at her bed. She imagined Ayden already in it, waiting for her as he'd done countless times before, the covers pulled neatly aside so she could slip in next to him with ease. She tried to recall his scent, the warmth of his skin, and the softness of his kisses. This would be the first weekend in many weeks they didn't spend together.

Deep in thought as she reviewed their dinner conversation, she heavy-handedly pulled down the bedcovers, sending her handbag to the floor, its contents scattered about. She'd gather them up in the morning, after a good night's sleep.

Then what she hoped for happened: the phone rang.

"Hello," she said in her sexiest voice.

"I wanted to hear your voice before I went to sleep." He spoke softly, just as he did when making love to her. "I guess things have settled down by now."

"I miss you. This bed seems too large and lonely without you, but with Drew home, you understand how a sleepover would be awkward."

"I fully understand. Besides, you need quality time with Drew."
He hesitated and, after what seemed to be a long silence, said, "We'll
get through this weekend, Leila. We'll be back on track soon."

This last remark didn't rest well with her. His words seemed
to suggest that the time they were about to spend with their families could be likened to a short prison sentence—something to be
endured rather than enjoyed.

"Why can't we spend time together after Thursday?" she asked.

"I don't want to be in the way while Drew is visiting."

"You'd never be in the way," she forcefully shot back.

Ayden went quiet. After a pause, he said, "Look, why don't I
come by on Sunday and take you to dinner?" When Leila didn't reply
immediately, he said playfully, "You'll need a kitchen break by then."

"And what about Friday and Saturday?" She anticipated his
answer would be disquieting.

"If you don't have plans with your kids, you could visit me. We'd
have some time to ourselves."

What was he implying? He seemed to focus mostly on the sexual
part of their relationship, and though Leila treasured their intimacy,
she needed more from him. She subdued her annoyance in order to
avoid an argument that would be difficult to resolve on the phone.
"I'll keep that idea in mind, although it may be a last-minute thing if
it does happen. I hope that's all right."

"I'm flexible." He waited for more from her. When she didn't offer
anything, he picked his old standby: "I love you."

"And I love you. Good night."

Leila hung up the phone, reached for her pillow, and screamed
into it, "What is your problem, Ayden Doyle!?" He loved her. She knew
that. And she was crazy about him. But his family avoidance issue
was undermining their relationship. Couldn't he see that his words
and attitude hurt her? Didn't he realize that the boundaries he'd
established for their relationship were too narrow, too exclusionary?

Her anxiety got the best of her. She needed to move and refocus. She jumped from her bed, pulled out her laundry basket, and began to sort clothes. She put a load in the wash. She dusted the bedroom and straightened the bathroom. Her frenzy stopped when she reached for a tissue to blow her nose. Only then did she become aware of her own tears.

Exhausted, she decided to go back to bed. She stopped to pick up her fallen handbag and gather up the things strewn on the floor. As she placed everything back into the bag, she found Eric Lowell's card. She brought it into bed with her. Once under the covers, she studied it intently. Most likely, she'd have thrown it away when she changed bags over the weekend; now, though, dark clouds hung over her future with Ayden. "Just in case," she whispered to herself, tucking the card under her pillow. She drifted into sleep.

It seemed to Leila that her eyes had just closed when the sound of the front door being secured brought her out of sleep.

"Mom, hi!" Drew called from the front hall. "It's me. Are you still up?"

"Of course, darling," Leila replied, her heart filled with happy anticipation. She threw on a robe and raced downstairs to greet him.

He grinned up at her as she came down the stairs.

"Look at you," she blurted out. "You're as handsome as ever. Just like your dad."

Drew wrapped his arms tightly around her. After a sustained hug, he pulled away and gave her a quick kiss on the cheek. "Good to see you, Mom. You're looking great yourself."

"Are you hungry?" she asked. "I can make you a sandwich."

"Definitely," he said. "But I'd like to take a shower first, if you don't mind."

"No, of course not. I'll wrap up the sandwich and leave it on the counter."

"Thanks, Mom. You're the best."

"Uh-huh." Leila went about making Drew his favorite sandwich: ham, turkey, cheese, lettuce, and tomato on rye with a generous application of mayonnaise.

Back in bed, she tucked her arms under her pillow and attempted to fall asleep, but all kinds of thoughts raced through her mind. Restless, her fingers stumbled upon Eric Lowell's card. She pulled it out and flipped over on her back, holding the card up to the moonlight streaming through the window. She examined the card for some time, turning it over and over again. Eric's handwriting was perfectly formed. *Funny, nothing like the stereotypical scribble often associated with doctors.*

In a short while, she fell asleep, the card resting in the palm of her hand.

35

Leila and Michelle agreed to close the shop early on Wednesday. They wanted to get a head start on their Thanksgiving dinners. Leila arrived at the shop around nine to finalize orders, pay the bills, and tidy up the selling floor. She'd tossed and turned most of the night—Ayden's remarks still weighed heavily on her heart and mind—so getting to work ahead of schedule hadn't been much of a challenge.

The front door opened with its familiar ring, alerting Leila to Michelle's arrival. She knew Michelle, a morning person, would appear within seconds, displaying her typical upbeat temperament—almost too cheerful for Leila on this particular morning—but she'd soon see that something was troubling Leila.

"Good morning, partner," Michelle said as she turned the corner. "How's it going?"

"Fine. I took care of orders and paid bills. How did the storefront look when you entered?"

"Certainly not terrible, or I'd have noticed. Let me bop out there and survey the place." Michelle threw her belongings onto her desk chair and returned to the front of the store to conduct the reconnaissance. "Looks perfect," she announced, raising her voice just enough for her to be heard back in the office.

Leila heard Michelle fidgeting with some merchandise for a few minutes before returning to the office and going through phone messages. Michelle often made things more perfect, just one of her attributes that endeared her to Leila.

"Did you get all your shopping done yesterday?"

"Most of it. I have a few things left to get after work." A yawn crept in when Leila replied.

"Up late with your lover?"

"No, I'm just tired. I didn't sleep well last night."

"Okay, give," Michelle instructed. "Something is on your mind. I sensed it the minute I entered the office."

"I finally leveled with Ayden. I told him I need his support on everything that matters in my life, especially family."

"How did he take it?" Michelle leaned in.

"Not great. He told me he loves me deeply but isn't cut out for the role of super dad—that he's not like Mike Brady of *The Brady Bunch*."

"Well, maybe he can grow into that role," Michelle said.

"Another thing. A situation arose at the market last night."

"Situation?"

"Okay, bear with me, because the situation was a bit involved . . ."

Leila told Michelle the whole story, from bumping heads with Eric at Whole Foods to Ayden's sullen jealousy at their dinner afterward.

Michelle whistled when she was through. "That's it?"

"That's it. Meanwhile, I'm in love with a man who resists becoming a part of my family and keeps me from knowing his. This resistance is slowly eroding our relationship. I have reason to be upset, right?"

"Yes. But at least you now have a backup," Michelle teased.

"Is that last comment supposed to be funny?"

"I'm sorry—a poor attempt to lighten things up. I see you're in the midst of emotional turmoil." Michelle rose and put her arms around Leila's shoulders. "I know things seem bleak at the moment, but love is a strong emotion. I believe all will work out in the end.

Besides, remember how Ayden responded to our dear client Susan? He enjoyed her advances to some extent. He just got a taste of his own medicine. It could prove quite therapeutic."

"You think?"

"Yes. Now, let's get to work so we can get out of here early."

❀

On Thursday morning, Leila's home became a beehive of activity. Her sister, Caroline, arrived at ten to help set the tables. The turkey roasted in the oven, filling the downstairs with savory smells that made Leila's stomach growl. Baked pumpkin pies cooled on the island. Their aroma mixed with the smell of brewed coffee.

"More coffee?" Leila asked her sister.

"Not just yet." Caroline finished munching on her third of Leila's recently baked chocolate chip cookies.

"Leave some of those cookies for later."

"I'll try." Caroline washed the last bit of cookie down with a gulp of coffee. "So, are we going to meet your handsome architect tonight?"

"Not tonight. He's spending the evening with his family."

"Really? I somehow feel he's avoiding us."

"Well, the truth be said, he's not keen on family-man duties. It could become a big problem." After this admission, tears formed in Leila's eyes. She tried to turn away so Caroline wouldn't see, but her sister wasn't fooled.

"Men!" she cried. "I've had a number of bad experiences with them. Remember the guy who broke up with me via voice mail?"

"I do. What a jerk!" Laughter spewed out, and their spirits lifted.

"How's your new guy working out?" Leila asked.

"I think he may be a keeper. I don't want to put a jinx on things, but it's been over four months since we began dating, and things are going along nicely. The kids have even told me they like him."

"Great. I'm happy for you."

Caroline slid off the stool and gave her sister a hug. "I'll get started on table two."

By midafternoon, Leila's family filled every room on the first floor. Her father and Caroline's kids were watching a football game in the den, munching on popcorn and downing cheese and crackers. Leila's mother was in the kitchen, making her special broccoli recipe and interrogating her girls about the men in their lives. Leila's cousins were in the living room, catching up on the happenings since last they were together.

"Where is this elusive Ayden Doyle?" her mother asked. "You've been together for months, and yet we haven't met him. I find it quite disconcerting."

"He's shy when it comes to family," Caroline blurted out.

"Caroline," Leila bellowed, giving her sister a guiding stare that told Caroline to keep her mouth shut. In a more measured tone, she said, "Mom, he's with his family today. I'll arrange something when I'm sure he's the one. Can we leave it at that for now?"

"Yes, I suppose. I just don't want you to be alone for the rest of your life."

Leila gave her mother a kiss on the cheek and began to carve the turkey.

❁

"The tables look gorgeous," Cousin Charlotte declared. "You are so adept at coordinating things. Plus, you're a great cook. I can't believe some guy hasn't snagged you yet."

Leila knew her cousin meant well, but considering the recent events with Ayden, she needed a quick topic change. "Does everyone have enough? Can I get anyone something?" She forced holiday gaiety into her voice.

"Everything is wonderful," her mother announced.

"Really, Mom, this may be your best Thanksgiving dinner ever," Drew mumbled around a mouth full of turkey.

"I'm glad you're all enjoying yourselves. I'll bring out more turkey. Hand me the plate, Chad."

Leila reached over heads and took the almost-empty platter from her son-in-law. Back in the kitchen, she arranged the turkey platter and decorated it with parsley.

Just as she was about to return to the dining room, the house phone rang. She thought it odd for someone to be calling her at dinnertime on Thanksgiving. She placed the turkey platter back on the island and reached for the phone. To her surprise, the ID indicated the caller was Ayden.

"Hello?"

"Hey, beautiful. How's everything going?"

"Just fine here. And how's it going at your family celebration?"

"Things went well."

Leila couldn't help noting that Ayden spoke in the past tense, as if the Doyles' Thanksgiving had already concluded.

"Listen, could you call me later? I'm in the midst of serving a second turkey platter. You caught me at a busy time. I can't talk right now."

"Oh, sounds like you've prepared enough food."

"Lots of everything. There certainly will be leftovers to feast upon."

"In other words, you could handle more guests?"

"What are you getting at? Please be quick."

"I'd like to come in and have dinner with you and your family, if that's all right. I'm actually at your front door this very moment. What do you say? Is there room?"

Leila stood still. She was beyond surprised. *Flabbergasted* would be a better description. All kinds of emotions surged through her being—anxiety, love, exhilaration, appreciation, and so forth. She nervously replied with quivering lips, "I'll be right there." She quickly grabbed the turkey platter and entered the dining room with such speed that she startled her guests.

"Please take the platter, Chad, and place it on the table. I think I heard the doorbell."

"The doorbell didn't ring," Caroline assured her.

"I need to make sure."

Leila sailed through the dining room and into the hall. She quickly checked her appearance in the mirror above the entry table, fussed with her hair a second or two, and gingerly opened the front door. Standing in front of her was Ayden, handsome as ever, dressed in khakis and a maroon sweater, wearing a big smile and holding a large box in one hand and a bottle of wine in the other.

Leila whispered a hello, hoping to keep her guests in the dark. "This is a surprise."

"I've been thinking."

"Yes?"

"I want a life with you. I love you. I want to make you happy. And if you'll help me, I'll become a family man you'll be proud of. Who knows, I may even enjoy it more than I imagine. What say you?"

"I don't want to force you into situations that make you uncomfortable."

"Being without you will make me very uncomfortable."

His words resounding in her head, she asked, "How about a kiss?"

Ayden leaned forward and gave Leila the very best kiss he could, considering his hands were laden with objects.

"What's going on?" Leila's dad shouted out. "Your dinner is getting cold."

"Come, let me introduce you to everyone." She took the wine bottle from Ayden's hand, slipped her arm through his, and guided him into the dining room, where her twenty-plus guests were devouring the food.

"Everyone," she said, "this is Ayden Doyle, my very significant other. Please welcome him to our family gathering while I get another place setting."

She put the wine bottle on the table and asked Chad to position a folding chair next to hers at the head of the table. Ayden set his package down. All the men rose and took turns introducing themselves and shaking hands with him. Leila's father took over the helm and introduced all the women. Ayden, with his wonderful smile and twinkling baby blues, charmed them all.

Once Chad had put the chair in place, Ayden made his way to his seat, carrying his package with him.

"What's in that box?" Leila heard Drew ask as she brought in a plate filled with all the Thanksgiving delights she'd prepared and placed it before Ayden.

"A present for your mom," Ayden said, his eyes on her.

Caroline filled water and wine glasses.

"You've been officially welcomed to our family Thanksgiving dinner," Leila announced. "So, what's in that box you're still clinging to?"

"It's for you," he said, raising it up to Leila. "Hope you like it."

Leila sat in her seat, placed the box on her lap, and carefully pried loose the lid. She struggled to remove the bubble wrap inside. Finally successful, she lifted a rather heavy object from its resting place and soon discovered it to be a bronze sculpture of a man and a woman sitting on a bench at a water's edge, the woman's head resting on the man's shoulder. In small letters and numbers, the inscription "Forever Yours, Number 1/1" had been carved into the center of the base.

"How lovely!" Leila's mother exclaimed.

"Marvelous," her father declared.

"Who's the artist?" Hillary asked.

"The artist is Ayden," Leila explained, a tear rolling down her cheek.

Another round of applause erupted. Leila turned to Ayden, gazed into his eyes, and in a loving voice said, "Thank you. Thank you for everything."

"You're welcome. It's a good start, right?"

"The best."

Acknowledgments

For as long as I can remember, I've been in love with stories involving romance and all those tangible things intricately associated with this sentiment—flowers, music, art, gardens, the sky at night with its stars bright, and, of course, chocolates.

My parents, Mona and Herbert Siegel, provided me with a secure and loving home and a wonderful neighborhood in which to build cherished childhood memories, and whose school district, Lower Merion, was rich with books and opportunities for writing and thinking about them. Novels by Thomas Hardy, Jane Austen, and the Brontë sisters were among my favorites and inspired me. For all of this, I am truly grateful.

Thank you to all my family and friends who have been so supportive over the last few years as I've devoted myself to conjuring up stories with romance in the forefront. To my sister Nancy Siegel and my baby sister, Stacy Gremminger—thank you for taking an entire Monday holiday when you could have attended to more pressing matters to read the first draft of the book and tell me you couldn't put it down. They continue to champion *And Now There's You,* and I'm most grateful for that.

A zillion "thank-yous" to my cousin, Adrienne Jones, for her numerous readings and editorial comments that helped me refine my story. And to her husband, Cecil Jones, who willingly added his most-needed masculine input.

To my cousin, Gail, thank you for your interest, advice, and introduction to your friend, Cathy Fiebach, owner of Main Point Books in Wayne, Pennsylvania.

And to my niece, Blair Manus, thank you for sharing your marketing genius with me, helping to create my website, and so much more. Many thanks to Beth Berkowitz, Reina Cohen, Sandy Shipon, and Bonnie Vandenberg for reading the ARC and identifying areas that needed attention.

Certainly, my deepest gratitude is extended to Brooke Warner, Lauren Wise, and Krissa Lagos of SparkPress who believed in *And Now There's You* and used their collective expertise to bring it to its full potential, and to Corinne Moulder, Sarah Gilbert, and their team at Smith Publicity who championed Leila's story. And many thanks to Mimi Bark for her enticing cover design.

My final tribute is to my late husband, Kenneth Lee Etkin, with whom I shared the most passionate and fulfilling thirty-seven years of my life.

Questions For Discussion

1. Leila Brandt experiences the loss of her beloved husband while in her fifties. For the years that follow, rather than seek a new companion to love, she invests all of her emotions, energy, and time into her business, family, and friends. How common do you think her reaction is to the loss of a husband?

2. Electronic dating has been successful for many singles. Why do you think Leila does not embrace this? Is Leila's story universal?

3. What is it about Ayden Doyle that awakens Leila's womanly needs and desires?

4. When Leila and Ayden first meet, they act competitively, vying for the Perkinses' attention and approval. What circumstances cause their relationship to become collaborative?

5. Why do you suppose Ayden has favored a life without commitment to one woman? What did Ayden's reaction to his younger client, Susan Fredericks, suggest? Has Ayden's role or responsibility as a father affected his reluctance to settle down with one woman?

6. What kind of father to Daniel has Ayden been over the years? What instances or circumstances in the book can you find to support your opinion?

7. Love always involves risk. Does a second chance at love later in life involve more risk than a young first love? Does Leila have particular attributes that allow her to take a second chance?

8. What does Michelle's friendship mean to Leila? Do we all need a "Michelle" in our lives?

9. Why is Drew less receptive to the idea of Leila dating than Hillary?

10. Why did Leila spend time with Eric Lowell? Do you think he would have been a better match for her?

11. How do both Leila and Ayden change, if at all, by the end of the story? Can people really change?

12. Considering what you now know about Leila and Ayden, do you see a positive and long-term outcome for their relationship?

About the Author

© Yael Pachino

Susan S. Etkin grew up on Philadelphia's Main Line and graduated from Temple University with a bachelor's in English for secondary education. She also holds a master's in literacy and a doctorate in curriculum and instruction, both earned at the University of Cincinnati. Her professional life has entailed writing and teaching experiences, as well as entrepreneurship in the art and design fields. Her husband's career within a large US conglomerate prompted numerous moves. Etkin and her two sons always viewed Dad's relocations, which took the family to four states on the East Coast, as well as to Ohio, as adventures. Etkin now lives in a suburb of Philadelphia and is grateful that her sons and daughters-in-law decided to raise their families nearby. She devotes her days to reading and writing novels that focus on romance and topics of interest to women.

SELECTED TITLES FROM SPARKPRESS

SparkPress is an independent boutique publisher delivering high-quality, entertaining, and engaging content that enhances readers' lives, with a special focus on female-driven work. www.gosparkpress.com

The Cast: A Novel, Amy Blumenfeld $16.95, 978-1-943006-72-4
Twenty-five years after a group of ninth graders produces a *Saturday Night Live*-style videotape to cheer up their cancer-stricken friend, they reunite to celebrate her good health—but the happy holiday card facades quickly crumble and give way to an unforgettable three days filled with moral dilemmas and life-altering choices.

The Opposite of Never:A Novel, Kathy Mehuron
$16.95, 978-1-943006-50-2
Devastated by the loss of their spouses, Georgia and Kenny think that the best times of their lives are long over until they find each other; meanwhile Kenny's teenage stepdaughter, Zelda, and Georgia's friend's son, Spencer, fall in love at first sight—only to fall prey to and suffer opiate addiction together.

Love Reconsidered:A Novel, Phyllis J. Piano $16.95, 978-1-943006-20-5
A page-turning contemporary tale of how three memorable characters seek to rebuild their lives after betrayal and tragedy with the help of new relationships, loyal corgi dogs, home-cooked meals, and the ritual of football Sundays.

The Legacy of Us:A Novel, Kristin Contino$17, 978-1-940716-17-6
Three generations of women are affected by love, loss, and a mysterious necklace that links them.

The Absence of Evelyn: A Novel, Jackie Townsend
$16.95, 978-1-943006-21-2
Nineteen-year-old Olivia's life takes a turn when she receives an overseas call from a man she doesn't know is her father; her mother Rhonda, meanwhile, haunted by her sister's ghost, must face long-buried truths. Four lives in all, spanning three continents, are now bound together and tell a powerful story about love in all its incarnations, filial and amorous, healing and destructive.

About SparkPress

SparkPress is an independent, hybrid imprint focused on merging the best of the traditional publishing model with new and innovative strategies. We deliver high-quality, entertaining, and engaging content that enhances readers' lives. We are proud to bring to market a list of *New York Times* best-selling, award-winning, and debut authors who represent a wide array of genres, as well as our established, industry-wide reputation for creative, results-driven success in working with authors. SparkPress, a BookSparks imprint, is a division of SparkPoint Studio LLC.

Learn more at GoSparkPress.com